LEE BROOK

The Echoes of Silence

First published by Middleton Park Press 2024

Copyright © 2024 by Lee Brook

All rights reserved. No part of this publication may be reproduced, stored or transmitted in any form or by any means, electronic, mechanical, photocopying, recording, scanning, or otherwise without written permission from the publisher. It is illegal to copy this book, post it to a website, or distribute it by any other means without permission.

This novel is entirely a work of fiction. The names, characters and incidents portrayed in it are the work of the author's imagination. Any resemblance to actual persons, living or dead, events or localities is entirely coincidental.

Lee Brook asserts the moral right to be identified as the author of this work.

Lee Brook has no responsibility for the persistence or accuracy of URLs for external or third-party Internet Websites referred to in this publication and does not guarantee that any content on such Websites is, or will remain, accurate or appropriate.

Designations used by companies to distinguish their products are often claimed as trademarks. All brand names and product names used in this book and on its cover are trade names, service marks, trademarks and registered trademarks of their respective owners. The publishers and the book are not associated with any product or vendor mentioned in this book. None of the companies referenced within the book have endorsed the book.

First edition

This book was professionally typeset on Reedsy.
Find out more at reedsy.com

For my wife—
For helping me somehow keep my sanity whilst overcomplicating this novel plot.
And for helping me finally finish it both realistically and satisfyingly.
Thank you.

Contents

Prologue	iii
Chapter One	1
Chapter Two	10
Chapter Three	17
Chapter Four	25
Chapter Five	34
Chapter Six	45
Chapter Seven	61
Chapter Eight	69
Chapter Nine	77
Chapter Ten	85
Chapter Eleven	94
Chapter Twelve	104
Chapter Thirteen	115
Chapter Fourteen	126
Chapter Fifteen	133
Chapter Sixteen	145
Chapter Seventeen	154
Chapter Eighteen	163
Chapter Nineteen	172
Chapter Twenty	182
Chapter Twenty-one	189
Chapter Twenty-two	197
Chapter Twenty-three	207

Chapter Twenty-four	217
Chapter Twenty-five	224
Chapter Twenty-six	233
Chapter Twenty-seven	246
Chapter Twenty-eight	251
Chapter Twenty-nine	264
Chapter Thirty	274
Chapter Thirty-one	284
Chapter Thirty-two	295
Chapter Thirty-three	306
Chapter Thirty-four	319
Chapter Thirty-five	330
Chapter Thirty-six	342
Chapter Thirty-seven	351
Chapter Thirty-eight	361
Chapter Thirty-nine	372
About the Author	384
Also by Lee Brook	385

Prologue

January 2012

Detective Constable George Beaumont's gaze was fixed on the decaying farmhouse, a silhouette against the night. He shifted in the passenger seat, his focus unwavering. The rural expanse of Leeds Country Way in Gildersome, unfamiliar territory for the city-bred detective, loomed around them, shrouded in the thick scent of damp earth. The occasional, distant sound of farm animals punctuated the silence.

Detective Inspector Arthur Grimes, beside him, studied the farmhouse through binoculars. "Quiet out here," he muttered, his breath fogging up the windscreen.

"It's a different world, sir," George replied, his voice low. He scanned the area, the darkness almost tangible compared to the city's perpetual glow. He felt an odd sense of unease creep in, a feeling he brushed off as a city dweller's discomfort in the countryside.

Grimes lowered the binoculars, turning to George. "We've got to be sure he's in there. Can't risk storming the place on a hunch."

George nodded, his thoughts racing. They had followed a trail of clues leading to this isolated farmhouse, believed to be a place suspected of being an organised crime group's drug drop.

He leaned forward, his eyes scanning for any movement.

"We wait, then, sir. Until we're certain."

Grimes grunted in agreement, his eyes returning to the farmhouse. The car's interior was cramped, the tension palpable as they settled in for a stakeout.

The night deepened, and the farmhouse remained still, almost as if it were abandoned. George's eyes never strayed far, the detective in him alert for any sign of life. The quiet of the countryside was unsettling, a stark reminder of how far they were from the backup.

As hours ticked by, George's thoughts drifted, the mundanity of the stakeout contrasting sharply with the potential danger of what might lie ahead. He found himself wishing for a quick resolution.

"Anything?" Grimes' voice cut through his reverie.

George shook his head. "Nothing yet, sir." He shifted uneasily in his seat, his discomfort growing as the darkness seemed to press down on them. The night, with its enveloping blackness, had always unnerved him. It was a fear rooted deep, stemming from a childhood incident locked away in the recesses of his mind, rarely spoken of, even to those closest to him.

Arthur, ever observant, noticed George's discomfort and leaned back, a wry smile playing on his lips. "You know, George, darkness is just another tool in our kit," he mused, his eyes still trained on the farmhouse. His tone was light, but his gaze remained as sharp as ever.

George glanced at Arthur, curiosity piqued despite his unease.

Arthur continued, his voice taking on a reminiscent quality. "Back in my early days on the force, I learned to move through the shadows, unseen yet ever-present." His eyes seemed to focus on a distant memory. "There was this one night, much like this, when we were tracking a suspect through the back alleys of Leeds. Pitch black, it was. I remember feeling like the darkness was a cloak, hiding us, protecting us, as we moved closer to our target."

George listened, the story drawing him in despite himself. Arthur's words painted a picture of a younger version of the detective, navigating the dark alleys with a mixture of caution and confidence.

"It's all about perception, George. Darkness can be an ally if you let it. It teaches you to rely on your other senses and sharpens your instincts," Arthur said, his voice now a soft murmur against the quiet of the night.

George considered Arthur's words, finding a certain comfort in them. He looked back out at the farmhouse, trying to see the darkness as Arthur did—an ally, a tool. He focused on the sounds of the night, the distant rustling of leaves, the occasional animal call. Slowly, his discomfort ebbed, replaced by a heightened awareness.

As the night wore on, George's gaze remained fixed on the farmhouse, embracing the darkness, allowing it to sharpen his focus, his senses attuned to any sign of movement. The fear that had once gripped him eased, replaced by a quiet determination.

Arthur broke the silence, his voice carrying a note of confidence that cut through the stillness. "The informant is solid, George. This tip about the drug drop here, it's as good as gold."

George nodded in response, his eyes fixed on the farmhouse. Despite Arthur's assurance, a hint of scepticism flickered in his gaze. They had been down this road before, led astray by tips that turned out to be less than reliable. The memory of those fruitless nights, the sting of wasted efforts, lingered in his mind.

Arthur, sensing George's doubt, turned to him. "I know we've been burned before," he acknowledged, "but this one's different. The informant has come through for us in the past. Has a track record that's hard to ignore."

George's cynicism wavered, replaced by a cautious optimism. Arthur's intuition, honed by years on the force, had rarely led them astray. It was one of the qualities George admired in his superior—the ability to sift through the noise and find the signal.

"You trust him, then?" George asked, seeking confirmation more than anything.

"I do," Arthur replied without hesitation. "He's got eyes and ears in places we can't reach. If he says the drop is happening here tonight, then I believe him."

George processed this, his gaze returning to the dark outline of the farmhouse, the blackness of the night mirroring his inner unease. Despite Arthur's confidence in their informant, a nagging sensation gnawed at him. It was a feeling that had slowly crept up and intensified since they had parked their unmarked car hours ago.

He tried to pinpoint the source of his discomfort, his eyes scanning the dark expanse. The farmhouse, an ominous silhouette against the night sky, seemed to hold secrets in its decaying walls. The rural silence, a stark contrast to the city's constant hum, felt oppressive, as if it were hiding something just out of sight.

George's instincts, honed by his years of being a cop on the beat, rarely misled him. There was something about this setup, this tip, that didn't sit right with him. He couldn't put his finger on it, but the unease was there, persistent and unsettling.

George glanced at Arthur, the older man's profile barely visible in the dim light of the car's dashboard. Arthur's trust in the informant was evident, his years of experience giving weight to his judgment. But George couldn't shake the feeling that they were missing something, a piece of the puzzle that was eluding them.

His mind raced through the details of the case, searching for any clue that might justify his apprehension. Was it the informant's credibility? The location? The timing? Each question led to more questions, a spiralling maze with no apparent exit.

The weight of responsibility pressed down on him. As a detective, his decisions could mean the difference between success and failure, safety and danger. The lives of others, including his colleagues, often hinged on his judgment.

George exhaled slowly, trying to calm the storm of thoughts. He needed to stay sharp and focused. He couldn't afford to be distracted by vague apprehensions. Yet, the feeling persisted, a silent alarm ringing in the back of his mind.

Then suddenly, two figures materialised from the shadows, cautiously moving towards the farmhouse. The sudden appearance of the suspects sent a jolt of adrenaline through George. His hand instinctively reached for his radio, ready to call for backup.

But Arthur, with a subtle yet firm gesture, signalled him to wait. His eyes were sharp, tracking every movement of the approaching figures. George's hand hovered over the radio, his instincts conflicted. The urge to act, to call it in, was strong, but he trusted Arthur's experience and judgment.

The figures, cloaked in darkness, moved with a cautious deliberation that suggested they were well aware of the risks. They paused intermittently, scanning the surroundings, as if sensing the presence of unseen eyes on them.

George watched intently, his initial impulse to immediately call for backup tempered by Arthur's restraint. He understood that timing was critical; acting too soon could spook the suspects, potentially jeopardising the operation.

Arthur's eyes never left the figures. "Let's see what they do. We need to be sure," he whispered, his voice barely audible. His calm under pressure was infectious, and George found himself easing into a more calculated mindset.

As they observed, the figures reached the farmhouse, their movements becoming more confident as they disappeared into the structure.

George's training kicked in. He noted their entry point, their mannerisms, and anything that might be useful later.

He glanced at Arthur, who gave a slight nod. It was a silent acknowledgement of the unfolding situation, a shared understanding of the stakes at play. They remained vigilant, ready to act, yet patient, allowing the scenario to unfold naturally.

But just as suddenly as the figures had arrived, the scene before them also took a sudden turn. The figures burst back out. They sprinted away, their movements frantic, a stark contrast to their earlier cautious approach.

From the distance, even in the dim light, their panic was palpable. George's eyes widened in surprise, his hand instinctively reaching for his radio again. But he paused, watching the scene unfold, trying to decipher the cause of this abrupt change.

Arthur, equally taken aback, scanned the area. "Something's spooked them," he muttered, his voice tense.

George followed Arthur's gaze, searching the dark expanse around the farmhouse. Then he saw it—a disturbance in the nearby beck, a shadowy movement that was out of place in the otherwise still night. Whatever it was, it had been enough to send the suspects fleeing in a blind panic.

The detectives exchanged a look, a mix of confusion and alertness. This was an unexpected twist, a variable they hadn't anticipated. George's mind raced, considering their options. Do they pursue the suspects or investigate what had startled them?

Arthur seemed to weigh the situation, his experienced eyes assessing the rapidly evolving scenario. "We need to check the beck," he decided swiftly. "If they were spooked, it could be someone else on our turf or something else entirely."

George nodded, his training kicking in. The priority was to maintain control of the situation and to gather as much information as possible. They exited the car quickly but quietly, making their way towards the beck with a blend of urgency and caution.

As they approached, the reasons behind the suspects' sudden departure remained a mystery, shrouded in the night's embrace. George's senses were heightened, every sound and movement amplified in the darkness.

As George and Arthur approached the beck, the moon broke through the clouds, casting a pale light over the scene. What it revealed sent a chill down George's spine—the lifeless body of a young brunette policewoman, her wrists bound with handcuffs, half-submerged in the shallow waters.

George's heart sank, a mix of anger and sorrow welling up inside him. The sight of the uniform, one of their own, made it personal. He felt a surge of protectiveness for his colleagues, a reminder of the dangers they all faced.

Arthur's reaction was more controlled but no less intense. His jaw clenched, a steely determination setting in his eyes. "We need to secure the scene," he said, his voice steady but tinged with an undercurrent of emotion.

George nodded, his professional instincts taking over despite the turmoil inside him. He reached for his radio, his voice calm as he called it in. "We need backup at Country Way, near the old farmhouse. We've got a body in the beck. Looks like a police officer."

As they waited for backup, George couldn't tear his eyes away from the young officer. Questions raced through his mind. Who was she? How did she end up here? Was this related to the suspects they were surveilling, or was it a separate, darker incident?

Arthur surveyed the area, his eyes searching for any clues, any signs that might explain what had happened. The grim discovery had shifted the focus of their investigation entirely. The stakes were higher now, the urgency greater.

George's voice was barely above a whisper, heavy with a mixture of grief and disbelief. "She's the third one, sir. The third policewoman." The weight of the revelation hung in the air, a grim pattern emerging in the darkness of the night.

Arthur, standing beside him, nodded solemnly. His eyes, usually a beacon of calm and wisdom, now reflected a fierce resolve. "We'll get him, George. We'll get this monster," he vowed, his tone infused with a steely determination.

The distant sound of sirens began to fill the night, a reminder that the world was still moving, even as they stood frozen by the grim discovery. The approach of their colleagues signalled the start of a long, challenging investigation.

George felt a renewed sense of purpose powered by Arthur's vow. The death of the policewoman, the third in a string of such tragedies, was a call to action that he could not ignore. It was more than just a duty; it was a moral imperative.

As the first of the backup cars arrived, flooding the scene with light and activity, George stood firm, his resolve hardening. This was a turning point, a moment that would define the course of their investigation.

The night, once a silent witness to their surveillance, was now alive with the urgency of the situation. Forensics teams moved in, their equipment casting eerie shadows on the ground as they began their meticulous work.

George glanced at Arthur, seeing him not just as his boss but as a partner in this quest for justice. Together, they would delve into the darkness of this case, driven by a shared vow to bring the perpetrator to justice.

The scene around them buzzed with activity, but George's thoughts were focused, his determination clear. They would find the monster behind these heinous acts. They had to. For the sake of their fallen colleagues, for the safety of the community, and for the integrity of the warrant cards they carried.

Chapter One

January 2024

Two weeks had elapsed since the Santa Claus murders had sent shock waves through Leeds. The city, usually bustling with life, still carried the echoes of those harrowing events. In the wake of the chaos, George Beaumont found himself in unfamiliar territory, not just geographically but professionally.

The diligent detective inspector had been catapulted into the role of detective chief inspector, a position that brought new responsibilities and challenges. His promotion, vigorously championed by Detective Superintendent Jim Smith, was more than just a change in title. It was a recognition of his unwavering dedication and sharp investigative skills that had been instrumental in solving the complex case.

George, seated in his new office, felt the weight of the change. The room was larger, the desk more imposing, but the sense of duty remained the same. The walls, adorned with commendations and case files, were a testament to his journey in the force.

He looked out the window, his green eyes reflecting a city still recovering, still grieving. The Santa Claus murders were not just another case; they had been a test of his resolve, a challenge to his abilities as a detective. And now, as a detective chief inspector, he knew the expectations would be higher, the scrutiny more intense.

The phone on his desk rang, jarring him from his thoughts. It was Jim Smith, his voice gruff but warm. "Congratulations, George. You've earned this," he said, a note of pride evident in his tone.

George thanked him, the reality of his new role settling in. "I won't let you down, sir," he replied, his voice steady, betraying none of the turmoil inside.

As he hung up, George took a deep breath. This promotion was not just a personal achievement; it was a commitment to uphold the values of the force and to lead with integrity and courage. He glanced at a photo of Isabella and their children, a reminder of the personal sacrifices that came with the job.

Stepping into the role of Detective Chief Inspector meant stepping into a world of greater complexity, where decisions had far-reaching consequences. But George Beaumont was ready. He had faced darkness before, both within and without, and had emerged stronger.

Later, in the bustling Incident Room at Elland Road Police Station, DCI George Beaumont stood before his team. The room, a hive of activity, buzzed with the energy of a team deep in the final stages of the Santa Claus investigation. The walls were still plastered with maps, photos, and whiteboards filled with notes—the lifeblood of the case.

George's presence commanded the room, his new role as DCI adding a layer of authority to his already respected stature. He scanned the faces before him, a mix of experience and youth, each member bringing their unique strengths to the table.

CHAPTER ONE

Detective Sergeant Yolanda Williams stood to his right, her sharp intellect and keen analytical skills making her an invaluable asset to the team. Her calm attitude was a stabilising force, especially in high-pressure situations.

Nearby, Detective Constables Tashan Blackburn and Jay Scott were deep in discussion. Tashan's imposing figure and analytical approach contrasted with Jay's lean build and creative methods. Jay's enthusiasm often brought a light-heartedness to the team's gruelling work, a much-needed respite from the gravity of their duties.

The atmosphere in the Incident Room was charged with a palpable sense of triumph. The walls, usually echoing with the seriousness of unsolved cases, now resonated with the sounds of celebration. George, standing at the forefront of the room, raised his voice above the jubilant noise.

"Everyone, your dedication has brought David Hardaker and his associates to justice. This is a significant blow to organised crime in Leeds," he announced, his words brimming with pride.

A cacophony of cheers erupted, the team's relief and satisfaction mingling in the air. Glasses clinked in a symphony of celebration as colleagues toasted to their hard-earned success.

In the midst of the celebration, Jason Scott, known for his quick wit, stepped forward. "Remember the stakeout at the warehouse?" he began, a mischievous glint in his eye. The room quieted, anticipation building for one of Jay's famous anecdotes.

He recounted the tale with dramatic flair, describing how an overly curious cat had almost blown their cover, leading to a series of comically improvised distractions. The room erupted into laughter, the story a perfect illustration of the unpredictability and lighter moments in their line of work.

George watched the scene unfold, a smile playing on his lips. The laughter and camaraderie momentarily lifted the weight of their demanding profession. It was moments like these that knit the team together, a necessary counterbalance to the challenges they faced daily.

He raised his glass, joining in the toast. "To the team," he said, his voice resonating with genuine affection and respect.

The room echoed his sentiment, glasses raised high. The shared success had not only strengthened their resolve but had also deepened their bond as a unit. In the demanding world of police work, these moments of light-heartedness and unity were rare and precious.

As the laughter and stories continued, George felt a deep sense of fulfilment. Leading this team and guiding them through the complexities of each case was more than a job; it was a calling. And tonight, they had every reason to celebrate their hard work and collective achievement.

The celebratory atmosphere in the Incident Room, however, subtly shifted as Detective Constable Candy Nichols entered. Known for her meticulous approach and keen eye for detail, her presence immediately drew George's attention. She approached him with a sense of purpose, holding an envelope that seemed out of place amidst the festivities.

George's expression turned serious as he accepted the envelope from Candy. His colleagues' laughter and chatter faded into the background as his focus narrowed on the mysterious delivery. He could sense Candy's anticipation, her usual composure tinged with a hint of urgency.

With a steady hand, George carefully opened the outer

envelope, his mind swirling with possibilities. The seriousness with which Candy had presented it suggested it was no ordinary correspondence.

Inside, he found another envelope, this one more personal, addressed directly to him. The room's energy seemed to pause, a collective breath held as George extracted its contents. His eyes widened slightly as he was confronted with a photograph.

The image was stark, commanding immediate attention. George studied it intently, his detective instincts kicking in. The photograph held a message, a clue, something significant enough to be delivered to him directly amidst a celebration.

Candy watched him, awaiting his reaction. The rest of the team, sensing the shift in mood, gradually quieted, their attention turning towards George and the mysterious envelope.

George's mind raced, piecing together the potential implications of the photograph. This unexpected development was a stark reminder of the ever-present undercurrents in their line of work. Even in moments of victory, the shadows of unresolved mysteries lingered.

He looked up from the photograph, meeting Candy's gaze. Raising his voice, he said, "We need to discuss this." The celebration around them seemed a distant memory now as they stepped into the familiar territory of analysis and investigation.

The mood in the room had transformed, the weight of their profession settling back onto their shoulders. But George, surrounded by his capable team, felt ready to face whatever challenge the photograph heralded. Their celebration was cut short, but their resolve remained unshaken, a testament to the ever-evolving world of police work because the photograph in George's hands was more than just an image; it was a ghost from the past, a haunting reminder of a case that had never truly left him. The scene depicted was unmistakable—the notorious cold case involving the murder of three young policewomen. It was a mystery that had lingered in his mind, an unresolved symphony of questions and dead ends that had stretched over 12 long years.

A shiver ran down his spine as he studied the image. The scene was eerily familiar, each element transporting him back to those early days of his career. The photograph held a morbid image—a chilling snapshot of a crime that had shaken the force to its core.

Memories flooded back, vivid and unbidden. He remembered the first time he had set eyes on the crime scene, the overwhelming sense of injustice, the determination to find the perpetrator. He recalled the long hours, the false leads, the growing frustration as the case grew colder with each passing day.

Beside him, the shadow of his former colleague, Detective Inspector Arthur Grimes, loomed large. Arthur had been his mentor, a guiding force in those early days. Together, they had poured over every detail, every clue, desperate to bring closure to the heinous crimes. But the answers had eluded them, slipping through their fingers like grains of sand.

George's eyes lingered on the photograph, each detail etched in his memory. The positioning of the bodies, the surroundings, the haunting expressions of the victims—it was a scene that had haunted his dreams, a case that had never quite let him go.

The room around him was still, his team watching him, waiting for his lead. George felt a surge of determination, a

CHAPTER ONE

rekindling of the fire that had driven him all those years ago. This photograph was not just a reminder of a failure; it was a call to action, a chance to right a wrong that had lingered for over a decade.

He looked up, his gaze steely. "This case isn't closed," he declared, his voice carrying a new resolve. "We're going to reopen the investigation. It's time we gave those women the justice they deserve."

The team rallied around him, the photograph now a symbol of their renewed commitment. The past had returned, but George Beaumont, now a DCI, was ready to face it head-on, armed with experience, a dedicated team, and an unwavering resolve to bring closure to one of the darkest chapters of his career.

George's resolve was firm, yet a knot of apprehension tightened in his stomach as he sought out Detective Inspector Luke Mason. Mason, a man whose words were sparing but packed with profound wisdom, was someone George trusted implicitly in matters of grave importance.

Finding Mason in the quiet corner of the station where he often reflected on cases, George presented the photograph without preamble. Mason's eyes narrowed as he studied the image, his expression betraying a hint of recognition.

"You need to report this, son," Mason said, his voice low and steady. His advice was unequivocal, a clear directive in the face of uncertainty.

With a heavy heart and the photograph in hand, George made his way to Detective Superintendent Jim Smith's office. His mind was a whirlwind of emotions as he walked. The image had ignited a fire of determination within him, but it was mixed with an uneasy sense of foreboding. The path ahead was shrouded in uncertainty, the ghosts of the past looming large.

Upon reaching Smith's office, George knocked and entered. Jim Smith looked up, his seasoned features rearranging into a look of concern as he took in George's serious expression.

"Sir, there's something you need to see," George began, extending the photograph towards Smith.

As Smith took the photograph, George watched his reaction closely. The Superintendent's eyes scanned the image, a shadow of recognition crossing his features. The weight of the case, its history, and its implications were not lost on him.

"This is the cold case from 12 years ago, the policewomen murders," Smith said, his tone serious. He looked up at George, his gaze sharp. "Where did you get this?"

George explained the mysterious delivery, his voice steady despite the turmoil inside. "It was just delivered to me anonymously." He paused. "I want to reopen the case... With your permission, of course."

Smith leaned back in his chair, the photograph in his hands. "This changes things, George. Reopening this case... it won't be easy."

George nodded, his jaw set. "I know, sir. But we owe it to them. We need to find out who's behind this and why now."

Smith regarded George for a long moment, the silence in the room heavy. Finally, he nodded. "Alright. We'll reopen the investigation. But tread carefully, George. This case... it's a maze with many turns."

George left the office with the Detective Superintendent's words echoing in his mind. He felt rattled, the image having stirred a deep-seated sense of duty but also a recognition of the complex and potentially treacherous journey ahead.

CHAPTER ONE

As he walked back to the Incident Room, the photograph now a catalyst for a renewed investigation, George felt the full weight of the task ahead. The path would be fraught with challenges, but his determination was unshaken. The fire within him, a blend of resolve and apprehension, was ready to face whatever secrets the photograph would unveil.

Chapter Two

As George descended the stairs, his thoughts preoccupied with the reopened investigation, he nearly collided with Detective Chief Inspector Alistair Atkinson. The suddenness of their encounter did little to ease the tension that always simmered between them, and the air instantly crackled with tension.

Atkinson's presence was commanding, yet his attitude carried an air of condescension that George knew all too well. The thinly veiled sneer on Atkinson's face as he glanced at the photograph in George's hand was unmistakable.

"Congrats on the promotion, Beaumont," Atkinson said sardonically, his words dripping with a bitterness that spoke of past disputes.

Atkinson, tall and imposing, leaned against the railing, a smirk playing on his lips as his eyes flicked to the photograph in George's hand. "Quite the detective work, Beaumont," he drawled, the sneer in his voice unmistakable. "Or should I say, quite the imagination? A mysterious letter right after your promotion—how very convenient."

George bristled at the insinuation. "It's a lead on an old case, Alistair. Not everything's a game or a ploy for attention."

Atkinson laughed, a hollow sound that echoed in the stairwell. "A lead? Or a desperate grab at proving yourself? Let's not forget who's really running things here. You may have the title, DCI Beaumont, but we all know who's the better detective."

The barb hit its mark, but George kept his composure. "The better detective doesn't need to undermine others to feel secure, Alistair."

A flicker of irritation crossed Atkinson's face, quickly masked by a mocking smile. "How does it feel commandeering my old crew? Enjoying playing the hero with them?"

George's eyes narrowed. "They were never 'your crew', Atkinson. They've always been a dedicated team, committed to justice, not to feeding someone's ego."

The disdain in Atkinson's eyes was evident, his voice dripping with condescension. "Watch yourself, Beaumont. These high-profile cases can be tricky. Wouldn't want you to trip over your newfound authority."

With that parting shot, Atkinson pushed off the railing and strode past George, leaving a trail of animosity in his wake. George watched him go, a momentary flare of anger giving way to a renewed sense of purpose. He didn't have time for Atkinson's games; he had a case to solve and a team to lead. With a determined step, he continued down the stairs, Atkinson's disdainful words dismissed to the back of his mind. The real work lay ahead, and George was more than ready to face it.

* * *

George sat across from Detective Inspector Luke Mason in his office. The photograph, now the epicentre of George's attention, lay on his desk.

"Take a look at this," George said, sliding the photograph to Mason. "It's definitely a scene from the Gildersome case, yet..."

Mason studied the image closely, his brow furrowing. "It's high-resolution, recent, I'd wager. The grave... it's disturbingly clear."

George leaned back in his chair. "Three crosses, made from branches. It's rudimentary, almost symbolic." He paused, a sense of unease evident in his voice. "Just like twelve years ago."

George's eyes returned to the photograph. "The starkness of it all... no people, no immediate clues. It's as if the scene itself is meant to convey a message."

Mason handed the photograph back to George. "Do you think it's a clue to revive the investigation? Or maybe a taunt?"

George sighed, the weight of the case evident in his expression. "It could be either, or something else entirely. And as you said, the clarity suggests it was taken recently, which raises even more questions about the sender's motives."

Mason pointed at the disturbed soil around the grave. "See here, the earth is darker. It suggests recent activity, maybe even a revisit to the site."

George nodded, and Mason added, "And in the background, there's an old structure, possibly a barn or an abandoned building. Could be significant, maybe a clue to the location."

George's eyes lingered on the photograph, particularly on the faint outline of the structure in the background. Mason's observation echoed in his mind. A flicker of recognition sparked in George's memory, transporting him back to a chilly night in 2012. He was back on the rural expanse of Country

Way in Gildersome, the night air thick, the scent of damp earth pervasive. He and Arthur Grimes were huddled in their vehicle, eyes fixed on a decaying farmhouse in the distance.

"It's the same farmhouse," George said abruptly, the realisation hitting him like a wave. "I was there with Arthur back in 2012. It's where we found Police Constable Emily Thompson..."

Mason looked at him, interest piqued. "The same farmhouse? That's more than a coincidence. It ties the location to you personally."

George nodded, his mind racing. The connection was undeniable now. The photograph wasn't just a random clue; it was intricately linked to his past.

"This changes things," Mason said thoughtfully. "It suggests whoever sent this knows about your involvement in the old case."

The implications of this revelation were profound. It meant the sender was not only familiar with the Gildersome case but also aware of George's personal connection to it. The photograph was a deliberate choice, a calculated move to draw him back into the mystery.

George felt a mix of apprehension and resolve. "We need to revisit everything about that night, any connections to this case. There's more to this than just an unsolved murder."

Mason nodded. "I'll dig into the archives and see what else we can find about your surveillance of the farmhouse. There might be more there than we realised at the time."

George nodded, his gaze fixed on the photograph. "It's like it's pulling me back into the past, forcing me to reopen old wounds." The haunting scene in the picture was more than just a reminder of an unsolved case; it was a personal challenge, a ghost from his early days in the force.

Mason suggested, "We should revisit the suspects from the original Gildersome case. There might be a connection we overlooked, something that seemed insignificant at the time."

George agreed, the wheels in his mind turning. "And what if the sender is trying to mislead us, to send us down the wrong path?" The possibility was a nagging concern, adding another layer of complexity to the puzzle.

"The timing is curious," Mason added. "It could be a warning, or maybe the sender wants to reignite the investigation for some reason."

George leaned back, the photograph's presence filling the room with an eerie sense of the past. "This case... it never really left me. There's a haunting personal impact to it, a feeling of unfinished business."

Mason nodded in understanding. "We'll need to tread carefully. Re-examining old leads discreetly, consulting with forensics for new insights. There might be advancements in technology that could shed new light on the evidence."

George felt a sense of resolve settle over him. "Let's start by pulling the old case files like you said, go over everything with a fresh perspective. We need to see this through, for the victims and for justice."

As Mason left the office, George remained seated, his thoughts deep in the shadows of the past. The photograph was more than just a piece of evidence; it was a catalyst, reigniting a quest for answers that had lain dormant for too long.

With a plan forming, George knew the road ahead would be challenging, filled with twists and turns. But the determination to solve this long-standing mystery, to finally bring closure to a case that had haunted him for years, was a fire that now burned brightly within him.

George held the photograph and envelopes with an air of solemn determination. There was a knock on the door.

"Come in."

He looked up as Detective Constable Tashan Blackburn entered.

"Tashan, I need you to handle the forensic analysis of these," he said, indicating the items on his desk. "It's crucial."

Tashan nodded, stepping closer to examine the evidence. "What are we looking for, sir?"

George's instructions were meticulous, showcasing his extensive knowledge and attention to detail. "Start with fingerprint analysis on both the photograph and the envelopes. Check for any latent prints. Then, move on to DNA analysis. Focus on the edges of the envelopes, where they were sealed."

He paused, ensuring Tashan was following. "And let's not overlook trace evidence analysis. We need to know where this photograph was taken, or at least where the envelope was posted from. Use whatever advanced techniques we have—digital image enhancement for the photo, chemical analysis for the age of the paper and ink."

Tashan listened intently, understanding the gravity of the task. "Got it, sir. Anything else?"

George emphasised the urgency. "This is high priority. It's potentially linked to an unsolved cold case. We need to act swiftly."

He then guided Tashan on maintaining the chain of custody. "Make sure you document everything. We need to preserve the integrity of the evidence. Use gloves, and transport them in sealed evidence bags."

Tashan assured him, "I understand, sir. I'll make sure everything's handled by the book."

George's expression softened slightly. "How soon can we expect results?"

"We'll push for a quick turnaround. With your permission, I'll personally ensure it's expedited," Tashan replied, sensing the eagerness in George's voice.

As Tashan left with the evidence, George sat back in his chair, his mind racing. The forensic results could be a turning point in the investigation. They might lead to a new suspect or confirm a connection to the old case. The possibilities were endless, and each one opened a different path in the investigation.

George knew that the answers they sought lay hidden within the minute details of the evidence. The outcome of the forensic analysis could either propel them forward or send them back to the drawing board. With a deep breath, he steeled himself for the next phase of the investigation, ready to follow wherever the evidence led.

Chapter Three

In the Incident Room at Elland Road Police Station, DCI George Beaumont assembled his team. The room, usually buzzing with the routine clamour of police work, had fallen into an expectant hush. The team members gathered around, their expressions a mix of curiosity and readiness.

DI Luke Mason, his face etched with experience, leaned against a table, his eyes sharp and focused. DS Yolanda Williams stood nearby, her posture straight, exuding a quiet strength. DC Jay Scott's youthful energy was evident in his eager stance, while DC Tashan Blackburn's composed manner hinted at his analytical mind. DC Candy Nichols, her red hair a stark contrast against the room's dull hues, watched George intently, ready for the challenge.

"Before we begin, I'd like to introduce a new member of our team, Detective Constable Alexis Mercer."

Alexis Mercer stepped forward, a confident yet approachable presence in the bustling incident room. In her mid-thirties, she exuded a sense of quiet authority that commanded respect. Her keen blue eyes, reminiscent of the North Sea on a clear day, scanned the room meticulously, missing little. These eyes, deep and probing, were a testament to her analytical nature, constantly soaking in the details of her surroundings.

Her hair, a cascade of blonde that varied in shades from golden to almost silvery, was pulled back into a practical ponytail, showcasing her no-nonsense approach to her work. The soft waves, however, lent a touch of softness to her otherwise sharp features, balancing her appearance between approachable and authoritative.

Alexis' stature, a touch above average, combined with her firm, athletic build, hinted at the strength and stamina required for her demanding role. She moved with a grace that was both measured and deliberate, each step purposeful and assured.

Her face, a blend of softness and angles, was marked by high cheekbones and a strong jawline. Her fair skin bore a slight flush, a testament to the long hours she spent in the field. Her expression, usually set in a line of concentration, now held a mix of anticipation and professionalism. There was a sense of eagerness about her, a readiness to dive into the intricacies of the case at hand.

Dressed in smart, well-fitted trousers paired with a crisp button-down shirt and a blazer, Alexis was the epitome of functional style. Her attire, sharp yet allowing ease of movement, was complemented by sensible shoes—flats that were perfect for hours of fieldwork. The simplicity of her thin gold chain and small stud earrings underscored her pragmatic approach to life.

"Alexis comes to us with an impressive background in criminal investigation," George continued. "She's not only a Leeds native but also a graduate with First-Class Honours in Criminology from the University of Leeds. Her local knowledge and expertise in digital forensics will be invaluable to our investigation."

As Alexis surveyed the room, her posture, upright and confident, reflected her inner resilience.

The team's interest was piqued. Detective Sergeant Yolanda Williams, always keen on welcoming new talent, stepped forward with a friendly smile. "Glad to have you with us, Alexis. Your experience, especially in digital forensics, will definitely come in handy."

Alexis stepped forward and nodded in acknowledgement; her movements, fluid and purposeful, betrayed an underlying agility. When she spoke, it was with a voice that was clear and concise, her words carefully chosen and delivered with a sense of assuredness. "Thank you, Detective Sergeant Williams. I'm excited to contribute to the team and help bring resolution to our cases."

George motioned towards Detective Constables Tashan Blackburn and Jay Scott. "Tashan. Jay. Alexis is also proficient in crime scene analysis. I'm sure she'll be a great asset in the field."

Jay, ever curious about new approaches, chimed in. "Welcome aboard, Alexis. Looking forward to seeing your analytical skills in action."

Tashan, always a bit more reserved, offered a nod of approval. "Good to have another sharp mind on the team."

Alexis turned to them, her tone respectful yet assured. "I'm eager to collaborate and learn from each of you. I believe in a meticulous approach to investigations, and I hope my skills will complement the team's efforts."

George then introduced her to Detective Constable Candy Nichols. "Candy, Alexis has spent several years in the Child Protection Unit. Her experience in dealing with sensitive cases will be a great addition to our work."

Candy extended her hand, her expression warm. "Welcome, Alexis. Your empathy will be a huge asset, especially in our more challenging cases."

Alexis responded with genuine appreciation. "Thank you, Candy. I've always believed in the importance of empathy in our line of work. It's crucial in understanding both victims and perpetrators."

As the introductions concluded, George addressed the entire team. "Alexis' addition to our team comes at a critical time. Her skills in digital forensics could be the key to untangling the web of this complex case, especially with the digital elements we're encountering."

Turning to Alexis, he added, "Your fresh perspective might also help us re-examine the evidence we've collected so far. Sometimes a new set of eyes is what we need to see what we've been missing."

Alexis, feeling the weight of her new role, nodded in agreement. "I'm ready to dive in, sir. Let's get to work."

George nodded and pointed towards a series of visual aids laid out before him—maps of Gildersome, haunting photos from the crime scene, and a detailed timeline of events. His tone was solemn, reflecting the gravity of the case they were about to revisit. "Twelve years ago, I faced a mystery that has remained unsolved," he began, his voice steady but imbued with a sense of resolve.

"Twelve years is a long time," George continued, his eyes sweeping across the team. He turned to Luke and Yolanda. "Luke. Yolanda. You were both here at the time. Your experience is invaluable, but I need you to look at this case with fresh eyes. Set aside any previous theories."

Yolanda nodded in understanding, her expression serious. Luke's nod was more subtle, but his agreement was evident in his attentive posture.

George turned his gaze to Alexis, his expression thoughtful. "Alexis, were you with West Yorkshire Police twelve years ago when these crimes occurred?"

Alexis nodded, her demeanour turning solemn as she recalled the time. "Yes, I was. I was just an officer on the beat back then." She paused, a distant look in her eyes as she delved into her memories. "It was a terrifying time, especially for us younger, female officers. The news of the murders, all involving policewomen, sent shock waves through the department."

The room fell silent, the weight of her words hanging in the air. George could see the impact the case had on Alexis, even as a rookie officer. It was a reminder of the far-reaching effects such crimes had on the police community, not just as professionals but as individuals.

Alexis continued, her voice steady despite the haunting memories. "We were all on edge, constantly looking over our shoulders. There was this palpable sense of fear but also a determination to find the perpetrator. It was a stark reminder of the dangers we face in this line of work."

George nodded in understanding. "That fear, that determination you felt back then, I want you to channel it into this investigation. Your perspective from the streets during that time could provide valuable insights that we might have missed."

Alexis met his gaze, her resolve clear. "I'll do everything I can, sir. Maybe now, with the skills and experience I've gained since then, I can help bring some closure to this case."

He walked them through the case, pointing to the visual aids. "We have a chance to revisit this with fresh eyes," he said, gesturing to the timeline. "New forensic technologies and investigative methods developed since then could provide the breakthrough we need."

Turning to individual assignments, George was methodical. "Tashan, as well as your previous instructions, I want you to dive into the technological aspects. Anything that can be enhanced or re-analysed, you're on it." Tashan nodded, his eyes already alight with ideas. "Alexis will assist you."

"Yolanda, you'll revisit witness interviews. There may be something we missed, or someone might be more willing to talk now." Yolanda acknowledged her task with a determined nod. "Alexis will speak with some of the victims' family members, so be sure to check in with her, OK?"

"Will do, sir," said Yolanda.

"Candy, Jay, you'll assist with fieldwork. Re-examine the crime scenes and look for overlooked clues." Both Candy and Jay responded with a readiness that spoke of their commitment.

George continued. "Each of you has talents that I do not. For example, Jay, your training in criminal psychology could give us new insights into the perpetrator's profile." Jay's eyes brightened, acknowledging the trust placed in his skills.

"Tashan," George continued, "your expertise in digital forensics could uncover details we previously missed." Tashan's nod was one of focused determination.

"And Candy," he said, turning to her, "your analytical approach to evidence gathering will be crucial in the field," Candy responded with a firm, confident nod, ready for the task.

CHAPTER THREE

"As we revisit this case, remember, we're not just looking for what's changed; we're looking for what we missed," George emphasised. "We have tools and methods now that weren't available back then." He pointed to a timeline chart, indicating key dates and events. "Every detail matters. Let's go over everything, no matter how small."

The team was fully engaged, each member mentally preparing for their role in the investigation. George's briefing had not only outlined the strategy but had also instilled a sense of unity and purpose; the team was a unified front, with each member aware of their role and the importance of the task ahead. The renewed investigation into the Gildersome murders was not just a case; it was a chance to right a wrong, to bring closure to a haunting chapter in their careers.

As George Beaumont distributed the comprehensive dossier of the Gildersome murders case to his team, the air in the Incident Room was thick with anticipation. The document was a culmination of everything he had compiled 12 years ago—case history, witness statements, and forensic reports.

As the team leafed through the pages, George's voice provided a backdrop, his tone clinical yet tinged with a solemn respect for the case's gravity. He used a projector to display maps of the crime scenes, photos that were as haunting today as they had been a decade ago, and a timeline that highlighted key events.

"While working this case 12 years ago, I was newer to the force, driven, but without the experience I have now," George reflected aloud, his gaze momentarily distant. "Looking at it now, with years under my belt, I see avenues we didn't explore, questions we didn't ask."

DI Luke Mason, looking up from the dossier, nodded

thoughtfully. "Hindsight is a powerful tool, son. We've now got a chance to make this right."

As the team engaged with the case, their reactions ranging from keen interest to quiet contemplation, George felt a sense of collective determination building in the room. The dossier, a testament to his past diligence, was now a foundation upon which they would build their investigation.

As the briefing wound down, George Beaumont addressed his team with a final instruction. "Take the evening to familiarise yourselves with the case history. We start fresh tomorrow."

The team members nodded, each holding a copy of the detailed dossier. The atmosphere in the room was a blend of solemn determination and keen interest.

DI Luke Mason flipped through the pages. "This is comprehensive, son. It'll give us a solid starting point."

As the meeting dispersed, Alexis stayed behind to review the case files, her eyes scanning the pages with an analytical sharpness. George watched her for a moment, confident in her ability to make a significant contribution. With Alexis on board, the team was stronger and more equipped to face the challenges ahead.

George's gaze lingering on the dossier. The Gildersome murders case, a complex puzzle from his past, was now a challenge for the present. With his skilled team and the benefit of advanced technology, George was ready to lead the charge in solving the mystery that had eluded him for over a decade.

Chapter Four

Maya Chen, a 34-year-old forensic scientist of East Asian descent who brought a combination of sharp analytical skills and meticulous attention to detail to her work in forensic analysis, was fully absorbed in the critical task at hand. With her black hair neatly styled in a practical bob, she moved with purpose among the array of high-tech equipment that filled the room.

Detective Constable Tashan Blackburn entered the lab with a folder of photographs in hand. "Maya, do you have a moment?" he asked, approaching her workstation.

Without looking up, Maya replied, "Just finishing up here, Tashan. What do you have for me?"

Tashan laid the photographs on the counter. "This was sent to my boss, a recent photo of an old crime scene," he explained. "We need your expertise on any chemical residues present."

As Maya prepared the necessary equipment for chemical analysis, Tashan watched in admiration. "Your ability to switch between different types of analysis is impressive," he commented.

Maya offered a small smile, her focus unwavering. "Every piece of evidence tells a story. It's just a matter of listening to what it has to say."

Her hands moved with practised ease as she prepared samples for testing. The atmosphere in the lab was one of quiet intensity, with Maya at the centre, orchestrating the intricate dance of forensic examination.

Once Tashan was gone, Maya worked methodically, starting with fingerprint analysis. She dusted each item carefully, her eyes focused and unblinking as she searched for latent prints. The concentration in the room was palpable; each swipe of her brush was a step closer to a possible breakthrough.

Moving on to DNA analysis, Maya's approach was equally meticulous. She sampled the edges of the envelopes, where they had been sealed, looking for traces of saliva or any other DNA evidence. The precision of her movements reflected the importance of the task; there was no room for error in this line of work.

With the fingerprint and DNA analysis underway, Maya then turned her attention to the digital enhancement of the photographs. Her fingers moved with practised ease over the keyboard, manipulating the images to bring out obscured details. As the features in the photos became clearer, Maya's eyes narrowed, focusing intently on the emerging patterns and elements.

The final part of her analysis involved a chemical examination of the paper and ink. Using various reagents and a spectrometer, Maya determined the composition and age of the materials, as well as clues that could provide context or link the items to a specific source.

* * *

CHAPTER FOUR

Detective Chief Inspector George Beaumont watched with keen interest as Detective Constable Alexis Mercer delved into the case files of their current investigation. It was her first day on the team, and George had assigned her to review the digital evidence, a task well-suited to her expertise in digital forensics.

Alexis sat at her workstation, her eyes intently scanning the screens in front of her. She was methodically analysing data from various electronic devices recovered from the crime scenes over a decade ago. Her fingers danced across the keyboard, pulling up files, cross-referencing data, and piecing together a digital timeline of the events leading up to the crimes.

They had a lot of information from back then, but it meant nothing at the time.

George approached her, curious about her findings. "Anything interesting, Detective Mercer?"

Alexis glanced up, a spark of determination in her eyes. "Call me Alexis, please, sir," she said with a grin. "And yes. There's a pattern in the communication data from the victims' phones. All three received texts from a number that's not in any of our databases. It's encrypted, but I'm working on tracing it."

Whilst her response reaffirmed DSU Smith's decision to add her to George's team, George already knew about the number. They'd had no luck tracing it twelve years ago. Hopefully, her expertise in digital forensics would prove invaluable in uncovering new leads in the case.

Moving on to her next task, Alexis prepared to conduct interviews with some of the victims' family members. Her empathetic nature, honed during her time in the Child Protection Unit, made her ideal for handling these sensitive conversations.

The more George watched her, the more he thought he recognised her.

"Have we met before, Alexis?"

Alexis paused her work, her gaze lifting from the computer screen to meet George's inquiring eyes. She studied his face for a brief moment, her expression unreadable. "Have we met before, Alexis?" George had asked, a hint of recognition in his voice.

Her response was measured, a hint of hesitation in her tone. "I don't believe we have, sir," she said, carefully maintaining a neutral expression. "Leeds is a big place, after all. It's easy to feel like you've seen someone before."

George, leaning against the edge of her desk, seemed to ponder her response. He was a seasoned detective, attuned to the nuances of human behaviour, but Alexis' demeanour gave nothing away.

"Perhaps you're right," George conceded with a slight nod, though a trace of curiosity lingered in his eyes. "I've been with the police force for a long time. Faces start to blend together after a while."

Alexis offered a polite smile, subtly steering the conversation back to the task at hand. "I really need to get on with these interviews, sir."

Whilst her change of subject was smooth, redirecting George's attention to the investigation, George noticed it.

Just as he couldn't shake the feeling of familiarity.

However, he respected her response and left her to her work.

* * *

CHAPTER FOUR

Under the cloak of evening, the streets of Leeds were quiet, their usual bustle subdued by the descending night. Streetlights cast a dim glow, creating long shadows that stretched across the pavement. In this twilight world, an unidentified person moved with purpose, their presence almost ghost-like.

Clad in a hooded tracksuit, they blended seamlessly into the shadows, their steps measured and silent except for the faint rustle of fabric. Every movement they made was cautious and calculated, as if they were acutely aware of the world around them. Their eyes darted about, scanning their surroundings with a wariness that suggested they were no ordinary shock waves.

They paused beside a red post box, their gaze flickering over their shoulder, a solitary figure against the dimly lit street. For a moment, they hesitated, their hand gripping an envelope tightly, almost an extension of the shadows that clung to them. The rustle of their tracksuit was a soft whisper in the quiet night as they moved. With a swift, almost furtive motion, they slid the envelope into the post box. The faint clatter of the letter hitting the side resonated in the still air, a solitary sound that seemed louder than it was.

Then, as quietly as the person had appeared, they retreated. The figure blended effortlessly into the shadows, merging with the darkness of the evening. They moved with a grace that belied their urgency, vanishing into the night, leaving behind a trail of unanswered questions and a lingering sense of intrigue.

The mood of the streets around them was sombre, the usual energy of the city subdued under the weight of the January evening. The air was frigid, carrying the faint scent of rain from earlier in the day, and the occasional sound of distant traffic was the only reminder of the city's pulse.

* * *

After a day immersed in the complexities of the Gildersome murders case, DCI George Beaumont welcomed the shift from his professional world to the personal sanctuary of his home. The moment he stepped through the door, the weight of the case seemed to lift, if only temporarily. The familiar comforts of home enveloped him, a stark contrast to the tension of the Incident Room.

His baby daughter, Olivia, greeted him with gleeful babbles from her playpen. George's face softened into a smile as he scooped her up, her tiny hands reaching for him with innocent joy. Holding Olivia, George felt a surge of love and responsibility. Here, in his arms, was a reminder of why he poured so much into his work—to make the world a safer place for her and others like her.

Carrying Olivia, he walked into the kitchen, where the aroma of a rustic stew filled the air. Isabella, his fiancée, stood by the stove, stirring the pot. The warmth in her smile as she looked up was the balm to the day's stress.

"Smells amazing," George said, as his stomach gave a loud, timely rumble.

Isabella laughed, a light, musical sound. "Timing as always, George. Your stomach knows when it's time for tea."

He chuckled, setting Olivia in her high chair. "It's got a mind of its own. Can't be helped when I come home to such delicious cooking."

The playful banter between them was effortless, a testament to the comfortable and loving relationship they shared.

CHAPTER FOUR

George watched Isabella move around the kitchen, a sense of deep gratitude washing over him. Here, away from the grit and grime of police work, he could be just George—a father, a fiancé, a man who cherished these quiet, ordinary moments.

As Isabella plated the stew, George took a moment to appreciate the normalcy. It was these moments that grounded him, that gave him the strength to face the challenges of his job. The laughter of his daughter, the warmth of his home, the love of his fiancée—these were the treasures he fought to protect, both in his personal life and through his work on the force.

The pair settled into their tea, the conversation flowing easily between George and Isabella. Isabella shared anecdotes from her day, detailing a shopping trip with Olivia. She mentioned a quaint little shop she discovered, filled with handcrafted toys and books, her eyes lighting up with enthusiasm. "I found the most adorable wooden puzzle for Olivia," she said, a hint of pride in her voice. "It's never too early to start challenging her mind, right?"

George smiled, appreciating Isabella's keen interest in nurturing Olivia's development. He loved this about her—her thoughtfulness, her eye for the unique and meaningful.

As George delved into the details of his day, Isabella's focus sharpened, her detective instincts kicking in despite her time away from work. Leaning forward, she interlaced her fingers, her eyes reflecting a familiar analytical spark.

"What about the forensic techniques? With all the advancements, there must be something new you can apply to the evidence," she mused, her tone suggesting a mind already sifting through possibilities.

George, noticing the shift, couldn't help but admire her

quick grasp of the situation. Her questions weren't just cursory; they cut to the heart of the investigation, echoing the very discussions he'd had at the station.

"And the witnesses," she continued, a thoughtful frown creasing her brow. "People's perspectives change over time. Maybe someone will remember something new."

Her insights were sharp, a reminder of her own skills as a detective. George responded, providing information while marvelling silently at how effortlessly she slipped back into her professional mindset.

"Do you think with the new technology you'll find something you missed before?" she asked, her tone casual but her eyes keenly focused on him.

George noticed the subtle shift in Isabella's demeanour. It was a familiar dance; though she was on maternity leave, her detective's instinct remained sharp. She had been more distant regarding work talk since her leave began, but now, there was a flicker of the old passion in her eyes.

He found himself curious about this change. It was clear that part of Izzy longed to be involved, to be back in the thick of solving cases. George trod carefully, sharing just enough to satisfy her curiosity but not enough to draw her too deeply into the case's complexities.

After dinner, they settled into their evening routine, a comforting rhythm of normalcy amidst their otherwise unpredictable lives. George bathed Olivia while Isabella cleaned up, the sounds of their daughter's giggles filling the house.

They ended the night with Olivia's bedtime story, a ritual George cherished. As they tucked her in, the stresses of his professional life seemed miles away. Here, in the warmth of their home, he found a balance, a peaceful counterpoint to the chaos of police work.

As Isabella and George retreated to the living room, a comfortable silence settled between them. Each lost in their thoughts; they enjoyed the simple pleasure of being together, a small island of tranquillity in the midst of life's relentless pace.

Chapter Five

As the first light of dawn filtered through the curtains, George Beaumont lay in bed, his mind slowly transitioning from the remnants of sleep to the realities of the waking world. He let out a heavy sigh, his thoughts drifting to the reflection he'd seen in the mirror recently—an image that reminded him of the relentless march of time.

Gone was the youthful officer who had joined the police, replaced by a man whose face bore the marks of long, sleepless nights and the stress of an often thankless job. The lines around his eyes were deeper, a testament to the years spent squinting at crime scenes and pouring over case files. His body, once athletic and agile, now carried the reminders of an accident that had left him more aware of his mortality and physical limits.

Lying there, George couldn't help but feel a twinge of nostalgia for his younger, more vigorous self. The demands of his job, both physical and mental, had taken their toll. He rubbed his shoulder, feeling the familiar ache, a souvenir from a pursuit gone awry years ago. He thought about his back where the Miss Murderer had stabbed him.

His thoughts then shifted to something that brought a soft smile to his face—his upcoming wedding to Isabella Wood.

CHAPTER FIVE

Isabella, with her unwavering support and understanding, had been his anchor through the tumultuous waves of his career. The thought of marrying her filled him with a warmth that offset the creeping chill of his ageing. She was his solace, the one who saw not just the detective, but the man behind the warrant card.

Yet, amidst this anticipation, there lurked a shadow of apprehension. The reopening of the Gildersome murders case was not just a professional challenge; it was a journey back into a chapter of his life filled with unresolved questions. His December had been filled with remnants of the past, and now his January was, too.

George wondered how the pressures of this case might affect his relationship with Isabella, especially with their wedding approaching. He wanted to shield her from the darker aspects of his work, but he also knew that she was more than capable of handling them.

As George prepared to start his day, these reflections stayed with him, colouring his thoughts. His ageing appearance and weakening body were reminders of his journey, while the upcoming wedding symbolised a future he longed to embrace fully. Balancing the weight of his past with the promise of his future, George Beaumont faced a day that was a microcosm of his life—a blend of professional challenges and personal commitments, each demanding a part of who he was.

* * *

George's morning drive to the station, usually a time for quiet contemplation, was abruptly interrupted by his phone ringing. Glancing at the caller ID, he saw it was Luke. He answered, expecting an update on the case, but nothing could have prepared him for what came next.

"George, I've received something strange this morning," Luke's voice came through the speaker, tinged with a mix of puzzlement and concern. "A letter, similar to what you got, with a photo of a car—a Vauxhall Corsa."

George's grip on the steering wheel tightened. His initial reaction was a blend of shock and a sinking sense of foreboding. "A Corsa?" he echoed, his mind racing. "Describe it to me. And give me the reg."

"It's an older model; it looks like it's from the early 2000s. Dark blue," Luke detailed, the confusion in his tone evident. He told George the reg number.

A chill ran down George's spine. "Luke, that matches the car seen twelve years ago near the scenes of the Gildersome killer." A man who had eluded George, DI Arthur Grimes, and the West Yorkshire Police. "Even down to the year of manufacture and the colour, Luke. This can't be a coincidence."

There was a brief silence on the line as the gravity of the statement settled in. Luke's voice, when he spoke again, carried a weight of concern. "What do you think it means, George? Someone playing games with us?"

George considered this. "Or the killer themselves, taunting us? It's as if they're pointing us towards clues we might have missed."

"There's an unsettling familiarity to this, George," Luke added. "Whoever's behind these letters knows the case inside out. They know about your involvement, and now this—it's like they're drawing us back in."

George's grip on the steering wheel tightened. "We need to tread carefully, Luke. This could be a trap, a way to mislead us.

Or it's a cry for attention—someone wanting the case back in the spotlight."

"The motive is what puzzles me, son," Luke said. "Are they seeking justice? Revenge? Or something more sinister?"

George pulled into the station car park, his thoughts heavy. "We'll figure it out, Luke. But let's keep this close for now. The last thing we need is panic or speculation among the team." He paused. "Regardless, we need to bring Detective Superintendent Smith into the loop," he said, his tone decisive. "He should see the photo."

"Agreed," Luke responded. "How do you want to approach this?"

George started walking towards the station. "We present it straightforwardly—the photo, its implications, and the connection to the Gildersome case. Smith needs to understand someone is dredging up the past for a reason. He might provide us with more resources."

"Right. And what about Grimes?" Luke inquired. "He was a key player back then. His insights could be invaluable."

George paused, his thoughts turning to Arthur Grimes. Their past working relationship had been complex—a mix of mentorship and occasional friction. "I'll suggest bringing Grimes in as a consultant. His perspective could be what we need to crack this. But I want to make sure Smith is on board."

Luke sensed the undercurrent in George's voice. "You think Smith will have reservations?"

"Possibly," George admitted. "There's history there, and Grimes wasn't always the easiest to work with. But his understanding of the case is unmatched."

They agreed to meet in George's office before heading to see Superintendent Smith. As George entered the building, his mind was already framing the conversation ahead. The introduction of Arthur Grimes into the investigation would be a significant step, one that could open new avenues but also old wounds.

The stakes were high, and George knew that every decision from this point forward would shape the course of the investigation. The path to uncovering the truth behind the Gildersome murders was becoming more intricate, and navigating it would require all the skill and experience at their disposal.

* * *

In Detective Superintendent Smith's office, George and Luke laid out the details of the mysterious photographs to Jim Smith. The seasoned Detective Superintendent listened intently, his expression growing increasingly troubled with each revelation.

"These photographs... they're sinister," Smith finally said, leaning back in his chair, his hands clasped together. "There's a calculated intent behind them. It's disturbing."

George nodded, his suspicions echoed by the Superintendent's words. "We believe they're directly linked to the Gildersome murders, sir. And we think speaking to retired DI Arthur Grimes could be our next step."

Smith's eyes narrowed thoughtfully. "Arthur Grimes, eh?" He paused, reminiscing. "I remember him. Sharp mind, relentless in his pursuit of justice. He lived in a white detached house on Suffield Road in Gildersome. Quite the detective, but a bit of a lone wolf."

George and Luke exchanged a glance, understanding the

implications. Grimes' intimate knowledge of the Gildersome case, coupled with his investigative prowess, could provide the breakthrough they needed.

"Grimes could have insights we've overlooked," Luke added. "His perspective on the case was always unique."

Smith nodded in agreement. "You're right. And if someone's bringing up the past, Grimes is the one who can help us understand why. I trust your judgment, George, and yours too, Luke. Go talk to him."

George felt a sense of validation from Smith's support. The dynamic in the room was one of mutual respect, a testament to their shared commitment to justice.

"Thank you, sir. We'll reach out to Grimes right away," George said, rising from his seat.

As they left the Detective Superintendent's office, George felt the weight of the case pressing down on him.

* * *

Back in George's office, he and Luke mulled over their next steps. The room was quiet, save for the occasional rustle of papers or the distant sound of activity from the station beyond the door. The atmosphere was one of focused deliberation, a testament to the gravity of their decision.

"Visiting Grimes... it's not without its risks," Luke started, leaning against the edge of George's desk. "He was brilliant, sure, but he was also known for being... unorthodox."

George nodded, his expression thoughtful. "True. His methods weren't always by the book, but his results were undeniable. His insight could be exactly what we need to see this case in a new light."

Luke crossed his arms, considering. "And there's the angle of how he'll receive us. It's been years since he was on the force. We don't know how he's changed."

George leaned back in his chair, his gaze distant. "There's only one way to find out. We need to tread carefully, though. Grimes was never one for unexpected visits."

The decision was made. They would visit Arthur Grimes at his home in Gildersome, a quiet, almost idyllic suburb that stood in contrast to the nature of their visit. As they prepared to leave, George couldn't help but feel a mix of anticipation and apprehension.

* * *

The drive to Gildersome was marked by a sense of quiet anticipation. As George and Luke entered the area, they were greeted by the tranquil, almost picturesque surroundings. The streets were lined with well-kept houses, each with its manicured garden, painting a serene picture of suburban life. It was a stark contrast to the gritty reality of their daily police work.

As they approached the address, George's eyes immediately fixed on a 'For Sale' sign that stood in front of a white detached house—Arthur Grimes' residence. The once-manicured garden showed signs of neglect, with overgrown bushes and a layer of fallen leaves covering the lawn. The house itself, though still stately, had a forlorn air about it, as if it had been quietly forgotten.

George and Luke exchanged a look of surprise and concern. "Didn't see this coming," Luke muttered, his brow furrowed.

"No, neither did I," George replied, his gaze still fixed on the house. "Let's take a closer look."

They stepped out of the car, their footsteps crunching softly on the gravel driveway. The area's quiet was almost oppressive, the silence amplifying their presence. As they approached the house, George peered through the windows, searching for any sign of recent activity. The rooms were visible but empty, devoid of the life and warmth that once might have filled them.

Luke walked around the perimeter, noting the layers of dust on the windowsills and the uncollected mail piling up at the front door. "Looks like Grimes left in a hurry," he observed.

George nodded, his mind racing with questions. Had Grimes moved on without a word to anyone? Was there more to his sudden departure? The discovery added another layer of mystery to their investigation, deepening the puzzle they were already struggling to piece together.

As they stood there, taking in the scene, a neighbour peeked out from behind a curtain in the house across the street. George caught the brief glance before the curtain was swiftly drawn. The slight movement was a reminder that they were being watched, that their presence in this quiet vicinity was noted.

"Let's ask around," George suggested. "Maybe the neighbours know something about Grimes' departure."

George and Luke decided to approach the neighbour who had peeked through the curtains earlier. The neighbourhood retained its quiet disposition, but there was a palpable undercurrent of curiosity as they approached the house across from Grimes'.

The door was answered by a middle-aged woman, her expression one of cautious interest. "Detectives?" she inquired, eyeing their warrant cards.

"Yes, ma'am. I'm Detective Chief Inspector Beaumont, and this is Detective Inspector Mason. We're looking into the whereabouts of Arthur Grimes. We understand he was your neighbour?" George asked, his tone polite but firm.

The woman nodded, ushering them inside. "I'm Mrs Harper. Please, come in. Arthur Grimes, yes, he lived just across there," she said, pointing towards the house with the white facade. "Haven't seen him for a few months now. He kept to himself mostly, but it was quite sudden, him leaving."

As they sat in Mrs Harper's neatly kept living room, George noted the contrast between the homeliness of her house and the desolate appearance of Grimes'. "Did you notice anything unusual before they left? Any visitors or perhaps some odd behaviour?"

Mrs Harper thought for a moment. "Well, it was odd. Arthur used to be quite the gardener. Then, a few months back, he just stopped. The garden went untended, which wasn't like him at all. And there was a van parked there a few times. Unmarked, but it seemed... out of place."

Luke exchanged a glance with George. "Did you happen to see who was in the van?"

"No, never did. But it was there, late at night, a few times. Then, one day, Grimes was just gone. No goodbyes, nothing."

"Did you get a reg number?"

Mrs Harper shook her head.

George's mind was working through the implications. The unmarked van and the sudden change in Grimes' routine were pieces of a puzzle that didn't quite fit yet.

"Thank you, Mrs Harper. Your information has been very helpful," Luke said as they stood to leave.

CHAPTER FIVE

Outside, George looked back at Grimes' house. "An unmarked van, late at night... It doesn't add up, Luke."

Luke nodded. "It raises more questions than answers. But it's clear there's more to Grimes' departure than meets the eye."

"Contact the estate agent and see if you can get any information out of them."

"It'd be easier getting blood from a stone, son."

* * *

The drive back to the station was a quiet affair. George navigated the streets, his thoughts clouded by the absence of Arthur Grimes. Beside him, Luke seemed equally pensive, the information from Mrs Harper replaying in his mind.

"It's like he vanished into thin air," Luke finally said, breaking the silence. Without a warrant, the estate agent would give them nothing. DSU Smith was working on it. "Do you think he knew we were coming?"

George considered the possibility. "It's hard to say. But Grimes was always a step ahead, even back in the day. If he didn't want to be found, he wouldn't be."

Luke drummed his fingers on the dashboard. "We should consider other ways to track him down. Maybe there are financial records, ANPR logs... something that points to where he went."

George nodded, his gaze fixed on the road. "Agreed. We'll need to dig deeper into his recent activities. In the meantime, we should revisit the case files. There might be something we missed, something Grimes knew that we didn't."

"As frustrating as this is, it might be a blessing in disguise,"

George mused. "We're forced to look at the case with fresh eyes, without Grimes' influence. It might lead us down new paths."

Luke nodded, a sense of resolve returning to his voice. "Let's brief the team. We'll need all hands on deck for this."

Chapter Six

Detective Constable Alexis Mercer was immersed in a world of the past in a quiet corner of the shared office, poring over transcripts of witness interviews from the original Gildersome murders case. Her desk was cluttered with files and notes, each piece a fragment of a larger, complex puzzle.

As she meticulously reviewed each interview, Alexis' keen eye for detail began to unravel threads that had been overlooked. Her fingers traced a line in one transcript where a witness mentioned seeing a car that didn't fit the area's usual traffic—a detail that had been dismissed at the time.

Leaning back in her chair, and thinking about the photo DI Mason received, Alexis mused aloud, "Could this be connected to the Corsa we're looking for?" Her instinct told her there was more to this witness statement than met the eye.

Later, in a strategy meeting with George and Luke, Alexis laid out her plan for the new interviews. "I want to revisit this witness, sir. If we consider the image DI Mason received, their account of the car could be a lead. I'm thinking of a more focused approach this time, probing the details they might have considered insignificant."

George nodded in agreement. "Good call, Alexis. We struggled to find anything last time. Let's not make the same mistake again."

Luke added, "Maybe cross-reference their statement with the times we know the Corsa was in the area. It could help corroborate their story."

As the meeting concluded, Alexis felt a renewed sense of purpose. The prospect of conducting new interviews, armed with the knowledge and context they now had, was an opportunity to shed new light on the case.

Back at her desk, Alexis organised her notes, preparing for the interviews ahead. The investigation was a complex tapestry of past and present, and her role in re-examining the witness statements was crucial.

Alexis was a vital thread; her attention to detail and persistence were critical to solving the Gildersome murders. As she delved deeper into the interviews, her contributions would prove invaluable in piecing together the truth.

* * *

Detective Constables Tashan Blackburn and Jason Scott stood at the edge of the overgrown field that once served as a crime scene in the Gildersome murders twelve years ago. The area, now quiet and seemingly undisturbed, held secrets from a past investigation that they were determined to uncover.

"Thanks for coming with me, mate," said Jay to which Tashan nodded.

"No problem."

Tashan, with his keen analytical mind, began methodically examining the layout of the scene. He took precise measurements and noted the positioning of landmarks that could have served as vantage points or escape routes. "If we can reconstruct the perpetrator's movements, we might find something the initial team missed," he suggested, his eyes scanning the terrain.

Jay, on the other hand, approached the scene with a different perspective. His creative methods led him to consider the psychological implications of the scene's arrangement. "Think about what this setting suggests," Jay mused, gesturing to the secluded nature of the field. "It's isolated, hidden from view. The killer chose this spot for a reason."

As they worked, the contrast in their methods became their strength. Tashan's focus on the tangible elements of the scene provided a solid foundation for their investigation, while Jay's imaginative approach offered new angles to consider.

At one point, Tashan's meticulous surveying led them to a spot where the ground seemed disturbed, hidden beneath overgrowth. Jay knelt down, sifting through the underbrush, and uncovered a small, rusted object partially buried in the soil. "Could be something the initial team overlooked," he said, holding the medal up for Tashan to see.

"Or it could have been recently planted by the killer?" said Tashan.

"Good point mate."

As they discussed the medal, their communication was seamless, a dance of differing styles that complemented each other perfectly. Tashan immediately bagged the object for analysis, his mind already cataloguing it and considering its potential relevance.

Back at the station, they reported their findings to George and Luke. Their collaboration had not only been productive but had also deepened their mutual respect for each other's abilities. "The field might hold more clues than we thought,"

Tashan explained. "And Jay's discovery could be a significant lead."

George nodded, impressed. "Good work. Let's get that object to forensics right away. And then get a SOC team out to search the area."

The efforts of Tashan and Jay were crucial pieces in the intricate puzzle of the investigation. Their unique skills and methods, blending the analytical with the creative, were invaluable assets in the team's pursuit of justice.

* * *

The sounds of the bustling station faded to a muted hum as George Beaumont made his way down one of the lesser-used hallways. Lost in thought, pondering the case, he almost didn't register the hushed voices around the next corner until a familiar voice made him pause—Alexis Mercer.

Curiosity piqued, George slowed his stride, footsteps softening instinctively. Peering around the edge of the wall, he spotted Alexis deep in a tense conversation with one of the civilian analysts. Her usual composure seemed fractured, one hand gripping her hip while the other gestured sharply.

"...his methods are questionable at best," Alexis was saying, an uncharacteristic heat lacing her words. "The way Atkinson handles cases and investigations, it's just... wrong."

The analyst's eyes widened slightly, but they nodded. "I've heard stories about DCI Atkinson," they admitted quietly. "Rumours of things that don't sit right with me either."

Alexis leaned closer, voice dropping further. "If even half of what people have said is true, he has no business being in his position. But who would believe us over a respected detective

CHAPTER SIX

chief inspector?"

A knot of concern formed in George's gut, every instinct blaring caution. While he shared some of Alexis' misgivings about Alistair Atkinson's attitude, this contempt went beyond professional critique. Her vendetta felt almost... personal.

Could her deep sense of justice have motivated Alexis to frame Atkinson for the murder and assaults? George hated to entertain the thought, but he couldn't ignore the possibility. He needed to grapple with this sensitively but directly before things escalated.

Craning his neck, George observed the conversation winding down, Alexis looking uncharacteristically agitated. As she and the analyst moved to part ways, George stepped back quickly before striding around the corner as if just arriving.

"Alexis, got a minute?" He kept his tone light but firm.

Alexis looked up, surprise flashing across her striking features. "Of course, sir. What can I do for you?"

"Let's discuss this in my office." George led the way, hyper-aware of Alexis assessing him curiously. Once the door was shut, he turned to her solemnly. "I don't wish to pry, but I accidentally overheard parts of your conversation just now."

Alexis visibly tensed, azure eyes guarded. "I see, sir. And what exactly did you hear?" Her tone remained neutral and professional.

George breathed deeply, choosing his following words with care. "I understand you have reservations about DCI Atkinson." He held her gaze. "But we must be cautious about how that frustration is expressed. Atkinson is still a high-ranking officer."

Alexis' jaw tightened almost imperceptibly. "Of course. I would never act unprofessionally or inappropriately, sir."

Each word rang with conviction.

Studying Alexis' rigidly controlled expression, George wrestled with his own conflicted emotions. His experiences made him inclined to trust her integrity. Yet the recording of Atkinson raised alarms he couldn't ignore. George hated entertaining even fleeting suspicions about Alexis, but the case demanded objectivity.

"I know you always operate by the book, Alexis, and value protocol," George said carefully. "But this case is...personal. For many of us. Strong emotions can cloud judgment."

Alexis' azure eyes flashed, the first crack in her composure. "With respect, sir, my emotions never dictate my actions on the job." An edge sharpened her voice despite her restraint.

George held up a conciliatory hand. "I just ask that you come to me if anything about this case, or Atkinson, becomes too overwhelming. My door is always open."

The stiffness seeped from Alexis' posture marginally. "I appreciate that, sir. And I assure you, seeking justice in this case remains my only motivation." Sincerity shone in her eyes.

George nodded slowly. His misgivings weren't fully settled, but he sensed Alexis' intentions were righteous, however personal her feelings toward Atkinson. He would maintain discreet vigilance, but she deserved the benefit of the doubt from a leader who should be supporting his team.

* * *

In the Incident Room, the team gathered around, their attention focused on Detective Constable Jay Scott. Jay, with his training in criminal psychology, was about to offer a fresh perspective on the perpetrator's profile, a perspective that could potentially open new avenues in the Gildersome Murders case.

As Jay began, his tone was confident yet open to collaboration. "Based on the crime scenes and behaviours observed, our perpetrator likely has a deep need for control and may exhibit signs of antisocial personality disorder," he started, pointing to the key traits on his mind map.

The team listened intently as Jay outlined the profile, highlighting the perpetrator's choice of isolated crime scenes, the intervals between crimes, and the need to leave a signature.

Jay Scott cleared his throat, his eyes scanning the attentive faces around the table as he prepared to delve into the victimology of the three victims from twelve years ago. "Let's continue with understanding our perpetrator's choice of victims," he began, pointing to the detailed mind map displayed on the screen behind him.

"The first victim, Laura Hughes, was a thirty-year-old detective inspector known for her work in serious crime investigations. The perpetrator's choice to target someone of her experience and status within the police force suggests a deliberate and bold statement. It's as if the perpetrator was not just challenging the police but directly confronting the authority and investigative prowess of the force."

"The second victim, Sarah Jennings, a police sergeant, was attacked while jogging early in the morning. Sarah was also a seasoned officer, but less so than Hughes, known for her involvement in community policing. The perpetrator's shift from an extremely experienced officer to a lesser ranking officer hints at an escalation in their approach, possibly seeking less of a challenge or a sense of triumph after already overcoming a more formidable victim in Laura Hughes," Jay continued, his analysis drawing a clear line of progression in the perpetrator's actions.

He then moved on to the third victim. "The final victim from twelve years ago, Emily Thompson, was a young police constable, new to the force. She was off-duty when targeted, suggesting that the perpetrator either knew her schedule or stalked her to find an opportune moment. Her choice as a victim indicates a specific grudge or a symbolic act against the West Yorkshire Police," Jay explained, his tone reflecting the gravity of the analysis.

Jay paused, letting the information sink in before adding, "This pattern of victimology points towards a perpetrator who not only harbours a deep-seated resentment towards the police and women, but also seeks to demonstrate their superiority over it and them. Each attack was more daring than the last, indicating a growing confidence and perhaps even a sense of invincibility in the perpetrator's psyche."

Concluding his presentation, Jay emphasised the importance of this analysis in their ongoing investigation. "Understanding the victim selection gives us insight into the murderer's motives and mindset. It's crucial we consider this pattern as we investigate current leads. This perpetrator is likely to continue targeting victims that symbolize their grievances or challenge their sense of control and superiority." His words resonated with the team, underscoring the critical need to apprehend the perpetrator before another life was claimed in this macabre sequence. "And given the escalating nature of the crimes, and the two images received so far, it's likely the perpetrator will strike again. We might be looking at shorter intervals between crimes moving forward."

CHAPTER SIX

Detective Sergeant Yolanda Williams chimed in, cross-referencing Jay's profile with their suspect list. "So, we're looking for someone with a history of control issues, possibly with a criminal record or known antisocial behaviour."

Detective Constable Tashan Blackburn, always meticulous, raised a question. "How does this profile help us narrow down suspects? We need to ensure we're not on a wild goose chase."

Jay acknowledged the concern. "It's about narrowing our focus, using behaviour to guide us where evidence might be lacking. We can also use this to predict and possibly intercept the next move."

Detective Chief Inspector George Beaumont, who had been listening closely, gave a nod of approval. "It's a different approach, but it complements our investigation. Let's cross-reference this profile with HOLMES and see where it leads us."

As the meeting progressed and Luke and George left the station, the team began formulating new strategies based on Jay's predictions. There was a renewed sense of direction, a feeling that they were piecing together the puzzle, one behavioural clue at a time.

* * *

The Incident Room hummed with activity as DCI George Beaumont's team worked diligently to uncover links between the murder victims. At the central desk, DC Alexis Mercer sorted through stacks of personnel files on the slain policewomen—Laura Hughes, Sarah Jennings, and Emily Thompson.

Her striking azure eyes skimmed over the pages intently, searching for any threads connecting the women's backgrounds, tenures on the force, or cases they handled. Anything that could indicate why a sadistic killer had targeted them.

So far, her detailed analysis was coming up short. Laura Hughes had been a formidable DI dealing with organised syndicates. Sarah Jennings worked robbery and burglary as a DS. Emily was just a probationary constable with scarce time on the job when her life was cut brutally short. On the surface, their professional spheres did not seem to intersect besides all working for The West Yorkshire Police.

"Nothing glaringly obvious so far," Alexis huffed in frustration, tossing down a folder. She pressed her fingertips to her temple, feeling a stress headache building after three hours hunched over files.

Across the table, DI Luke Mason glanced up from his own stack of documents—archival personnel logs. "Careers don't always tell the full tale of a copper's life," he remarked sagely. "Maybe we need to dig into their personal connections, too."

Alexis nodded thoughtfully. Wise, experienced Luke often provided valuable perspective to balance her laser focus. "We should re-interview any family, friends, partners. Someone must recall if these women's paths ever crossed in any capacity."

At his desk in the corner, DC Jay Scott ended a phone call and swivelled to face them. "That was the archives office. They're pulling every file on past and present female personnel for us to review. Should be heaps to sift through." He raised his eyebrows meaningfully.

Luke blew out a breath. "Let's rope in some bright-eyed coppers on the rise to tackle that mountain of paper, eh?" His weathered eyes glinted wryly.

CHAPTER SIX

Alexis allowed herself a small smile at the banter lightening the room's mood despite the grim purpose of their task. Levity was scarce these days, with the murder count climbing. She was grateful to colleagues like playful Jay and dependable Luke, who lifted spirits when tensions ran high.

The door swung open to admit DCI Beaumont, his athletic frame radiating restless energy. "Status update?" he prompted without preamble, scanning the room.

"Collecting background data to cross-check connections between victims," Alexis reported. She passed George the hefty stack of personnel files. "So far, no professional overlap that we can tell."

George said, "Right. We'll need to dig deeper, approach this from new angles." His piercing green eyes took on a familiar, steely light. "Alexis, you and Jay start compiling detailed profiles on each woman—personal relationships, hobbies, routines," George directed decisively. "If this is someone with a vendetta, those details could prove enlightening."

Alexis nodded briskly. "I'll conduct interviews with their inner circles again, probe for any common threads." Beside her, Jay straightened with an eager expression.

"Good." George turned to Luke. "Get Blackburn and Nichols canvassing known haunts of the victims—pubs, cafes, gyms. I know it was twelve years ago, but we need fresh recollections, however minor."

Luke dipped his chin. "They'll squeeze every grain from those regulars if it kills 'em." His weathered face creased into a wry grin.

"Right, the archives team should have those personnel files soon," George said decisively. "Let's divide and conquer. I want every page scrutinised for even the vaguest connections."

He surveyed the room. "Somewhere in these women's shared history lies the missing piece. We find that, and we're one step closer to nailing this bastard."

As the team filed out to their assignments, Alexis paused, laying a hand lightly on George's forearm. "We'll find the pattern, sir. Your insights have put us on the right path," she said earnestly, holding his gaze.

George looked down at her hand, which she immediately moved, a blush starting to tinge her cheeks.

Stepping out into the frigid winter air, Alexis tipped her face up to the muted sunlight, rallying her energy reserves. She would need every ounce of her focus and analytical prowess to sift through the avalanche of data headed their way. But she relished the challenge. Each fact pried free brought them closer to ending this killer's depraved spree.

* * *

Detective Constable Candy Nichols was on-site at one of another of the original Gildersome murder crime scenes, a now overgrown area that once played host to unspeakable acts. Accompanied by Tashan Blackburn, she moved meticulously through the scene, her eyes scanning every inch of the ground, searching for anything the initial investigation might have missed.

Candy's methodical approach was her greatest strength. She took her time, carefully examining each potential piece of evidence, no matter how insignificant it might have seemed. Tashan, observing her process, appreciated the thoroughness she brought to their work.

As Candy sifted through some underbrush, her keen eye

caught a glint of metal partially buried in the soil. "Tashan, over here," she called out softly. Kneeling, she used her tools to gently unearth what appeared to be a small, rusted metal object. It was delicate work, requiring patience and precision.

Tashan joined her, watching as she carefully extracted the object. "What have you found?" he asked, intrigued.

"It looks like some sort of metal badge, medal or emblem. Could be related to the perpetrator or the victim," Candy speculated, her mind racing with the possibilities of this new clue.

"That looks exactly the same kind of medal Jay and I found at a different crime scene," said Tashan.

Back at the station, Candy presented the find to George and Luke. "I found this at the Gildersome scene. It was well-hidden, easy to miss in the initial sweep."

George examined the object closely, realising the similarities to the one Jay and Tashan found. "This could be significant. Great work, Candy. Let's get this to forensics immediately."

Candy's discovery was a testament to her meticulous nature and her invaluable role in the investigation. Her attention to detail had unearthed a clue that could potentially lead them down a new investigative path.

As the team discussed the implications of Candy's findings, there was a sense of renewed energy in the room. George acknowledged the contribution of each team member, emphasising how their unique skills were integral to the progress of the case.

Candy, while modest about her role, couldn't help but feel a sense of accomplishment. Her diligence had paid off, providing the team with a new piece of the puzzle.

***

The quaint café on Otley Road was a far cry from the stark precincts and dusty archives. Its warm lighting and the soft hum of conversation created a cosy atmosphere, a peaceful backdrop for their meeting with retired Police Sergeant Ellen Hartley.

As George and Luke settled into a corner table, they observed Ellen approaching. Her demeanour was calm, yet her eyes carried the sharpness of someone who had spent years in the force. She greeted them with a polite nod and sat down, her hands clasped tightly in front of her.

The café's chatter faded into the background as Ellen began to speak about Arthur Grimes. "Arthur was brilliant, but the Leeds Lurker case consumed him," she said, her voice tinged with a mix of admiration and concern. "He believed there was a connection to the Gildersome murders, something everyone else missed."

George leaned in, intrigued. "What sort of connection?"

Ellen sighed, her gaze distant. "He never specified, but it became an obsession. He'd spend hours going over old files, looking for patterns, any link between the two cases."

Luke, his expression thoughtful, asked, "Did he find anything concrete?"

"Not that he shared. But I remember this one time," Ellen continued, "he came to me, wild-eyed, claiming he'd found a pattern in the dates of the incidents. Said it was too systematic, too precise to be a coincidence. But he wouldn't elaborate, just mumbled about needing to dig deeper."

She paused, her eyes meeting George's. "In his last months before retiring, Arthur became increasingly isolated. Paranoia, perhaps. He believed someone was always watching, that he was being followed."

George exchanged a glance with Luke, both sensing the gravity of her words. "Do you think he might have gone underground to continue his investigation?" George asked.

Ellen nodded slowly. "Wouldn't surprise me. Arthur was the type to go to any lengths for the truth. If he believed the Leeds Lurker and Gildersome cases were connected, he wouldn't rest until he proved it."

As they wrapped up their meeting, George and Luke thanked Ellen for her insights. Stepping out of the café, the mood was contemplative. The pieces of the puzzle were slowly coming together, forming a picture of Arthur Grimes as a man driven to the brink by a case that consumed him.

George's mind was racing with possibilities. If Grimes had indeed gone underground, finding him would be crucial. Ellen's account had provided a new perspective, one that highlighted the depth of Grimes' obsession and the potential risks he posed to himself and possibly others.

After their revealing conversation with Ellen Hartley, George Beaumont stepped aside to make a crucial phone call. He dialled DS Yolanda Williams, who was back at the station, coordinating various aspects of their investigation.

"Yolanda, it's George. Have we got anything back on Grimes' financial records?" George's voice was brisk, the urgency clear.

Yolanda's response came quickly. "Yes, sir, something interesting. Grimes was making regular payments for a warehouse in Holbeck. It's been going on for years."

"A warehouse in Holbeck?" A spark of realisation ignited in George's mind, linking with what Ellen had said. "That could be significant. Thanks, Yolanda. We're on it."

He ended the call and turned to Luke, who was waiting nearby. "Grimes has been paying for a warehouse in Holbeck. Could be his base of operations or something more. We need to check it out."

Without hesitation, they set off for Holbeck. The area was a stark reminder of the city's industrial past, now a shadow of its former self. As they arrived at the warehouse Yolanda had mentioned, the sheer size of the building loomed over them, its façade a mute witness to countless untold stories.

Chapter Seven

The warehouse stood desolate, its vast, empty spaces echoing with the ghosts of its past. George and Luke made their way through its dimly lit corridors, the air thick with the dust of neglect. Each step they took was cautious, aware of the unknown that awaited them.

The atmosphere was heavy, the silence of the warehouse punctuated only by their footsteps and the distant sound of the city outside. It felt like stepping into a forgotten world, a place untouched by time and yet full of hidden secrets.

Their search led them to a secluded part of the warehouse, hidden away from prying eyes. With a sense of anticipation and apprehension, George and Luke discovered what they had come for—the hidden office of Arthur Grimes.

The office was cramped, its walls plastered with clippings from newspapers, maps with areas circled and annotated, and a plethora of notes scrawled in Grimes' unmistakable handwriting. The room was a visual representation of a mind consumed by an unsolvable puzzle. The air was stale, heavy with the scent of old paper and ink.

George's gaze was drawn to a giant cork board, where photos and notes were pinned in a seemingly haphazard manner. But as he looked closer, he realised there was a method to the madness. Timelines, suspect lists, and theories were all laid out, showing Grimes' relentless pursuit of connections between the Leeds Lurker and the Gildersome murders.

Luke sifted through a stack of notebooks on the desk. "He was thorough; I'll give him that," he said, flipping through pages filled with meticulous observations and deductions.

It was then that George noticed a recent photograph pinned among the clippings. It was of the same Vauxhall Corsa showed in Luke's mysterious photo. The car was parked on a dimly lit street, its details matching exactly. The realisation hit him like a wave—the link between Grimes and the mysterious correspondence was undeniable.

"This is it, Luke," George said, his voice a mix of excitement and apprehension. "Grimes is involved in this somehow. The letters, the photographs—it's all connected. It has to be!"

Luke joined him, studying the photograph. "It's like he's trying to communicate with us, but why this way?"

The atmosphere in the office was thick with the gravity of their discovery. George's and Luke's investigative styles —George's instinct-driven approach and Luke's methodical analysis—had complemented each other perfectly, leading them to this crucial breakthrough.

As they prepared to leave the office, the weight of what they had found settled upon them. Arthur Grimes' hidden office had provided more questions than answers, but it was a significant step closer to understanding the tangled web of the Gildersome case.

Long shadows caused by the fading light were cast across the warehouse as George Beaumont and Luke Mason made their way out, their minds still reeling from the discoveries in

Grimes' hidden office. The sudden appearance of DCI Alistair Atkinson, emerging from the shadows, was a jolt to their already heightened senses.

Atkinson's figure was imposing, his expression taut with accusation. "Going a bit rogue, aren't we, George?" he said, his voice laced with a barely concealed disdain.

George, taken aback by Atkinson's sudden confrontation, replied with a guarded tone. "Alistair, what are you doing here?"

Atkinson stepped closer, his eyes hard. "I've been keeping tabs on Grimes myself. I don't appreciate being left out of the loop, especially by someone who used to work under me."

Luke, sensing the rising tension, interjected, "This isn't about territory, Atkinson. We're following a lead."

Atkinson's gaze shifted between the two, his suspicion evident. "Grimes was always a wildcard. I had my run-ins with him in the past. But what's your angle here, George? Trying to outshine everyone again?"

George, maintaining his composure, responded, "This isn't about outshining anyone. It's about finding the truth behind the Gildersome murders."

The air was thick with unspoken animosity. George's and Luke's reactions were a blend of surprise and wariness, their instinctive distrust of Atkinson's motivations clear.

Atkinson scoffed. "Well, just be careful, Beaumont. You might uncover more than you bargained for."

With that cryptic warning, Atkinson turned and walked away, disappearing into the fading light. His interest in Grimes and the veiled threats left George and Luke with a sense of unease.

As they headed back to the car, Luke voiced his concern.

"What's Atkinson's game? His interest in Grimes doesn't add up."

George shook his head, his thoughts clouded with the same questions. "I don't know, but it's clear he's got his own agenda. We need to stay one step ahead."

* * *

Later, in the Incident Room at the station, George, Luke, and Tashan Blackburn were hunched over Grimes' notes, a sense of urgency palpable in the air. The clutter of papers, photographs, and maps around them was a testament to the intensity of their investigation.

Tashan, his eyes focused on a computer screen, was skilfully manipulating the images of Grimes' photographs. "I'm using a digital enhancement program to bring out the finer details," he explained, his fingers moving deftly over the keyboard. "Enhancing contrast, sharpening the image... here, look at this."

The others leaned in as Tashan zoomed in on a photo of the Vauxhall Corsa. The enhancement process had made a partial license plate visible, a breakthrough that had previously eluded them.

George's eyes widened. "That's it. Can we trace the plate?"

Tashan nodded, already running the partial number through their database. "I'll cross-reference it with vehicle registrations and see what comes up."

The room fell into a tense silence as they waited. Moments later, Tashan looked up, a look of surprise crossing his features. "Got something. The car was registered to a retired policeman named Langton. Worked at Millgarth police station

CHAPTER SEVEN

back in the day, the same as Grimes."

* * *

George Beaumont and Luke Mason were knee-deep in a journey through time once again in the archives, exploring the cold case known as the Bramley Woods Murder in the nineties and involving the Leeds Lurker from the 1980s.

The archives were a labyrinth of towering shelves, each laden with ageing files and long-forgotten records. Luke, his eyes weary from hours of searching, sifted through a box marked 'Bramley Woods—1980s.' Dust particles danced in the beams of light filtering through the small window. Across the table, George sat, rubbing his temples, burdened by the weight of their relentless investigation.

The air was thick with the musty scent of old paper, and the quiet rustling of pages seemed to echo the whispers of the past.

As they pored over the case files, the parallels between the Bramley Woods Murder and the Gildersome murders became increasingly apparent. Both cases featured eerily similar symbols at the crime scenes, symbols that had baffled investigators decades ago.

"These symbols," Luke said, tracing a finger over a faded crime scene photograph, "they were considered the work of a deranged mind back then. But now, it looks like we're dealing with something more calculated, the signature of a possible serial killer."

George nodded, his expression sombre. "It's chilling to think these cases might be connected. Decades apart, yet bound by a sinister thread." He paused, his thoughts turning to the victims' families. "For these families, the pain never really goes away. Cases like these... they leave scars that last generations."

Luke, his eyes still on the files, sighed. "We owe it to them to find the truth, no matter how long it's been."

As they delved deeper, it became clear that criminal profiling and forensic analysis had evolved significantly since the Bramley Woods Murder. What was once dismissed as the erratic behaviour of a lone individual now pointed to the methodical actions of a serial killer.

"The way we understand these symbols now could be key to unlocking both cases," George mused, his mind racing with possibilities.

"And there's something else, son," said Luke.

George leaned in, his focus intensifying as he read over Luke's shoulder. The notes, penned in a hurried yet deliberate hand, detailed suppressed evidence and jury tampering, signed at the bottom—'R. Whitaker.'

"Whitaker had reservations about the trial," Luke murmured, his finger tracing the lines of text. "He's referring to external influence, George. This could be significant."

George's eyes narrowed, a glimmer of intrigue illuminating his weary features. "Whitaker was the judge, wasn't he? If he suspected foul play..."

"Then he might be privy to more than what's in these records," Luke finished the thought, snapping the folder shut with a renewed sense of purpose. "We ought to speak with him. Now that he's retired, he might be more open to talking."

George nodded in agreement, standing and stretching his back. "Let's find him. This 'shadow' he mentions... it might be the link between the Gildersome and Bramley Woods cases."

Luke tucked the folder under his arm, his face set with determination. "If Whitaker felt justice wasn't achieved, he might just be the ally we need."

George nodded. "Let's visit him as soon as possible."

They left the archives, their minds burdened yet determined; the weight of their discovery hung heavily between them. The connection between the two cases had opened a new avenue of investigation, one that spanned decades and challenged their every assumption.

As the pair headed upstairs, George found himself yet again face-to-face with DCI Alistair Atkinson, the air between them charged with unspoken animosity.

Atkinson's posture was rigid, his gaze sharp and probing. "Beaumont, digging up the past can have unforeseen consequences," he threatened again, his voice low but carrying an edge that made a nearby junior officer pause in her tracks.

George, maintaining a calm exterior, felt a surge of suspicion. "What are you implying, Alistair?" he asked, his mind racing to decipher Atkinson's true intentions.

Atkinson leaned in, his voice barely a whisper. "The Bramley Woods connection—leave it alone. It's for your own good."

George's jaw tightened. He could feel the eyes of a police constable named Sally Jenkins, a constable who had worked on the initial murders twelve years ago, on them. "I'll follow the evidence where it leads, Alistair. If there's something you know, you should come forward."

Atkinson straightened, a cold smile playing on his lips. "Just a friendly warning to my newly promoted colleague." He paused and eyed George. "Don't dig too deep."

As Atkinson walked away, the tension in the air slowly

dissipated, leaving George deep in thought. His mind was a whirlwind of questions. What did Atkinson know about the Bramley Woods connection? And why was he so insistent on warning him off?

Later, back at his desk, George was approached by Sally Jenkins, the officer who had witnessed the exchange. She hesitated for a moment before speaking. "DCI Beaumont, I overheard your conversation with DCI Atkinson. There's something you should know."

George looked up, his interest piqued. And as Sally began to speak, George listened intently.

Chapter Eight

Detective Constable Candy Nichols arrived at the site of the first Gildersome murder from twelve years ago, a now tranquil meadow that once witnessed a brutal crime. Clad in her forensic suit and with Stuart Kent at her side, she carried her kit, which contained an array of tools essential for meticulous examination: tape measures, evidence markers, a high-resolution camera, and more.

Candy began her work with a calm and methodical approach. She moved through the scene with a keen eye, marking areas of interest with small flags. Every few steps, she paused to take measurements, jotting down notes on her pad. Her camera clicked continuously, capturing every angle of the scene.

As she worked, Candy's mind was entirely focused on the task at hand. Her meticulous nature was not just a professional trait but a personal commitment to justice. Each crime scene was a puzzle, and she believed every piece mattered, no matter how small.

At Stuart's advice, Candy carefully cross-referenced her observations with the original investigation reports. She was looking for discrepancies, anything the initial team might have overlooked. Her process was thorough, ensuring that no stone was left unturned and no clue was missed.

After several hours of intense examination, Candy stepped back to survey the scene. Her keen eyes caught a slight irregularity in the soil near a cluster of trees—an area that seemed undisturbed at first glance. Kneeling down, she uncovered a small, partially buried item. With careful hands, she collected it as potential evidence.

"Good work, young lady," Kent said. "The DI will be proud of you for that."

Candy grinned. "Don't let DCI Beaumont hear you still calling him a DI, Stuart."

Kent mirrored her grin. "I'd forgotten about his promotion, to be honest; I must congratulate him when I see him."

"Come with me now, Stuart. You helped me find this."

"I did nothing but guide you, Candy. You deserve the credit."

Back at Elland Road Police Station, Candy prepared to report her findings to DCI George Beaumont and the team. Because George and Luke were about to head into the city centre, her presentation in the Incident Room was detailed but concise, showcasing the thoroughness of her work.

"I found something that was missed in the initial sweep," she explained, displaying photos of the item she had discovered. Another medal encased in dirt. "It's too early to say if it's connected, but it was definitely overlooked by forensics before."

George listened intently, nodding in acknowledgement of Candy's dedication. "Excellent work, Candy. Let's get this to forensics right away. It could be the break we need."

* * *

CHAPTER EIGHT

The café on Briggate was a quiet haven amidst the hustle of the city, its cosy ambience a stark contrast to the tension of the police station. George and Luke sat at a secluded table near the back, the murmur of hushed conversations and the clink of coffee cups surrounding them. They waited for Sally Jenkins, their anticipation growing with every passing minute.

Sally arrived, a look a mix of determination and apprehension upon her face. She scanned the café before approaching George and Luke, her steps measured and cautious. As she sat down, her hands were visibly trembling, betraying the fear she was trying to conceal.

"Thank you for meeting us, Sally," George said, his tone gentle, aiming to put her at ease.

Sally nodded, taking a deep breath before speaking. "I overheard DCI Atkinson in a conversation about the Gildersome case, sir. He mentioned a cover-up," she said, her voice barely above a whisper. "I managed to record a part of it."

Luke leaned forward, his expression serious. "Can we hear it?"

Sally hesitated for a moment before handing over a small digital recorder. As George pressed play, the low, muffled voice of Atkinson filled their ears, discussing details of the case with an unidentified person. The words 'cover-up', 'Operation Redwood', and 'Gildersome' were unmistakable.

The revelation sent a chill down George's spine. The recording was a significant piece of evidence, hinting at a depth of corruption that went beyond anything they had anticipated.

"We need to tread carefully," Luke said, his eyes meeting George's. "This could be bigger than we thought."

George nodded, his mind racing with the implications of

the recording. "Sally, this is crucial evidence. Thank you for bringing it to us." He paused, pondering what to do. "I'll need you to give your device to my detective constable, Tashan Blackburn, once back at Elland Road, please," he explained. "And let's keep this between us for now, yeah?"

"Yeah," Sally said and nodded.

As Sally left the café, a sense of urgency enveloped George and Luke. The discovery of the recording added a new dimension to their investigation, suggesting that the Gildersome murders were entangled in a web of deceit that extended to the upper echelons of the police force.

As they stood up to leave, George knew that they were on the brink of uncovering a truth that someone had gone to great lengths to keep hidden.

* * *

The drive to Roundhay took George and Luke through leafy suburbs, a world away from the gritty streets of central Leeds. As they approached Judge Robert Whitaker's estate, the grandeur of the stately home was imposing, its manicured gardens a testament to a life of privilege and order.

Judge Whitaker, retired yet still commanding in presence, greeted them with a measured curiosity. His years on the bench had given him a discerning eye, and he appraised George and Luke with a keen, almost scrutinising gaze.

"Detective Chief Inspector Beaumont, Detective Inspector Mason," he began, his voice rich with the gravitas of his former office. "To what do I owe this unexpected visit?"

George, sensing the judge's guarded nature, was direct. "Your Honour, we're investigating connections between the

CHAPTER EIGHT

Bramley Woods Murder and the re-opening of a cold case. We believe there's more to the story."

Whitaker's expression changed subtly, a flicker of recognition, perhaps even apprehension, passing over his features. "Ah, the Bramley Woods case," he said, leading them into a study lined with shelves of legal tomes. "A troubling matter. I always suspected there was something amiss during the trial."

Luke leaned forward. "In what way, Your Honour?"

Whitaker sighed, settling into an armchair. "Key evidence was... overlooked. Or perhaps, suppressed. It suggested a conspiracy, reaching higher than a mere trial."

George's pulse quickened at the judge's words. "Suppressed evidence? Could you elaborate?"

Whitaker hesitated, his gaze shifting to a portrait on the wall. "Let's just say not all parties wanted the truth to come out. It was a delicate matter, politically charged. My hands were tied."

George leaned forward, a determined look in his eyes. "Your Honour, if there was suppressed evidence, it could be crucial to our investigation. Can you tell us anything more about it?"

Judge Whitaker, sitting behind his polished mahogany desk, regarded George with a measured gaze. He sighed, his hands clasped tightly in front of him. "Detective, I understand your position, but you must realise my constraints at the time. There were... external pressures."

"But surely the truth must come out, especially in a murder investigation," George pressed, his voice tinged with frustration. "Any detail you remember could make a difference."

The judge's eyes drifted to the portrait on the wall again, a silent witness to the conversation. "I wish I could help more,

Detective Beaumont. The case was complex, entangled in affairs beyond the usual scope of law enforcement."

George sensed the walls closing in on the conversation. "Were there specific individuals who influenced the case? Any names you can give us?"

Judge Whitaker's expression hardened slightly, a mix of regret and caution. "I'm sorry, Detective. I've said all I can. The less you dig into this, the safer you'll be. It's a matter I'd advise you to approach with utmost caution."

The judge's vague warnings and reluctance to divulge more left George with a sense of deepening intrigue. He realised that whatever had been buried in the past was guarded by powerful forces, ones that even a retired judge was hesitant to challenge. The hint at a deeper conspiracy was both illuminating and frustrating. It raised more questions than answers, suggesting layers of corruption and manipulation that extended beyond the confines of a single murder case.

As they left Whitaker's estate, the air of Roundhay felt different, charged with the weight of the judge's implications. George and Luke exchanged a look of mutual understanding—they were on the cusp of uncovering something significant.

The ride back to the station was filled with a tense silence, each man lost in thought. The pieces of the puzzle were slowly coming together, forming a picture that was as disturbing as it was compelling.

George knew they were delving into dangerous territory, where the stakes were higher than they had ever imagined. But the truth was within reach, and he was determined to pursue it, no matter the cost.

* * *

CHAPTER EIGHT

Forensic Scientist Maya Chen was in her element, surrounded by advanced equipment and technology. She was deep in the process of analysing the photographs and envelopes received by George Beaumont and now Luke Mason, a task that required her full array of forensic expertise.

As Maya examined the fingerprints on the envelopes, her movements were precise and methodical. She carefully applied fingerprint powder, her eyes keenly observing the patterns that began to emerge under her magnifying lens. Each print was meticulously documented and then scanned into the database for potential matches.

Next, she turned her attention to the DNA analysis. Donning her gloves, Maya carefully swabbed the edges of the envelopes where they had been sealed, looking for traces of saliva. She placed the swabs into the DNA analyser, her mind already considering the potential implications of any matches that might be found.

The digital enhancement of the photographs was equally intricate. Maya adjusted the settings on her computer, enhancing the images to reveal hidden details. She focused on bringing out obscured features in the background, zooming in on specific areas that might hold clues.

Her chemical examination of the paper and ink was a testament to her background in chemical engineering. Using chromatography and spectrometry, she analysed the composition of the materials, determining their age and potentially identifying their source.

Throughout her analysis, Maya's approach was a blend of passion for forensic science and a natural aptitude for solving complex puzzles. She was methodical yet creative, her mind always working a step ahead.

After hours of painstaking work, Maya finally had an answer.

Half an hour later, George sat across from Maya and listened to the forensic scientist.

Her presentation was clear and concise, yet filled with the enthusiasm of someone who loved their work. "I have managed to isolate a fingerprint," she explained. "I have an expert working on it as we speak."

Chapter Nine

"I'm getting fed up with this place already, son," Luke Mason said to George Beaumont as he navigated through the archive's rows of metal shelving with a clear purpose.

Reaching a section marked with dates corresponding to Grimes' departure, they began their search. The area was a time capsule, each box and file a piece of history, some potentially holding the keys to unresolved mysteries like the Gildersome murders and the Bramley Woods Murder.

It was Luke who first noticed a mislabelled box tucked away, almost as if to evade discovery. "George, over here," he whispered, his voice barely audible.

The box was heavy with contents, and as they sifted through, a sense of anticipation grew. Then, almost hidden between old reports, Luke pulled out a dossier labelled 'Operation Redwood.' Its worn cover hinted at the secrets that lay within.

The dossier was a revelation. Page after page contained names of high-ranking officials, some still active, entwined in cryptic references connecting them to both the Gildersome and Bramley Woods cases. The magnitude of what they held was staggering, suggesting a web of corruption woven into the very fabric of the force.

George's face mirrored the shock and gravity of their discovery. "This is explosive, Luke. If these names are involved... it's going to shake the entire department to its core."

Luke, still scanning the documents, nodded in agreement. "Grimes knew something big. Operation Redwood... it's like he was trying to expose a conspiracy at the heart of the police force."

Their initial shock slowly transformed into an unwavering sense of duty. Holding the dossier, they realised the weight of responsibility that now rested on their shoulders. Grimes had compiled this at significant risk, and now it was up to them to pursue the truth he had unearthed.

Carefully replacing the dossier, George and Luke understood the path ahead would be fraught with challenges.

As they left the archive, blending into the night, the gravity of their discovery loomed large. The unearthed secrets of 'Operation Redwood' had irrevocably altered the course of their investigation, for they were now on a path that promised danger and revelations, a path that demanded courage and resolve in the face of daunting odds.

* * *

Detective Constable Alexis Mercer took in the shop. The walls, lined with shelves of various goods, created an intimate setting, a stark contrast to the weight of the conversation about to unfold.

As Martin greeted her, his appearance was a blend of curiosity and mild apprehension. He remembered the initial interview from over a decade ago and seemed unsure about what new information he could offer.

Alexis began with a reassuring smile. "Mr Hughes, I

appreciate your time. I'm here to discuss the Corsa you mentioned in your statement. Anything you remember could be crucial."

Martin nodded, his hands fidgeting with a pen. "Well, I told the officers everything I remembered last time," he said, a hint of nervousness in his voice.

Alexis leaned forward slightly, her tone gentle yet persuasive. "Sometimes it's the small details that matter most. Can you recall what time of day you usually saw the car? Or if there was anything unusual about those days—maybe the weather or something else happening in the area?"

Martin paused, his eyes drifting upwards as he tried to recall. "Well, now that you mention it, it was often early in the morning. And I remember it was quite foggy on a few of those days. Made it hard to see much, but that car... it just seemed out of place."

Alexis' keen eyes didn't miss the slight change in his body language, the way he leaned in as he spoke, indicating he was starting to remember more clearly. "Did you ever notice anything about the driver? Or maybe if they met with anyone?"

Martin shook his head slowly. "No, never saw who was driving. But there was this one time I saw someone walking away from the car, heading towards the park. Couldn't see their face, though."

Alexis made careful notes, her mind already correlating this new information with the known movements of the Corsa. "This is very helpful, Mr Hughes. These details, they might seem small, but they can make a big difference."

As the interview concluded, Alexis thanked Martin for his cooperation. Stepping out of the shop, she felt a sense of accomplishment. Her skilful probing had uncovered new details that could potentially place the Corsa at the scene of the crime, a testament to her thoroughness and dedication to the case.

Back at the station, Alexis updated George and Luke on her findings. They looked busy, but Alexis knocked on the door and was permitted access. "Hughes remembered seeing the Corsa early in the mornings, often on foggy days. There's also a mention of an unidentified individual heading towards the park."

George nodded, impressed. "Excellent work, Alexis. Let's cross-reference this with our timeline for the Corsa. We might be closer to placing our suspect at the scene."

* * *

Tired from the day but raring to go, George Beaumont sat across from Luke Mason in his office, the contents of the 'Operation Redwood' dossier spread out across George's desk. The room was quiet except for the rustling of papers, the tension palpable as they began to unravel the layers of surveillance logs, photographs, and notes.

As they sifted through the documents, it became increasingly clear that they were uncovering a scandal of unprecedented proportions. Among the names implicated was Chief Superintendent Elaine Harwood, a revelation that sent a shock wave through both men.

George's hands paused over a photograph of Harwood in a clandestine meeting. "This... this is huge, Luke," he said, his voice a mix of disbelief and resolve. "If Harwood is involved, who knows how deep this goes."

Luke, usually composed, looked equally shaken. "It suggests a network, George. Influencing case outcomes, manipulating investigations... this is beyond corruption. It's a complete subversion of justice."

The gravity of their discovery was overwhelming. George felt a surge of determination, a deep-seated commitment to justice that had always guided him. "We have to pursue this, Luke. No matter how high it goes."

Luke nodded, a firm look of agreement in his eyes. "Right. We can't let this stand. But we need to be careful. People this powerful won't go down without a fight."

As they continued to examine the dossier, George couldn't help but think about the threats to his family and career that pursuing this could entail. Yet, the need to expose the truth, to shine a light on this darkness, overrode his fears. His resolve solidified; he was ready to face whatever consequences came with uncovering this web of corruption.

The atmosphere in the office was charged with a sense of urgency. With each document they reviewed, the stakes grew higher, and the danger more real. But George and Luke were undeterred, their dedication to justice driving them forward.

* * *

After speaking with George and Luke, Alexis Mercer returned to the shared office, her mind buzzing with the new information she had gathered. Settling into her workspace, she spread out the timeline of the Corsa's known movements alongside her freshly written interview notes. The walls around her desk were adorned with maps and timelines, each a crucial part of the intricate tapestry they were weaving in the Gildersome murder investigation.

Alexis began the meticulous process of cross-referencing Hughes' statements with the Corsa's timeline. She plotted each sighting of the car on a map, her brow furrowed in concentration. The early mornings, the foggy days—all these details were pieces of a larger puzzle. "Could Hughes have unwittingly witnessed something crucial?" she wondered to herself.

As she worked, Detective Constable Jay Scott approached her desk. "How did the interview with Hughes go, Alexis?" he asked, leaning against the edge of her desk.

Alexis looked up, a glint of determination in her eyes. "It went well. He mentioned seeing the Corsa early in the mornings, particularly on foggy days. I'm trying to see if this fits into the Corsa's known movements."

Jay nodded, his gaze following the lines and markers on her map. "That could be a significant pattern. Maybe the fog was used as a cover."

Alexis' fingers traced along the routes on the map. "Exactly my thought, young man. It's all about finding the connections." Her mind was racing, considering the possibilities. "If we can place the Corsa at or near the crime scenes based on Hughes' sightings, it could be the breakthrough we need."

"Young man?" Jay asked. "You're what, twenty-six?"

Alexis narrowed her eyes. "Oh, I wish."

As Alexis continued to piece together the timelines, her mind returned to the interview. Hughes had seemed genuine, his observations unfiltered by the passage of time. It was this raw, untainted perspective that could sometimes provide the most valuable insights.

Alexis' dedication to the case was evident in her methodical

CHAPTER NINE

approach. She was a sentinel of justice, her every effort bringing them closer to solving the mystery that had long cast a twelve-year-shadow over Gildersome.

* * *

Upstairs in the forensic lab, Forensic Scientist Maya Chen presented the three cleaned medals to Candy Nichols.

"You said these were buried?" asked Maya.

Candy picked up the three bags, examining the medals through the plastic. Candy nodded. "I found two of them at two of the crime scenes from twelve years ago, and DC Scott found the third at the third Gildersome crime scene," Candy explained, her voice steady but tinged with excitement. "They were buried, almost as if they were meant not to be found. I think it could be significant."

"Any ideas what this symbol could represent?" Candy asked.

Maya held out her hand and when Candy handed one over, Maya held the medal in nearer for a closer look. "From the symbols I can only imagine they will be linked to a specific group or organisation. We should run it through our databases and see if it matches any known symbols."

Candy speculated about the medal's origins—were they personal items of the perpetrator, tokens left intentionally, or perhaps a clue to their identity? The possibilities were numerous, and the discovery opened a new line of inquiry in the case.

DC Nichols watched as Maya took the badge for further analysis. Her find had reignited a sense of momentum in the investigation. The small, rusted emblem, once hidden beneath layers of time and earth, was now a beacon of hope in resolving the secret that shrouded the Gildersome murders. Her attention to detail and commitment to preserving evidence integrity had potentially brought the team one step closer to understanding the perpetrator's identity and motives.

Chapter Ten

George Beaumont, dossier in hand, stood resolutely across from Chief Superintendent Elaine Harwood, who sat behind her desk, an image of composed authority. The air was thick with unspoken tension. The slight tightening of her jaw betrayed her calm exterior.

Detective Superintendent Jim Smith nodded, and George took a step forward.

"Chief Superintendent, I need answers about your involvement in 'Operation Redwood,'" George began, his tone even but firm.

Harwood's eyes narrowed slightly, a flash of surprise flickering across her features before she regained her composure. "Involvement? That's a serious accusation, Beaumont. I suggest you tread carefully," she said, her voice steady but laced with an undercurrent of warning.

"George isn't accusing you of anything, ma'am—"

George slammed the photographs from the dossier on her desk, interrupting his boss. "These suggest otherwise. They show you in meetings that were never on the record, with individuals linked to the Gildersome and Bramley Woods cases."

As Harwood's eyes fell on the photographs, her facade of

control wavered. She leaned forward, her fingers trembling ever so slightly as she rifled through the evidence. Her denial came quickly, almost too quickly. "These are circumstantial at best. Doctored photographs don't prove anything."

Despite her words, the slight quiver in her voice and the way her gaze avoided George's spoke volumes. Attempting to regain control, she fixed George with a steely look. "Why are you really here, Beaumont? Who's pulling your strings? This isn't like you." She looked at Jim Smith. "Is he here because of you?"

"No, ma'am," the Geordie replied.

George stood his ground, unfazed by her attempt to deflect. "No one's pulling my strings, Superintendent. This is about justice, about corruption that's undermining everything we stand for."

Harwood's attitude shifted, a mask of warning replacing her initial shock. "You're playing a dangerous game, Beaumont. Digging into this will not only endanger your career but also those around you. Is it worth it?"

George's resolve didn't waver, his commitment to uncovering the truth unwavering. "If we ignore this, we're part of the problem. I won't let that happen." He paused, not wanting to look at Smith as he said, "If you're innocent, then you have nothing to hide, right?"

"Get out, Beaumont, before I lose my temper and say something I regret."

As George left Harwood's office, the weight of her words hung heavy in the air. The confrontation had only deepened his determination, solidifying his resolve to expose the truth. George knew the path ahead was fraught with risks, but the stakes were too high to back down now.

CHAPTER TEN

Stepping out into the bustling corridor of the police station, George was more aware than ever of the intricate web of deceit and power he was unravelling. Detective Superintendent Jim Smith had ordered George to leave Operation Redwood to Professional Standards, but that wasn't George's way. He even knew just the person he could visit to ask for help.

* * *

The late afternoon sun cast long shadows across Hyde Park, creating a secluded and secretive atmosphere perfect for clandestine meetings. George Beaumont and Luke Mason waited on a quiet path, far from prying eyes, their anticipation growing with each passing moment.

Their informant, a figure emerging from the shelter of an old oak tree, was Ian Foster, a retired detective who had worked on the original Bramley Woods case. DI Mason had managed to get in touch with Foster so instead of heading to Cookridge, George had agreed to head to Hyde Park first.

Foster's expression was one of weary regret, the lines on his face telling the story of a career weighed down by unsolved mysteries and unspoken truths.

"Detective Foster," George greeted, extending his hand. "Thank you for meeting us."

Foster's handshake was firm, but his eyes were troubled, darting around as if fearing they were being watched. "I should've come forward sooner," he said, his voice low. "What happened in Bramley Woods... it was never right. The investigation was steered away from the truth."

Luke, observant as ever, noted Foster's anxious glances. "What truth are you referring to?"

Foster reached into his coat, producing a small, carefully wrapped package. "This," he said, unwrapping it to reveal a medal. It was unique, an intricate design that seemed to belong to another era, its metalwork aged but distinctly recognisable.

George examined the pendant, a sense of realisation dawning. "This is similar to three we recently found related to the Gildersome case. Where did you find it?"

"It was at the Bramley Woods murder scene," Foster replied, his voice tinged with a mix of sadness and determination. "But it was never logged as evidence. I kept it, knowing something wasn't right. Now I see the connection."

The revelation was a significant breakthrough. The medal, a link between the two cases, suggested a serial killer whose actions spanned decades. But George was suspicious of Foster. Who would take a piece of crucial evidence away from a crime scene?

Regardless, George's mind raced with the implications. "This could be the key to unravelling both cases," he said, his determination evident. "We appreciate you coming forward, Ian. This takes courage."

Foster nodded, a hint of relief in his expression. "It's time the truth came out. I just hope it's not too late."

As they parted ways, the weight of Foster's revelations hung heavily in the air. George and Luke walked back through the park, their path illuminated by the fading light. The discovery of the pendant was a turning point, a piece of evidence that could unlock the mysteries that had eluded them.

They got to the car, and as soon as George fired up the engine, Luke said, "I don't trust him."

"I don't either," replied George.

CHAPTER TEN

* * *

George sat hunched at the central table in their Incident Room, brow furrowed in concentration as he studied the sparse notes and forensic reports related to the perplexing medals discovered at the Gildersome crime scenes.

The room felt stuffy, almost claustrophobic, with the pressure bearing down on the investigation. George raked a hand through his hair in frustration, the words on the pages before him beginning to blur together. He desperately needed a breakthrough to reinvigorate this stagnating case.

As if on cue, the shrill ring of George's mobile phone pierced the ambient noise. Snatching it up eagerly, he saw the call was from the forensics lab. "Maya, please tell me you've got something," George answered without preamble, pulse already quickening. Even a fragment of new evidence could spark fresh momentum in the case.

Maya Chen's voice held a note of surprise layered beneath her usual brisk professionalism. "Apologies for taking some time analysing those photographs and envelopes related to the Gildersome cold case, DCI Beaumont. But I have uncovered something rather unexpected." She hesitated briefly. "The DNA and fingerprint results came back conclusively matching one individual: Arthur Grimes."

George sat bolt upright, the name jolting through him like an electric shock. "Did you say the evidence matched Arthur Grimes?" he repeated sharply, certain he had misheard.

"Yes, sir," Maya affirmed. "I ran the samples multiple times against our database to be certain. But the fingerprints and DNA profile from skin epithelial cells on the envelopes match Inspector Grimes definitively."

George's mind reeled, thoughts racing to process the implications. The revelation of Arthur Grimes' apparent involvement meant one of two things. One, he was trying to help them or two, he was the culprit. It had to be the former. Grimes dedicated his career to putting away criminals and exposing corruption. Why would his prints turn up on something connected to sadistic murders?

"Thanks for the great work, Maya," George said and ended the call, mind spinning from the scenarios already. This startling revelation introduced new variables that could drastically impact the trajectory of the entire investigation depending on what Grimes did or didn't know. George realised he was navigating treacherous waters now.

But it was clear Grimes held intimate knowledge related to the murders twelve years ago, and George was determined to unravel the full extent of the retired inspector's apparent entanglement in this deepening web of mystery and corruption. The answers were out there if he was willing to pursue them, regardless of potential consequences.

* * *

George Beaumont's phone rang just as the evening sky began to darken, the call from Detective Sergeant Yolanda Williams sending a jolt of alarm through him. "Sir, it's Yolanda. Police Constable Sally Jenkins hasn't signed back in and provided the recording device like you asked," she explained. And before George could answer, Yolanda added, "Sally also hasn't arrived home yet." She paused, the tension palpable. "Her partner thinks Sally's missing."

The news hit George like a punch to the gut. Sally's recent

involvement in providing information about Alistair Atkinson immediately raised a red flag. "Alright, Yolanda, get everyone on this now. I'll be back at the station in twenty minutes," George responded, his voice taut with urgency. He and Luke were on their way to Cookridge and had stopped off for some food, but seeing his father would now have to wait.

As he ended the call, Luke Mason looked up, still chewing his Greggs sausage roll but clearly sensing the seriousness of the situation. "What's happened?"

"Sally Jenkins is missing. We need to move fast. She could be in danger because of what she knows about Atkinson," George explained as they hurried out of the office.

Arriving at the station, George and Luke wasted no time. They coordinated with other officers, instructing them to check security footage from around the station and to canvas areas Sally frequented. Every resource available was mobilised.

George's mind was racing. Sally's disappearance couldn't be a coincidence. It was too closely tied to her revelations about Atkinson. "Check her phone records, bank transactions, anything that might give us a lead," he instructed Yolanda.

Luke, meanwhile, was on the phone with the tech team, asking for an urgent trace on Sally's last known location from her phone's GPS.

The station was a flurry of activity, the air charged with a mix of concern and determination. As officers moved quickly, poring over computer screens and making calls, George felt the weight of responsibility bearing down on him. Sally's safety, potentially compromised by her involvement in their investigation, was now his top priority.

"Let's also get a team over to her flat," George said, his

expression hardening. The urgency of the situation demanded swift action, and he was prepared to push boundaries to ensure Sally's safety.

As they coordinated the search, the atmosphere in the station was tense. Every officer understood the stakes were high, and time was of the essence. George's leadership and sense of justice were guiding forces in the frantic search for Sally.

But George was conflicted. And angry. He was sure somebody within the police was responsible for Sally being missing, but he wasn't sure whether it was Grimes, Atkinson, or Harwood.

* * *

The piercing ring of the security alert on his phone jolted George Beaumont from the urgency of the search for Sally Jenkins. The message was stark: a break-in at his home in Morley. His heart pounding, George excused himself from the station, a sense of dread washing over him. As he raced through the night streets, his first thought was for the safety of his family.

He made a frantic call to Isabella, who, luckily, had taken Rex and Olivia to her grandparent's house for an evening visit with Granny Annie and Grandad Eric. Hearing her voice, confirming they were safe and away from home, brought a momentary relief, but it was quickly overshadowed by fear of what he might find at their house.

Arriving home, the scene that greeted him was one of chaos. The front door was ajar, its lock broken. Inside, his once orderly home was a landscape of upheaval, drawers pulled out, contents strewn across the floor. George's pulse quickened as he surveyed the damage, grateful now more than ever that Isabella and Olivia were not there to witness it.

But it was the living room that brought him to a standstill. On the wall, in bold, menacing crimson letters, was a message: 'Stop digging, or else.'

George's mind reeled at the sight. The unambiguous threat was a chilling wake-up call to the reality of the danger he faced—a threat that had now invaded his own home.

The personal risk had escalated beyond what George had anticipated. His family, although safe for the moment, were unwittingly in the crosshairs of this shadowy threat. The thought of Isabella and Olivia being targeted because of his investigation filled him with a fear that was new and raw.

Standing amidst the wreckage of his living room, George's usually unshakeable character gave way to a moment of vulnerability. The walls of his home, once a sanctuary, now echoed with the menace of the warning left behind.

After contacting the police to report the break-in, George waited, his mind a whirlwind of emotion and determination. The message on the wall was a stark reminder that his pursuit of justice came at a high personal cost.

Yet, even as fear for his family's safety gnawed at him, George's resolve to uncover the truth and protect those he loved only grew stronger. The break-in at his home, far from deterring him, had steeled his determination to bring the culprits to justice.

Chapter Eleven

Wearing a Scene of Crime suit that he had in his boot, shoe covers, gloves and a mask, Detective Chief Inspector George Beaumont stood amidst the chaos of his once serene home. The stark message scrawled on the wall in crimson was a visceral punch, a blatant threat that shook the foundations of his world.

As he waited, the sound of vehicles pulling up broke the eerie silence. The forensics team arrived, their arrival marked by the soft murmur of voices and the clatter of equipment being unloaded. The lead forensic specialist, Helen Carter, a seasoned professional forensics manager with whom George had worked on numerous cases, though albeit not recently, stepped into the chaos.

"DCI Beaumont, we got here as fast as we could," Helen said, her voice a mix of professionalism and concern.

George nodded, his eyes lingering on the menacing message. "Thanks, Helen. I appreciate it."

The team set to work immediately, their movements precise and methodical. Flashbulbs flickered, casting stark shadows against the walls as photographs were taken. Every drawer pulled out and every item strewn across the floor was documented, becoming part of the narrative of the intrusion.

George watched them work, a silent sentinel amidst the flurry of activity. He found a strange comfort in their efficiency, a reminder that even in chaos, there was order to be found.

Helen approached him, her gaze following his to the message on the wall. "This is brazen, DCI Beaumont. It's a clear message to you."

"I know," he replied, his jaw tightening. "It's a warning but also a sign of desperation."

As the team continued their meticulous work, George's mind wandered. He thought of past cases, of the countless criminals he had pursued, each with their own motives and methods. He thought of the Miss Murderer, the Bone Saw Ripper, the Blonde Delilah, and the Rothwell Killer. Why did it always end up being personal?

Helen's voice brought him back to the present. "We've found some footprints, and there might be fibres we can work with. We'll know more once we get everything back to the lab."

George nodded, his detective instincts kicking in. "Anything out of place, anything they might have left behind, could be the key."

As the night wore on, the forensics team gathered evidence, filling bags and containers with potential leads. George stepped outside for a moment, the cool night air a stark contrast to the heavy atmosphere inside. He gazed up at the stars, a brief respite from the weight of his thoughts. His family was safe, but the danger was far from over.

He thought of Isabella and Olivia, the life he had built with them. The intrusion into his home was a violation of their sanctuary, a place where they should have felt safest. The fear for their safety fuelled his resolve; he would not let this threat linger.

Returning inside, Helen approached him with a small bag in her hand. "We found something."

George's eyes narrowed in interest. "What is it?"

Helen handed over a plastic bag, and upon inspection, George saw a black and white landscape photograph of the countryside. It seemed oddly out of place amidst the chaos of the break-in. The picture, depicting a serene rural setting, contrasted sharply with the menacing message left on the living room wall.

George, still processing the violation of his family home, was immediately drawn to it. "Where did you find this?" he asked, his eyes narrowing as he examined the photograph.

"Upstairs in your daughter's bedroom."

Clenching his fists and grinding his teeth, George took a closer look at the photograph. It depicted a tranquil countryside scene, but something about it seemed deliberate, intentional.

George's hand trembled slightly as he flipped the photograph over. On the back, in stark, black marker pen, were the words: "PC Sally Jenkins." The name, written so abruptly, sent a jolt through him. Sally Jenkins—the very person at the centre of their current investigation. How did this serene countryside image connect to her? And more importantly, why was it left in his house?

"I need a copy of this immediately," he said decisively. "And can we fast-track the forensics on this? Prints, paper type, anything."

Helen nodded, understanding the urgency in his voice. "We'll prioritize this, DCI Beaumont. I'll get you a copy and

CHAPTER ELEVEN

start the analysis right away."

As Helen and her team continued their work, George's mind raced. The photograph was clearly a piece of this twisted puzzle, but how it fit in was a mystery he needed to unravel. With the promise he'd receive a copy immediately by email, George stepped outside into the crisp midnight air. The street was quiet, the normality of the scene a stark contrast to the turmoil he felt inside.

He slid into his car, and as he started the engine, his thoughts were a whirlwind of speculation and determination. This photograph, this seemingly innocuous piece of paper, could be the key to understanding the threat against him and his family.

Driving through the streets of Morley, George's detective instincts were in overdrive. The picture added a new, urgent dimension to the investigation. It was no longer just a clue; it was a direct message, a piece of the puzzle intricately linked to Sally Jenkins. George's mind raced with possibilities. Was this a location significant to her? A message from the perpetrator about her whereabouts or involvement?

He mulled over the possibilities, each more perplexing than the last.

* * *

George Beaumont entered the bustling station, the energy of unresolved cases palpable in the air. Jay, Tashan, and Candy were huddled over their desks, immersed in various leads. George was proud of his team for coming in despite having worked a full day already. They looked up as he approached, their faces a mix of anticipation and weariness. "Where's

Yolanda and Alexis?" George asked.

"Alexis couldn't get anybody to watch her daughter at short notice, boss," Jay said.

George nodded. "And Yolanda?"

"Phone kept ringing, sir," said Candy.

"OK, I'll give her another ring in a bit, but I have to show you this." George held up the evidence bag containing the black and white landscape photograph, their attention instantly sharpening at the stark message: 'Stop digging, or else!'

"It's what somebody wrote on my living room wall," he said, his voice low but carrying a weight of significance.

As his team gasped, he laid out the photograph for them to see, too; the serene countryside image created a jarring contrast.

Jay leaned in closer, his brow furrowing. "Where did you find this, boss?" he asked, pointing to the photograph.

"In Olivia's bedroom," George replied, his tone even, but the undercurrent of concern was evident.

"Jesus Christ." Jay picked it up. "What's it supposed to mean?"

Tashan, always quick to connect the dots, chimed in, "There's something on the back." He turned the photograph over, revealing the handwritten note: "PC Sally Jenkins."

Candy, the newest member of the team, looked between the photograph and the message on the wall. "Is this a threat? Or a clue?"

"That's what we need to figure out," George said, his gaze moving over the two pieces of evidence. "This photograph was deliberately placed in my home. It's connected to Sally Jenkins, and whoever did this clearly wanted me to find it."

The team absorbed this information, the gears of their

CHAPTER ELEVEN

trained minds turning. George continued, "We need to dig deeper into Sally Jenkins' background. Any connection to this location, any link that can explain why this photograph was left for me."

Jay nodded, already pulling up Jenkins' file on his computer. "I'll cross-reference her known associates, her case history. There might be a connection we've overlooked."

Tashan was already on his feet. "I'll make a plan to hit the streets in the morning and talk to some informants. Someone might have seen something that ties back to this." He paused, looking at the photo. "Somebody is bound to have seen Sally."

Candy, thoughtful, added, "I'll research the local photography shops and clubs online now and visit them in the morning when they open. Maybe this landscape is a known spot among photographers."

George looked at his team, a sense of pride mixed with the gravity of the situation. "That's a great idea, Candy. And thank you, Tashan." He looked at each member of his team, meeting their eyes and nodding as he said, "Keep me updated on any leads. This photograph is a piece of the puzzle we can't ignore."

As the team dispersed to their tasks, George's thoughts lingered on the photograph and the menacing message. The connection to Sally Jenkins was a significant lead, but the motivations behind it were still shrouded in mystery. He knew that unravelling this clue was vital to understanding the threat against him and his investigation.

George took a moment to step aside, pulling out his phone to try contacting Yolanda again. This time, after several rings, the call connected.

"Yolanda, it's George. We've had a development, and I'm

glad to hear your voice," he said, his voice a blend of relief and annoyance.

Yolanda replied, her tone brisk and professional, "I'm on my way, sir. I was... I'd been out on a date and..."

"No need to explain; I'm just glad you're safe. See you soon." George ended the call, a sense of relief mixed with the ever-present tension of the case.

In his office, George leaned back in his chair, the photograph and the chilling message still occupying his thoughts.

Then, like a lightbulb moment, he thought of Alexis Mercer. Her expertise in cybercrime could be precisely what they need right now. If there were a digital trail connected to this photograph, she would be the one to find it.

He picked up his phone and dialled her number. The call connected, and Alexis' voice came through, apologetic yet firm. "Sir, I'm really sorry, I couldn't find anyone to watch Georgia on such short notice."

The DCI had been so obsessed with the case that he hadn't thought about the detectives who worked under him or the lives they led outside the station.

"I didn't know you had a child," George said. "I'm sorry, I should have known that."

"That's OK, sir; we haven't had much chance to speak since I joined, have we?"

"No, and I'll remedy that when we can."

"Was there a reason you called me, sir?"

"Nothing that can't wait until tomorrow," George said.

George explained about the break-in at his house, the photograph, and the message on the wall. He spoke of the inscription on the back of the photograph, 'PC Sally Jenkins,' and how it could potentially lead to a breakthrough in their case.

"I need someone with your expertise to take a look at this photograph. We need to scan it, see if there's anything digitally we're missing—any hidden data, anything that could lead us to where it came from or why it was left for me," George said, his voice a mix of urgency and hope. He also remembered the training he'd received before Christmas. It was similar to Google Lens, but it was a more powerful version that the police had access to.

"I know the program you mean, sir," Alexis said, promising to get in early and get started. She also said, "I can use the digital imaging software at the station to scan the photograph for any hidden metadata or even to see if it's been digitally altered in any way. We might also be able to trace its origin if it's been uploaded or shared online."

"Excellent," George replied, a sense of relief washing over him. "See you bright and early, Alexis."

Hanging up the phone, George felt a renewed sense of momentum. Alexis' skills in digital forensics could open up new avenues in their investigation, avenues that traditional methods might not reveal. He placed the photograph safely in an evidence bag, ready for Alexis to analyse when she arrived in the morning.

As he waited for information to filter through to him from Jay, Candy, and Tashan, George couldn't help but feel that they were on the verge of a significant breakthrough. The photograph, a silent witness to the turmoil that had invaded his life, held secrets that they were just beginning to uncover.

* * *

Fatigued, George was ordered to go home by DSU Smith, who had called for a quick update, having heard about the break-in and the photograph.

And he did, shocked to find forensics were still there as he pulled his Mercedes into the drive.

An hour later, as the forensics team wrapped up their work, George's mind was a whirlwind of emotion and determination. The message on the wall was a clear indication that the stakes had been raised, but so had his resolve.

The team left, promising to expedite the analysis of the evidence collected. George lingered in the living room, the silence now filled with the echo of their findings.

His thoughts were interrupted by his phone vibrating in his pocket. It was Isabella, checking in. "George, are you alright?" her voice was laced with worry.

"I'm fine, love. The team's just left. They've found some things that might help," he reassured her, though the tightness in his voice betrayed his concern.

"Please, be careful," she whispered, a sentiment that hung heavily in the air as they ended the call.

George's gaze fell once more on the menacing message on the wall. 'Stop digging, or else.' It was a stark reminder of the peril he now faced, not just as a detective but as a husband and father. This case had crossed into his personal life in the most alarming way, yet it only served to strengthen his resolve.

He knew the risks and understood that each step closer to the truth put him and his family in greater jeopardy. But backing down was not in his nature. The pursuit of justice, the safety of his city, his family—these were the things that drove him, that had defined his career.

Alone in the quiet of his disrupted home, George's thoughts

turned to strategy. The evidence gathered tonight would be analysed, and leads followed. But he needed more. His instincts told him that this wasn't just a random act to scare him off. It was calculated, a move by someone who felt threatened by the investigation.

As George tried to sleep, the bed feeling far too large and cold without Isabella, the hours ticked by as he sifted through the events leading up to tonight. Connections, motives, suspects—his mind raced through the possibilities. As dawn began to break, painting the sky with the first light of morning, a plan began to take shape.

He would need to be cautious, more so now than ever. But he was not alone. His team, trusted colleagues like Helen, and now Alexis Mercer, with her keen eye and fresh perspective, were assets. Together, they would peel back the layers of this case and expose the corruption that lay beneath.

As the new day began, George Beaumont was more than a detective; he was a man on a mission. The risks were clear, the path fraught with danger, but his course was set. He would do whatever it took to protect his family, to serve justice. And as he stepped out of his house, locking the door to the remnants of last night's chaos, he carried with him a renewed sense of purpose.

The game had changed, the stakes higher than ever, but so was his determination. The message on his wall was meant to be a warning, but for George, it was a call to action. And he was ready to answer it.

Chapter Twelve

The shadows crept along the damp brick walls, swallowing the dim light that strained to illuminate the narrow alley. George's breath caught in his throat as he crept forward, senses hyper-aware of any movement or sound. The distant wail of sirens echoed somewhere in the city, but here, there was only tense silence.

He knew she was close. The killer had chosen his hiding place well—this neglected urban crevice where no help would find them. George's gut twisted with anger, the hunt so near completion. Just a bit further now.

Rounding the corner, the sight stole his breath. Sally Jenkins lay crumpled on the ground, ropes cutting into her wrists and ankles. Fresh blood trickled from the gag over her mouth. But those wide, terrified eyes—they pierced George to his core.

"Well, well. Right on time, Detective."

Alistair Atkinson emerged from the shadows, smug satisfaction etched on his face. The glint of a hunting knife reflected in the low light as he toyed with it casually. Anger and hatred coursed through George like fire.

"Let her go, Atkinson. Now!"

"I don't think so. We're just getting to the fun part."

CHAPTER TWELVE

Atkinson's lip curled as he leaned down, pressing the knife against Sally's throat. She whimpered, trembling.

George's fingers twitched toward his holster before he froze. He was unarmed. Helpless. Sally's frantic eyes found his, pleading. "Please..." he begged hoarsely. Atkinson just smiled.

The knife slashed downward in a vicious arc. Blood sprayed across the brickwork. Sally's final, gurgling gasp echoed in George's ears.

"No!"

He jolted awake, pulse hammering. The familiar surroundings of his bedroom filtered into focus, but his skin still crawled from the haunting images. Just a nightmare. One of many lately.

George rubbed his eyes, trying to slow his breathing. But the sick feeling in his gut remained. Sally Jenkins was still out there, and they were no closer to finding her. And Atkinson... What the hell was going on?

Clenching his jaw, George threw off the covers. He wouldn't be getting any more sleep tonight. Lying there, replaying the nightmare, would drive him mad.

His feet hit the cold floor, and he stood, muscles tight and tense. A glimpse of the clock showed it was nearing 5 am. He thought about Isabella, hoping she was sleeping soundly still at her grandparents' house, daydreaming about her dark curls as they splayed across her pillow.

George envied her peaceful rest.

After a quick trip to the bathroom, he found himself drawn almost automatically to the small home gym they'd set up. Physical exertion often helped clear his mind and provide focus. And God knows he needed that right now.

The weights felt comforting and familiar in his hands as he started his reps. The metal bar strained against his palms, the heavy plates clanking softly with each curl. Up, down. Up, down. He embraced the burning in his biceps, channelling his energy there.

But the images flickered behind his eyes still. Sally's pale, bloody face. Atkinson's cold smile. Anger simmered in his gut. With a tight exhale, George increased his pace, teeth gritted.

Up, down. Up, down. Ten reps turned to fifteen, to twenty, muscles screaming. Still, that sick rage and shame lingered. He saw Sally crying, helpless. Heard her frantic pleading. George's arms quivered, exhaustion seeping in, but he pushed harder. Sweat beaded on his forehead.

"Come on," he grunted through ragged breaths. "Come on!"

The bar slipped from his slick grip, crashing to the mats. The metallic clang echoed through the room. George braced his hands on his knees, chest heaving. Fuck!

Frustration simmered, but the red haze over his mind felt thinner now. His shoulders slumped as he scooped up the fallen weights and restored them to the rack with care. He winced, flexing his fingers gingerly. No real damage was done; it was just overexertion.

Rolling his neck with a sigh, George moved for the treadmill next. The rhythmic pounding of feet on the belt drowned out the lingering echoes of the nightmare still clawing at him. He started off slow, then built to a steady jog, embracing the burn in his lungs. Mile after mile, he lost himself in the motion and the shrill whir of the machine.

By six miles, a sheen of sweat covered George's skin. But his mind did feel clearer, tensions slowly easing from his muscles.

Small blessings. Especially since six months ago he couldn't even jog down the stairs.

Steps slowing to a brisk walk, George gradually brought his heartbeat down. As his feet carried him nowhere, his thoughts turned to the case, examining it with fresh eyes. They were missing something; he knew it. Some clue, some thread that could unravel this whole mystery. It lurked at the edges of his awareness, taunting him.

A hot shower would help shake things loose. Cut through the haze still clouding his focus. Peeling off his sweat-soaked shirt, George made for the bathroom.

The scalding hot water cascaded over George's muscular frame as he stood motionless in the shower, lost in thought. The events of the previous night played over and over in his mind—the break-in at his house, the message on the wall, the landscape photograph of the countryside, and the unsettling feeling that there was something they had missed all those years ago.

It washed away the stale sweat and lingering unease from the vivid nightmare. Bracing his hands against the slick tiles, George hung his head under the stream, letting it drum against his weary muscles. Twisted memories of the dream still flashed behind his eyes, intermingling with case details.

He saw Alistair Atkinson's face morph into Ethan Holloway's, a man he hadn't seen or thought of in over ten years. George shook his head, frustrated with himself for not making the connection sooner. How could he have forgotten about Ethan? He was their prime suspect at the time—a disturbed young man with a dark family history of abuse and violence. They had interrogated Ethan relentlessly but could never directly tie him to the crimes. There was circumstantial evidence, sure—Ethan's proximity, his lack of alibi, the tension between him and his stepfather—but nothing concrete enough for an arrest. George realised now that Ethan's recent return to Leeds after over a decade away was too much of a coincidence to ignore.

The crime scene photos from twelve years ago mingled with imagined scenes of Sally's torment. George ground his teeth, struggling to reconcile the two cases that refused to stop haunting him.

There had to be something he was missing. Some evidence he'd overlooked, some connection his tired mind couldn't make.

Scrubbing a hand over his face, George shut off the water, reaching for a towel and feeling uneasy about how this face from his past was re-emerging. There were too many questions that needed to be answered, questions he should have pursued more vigorously. George had been younger, less experienced. Now he knew better. He had to keep looking. Had to find that missing piece before Sally's nightmare became real. Before someone could take another innocent life.

The other officers would already be gathering at the station, comparing notes and chasing down leads. But that underlying dread lingered in George's gut, the helplessness of his nightmare still fresh. He had to get down there himself, had to feel like he was doing something. Anything.

Drying himself off with the worn grey towel Isabella always scolded him about; he vowed not to let this second chance slip away. Ethan Holloway was either a very unlucky man... or a very guilty one. George needed to figure out which.

After towelling off briskly, George pulled on a clean shirt and pair of trousers, running wax through his blond hair

CHAPTER TWELVE

to tame it. The familiar routine soothed his rattled nerves somewhat. A glimpse in the mirror showed tension still pinching his features, faint circles under his eyes. But he looked presentable enough. Ready for another long day on the trail of a killer.

George crept back to the bedroom, thinking about Isabella and Olivia, and a bittersweet pang touched George's heart. They should be here, safe in their home, spending this time with him. Not that he could be at home at the moment; he couldn't abandon Sally. However long it took, he had to find her.

He was surprised when he didn't immediately see Isabella bustling around the kitchen, singing softly to their baby Olivia while brewing a fresh pot of coffee for him like she did most mornings. Usually, he would sneak up behind her while she swayed and cooed at Olivia in her arms, kissing Isabella's neck and breathing in the comforting smell of her lavender shampoo mixed with the refreshing aroma of the dark roast brewing. Instead, the silence of the kitchen enveloped him as George prepared a simple breakfast of coffee and toast, mentally running through the day ahead. He washed up quickly, thoughts already returning to the case.

Locking the door behind him, George headed out into the cool morning air. It washed over his skin, helping dispel the last clinging unease from his unsettling dreams. Jogging down his front steps, he slid into the driver's seat of his Mercedes, turning the key in the ignition with a sense of renewed purpose.

No more wallowing in helplessness. If the killer wanted to turn this into a battle of wills, George would rise to meet the challenge. He refused to fail Sally Jenkins like in his nightmare.

Failure was not an option. Not when lives hung in the balance.

* * *

The twenty-minute drive to the Elland Road Police Station gave him time to mentally prepare for the day ahead. As he steered his Mercedes through the streets, the uneasiness from earlier settled into focused determination. He knew what needed to be done. Ethan Holloway had to be brought in for further questioning immediately. George felt confident that his seasoned interrogation skills could extract a confession if Ethan were indeed guilty.

He also needed updated background checks run on Ethan, as well as new statements taken from key witnesses in the original investigation. George was eager to dig back through the old case files again and re-examine the evidence with fresh eyes now that Ethan was back on the radar. New connections or leads could emerge that might finally close this case that had haunted him for over a decade.

Inside, George strode purposefully towards Detective Superintendent Jim Smith's office, his mind racing as he mentally prepared to present his disturbing theories about Alistair Atkinson and Ethan Holloway's potential involvement in Sally Jenkins' kidnapping. The rhythmic tapping of his shoes against the meticulously polished floor echoed through the hallway, punctuating the tense silence that had fallen over the usually bustling station.

Turning the final corner, he was greeted by the sight of Smith's closed door. Pausing for a brief moment to gather his thoughts, he raised his hand and gave three sharp knocks.

"Come in," Smith's muffled voice called out. Taking a deep

breath, George entered the office.

Superintendent Smith was seated behind an imposing oak desk, stoically reviewing a stack of paperwork. He raised his eyes as George stepped inside, gazing at him over the rim of his reading glasses.

"Ah, Beaumont, take a seat," he said, gesturing to the empty chair across from him. George obliged, sitting upright with his shoulders squared, meeting the Superintendent's scrutinising stare.

"I take it you're here with an update on the Jenkins case?" Smith queried, setting aside the papers in his hands.

George nodded. "Yes, sir. I have..." He hesitated, internally debating just how much to reveal of his suspicions. Smith maintained his steely gaze, waiting expectantly.

"Go on, Beaumont."

"I have concerns about two individuals who I believe may be involved in Sally's kidnapping." He paused. "One of the individuals is from within the force," he stated carefully.

Smith's brows furrowed ever so slightly, the only indication of his surprise. "Go on," he prompted.

George clasped his hands together, choosing his following words cautiously. "During our investigation, we heard from Sally Jenkins that she overheard DCI Atkinson in a conversation about the Gildersome case and a cover-up, sir," he said. "She managed to record a part of it."

"OK? May I hear the recording?" asked Smith.

"That's the problem, sir," said George. "She went missing the moment we asked her to return to the station and hand the recording device in."

"I'm struggling to understand how Alistair is a concern, Beaumont," Smith said.

Deciding full disclosure was necessary, George continued, "Well, think about it, sir, the only person to gain over Sally going missing is Atkinson, so I have reason to believe Atkinson was directly involved in the abduction." George shrugged. "And whether that's coerced or bribed by an outside party, I don't know, but I wanted to make you aware of the situation, sir, and get your recommendation on how to proceed with a high-ranking member of the force under suspicion."

Silence permeated the room as Smith digested this information, his expression unreadable. George sat rigidly, muscles tensed as he awaited the Superintendent's response.

Finally, Smith let out a slow breath and removed his glasses, carefully folding them and setting them on his desk. "These are grave allegations, Beaumont," he began gravely. "I understand you would not make such claims without compelling evidence."

George felt a simultaneous sense of relief and foreboding at Smith's words. At least the Superintendent was taking him seriously rather than dismissing the accusations outright.

"How substantial is this evidence against Atkinson?" Smith questioned.

George narrowed his eyes. "I have nothing substantial, just the statement from Officer Sally Jenkins," George reported. "My team is still gathering additional details, but the implications are clear." He paused. "And if we consider that Chief Superintendent Elaine Harwood is guilty, then who knows how deep this goes."

Smith nodded slowly, brows drawn together as he processed this information.

"This is deeply troubling, Beaumont. Two high-level officers suspected of aiding in a kidnapping," he murmured.

CHAPTER TWELVE

Raising his eyes to meet George's steady gaze, Smith's expression hardened with resolve. "Right then. This is how we will proceed," he began decisively. "I will personally handle the investigation into Atkinson. As a DCI, he has connections that could impede an impartial inquiry, and we must act swiftly but cautiously given his rank."

George opened his mouth to respond, but Smith raised a hand to forestall any objections.

"You and your team will remain focused on locating Police Constable Jenkins and uncovering the outside parties responsible for her abduction," he continued. "Leave Atkinson to me. Your priority is recovering the girl safely."

George hesitated, uncertainty gnawing at him. Could he really leave a senior officer under suspicion solely in Smith's hands?

Yet George could not deny the logic behind the Superintendent's command. This case stretched far beyond the walls of the station and into the territory of dangerous syndicates who had evaded justice for years. Stopping them and saving Sally Jenkins had to take precedence.

"You have reservations," Smith observed, interrupting George's internal debate.

George met his superior's steady gaze. "I do not doubt we require separate strategies in investigating Atkinson versus the larger criminal network, sir," he conceded carefully. "But with all due respect, Atkinson has deep roots here. If any whisper of suspicion reaches him..."

He trailed off meaningfully. Smith's expression remained impassive, though George detected a flicker of approval in his eyes.

"Your concern is understandable, Detective Chief Inspector,

and not unfounded," Smith acknowledged. "But I assure you, I can operate with the utmost discretion in looking into Atkinson. We cannot risk dual investigations tipping him off. You must keep your team's sights set squarely on locating Miss Jenkins and unmasking the perpetrators."

Smith's voice brooked no argument. George inclined his head in assent. "Of course, sir. My team will remain focused on Sally's safe return and bringing justice to those responsible," he affirmed.

Satisfied, Smith gave a brief nod. "Right then. Keep me informed of any developments. And Beaumont—" He paused, meeting George's gaze directly. "You and your team watch each other's backs out there. We don't know how far this rot spreads."

A chill crept down George's spine at the quiet warning. Wordlessly, he rose and moved toward the door. Pausing with his hand on the knob, he glanced back.

"Yes, sir. We'll be vigilant."

As George made his way briskly down the hall, the full weight of responsibility settled upon his shoulders. Far more now rested on him and his colleagues than just Sally Jenkins' life. They were unravelling a web of corruption that could penetrate deeply into the heart of the force.

Chapter Thirteen

George stepped into the Homicide and Major Enquiry Team office, his sharp green eyes scanning. Phones rang incessantly. Harried detectives shuffled back and forth, clutching files and printouts. The acrid tang of stale coffee permeated the thick air.

He took a deep breath, broad shoulders rising and falling beneath his fitted jacket. In the eye of the storm, George had learned to project an air of calm authority. It steadied subordinates and inspired public confidence in the competence of the force.

Yet privately, tension coiled in his muscular frame. Twelve years since Ethan Holloway eluded justice for sadistic serial murder. A dozen years of festering darkness left to spread. George pressed his lips together. Not this time. However long it took, Holloway would answer for his crimes.

"Right, team," George called out, voice crisp and commanding attention. "I need you in the Incident Room in two minutes."

He crossed the crowded floor with his long stride, team members falling in step behind him. Tashan Blackburn loomed at his right shoulder, imposing even with his habitual stoic expression. To his left, Jay Scott bobbed along enthusiastically as ever while slender Candy Nichols matched their brisk pace.

At the end of the hall, George pulled open the frosted glass door emblazoned with 'Incident Room 2' in imposing block letters. As he flicked on the fluorescent lights, the others filed inside the cramped space dominated by a long table ringed with wheeled office chairs.

George lowered himself into a seat at the head of the table, clasping his hands together atop the scuffed wood surface. His team arrayed themselves around him, their focus absolute. George met each of their intent gazes in turn. Even after only a week together, he could already sense the distinctive skills and attributes they brought to this partnership.

Jay's keen intuition and creative insight. Candy's unwavering determination and insight. And Tashan's analytic rigour and unflinching sense of justice. United by a shared commitment to protect the innocent and punish the guilty.

George cleared his throat before beginning, modulated voice carrying clearly in the small room. "Right then. Our first priority is locating Ethan Holloway. His name's resurfaced after twelve years off the radar. We need to know what he's been up to all this time."

George paused, brows lowering. "He's dangerous. Savage. Grimes and his team couldn't get anything to stick back then. But we have a second chance to get justice for those women."

Around the table, his team sat rapt with attention. George sensed their excitement, their hunger to right past wrongs.

"Finding Holloway is our first challenge," George continued. "We'll put his name and known aliases out to every informant and snitch on the streets straight away. He can't hide forever."

CHAPTER THIRTEEN

George looked to Tashan. "Get a list of Holloway's known associates from the old case file. We'll have uniforms bring them in one by one for questioning."

Tashan nodded. "I'll compile complete profiles on each one, sir. We'll map their networks to identify Holloway's most likely connections."

"Good man," George affirmed. He knew Tashan's tireless, systematic approach would uncover every scrap of potential evidence.

Next, George addressed Jay. "Check virology and pathology databases for Holloway's medical records. See if he's turned up at any clinics or hospitals in the past decade. Discreetly contact administrators to monitor for future visits."

Jay bounced his leg with enthusiasm. "Consider it done, boss. I can request surveillance notifications as well. The second he steps in for an appointment or a prescription, we'll have him."

George nodded, the faintest smile twitching his lips. He appreciated Jay's creative angles, no matter how unorthodox. The lad's innovation might crack this case wide open.

Finally, George turned to Candy. Her delicate features were set with solemn determination, red hair blazing under the harsh light.

"Candy, you'll take point interfacing with the SOC team for updates on forensics," George instructed. "Light a fire under them if you have to. We need those lab results yesterday."

Candy straightened. "You can count on me, sir."

George knew Candy would use her trademark blend of charm and tenacity to spur the technicians to accelerate the slowed momentum of their investigation.

Leaning back in his chair, George surveyed his team with

a swell of pride. He recognised their competencies meshed superbly under his experienced direction. Each member eagerly anticipated their assignments like athletes before a match.

Yet hovering beneath their game faces, George sensed hints of unease. Candy bit her lip pensively. Jay's knee bounced even faster. And Tashan stared down at his steepled fingers.

The spectre of their elusive suspect dampened the team's zeal, George realised. Ethan Holloway—sadist, defiler, murderer. Roaming free despite their best efforts.

George straightened. "I know this Holloway is a nasty piece of work," he said bluntly. "Grimes couldn't nail him back then. But we will. Because we're smarter. Because we're relentless. And because justice doesn't have a damn statute of limitations."

George held their gazes, radiating certainty. "It may take days or weeks. But we will track him down. And we will lock him away for good. Understood?"

Around the table, spines straightened, and shoulders squared.

"Understood, sir," Tashan replied, rich voice resonant.

Jay nodded eagerly. "We've got this, boss."

"Too right," Candy chimed in fiercely. "We'll get him."

George allowed himself a small smile. The spectre banished for now, replaced by steadfast commitment.

"Excellent," he said crisply. "Then let's get to it. We all know the clock's ticking on this bastard. Dismissed."

Chairs scraped and shuffled as the team began gathering documents and supplies to launch their respective missions. Eagerness and purpose electrified the air. George felt it, too, the thrill of the hunt. After a week of fruitless waiting,

CHAPTER THIRTEEN

momentum surged through their investigation again.

As the others filed out, Candy hesitated in the doorway. "One more thing, sir."

George raised a brow. "Go on."

"We're still no closer to figuring out the insignias from the medals, sir," Candy said.

George nodded slowly. "What's the progress on the analysis? If we can trace their origin, it may tell us more about our culprit and his motives."

"Slow, sir," Candy chirped. "Maya reported back that the unusual symbol didn't produce any definitive database matches. She suggested consulting external experts, which would take more time. I'll stay on top of the lab, but I know it's frustrating, sir."

As she disappeared down the hallway, George smiled to himself. For all her bubbly charm, Candy was as sharp as a tack. The team was coming together perfectly, he mused. Each member complementing the others' skills and driving the investigation forward. Together, they would uncover the truth.

For the next two hours, George spent time in his office, looking through old files.

Leaning back in his chair, he rolled his shoulders, stiff from hunching toward the monitor. His eyes burned from staring at the distorted shapes and pixels. George blinked hard, then turned to observe the shared office.

Outside, an array of intense activity unfolded across the HMET floor. Uniforms arrived to speak with detectives, explaining they'd escorted sullen, tattooed men to interview rooms for questioning about Holloway. Tashan huddled with two analysts, pointing emphatically at his monitor.

Candy laughed brightly on the phone, undoubtedly cajoling the pathology lab. And Jay gesticulated wildly, explaining something to a bemused sergeant.

Pride swelled in George's chest at the industrious momentum. Their commitment and competence affirmed George's certainty they would prevail no matter the obstacles.

* * *

George cleared his throat, the reverberating sound slicing through the anticipatory silence. Four faces turned towards him expectantly. "Right, a quick recap on where we are. Sally Jenkins has now been missing for 20 hours. There's been no contact, no sightings and no leads."

George pointed to the time-stamped CCTV image displayed on the board. It showed Sally striding purposefully towards her car after meeting with George and Luke yesterday. Her long brown ponytail swished behind her as she walked.

"This is the last visual confirmation we have of Sally before she disappeared. I want to review the progress on the tasks I assigned last night. Blackburn, you were going to liaise with Sergeant Greenwood about canvassing Gildersome. Have you spoken to him yet?"

Dark eyes met George's gaze steadily. "Yes sir," Tashan Blackburn responded, his deep voice crisp and assured. "Sergeant Greenwood has teams ready, so I'll head over straight after this briefing to coordinate with Sergeant Greenwood's team."

George nodded, studying the intensive notes scattered around the focused detective. Meticulous and uncompromising, qualities he admired in Tashan. "Good. Let me know if you turn up anything significant."

Turning his attention to his right, George addressed the next team member. "DC Nichols, what do you have on the photography angle? Any leads on who took that unsettling photo?"

Candy Nichols sat up straight, her signature red hair shimmering as she flipped open a journal filled with vibrant post-it notes marking key pages. Her eyes shone with a lively determination that lifted George's spirits despite the oppressive gloom outside.

"Yes, sir, I've been looking into photography clubs and studios in Gildersome to track down where that photo may have been taken. There's a small professional studio on Moorland Avenue called Alfred Hill Photography. The owner, Ronnie Hill, is a bit of a creep by all accounts. Known for taking intimate photos of female models. His club has regular exhibitions at a gallery on Gildersome Town Street—very exclusive, invitation-only events."

George nodded.

"I have an appointment to speak to Ronnie Hill this morning. And then I'm heading over to the Gildersome Gallery to talk to the curator, Nina Flynn."

"Good initiative," George affirmed. "Let me know what you find out. We need more information about this photograph."

Candy nodded, azure eyes glinting with determination as she neatly slid the photo back into a file. George was grateful for her energetic tenacity. They would need her resilience and innovation before this case was through.

"DC Scott, what did you learn from reviewing Sally's background and known associates?" George prompted, turning to the pensive young man leaning casually against the far wall instead of sitting.

"Right, so Sally's been on the force for five years now. Stellar record and is known for having incredible intuition when interviewing suspects or witnesses. Can get them to open up like no one else. Bit unorthodox in her methods at times, but gets results."

George nodded. "That matches what I know of her. Promising officer, naive at times given her age but good instincts."

"Exactly," Jay continued. "Now, in terms of connections, I didn't find any major red flags. No ties to organised crime or anything like that. She keeps a pretty tight inner circle. Parents still local, older sister moved to Edinburgh last year. Been in a steady relationship with boyfriend Liam Rhodes, an accountant, for about three years now."

"Any issues there? On the rocks lately, any jealousy or controlling behaviour?" George asked.

"Nothing in her file to indicate that, boss," Jay said. "From what I gather, it's pretty solid. Liam seems clean on the surface, too, with no record. Though we may want to question him, see if he knows anything relevant."

"Good thought," George said, leaning forward intently. "We'll bring him in. Even if he's not involved, he might have some insight into where Sally went instead of coming back to the station. Who else does she interact with regularly?"

Jay rifled through some papers. "Usual colleagues here at the station, of course. Punching way above her weight, though, that one. Barely twenty-five and handles cases like a pro. Outside of work, main friend is Alice Carter. They go way back, grew up on the same estate."

"Interesting," George muttered. "And this Carter woman, anything notable there?"

CHAPTER THIRTEEN

"A bit more chequered history," Jay admitted. "Few petty crimes in her teens and early twenties. Shoplifting, minor drug possession charges. But she seems clean past few years. Works as a bartender now at O'Malley's Pub in the city centre. Sally often pops by there after shifts, apparently."

George stood up and began pacing, piecing together this new information. Jay followed his movement like a puppy awaiting approval.

"Good work, Jay. This gives us some solid leads. Haul in the boyfriend first thing for questioning. And let's get uniform to bring Carter in as well. I want to know what they were chatting about in those late-night drinks at the pub. It could be the key to Sally's disappearance."

Jay beamed, snapping the folder closed crisply. "Right you are, boss. I'll get right on it."

Footsteps at the door announced the arrival of the final team member, with Luke and Yolanda elsewhere in the station, following up on leads and looking at CCTV, respectively. Detective Constable Alexis Mercer entered briskly, her cascade of golden hair swaying as she walked. An athletic grace characterised her movements, and her expression was calmly professional. But George noted she was nearly half an hour late now. Unacceptable, given the urgency of their case. He made a mental note to address it once they wrapped up the briefing.

"Morning, DC Mercer; thanks for joining us," George said evenly. "We were just covering the leads so far. Scott has a promising new angle with the stalker Sally Jenkins had back at university. Bring Mercer up to speed, Scott."

As Jay rapidly summarised his findings, George studied Alexis carefully. Her azure eyes remained fixed on Jay, absorbing the details with analytical precision. She asked a few concise clarifying questions, then neatly jotted down notes in shorthand cursive. George was relieved to see no defensiveness at her late arrival. Just that pragmatic focus he depended on from Alexis. Her resilience and logic were anchoring elements for this team. He would tread cautiously in addressing her tardiness later.

Once Jay had finished, George quickly summarised the updates from Tashan and Candy. Alexis listened intently, gaze steadily meeting George's as she integrated each new piece of information into her meticulous mental file. He was struck by her quietly commanding presence. Alexis inspired confidence in her diligence and capability. George hoped she would continue exemplifying resilience and stability as pressures mounted on this case. They would sorely need her pragmatic competence in the days ahead.

"Right, we have plenty of threads to follow up on today," George said decisively, rising from his chair as the team began gathering papers and laptops. "Let's get out there and find Sally Jenkins. Call in regularly with updates. And get some rest when you can—we'll need to be at our sharpest to crack this case."

As his team filed purposefully out into the bustling station, George felt a swell of pride in their commitment, initiative and diverse skills. But lingering beneath it coiled a cold thread of unease. A young woman's life hung precariously in the balance. And the clock was ticking down.

George turned back to the Big Board, staring intently at Sally Jenkins' youthful smile. "Where are you, Sally?" he murmured under his breath. "What happened to you yesterday?"

CHAPTER THIRTEEN

The empty Incident Room held no answers. Only the silent faces of the dead and missing were pinned in neat rows across the walls. George sighed, scrubbing a hand over his tired eyes. It had already been a long two days. And something told him the real challenges lay ahead.

But as George strode out to begin coordinating the wider investigation, he carried with him the image of Sally's smile. A reminder of the young, vibrant life at stake. And the possibility that, together, his team could find the truth that would bring her home.

Chapter Fourteen

Finally alone to gather his thoughts on this troubling case, George sank into the worn leather chair behind his desk, the dark wood surface strewn with case files and coffee rings marking each stressful late-night brainstorming session. George kneaded his temples, the ache behind his eyes beginning to form once again.

Police Constable Sally Jenkins had been missing for nearly 24 hours now with no trace or contact. As a fellow officer, her disappearance weighed heavily on them all, but especially on George. He stared through the blinds to the hive of activity beyond, the urgency palpable even through the glass as teams followed every possible lead to find Jenkins. But they kept hitting dead ends.

A sharp rap at the door drew his attention. "Come in," George called, straightening in his chair.

Detective Inspector Luke Mason entered briskly, a serious set to his unshaven jaw and dark circles lining his grey eyes. "You wanted to see me, son?" he asked, standing at attention before George's desk.

George gestured to a chair. "Aye. Have a seat, Luke."

Mason sank into the chair, elbows on knees as he leaned forward intently. "I assume this concerns Jenkins?"

CHAPTER FOURTEEN

George nodded gravely. "No question. It's been a full day without contact, well past the point of her just needing some time off the grid. Something is very wrong here."

Mason scrubbed a hand through his greying hair in frustration. "I just can't wrap my head around it. Sally was a model officer, totally dedicated. No enemies that we know of, nothing in her file to indicate she'd just take off. And no signs of a struggle at her place. It's like she just vanished into thin air."

"I know," George sighed. "We're running down every possible lead, but so far nothing to go on. No digital footprint, bank activity normal until she disappeared. No texts or calls before she went dark. Her vehicle was still parked in the city centre until Kent and his team took it away." Forensics were sweeping it as they spoke. "It doesn't make any sense."

He swivelled his chair to gaze out the window, watching a pair of uniformed officers exit the building, heading out to canvass Jenkins' neighbourhood yet again. George said, "So far, the inquiries had turned up little. Sally was friendly with her neighbours but kept to herself for the most part. The boyfriend was a dead end, too. Absolutely mortified, according to DC Mercer."

"There has to be something we're missing," George mused, almost to himself. He turned back to Mason. "We need to go over every facet of this investigation again from the top. Re-interview her colleagues and neighbours and dig deeper into her phone and financials. Leave no stone unturned."

Mason nodded. "Agreed. I can coordinate with Forensics to sweep her flat again and take it apart piece by piece. And I'll take the lead on re-interviewing the neighbours myself. Someone had to see or hear something out of the ordinary."

He clenched a fist tightly, knuckles whitening. "This job comes with risks, but we look out for our own. If someone has taken Jenkins..." His jaw tightened, the unspoken threat hanging ominously between them.

George studied the determined set of Mason's face and hoped fervently that Sally was somehow safe and soon to be found. Because once Luke got on someone's trail, he was like a bulldog with a bone. Relentless. Unshakeable. And liable to take things too far if that someone had harmed a fellow officer.

"We'll find her, Luke," Beaumont said firmly.

Pushing down his misgivings, Beaumont attempted to steer the conversation to more constructive matters. "While we're reworking every angle on Jenkins' disappearance, we can't lose momentum on the Hardaker case. The trial is coming up fast, and we need to verify all evidence and testimony are air-tight."

Mason nodded reluctantly, some of the tension easing from his shoulders at the change of topic. "You're right, son. Cracking the organised crime syndicate wide open will be one of the biggest collars of our careers. Especially nailing Hardaker. All we need is Schmidt. Cut off the head of the snake and all that."

"Exactly," George agreed. "Tighten up witness protection protocols as well. No way Hardaker goes down without taking a few vicious bites first."

They discussed logistics on the case for several more minutes before Mason checked his watch and stood. "I'll get back to my team now and get them cracking on those new canvasses and interviews. And you let me know the instant we get any break on Jenkins, yeah?"

CHAPTER FOURTEEN

"Absolutely," George assured him.

After Mason left, Beaumont rifled through a stack of folders until he found the one labelled 'PC Sally Jenkins.' He spread out the sparse contents and got back to work, determined to find the answer they so desperately needed.

George's mobile rang, jerking him from his thoughts. The name flashing on the screen spiked his pulse. Mia. Jack's mother rarely called, only when something was wrong. A dozen dire scenarios flashed through George's mind as he quickly answered.

"Mia? Is everything okay? Is Jack alright?" He could hear the tension in his own voice.

"Yes, don't worry, he's fine," Mia replied briskly, immediately putting George on edge. "But he's been asking for you repeatedly last night and the night before. Crying that he misses you. I finally got him to sleep last night, but it took ages to calm him down." She paused. "And I have to be up early for work, so I'm shattered today, too!"

Guilt twisted George's gut. He hadn't seen Jack in three days with this case taking over. "I'm so sorry, Mia. I should have come by—"

"Sorry doesn't cut it!" she snapped. "He needs his father, George. But clearly, your job matters more than your own son. This isn't the first time work has made you neglect him. It's unacceptable."

George ran a hand through his hair in frustration. She knew he didn't have a choice right now. "Mia, please, you know I would never abandon Jack. This case...a young officer's life is at stake. I have to find her—"

"Don't," she cut him off sharply. "I've heard it all before and heard every excuse when Jack stays up crying for you. I won't let you keep doing this to him. He needs stability, not a father who's never there."

"What exactly are you saying?" George asked slowly, ice creeping into his veins.

"I'm filing for sole custody of Jack. It's clearly in his best interest to live with me full-time. You'll get supervised visitation, but only if your job allows it. I'll be in touch with my solicitor to start the paperwork." Her voice rang with cold finality.

"Mia, please don't do this," George pleaded urgently. "You know how much Jack means to me. I'll make more time, just please..."

But the line was already dead. She'd hung up on him. George stared down at the silent mobile, heart pounding. He couldn't lose Jack. Couldn't let Mia use his son as leverage like this. But she had all the power unless he made radical career changes. Changes he wasn't sure he could make, even for Jack.

Numbness crept through George's body. This case suddenly felt inconsequential compared to the custody battle ahead. Sally's life hung in the balance, but so did George's future with his son. He sank back into the desk chair, head in hands. How had his world unravelled so spectacularly in just one phone call?

* * *

George ended the call and leaned back in his chair, steepled his fingers and exhaled slowly as he processed this new information from Candy. The photography club lead had yielded a critical breakthrough—the rural tracts of Leeds Country Way were now firmly in focus as the potential location of the

CHAPTER FOURTEEN

abducted policewoman. Candy's unrelenting pursuit of this slender lead had uncovered a vital piece of the investigational puzzle that had eluded the rest of the team.

George made a mental note to commend the young detective constable for her perseverance once this crisis was resolved. Her diligence deserved acknowledgement. Though Candy's energetic zeal could border on overeagerness at times, her commitment never wavered. She was proving herself to be a tenacious asset to the team with each demanding case.

Instead, he quickly typed out a text update to his fiancée summarising this incremental progress. Isabella's SMS came through straight away—a heart emoji and thumbs up of encouragement. George allowed himself a brief smile before setting the mobile face down and gathering his notes to brief the team.

A crisp knock at the door stirred George. "Enter," he called, steeling himself for the conversation ahead.

The door swung open, and Detective Constable Alexis Mercer strode in. "Apologies for being late today, sir," Mercer said briskly, maintaining eye contact. "I may have a development on the photo you'll want to hear straight away."

George tensed. His planned reprimand about her tardiness evaporated as wary optimism flooded in. Mercer had proven herself an astute investigator. If she claimed a lead on their only evidence, he trusted her assessment.

"Go on," George said, leaning forward intently.

"I've been running the image through our recognition software, and I've got something." Mercer opened a file folder and slapped a photo on George's desk.

"Good work," he said.

Mercer gave a curt nod. She turned sharply, ready to rush

back into the fray.

"Hold on," George said. Mercer paused, casting an inquisitive glance over her shoulder.

"You rushed straight here to update me on this development," George continued. "Left me waiting when I expected your prompt arrival this morning. But I see now your priority was the case, not protocol."

Mercer faced him directly again. George watched emotions ripple across her striking azure eyes—surprise, wariness, sheepishness at the mild admonishment about her tardiness. Her jaw set, awaiting his verdict. "Yes, sir."

Chapter Fifteen

The rural expanse of Leeds Country Way felt desolate under the white winter sky. A damp chill hung in the air at noon as Detective Chief Inspector George Beaumont stepped carefully through the long grass and brambles, his breath rising in faint puffs of mist. Somewhere out here, among these isolated fields, they hoped to find Sally Jenkins' remains.

George glanced over as Detective Inspector Luke Mason conferred quietly with the search team coordinator, Andrea Mills. The specialist officers moved with practised precision, spaced out in a long line, sweeping methodically through the vegetation. Years on the force honed Luke into a consummate professional, his salt and pepper hair neatly combed and his expression serious as he issued instructions.

George felt that familiar tense knot in his stomach that came with the hunt for a body. It never got easier, no matter how many years went by. He vividly remembered another search over a decade ago when he and Arthur Grimes had staked out a decrepit farmhouse much like the one now looming in the distance. They, too, had combed these rural acres for a missing policewoman.

Like Emily Thompson, George feared they were far past hope of finding her breathing. But they might still recover her remains and bring some small measure of closure to her grieving family. And find the evidence to convict the monster who killed her.

George blinked, banishing old ghosts, and focused on the task at hand. He nodded briskly to DC Alexis Mercer as she approached, her blonde hair neatly pulled back and a determined glint in her eye.

"No sign of anything yet, sir," she reported crisply. "But we're expanding the search area based on the most likely approaches to the farmhouse. Hopefully, we'll turn something up soon."

Her pragmatic approach heartened him. "Good work. I know it's grim going, but we'll keep at it as long as it takes."

Alexis offered a brisk nod before moving off, her athletic stride unfaltered by the rough terrain. A hint of a smile lifted George's bearded face as he watched her. If anyone could maintain morale during a gruelling search, it appeared was Alexis.

Nearby, eager young DC Jay Scott bounced on the balls of his feet, wisps of brown hair escaping from under his wool cap.

"This place gives me the proper creeps, boss," Jay said with a dramatic shiver, rubbing his hands against the cold. "Like something from a horror movie, all foggy and decrepit. Reckon our killer stashed more bodies out here?"

George shot him a wry look. "Let's find Sally first. No use borrowing trouble."

Jay nodded, chastened. For all his enthusiasm, he was still green.

They pushed onwards, the looming derelict farmhouse growing closer through the misty air. George's jaw tightened as he observed the peeling paint and cracked windows of the dilapidated structure. It was eerily similar to another decaying ruin, a recurring nightmare from his past.

Would today offer a resolution or another haunted memory to torment his darker moments? There was no telling until the search concluded.

So he carried on, boots wet with dew, carefully scanning the winter-browned grass. Until a shout rang out that froze his blood.

"This is Search Team Coordinator Mills. I've found something!"

George broke into a run, his heart lurching. This was the moment they had both sought and dreaded since Sally first went missing.

He slowed as he approached the huddled search team, steeling himself before pushing through to the epicentre. The officers shifted aside, revealing a slender figure.

* * *

Moments earlier, Andrea Mills navigated the rugged terrain. She scanned the landscape diligently, searching for any sign of Sally Jenkins.

Andrea suppressed a frustrated sigh, her keen eyes raking the underbrush for clues. It was like Sally had vanished into thin air. With each hour that passed, the hope of finding her alive diminished. But Andrea refused to give up. She owed that much to Sally's partner, who anxiously awaited news. And to DCI George Beaumont, who drove the investigation relentlessly, haunted by a case gone wrong years ago when three missing policewomen turned up dead after his boss, DI

Arthur Grimes, assured the public they'd all be found alive.

A flash of colour up ahead caught Andrea's attention. She hastened towards it, pulse quickening. Draped over a lichen-encrusted stone wall, almost blending into the surroundings, was a lifeless form. Andrea's chest constricted. She didn't need to look closer to recognize the build, hair colour, and uniform.

"Sally..." she breathed, knees buckling. Andrea squeezed her eyes shut, composing herself before radioing it in. "This is Search Team Coordinator Mills. I've found something!" She paused to catch her breath. "I've located Sally Jenkins' body approximately two kilometres west of the trailhead. Requesting immediate assistance." Her voice remained steady, belying the upheaval of emotion beneath.

The flurry of activity that followed seemed a blur. Andrea cordoned off the area, blinking back tears as she regarded the battered body of the vibrant woman she'd hoped to bring home safely. Forensics personnel swarmed in, along with a contingent of uniformed officers. Andrea provided a statement, clinging to professionalism like a life raft in a stormy sea.

Detective Chief Inspector George Beaumont emerged, his athletic frame radiating restless energy, blond hair ruffled, and jaw clenched. Andrea squared her shoulders. She had promised to bring Sally home instead of delivering this devastating outcome.

George's piercing green eyes assessed the scene. "You're certain it's her?" His gravelly voice was tight.

Andrea nodded grimly. "No doubt, sir."

George scrubbed a hand down his face. "Let's get a perimeter set up. I want this processed swiftly and thoroughly. We're losing daylight as it is."

His authoritative tone propelled people into action.

Andrea sensed George's boiling urgency. He wanted—needed—to apprehend whoever was responsible. Now.

* * *

It was undeniably a woman, her blank eyes staring vacantly upward, mouth stretched in a frozen scream. The pale flesh of her body was streaked with dirt, her uniform tattered rags. Bruises marred her throat in the distinct outline of strangulation.

George's breath left him in a quiet rush. There was no doubt, just from the context clues. But protocol demanded confirmation.

"It's her," he said heavily. "It's Sally."

A sombre silence descended on the group. George sensed the wave of sadness, frustration, and determination emanating from the search team. Despite their professionalism, a discovery like this always struck hard.

He found Luke coordinating with Stuart Kent and the forensic team that had arrived on the scene. Stuart's hair had gone silver in the two years since the attempt on his life, but his movements were just as swift and methodical as he prepared to document and collect Sally's remains. Luke glanced up and met George's gaze, fatigue and frustration etched in the lines around his eyes.

"This is a right bloody mess," Luke bit out. "Poor girl. At least we can call off the search now; let her family know for certain while we start hunting the bastard down."

George folded his arms across his chest, disappointment

sitting heavily despite the fact they had found Sally's body. "Fuck."

Luke's mouth twisted wryly. "We'll get the bastard, son. We always do."

Before George could reply, Alexis stepped up, features set with quiet determination.

"Regardless of past suspects, we need to remain objective and follow the evidence from this specific case," she said calmly. "If Holloway is guilty, forensics will link him to Sally. We owe it to her not to let assumptions close our minds. All possibilities must be considered before her killer sees justice."

George shot her an approving look. Trust Alexis to keep a cool head at a time like this.

"You're absolutely right," he agreed. "Let's secure the scene and get Sally's remains properly collected. Then, we can refocus our investigation based on what we recover here today. One step at a time."

Luke looked unhappy but dipped his head in acquiescence.

DCI George Beaumont surveyed the now depressingly familiar scene, Sally Jenkins' battered body splayed brokenly across a lichen-covered stone wall deep in the Leeds Country Way. Swallowing hard, he mentally steeled himself against the roiling emotions elicited by the gruesome sight. This was about securing justice for Sally, not his own absolution. Still, icy guilt slithered down his spine. If only he'd found her sooner...

Ruthlessly suppressing those thoughts, George refocused on the task at hand. His gaze tracked the forensic team meticulously processing the scene under Crime Scene Manager Stuart Kent's oversight. George noted each piece of potential evidence bagged and tagged with clinical precision.

CHAPTER FIFTEEN

Stuart's steel-grey hair and wire-rimmed glasses lent him an academic air, belying the decades of experience that made him a valued lead on murder investigations. George trusted Stuart's unwavering methodicalness, knowing no detail would be overlooked.

Satisfied the scene was secured, George began barking orders, urgency bleeding into his gravelly baritone. "Widen the search radius. Get K9 units combing those woods." Adrenaline flooded his veins as pieces clicked into place. The killer, whilst most likely nowhere nearby, could have left a trace. And George would find the bastard.

George saw Andrea leaning against a tree trunk, clearly winded. "Are you OK, Andrea?"

"I'm OK, sir; it just never gets any easier."

The DCI nodded. The frigid January air enveloped the crime scene in a haunting chill. George pulled the collar of his overcoat tight, bracing against the cold as he assessed the solemn scene.

Pathologist Lindsey Yardley approached brusquely, kit in hand. An icy gust whipped at her long blonde hair, but her expression stayed stony. She offered George the slightest nod before moving past him to the body. George remained silent as Lindsey set her case down, pulled on gloves and knelt by Sally's body, beginning her grim task with compassionate efficiency.

She worked with clinical precision, photographing Sally from various angles and then scrutinising her injuries. Peeling back each eyelid, Lindsey shone a penlight at the clouded irises. Pursing her lips, she hummed softly as if confirming some unspoken suspicion.

With gloved hands, she probed at the vivid bruises ringing

Sally's slender neck, nodding grimly at the damage inflicted.

Rising, Lindsey exchanged solemn words with George. "Blunt force trauma to the head," Lindsey murmured, gently examining Sally's battered form. "And ligature marks on the neck. I'll know more once I get her on the table." Lindsey's voice was cool and impersonal, as if delivering a weather report. George listened intently, watching her work.

"With the weather as it is, I can't give you a time of death. My apologies."

George crouched down beside her. "Any indications of sexual assault?"

Lindsey shook her head. "I won't know for certain until I can perform a full postmortem, but I'm not seeing overt signs."

She leaned in close, scrutinising Sally's face. "Notice the petechiae in the eyes and eyelids. That happens when the oxygen supply is cut off. The capillaries rupture, leaving these tiny haemorrhages."

George followed her gaze, observing the dark red dots marring Sally's pale skin.

"The murderer used substantial force," Lindsey continued. "My preliminary assessment is death by manual strangulation, possibly preceded by a violent struggle."

She sat back on her heels, scanning the crime scene pensively as if viewing a troubling portrait she longed to understand.

George swallowed tightly. "This was personal, Lindsey. Whoever did this... he's dangerous."

Her gaze was sympathetic. "I'll expedite forensics." She called Kent's SOC team over, who immediately set to work chronicling the grim tableau, their camera shutters clicking rapidly. Lindsey directed them to take close-ups of Sally's injuries while also capturing wider shots of the surrounding area.

As the team documented the scene, Lindsey returned her attention to the body. She swabbed Sally's hands, scraping beneath each fingernail and sealing the samples in labelled vials. Next, she used an iris clamp to hold Sally's arm still as she drew several vials of blood. Each step was handled with clinical precision, preserving critical trace evidence.

George observed Lindsey's exhaustive efforts. In their previous case, she had been just a suspect—a phantom menace he pursued mindlessly. Now they stood united in sombre purpose. Her skills would help illuminate the dark circumstances surrounding Sally's tragic end. George felt unexpectedly reassured by her presence.

The biting air seemed to grow colder as the morning light remained muted and wan. George bounced on the balls of his feet, trying to keep warm as he maintained vigil over the unfolding investigation. It seemed even the elements themselves conspired against them today.

Before long, Lindsey had finished collecting samples. She meticulously labelled each specimen and then stowed them securely into her kit. Standing smoothly, she turned to George.

"That's all I can accomplish here. I'll get the body transported to the mortuary for a full postmortem examination immediately."

George nodded. "Keep me informed of any developments. And let me know when you start the postmortem. I'll send someone from the team to observe."

Lindsey offered a thin smile. "Of course. I imagine my

schedule will permit me to begin later today or first thing tomorrow morning at the latest."

With that, she pulled off her gloves and disposed of them in a waste bag before slipping on a fresh pair. After wrapping up Sally's hands and feet, Lindsey then assisted the responding officers in carefully moving Sally's body into a body bag. Her pale, lifeless form disappeared from view as they slowly zipped the bag closed.

George watched as the officers respectfully loaded the trolley into the back of a private ambulance. Crime scene technicians would remain to continue documenting and processing evidence, but Sally was now in Lindsey's trusted hands.

Pulling out his mobile, George paced as he punched in a number. "Detective Superintendent Smith? DCI Beaumont here. We've found her." He paused. "She's gone, sir. Appears to have been brutalised."

Andrea strained to hear the response, watching emotions ripple across George's face—anger, regret, resolve.

"I'll keep you informed, sir. We'll get forensic evidence expedited. I want this bastard caught." George's eyes again tracked the tree line as he listened. "Understood, sir. I'll coordinate with DC Scott. And thank you for getting Dr Yardley on the scene so promptly."

Ending the call, George scanned the area until his gaze landed on Andrea. His muscular frame radiated coiled tension as he approached. "Reconvene your search team, focusing on areas north-east of the body. I believe our suspect fled that direction. Look for any signs of a trail."

Andrea straightened. "Right away, sir." This she could do—pour her energy into finding Sally's killer.

CHAPTER FIFTEEN

As she set off, Andrea glimpsed George's stoic façade crack, pain flashing across his rugged features. For a moment, his broad shoulders sagged under the weight. Then he drew a bracing breath and turned back to the investigation, tireless drive evident in his purposeful stride.

Andrea understood his torment. They'd been too late for Sally. But not for justice.

Squaring his shoulders, George turned back to the scene and Detective Constables Mercer and Scott. The DCI nodded at his DI, a look in his eye that showed he would breathe down the killer's neck until the bastard had nowhere left to run. This was only the beginning. George silently vowed to chase this predator to the ends of the earth if that's what it took. The fire of relentlessness kindled in his gut. There would be justice for Sally.

Together, the four detectives stood and watched as the ambulance pulled away, blue lights flashing silently. George exhaled heavily, feeling the weight of this new burden. A killer was loose in his city, and the clock was already ticking to find them.

Turning to his team, George squared his shoulders. "Right. We have our work cut out for us. But now we can give Sally's family some closure while we track down the truth. Let's get started."

Alexis and Luke moved off purposefully to coordinate with forensics. George observed as Jay watched the van drive away.

George clapped him on the back. "You OK, Jay?"

"Pissed off, boss!"

Together, they headed off to rejoin the others, spirits lifted by shared purpose. The grief of this day would linger, but progress helped to heal the pain. Step by step, they would uncover the truth about Sally Jenkins' death. And in those hard-won answers, find some measure of peace.

Chapter Sixteen

Detective Chief Inspector George Beaumont surveyed the Incident Room with a sombre expression. The landscape photograph, enigmatic and unsettling with its stark connection to Sally Jenkins, weighed heavily in the tense atmosphere.

"Why reveal the location of Sally's body?" George asked without preamble, holding his team in an uncompromising gaze. "This elaborate taunt feels personal—directed at us, at me. Playing games when lives hang in jeopardy."

The detectives exchanged uneasy looks around the room as the significance of his words sank in. The ruthless perpetrator had shifted tactics, escalating the stakes by drawing the police deeper into their twisted machinations. But toward what endgame? Nobody knew.

Glancing around at their conflicted faces, George gentled his tone by increments, clasping his hands on the table. "Speculation breeds assumptions. So let's examine this analytically—why provide a precise marker leading us to Sally? The killer must have known we'd find out. And fast. So why?"

Jay Scott straightened in his chair, amber eyes glinting with fresh insight beneath his tousled fringe. "What if we're his latest entertainment, boss? A new challenge to replace the escalating thrill of the kills?" He gestured emphatically with his lean hands. "Bragging by saying 'look what I did under your noses, now try stopping my next artful conquest.'"

Luke Mason leaned forward; salt-and-pepper brows knitted critically. "Possible. But risky revealing his puppet mastery so overtly mid-performance, eh?" He steepled his fingers thoughtfully. "This probing attack feels personal."

Tashan Blackburn added solemnly, "True, but extreme narcissists perceive themselves impervious and enjoy flaunting that supposed invincibility." He tapped a pencil against his notepad. "I suggest compiling a profile on behavioural patterns and motivations, the psychological framework of our suspect."

George considered this, arms folded across his broad chest. Frank insights could prove pivotal puzzle pieces. Yet danger lurked when presuming facts not yet in evidence, allowing bias to cloud truth-seeking. Details matter! His jaw tightened. "We only have theory, not fact, I'm afraid."

Murmurs of assent answered around the room. Then Jay tilted his head, expression troubled. "But what if the killer is controlling the facts?" He held George's gaze unblinkingly, jaw set with conviction. "Think about Sally and the tape, boss."

A weighty silence met his bold assertion as breaths collectively caught. George absorbed the accusation, schooling his features to remain neutral through sheer force of will when inside, all he could do was cheer Jay as he, too, was thinking about only Atkinson.

"Speculation proves nothing without corroborating facts," George said gently and strategically, straightening in his chair. "For now, we stick to what we know are facts." He paused, unsure how to proceed. "If Atkinson's prints or DNA show up, then fine. If not, we keep digging."

Subdued nods acknowledged the boss and his words. Standing decisively, George gathered the landscape photo and pinned it to the case board with sharp movements. "Sally's killer wanted us to find the body, and I want to know why. So, scour Sally's history with fresh eyes."

"Has Forensics finished with Sally's house yet, boss?" asked Jay.

"Not yet, DC Scott. But they will soon, and hopefully, they'll find a copy of Sally's recording."

Both detectives met eyes. They were both hoping for the same outcome.

As the others moved to their assigned tasks with renewed focus, George lingered, contemplating the photograph and the person's reason for giving it to him. But whatever the reason, George would make the culprit pay for what they'd done. Sending the picture to George was a mistake, a mistake that George would ensure would be paid for with the highest price.

* * *

The familiar controlled chaos of the shared office enveloped George Beaumont as he strode through the door. He wove between desks cluttered with case files and coffee-stained mugs to reach his own office, the background hum fading slightly as he pulled the door shut.

George sank into his desk chair, scrubbing a hand over his tired eyes. The investigation felt mired, struggling to build momentum after each new lead hit a dead end. Grimes had vanished without a trace, and George felt the man's ghost taunting them around every corner.

A sharp rap at the door jarred him from his thoughts. "Come in," George called, straightening in anticipation.

The door swung open, and Tashan Blackburn stepped through, an air of urgency radiating from his imposing frame. "Boss, I've got something promising," he announced without preamble.

George leaned forward intently as Tashan continued. "I've managed to trace the white van spotted at Grimes' residence back to a Leonard Beedham, residing on Scott Green Drive in Gildersome."

"Excellent work, Tashan," George said approvingly, senses sharpening. This could be the break they desperately needed; he could feel it in his gut. "What do we know about this Beedham character? Any apparent connections to Grimes?"

Tashan consulted a slim black notebook. "Leonard Beedham, aged 46. No criminal history I could find. He does, however, seem to run in some of the same social circles as our missing DI. Specifically, Beedham was once a member of the White Roses, a group Grimes investigated back in his early days on the force."

George's green eyes narrowed, thoughts racing. The White Roses had been a shadowy organization linked to racketeering and extortion before Grimes took them down. If Beedham was a former member, he might harbour old grudges against the former detective inspector.

"Right, we need to have a chat with Mr Beedham straight away," George decided, grabbing his coat from the stand by the door. "No time to waste. Let's see what he knows about that van's ties to Grimes."

Tashan nodded, falling into step as George strode rapidly from his office, barely pausing to notify the desk sergeant of their destination. As they navigated the bustling main floor, George asked, "What's Beedham's neighbourhood like? Any known criminal activity there?"

Tashan shook his head. "Quiet residential area in Gildersome, mostly families and elderly. The few photos I found of Beedham's house show a modest brick semi-detached. Nothing remarkable."

George absorbed this as they exited the station into the brisk late autumn air. No obvious red flags so far. Perhaps Beedham's link to Grimes was innocuous. But George's gut urged caution. In his experience, coincidences were seldom just coincidences.

They soon arrived on Scott Green Drive, a sleepy tree-lined street of near-identical redbrick houses and neatly kept gardens. Beedham's residence matched Tashan's description, indistinguishable from its neighbours. The utter ordinary nature of the place gave George pause. Somehow, he had expected anyone connected to the bizarre disappearance of Grimes to reside in conspicuous surroundings.

Exchanging a glance with Tashan, George said, "Let's play this first interview low-key. Get Beedham comfortable opening up to us before we reveal why we're really here."

Tashan nodded. "Understood, sir."

They mounted the steps and George firmly pressed the bell. A shuffling was heard within before the door opened partway, revealing a man in grease-stained coveralls squinting at them uncertainly.

"Leonard Beedham?" George inquired in a pleasant tone, holding up his warrant card.

The man's eyes flicked over the warrant card. "Can I help you officers with something?" His tone was wary but cooperative.

"Detectives, Mr Beedham," George said as he offered a disarming smile. "I'm Detective Chief Inspector Beaumont, and this is my colleague, Detective Constable Blackburn. We just had a few routine questions for residents around this neighbourhood. Do you have a moment to chat?"

Beedham hesitated, then stepped back, gesturing them inside. "Come in then, I suppose."

The living room was as nondescript as the exterior, the worn furniture tidy but outdated. Beedham perched stiffly on a recliner while George and Tashan seated themselves on the sofa.

"So what's this about then?" Beedham asked, fidgeting with a loose thread on his coveralls.

"Nothing to worry about," George assured lightly. "We've just had a few recent incidents in the area—vandalism, that sort of thing—and wondered if you might have noticed anything out of the ordinary recently?"

Beedham's shoulders loosened slightly in evident relief. "Can't say as I have. It's been quiet round here, least as far as I've seen."

George nodded encouragingly. "And have you lived in this neighbourhood long yourself?"

"Going on twelve, thirteen years now," Beedham replied.

"Lovely area," George commented conversationally. "Very community-oriented, from what I've heard. Have you gotten to know many of the other residents well over the years?"

Beedham gave a non-committal shrug. "I keep to myself for the most part. But sure, I know some of them to chat with in passing."

"Did you ever come across a gentleman named Arthur Grimes?" George asked casually, watching Beedham closely. "He lived just a few streets over on Suffield Close until recently."

Beedham froze almost imperceptibly before recovering quickly. "The name sounds vaguely familiar. I may have seen him around the neighbourhood once or twice." He shifted in his seat, not quite meeting George's eye. "But I can't say I knew him personally."

George nodded thoughtfully. "Of course. Though we did have a report of a white van registered to you parked outside his residence on several occasions over the last few months. You wouldn't happen to know anything about that, would you?"

Beedham paled, his eyes darting towards the front window as if gauging escape routes. He seemed to wrestle internally before heaving a resigned sigh.

"Right, that was my van you saw. But it was nothing sinister." Beedham looked decidedly uncomfortable but continued. "Arthur—Mr Grimes that is—he'd mentioned needing help moving some boxes and furniture to a new place. I owed him a favour, so I volunteered my van to transport the items a few times."

Tashan's dark gaze was piercing. "Can you confirm the exact dates you were present at Mr Grimes' home?" His tone brooked no evasion.

Beedham raked a hand through his thinning hair. "I'd have to check my logs. It was maybe four times last month? Or it could have been November. I really didn't take much notice..." He trailed off under Tashan's intent stare.

"We'll need those precise dates and durations," Tashan pressed. "And anything you can recall about the items you moved or any interactions with Mr Grimes."

Sweat beaded on Beedham's brow as his eyes flicked between the two detectives. George could almost see the calculations running behind the man's panicked expression.

"Is Mr Grimes... in some sort of trouble?" Beedham asked hesitantly.

"He's currently missing," George said bluntly, watching Beedham's reaction closely. Was that a flash of shock or feigned surprise? "And any information related to his disappearance could be crucial."

Beedham held up his hands defensively. "Look, I don't know anything about that. I just did the odd job ferrying boxes. Didn't even go inside his house."

His obvious discomfort hinted at more he wasn't admitting. But pressing further now seemed unwise. George stood smoothly, Tashan following suit.

"If you can get us those logs of your trips to Grimes' house that would be very helpful," George said pleasantly but firmly. He withdrew a business card from his coat pocket and passed it over.

"Anything at all you can recall may prove useful. Don't hesitate to ring if you remember additional details."

Beedham fidgeted with the card. "Yeah, alright. I'll dig up what records I have from those jobs."

George gave a benign smile that didn't reach his eyes. "Much appreciated, Mr Beedham. Thank you for your time."

They left Beedham shifting uneasily in his foyer, clearly unsettled by the encounter. As George and Tashan descended the steps, Tashan murmured under his breath, "He's hiding something. Could see it in his reactions."

George made a sound of agreement. "No question. He knows more than he's saying."

Reaching the car, he turned to Tashan. "But we have to tread lightly. Can't risk spooking him into clamming up or doing something rash."

Tashan's dark eyes were thoughtful. "Agreed. But we'll keep up the pressure. If he's lying about the van logs, I'll catch it. And if he destroyed any evidence, Forensics might still turn something up at Grimes' place linking him."

George nodded. "Too right. We stick to Beedham like glue but keep him believing we don't suspect his involvement."

As they pulled away down the quiet street, George added, "For now, we verify his story. But I want full background checks run on Beedham and any known associates. And have tech compile a timeline of his movements over the past year cross-referenced against Grimes."

Tashan jotted rapid notes. "Consider it done, boss."

Chapter Seventeen

The Incident Room hummed with focused activity, detectives sifting through piles of documents and forensics reports searching for leads. At a desk, Tashan Blackburn sat hunched toward a monitor, engrossed in deciphering the partial license plate glimpse they had captured on CCTV footage. His fingers scurried over the keyboard as he ran image-enhancing algorithms.

After hours of painstaking pixel-by-pixel analysis, Tashan finally isolated a few legible letters and numbers. His eyes narrowed, thoughts already leaping ahead as he cross-referenced vehicle registration databases. Moments later, a match popped up on the screen, and he leaned back, eyebrows raised in surprise. This was an unexpected development.

Tashan quickly located DCI George Beaumont and DI Luke Mason across the room, gesturing them over. As they approached, fatigue evident in their facial lines and the slump of their shoulders, Tashan announced, "The Corsa that was spotted parked near the Grimes house belongs—or belonged— to Alfred Langton." He swivelled his monitor to show his findings. "Langton's deceased now, but he was a retired detective inspector with the West Yorkshire Police a couple of years back. I mentioned him before if you remember?"

George and Luke exchanged startled looks.

"Deceased?" George echoed. "So, who the hell is driving his car lurking around Grimes' place?"

Luke gripped the back of Tashan's chair, knuckles whitening. "Could be a relative, someone who inherited from the old man? Or the car was stolen or sold without transferring ownership?" His tired eyes took on a sudden intensity.

"If Langton and Grimes crossed paths, maybe someone from Langton's past is involved here," George suggested, folding his arms across his chest.

Tashan's fingers were already flying across the keyboard, picking through layers of records. "I'm digging into Langton's history on the force and known associates. I also have an ANPR inquiry out for sightings of the Corsa based on those partial plate numbers."

He glanced up. "It's a solid lead. If we can track the vehicle's movements in the last few months, we may identify suspects."

George clapped a hand on Tashan's shoulder. "Good work. Stay on it. That car is a vital piece of this puzzle."

Luke began pacing, lost in thought. "If Langton is connected to our culprit, it may explain how they knew so much about Grimes' schedule. Hell, maybe they even worked together back in the day."

He turned back to George. "We need to dig into both Langton and Grimes' backgrounds on the force. Old case files, employee records, anything linking them."

George nodded decisively. "I agree. We widen the scope and learn everything about Langton, his past, his family and known associates. Look for overlap with Grimes."

Determination welled up in George's chest, driving back the blank fatigue from hours of fruitless analysis. Finally, they had a thread to pull that could unravel this whole tangled affair.

"Right, you two start digging into Langton's history and cross-check for connections to Grimes," George decided, grabbing his jacket off the back of a chair.

"I'm going to notify the desk sergeant to allocate more bodies for document analysis. We'll likely be pulling old case files, so we'll need all hands on deck."

Luke nodded, already rolling up his sleeves with renewed vigour. "We're onto something here, George. I can feel it."

A fierce light of determination blazed in Luke's eyes that George knew all too well. Like a bulldog scenting prey, Luke wouldn't let go of this trail now that they had a promising lead.

* * *

Three Big Boards now dominated the Incident Room, plastered with maps, timelines, and photos connected by a maze of coloured string. The sterile glow of computer monitors illuminated the room further as the detectives took their seats around the central table.

Detective Chief Inspector George Beaumont stood at the head, broad shoulders back, an intent gleam in his green eyes. "Let's get straight into updates."

He nodded to Tashan Blackburn, who rose smoothly, clasping his hands behind him. "I've compiled thorough profiles on all of Holloway's known associates from the old Grimes case file," Tashan reported, his rich baritone crisp and assured.

With a click of the remote, he brought up slides detailing the associates' known haunts, rap sheets, networks. "We brought several in for interviews today. I've also mapped their relationships to identify Holloway's most likely current connections."

Tashan advanced to an intricate web of head shots linked by flowing lines representing affiliation, hierarchy and family ties.

Tashan tapped a mugshot of a stern, bald man. "Clive Stokes. Long rap sheet including aggravated assault, extortion, trafficking. Did a five-year stint back in 2008. Holloway's name came up during questioning about an arson case, suggesting they were associates at the time."

He moved to a scruffy face half-obscured by long unkempt hair. "Angus White. Petty criminal, mostly drugs and burglary convictions. Reportedly ran into Holloway a few months back at a pub and described him as wired, going on about conspiracies."

Tapping a photo of a smirking man with cold blue eyes, Tashan continued. "Vincent Shaw. Violent reputation enforcer for local crime rings. His brother was an early suspect in the disappearance of one of Holloway's victims, though never charged. Bad blood there."

Tashan indicated the connections between photos. "Mapping the known relationships shows these three may still be in indirect contact with Holloway based on overlapping social and criminal networks. They're our strongest links currently."

He crossed his arms. "Unfortunately, none have divulged useful information so far in interviews. But inconsistencies and defensiveness in their statements suggest they know more than they claim about Holloway's recent activities."

Tashan gave a curt nod to punctuate his summary before

taking his seat.

George listened intently, absorbing the intelligence. "Well done, Tashan. This provides a solid foundation."

Detective Inspector Luke Mason stood next, silver hair neatly combed, his wiry frame coiled with energy. "The interviews proved largely unproductive," he admitted with thinly veiled frustration. "Most claim no recent contact with Holloway. A few suggest he reached out several years back, ranting conspiracies. Sounded paranoid."

Luke's steely eyes narrowed. "Regardless, they're a cagey bunch. Suspect some are protecting Holloway out of loyalty or fear." He clenched a veined fist. "We're keeping the pressure on and monitoring their communications."

George nodded thoughtfully. Even stubborn silence told them something.

Eager Jay Scott bounced up, tousled hair sticking out at all angles beneath his vintage band tee. "Bad news on the medical records front," he reported, a touch sheepishly. "No sign of Holloway turning up at clinics or hospitals in the past decade."

Jay hastened to add, "But! I've set alerts with administrators to notify us the second he shows up anywhere in the region, boss. We'll nab him if he gets so much as a bloody nose treated."

Luke rolled his eyes at Jay's casual language, but George smiled faintly at the lad's enthusiasm. "Keep monitoring it. He'll surface eventually if he's still in the area."

Leaning forward on the table, George surveyed the gathered team, feeling the crackle of their combined focus like electricity.

"Excellent work, all of you. We're making progress piecing

together Holloway's life since he slipped away last time." George's gaze grew distant for a moment before sharpening again. "Our leads may be thin now, but we only need one thread to unravel everything. So keep digging."

He doled out assignments. "Yolanda, Alexis—work with Tashan and Luke to analyse known associates and their links to Holloway. Look for fresh angles."

The women nodded solemnly, exchanging determined looks.

"Candy, you team up with Jay on medical records. Help him brainstorm any other traceable care Holloway may seek—pharmaceuticals, physiotherapy under the table, anything."

"You got it, boss!" Jay chimed as Candy grinned brightly, ponytail swishing.

George stood tall, hands braced on the back of his chair. "It's a tough nut to crack. But we've cracked worse. Let's show Holloway he can't hide in the shadows forever."

Around the room, spines straightened with shared purpose. For all the bleak dead ends so far, George saw the steely glint of perseverance in his team's eyes. They would uncover the truth wherever it led. Failure was not an option when lives hung in the balance.

As the team filed out to pursue their assignments, George watched them with a swell of fierce pride. Whatever Holloway's secrets, this group would lay them bare. Each member brought vital skills to the hunt—Luke's bulldog tenacity, Tashan's analytic insight, Jay and Candy's creative determination, Yolanda and Alexis' sharp intuition. And George's own uncompromising drive fused them together.

* * *

The periodic trill of ringing phones filtered through the closed office door as George Beaumont sat hunched over his desk, files and notes strewn across its surface. He rubbed his tired eyes, the words on the pages blurring together. It had been another long day sifting through evidence, trying to shake loose any clue that could break open this confounding case.

When his mobile rang, George snatched it up quickly. Seeing it was Maya Chen from the forensics lab, his pulse spiked with anticipation. Perhaps she had finally extracted some revelation from the microscopic grains they had collected.

"Maya, what have you got for me?" George answered without preamble, unable to keep the eagerness from his gravelly voice. Any progress would be a lifeline right now.

"DCI Beaumont, I've been consulting with a specialist, Professor Patricia Gloucestershire, about the pollen samples we found," Maya responded briskly. George immediately sensed a conflicting mix of excitement and regret in her tone that made his heart sink even before she continued.

"Professor Gloucestershire is one of the nation's leading experts in palynology—the study of pollen grains. I sent her the data of the samples we recovered, hoping she could isolate the plant species and locations to pin down where the photo had been mailed from."

Maya paused, and George could envision her slight frown. "Unfortunately, she analysed the pollen and reported back that the samples contained quite common species widespread across the region. Nothing rare or distinct enough to conclusively trace their origin."

George exhaled heavily, shoulders slumping. He had hoped the microscopic grains might illuminate critical clues about where the photo had been mailed from. But it seemed another promising thread had snapped.

"So we've hit another dead end on that front," he acknowledged heavily, scrubbing a hand across his beard.

"I'm sorry, DCI Beaumont," Maya said, audibly frustrated. "I know you were hoping the pollen would give us a solid lead. But the professor said often trace evidence only yields general areas spanning hundreds of miles. It's just the nature of pollen dispersal on the wind."

George nodded. He appreciated her dedication; the setback was no fault of her skills. "I understand, Maya. We'll just have to pursue other avenues."

Maya's tone regained a hint of optimism. "It's not a total loss. Professor Gloucestershire was quite eager to aid our investigation in any way she could. She's offered to analyse any future samples we uncover to compare and potentially triangulate an origin point."

George sat up a bit straighter. Having an eminent expert assisting them could prove invaluable if they located additional crime scenes or evidence linked to their suspect.

"That's good to know, Maya. Please extend my sincere thanks to the professor for offering her services. Her insights could prove pivotal down the line."

"Of course, I'll let her know," Maya assured him. "And I'll keep searching for any other trace evidence we may have overlooked initially. We'll find the break we need, DCI Beaumont. Just have to keep looking."

George felt a swell of gratitude for her stalwart persistence despite this demoralising development. The professor's participation was a ray of hope piercing the gloom.

"I appreciate that, Maya. Your skills and determination have been indispensable. We'll get there, one piece at a time."

After a few more words of encouragement, George ended the call, exhaling slowly as he set down the phone. So much rode on each analysis yielding that one pivotal clue. The lack of answers from the pollen data felt like a physical blow.

Leaning back in his worn leather chair, George reflected on where they stood. The case was proving more complex and confounding than he had anticipated. The killer left frustratingly little evidence, and what traces existed failed to illuminate his identity or location.

Chapter Eighteen

George Beaumont stood silently, steeling himself against the clinical sights and scents of death. The relentless hum of ventilation and muted beeps of equipment underpinned the heavy atmosphere.

He studied the lifeless form laid out before him under a sheet with a frown creasing his rugged features.

It was a sight he never could fully numb himself to, no matter how many years passed investigating murders. Sally Jenkins, vibrant and full of promise, was reduced to a battered corpse on a frigid slab covered by a bland sheet. George gritted his teeth. Seeing the violence inflicted always ignited that seething drive for justice in his gut. Made the hunt for her killer feel that much more urgent. Personal.

Footsteps echoed crisply on the tiled floor as Detective Inspector Luke Mason strode in through the swinging doors into the frigid cold of the mortuary, the sterile tang of antiseptic greeting him. His breath misted in the chilled air as he nodded briskly to George.

"OK, now that you're both here, we can begin," Lindsey Yardley said. Petite but imposing, she swept towards the table with practised purpose, chart in hand. Her blonde hair was swept back in a neat twist, and silver glasses perched atop her nose, lending her an academic air. The pathologist was garbed in a disposable gown and gloves; her expression remained impassive as she regarded the shrouded form on the steel table before her.

Mason crossed to a supply cabinet, removing a protective gown and gloves. DCI Beaumont, who stood tense and silent nearby, was already attired. Donning the outfit, Mason joined Yardley at the table. Without a word, she drew back the sheet. The detectives stiffened at the sight of Sally Jenkins' battered corpse.

Mason surveyed her dispassionately. Bruises still livid across the slender throat. Darkened eyes sunk deep in their sockets, petechial haemorrhages spidering across the lids. Her auburn hair was matted and dull. Mason took it all in with clinical detachment.

In contrast, George averted his gaze briefly. He steeled himself before looking back at Sally's ruined form, mouth tightening. Mason observed his superior officer subtly brace his hands on the edge of the table, grounding himself.

Lindsey launched straight into the technical details. "Starting with cause of death, she did indeed succumb to manual strangulation. The hyoid bone was fractured, likely from the assailant gripping her throat and throttling violently."

George's jaw tightened, imagining Sally's panic as she fought for breath.

"I also noted muscle haemorrhages and petechiae in the eyes and eyelids," Lindsey continued matter-of-factly. "Those occur when oxygen flow to the brain is violently cut off."

She indicated faint red dots beneath Sally's clouded eyes. Mason nodded. It lined up with his initial impression at the scene. George's fists clenched involuntarily even as he maintained a stoic façade. He had to keep perspective despite the dark fury kindling inside him.

"In addition to the neck trauma, Sally had extensive blunt force injuries to her torso and upper body. Focused largely on the front, indicating she was facing her attacker." Lindsey indicated the lurid purple contusions stark against Sally's pallid flesh.

"Defensive wounds present on her hands and forearms reveal she fought back against a violent, sustained assault prior to being strangled."

George studied the deep gouges and cuts across Sally's knuckles and arms. He felt that familiar ache in his chest at the confirmation of her struggle. Sally had fought bravely, just as fiercely as she pursued justice in life. But ultimately, her killer had overpowered her through ruthless savagery.

George ground his teeth at a sudden thought. "Any signs she was... violated after death?" Just voicing the possibility made bile rise in his throat.

But Lindsey gently shook her head. "I examined thoroughly and found no indications of sexual assault pre-mortem or postmortem. Small consolation given what she endured, but I hope it offers some slight comfort to her loved ones."

George released a tight breath, relief washing through him—one less horror for him to avenge.

"I did find one peculiar detail during the examination," Lindsey added. She gently pried open Sally's mouth, revealing a tuft of coarse fibres clinging to her tongue and inner cheek. "It appears her attacker attempted to gag her with some sort of crude cloth. I've sent samples to the lab for analysis."

George and Luke leaned in, peering closely at the filthy

wad extracted from Sally's mouth. George's pulse quickened. "That could be our first solid forensic lead," George said. If they could trace the gag's origin, it might point them right to the killer.

"There's also no ligature markings that I can see," Lindsey murmured, almost to herself. "The assailant used brute manual force to strangle her."

She sat back on her heels, scanning the crime scene pensively. "In fact, aside from the localised throat trauma, there are no binding marks on the wrists or ankles. No indication she was restrained during the assault."

Luke Mason straightened at this observation, a frown creasing his unshaven face. "That's odd. I would have expected restraints if she'd been held captive for any period." He shrugged. "Maybe the bastard used soft tie-downs that didn't leave marks?"

But Lindsey shook her head. "While possible, in my experience, victims restrained against their will almost always exhibit chafing or contusions at the points of contact. I don't see evidence of that here."

She turned her cool grey gaze up to Luke. "The lack of defensive wounds on the palms also suggests she wasn't fighting restraints. No torn fingernails or soft tissue damage consistent with struggling at tight bindings."

George's brows furrowed as he listened. Lindsey's analysis didn't align with his working theory that Sally had been held somewhere and assaulted prior to her murder. But the pathologist's expertise gave him pause.

Sensing the detectives' scepticism, Lindsey spoke again. "I know you're hoping for clear signs she was a captive. But objectively, the body lacks conclusive evidence of long-term restraint. She may have been conscious and mobile in the period preceding the attack."

Luke shook his head. "That makes no sense. Why aren't there ligature marks or bruising from resistance, then? She must have been incapacitated somehow before the bastard choked the life out of her."

"Perhaps she was impaired by intoxicants or a head injury instead of physical bonds?" Lindsey suggested calmly. "I'm just presenting possibilities supported by my medical findings."

Sensing rising tension, George interjected. "You both raise valid points. Restraints may have been used that left no marks. But we also can't ignore Lindsey's expert analysis that Sally wasn't a prisoner immediately preceding her death."

He looked between them imploringly.

"I know it's difficult when the evidence challenges our assumptions. But we must account for all possibilities right now. There is still much we don't understand about what happened to Sally that day."

Luke's mouth twisted in displeasure, but he gave a grudging nod. Lindsey offered an appreciative glance to George for his diplomacy. She turned back to the body, pausing in consideration.

"We may find more clarity from the additional evidence I can collect here," Lindsey offered gently, holding out an olive branch. She reached for her kit to retrieve several small evidence bags and sterile swabs.

"I'll take fingernail scrapings, oral and nasal swabs, ligature samples, and any biological traces left by the killer. Those may yield DNA or particulates to indicate Sally's location and other key factors."

She set to work methodically, first taking a swab from inside Sally's cheek, explaining the oral sample could contain her attacker's epithelial cells if he forced intimate contact. Another swab gathered dried nasal secretions that might point to inhaled substances used to incapacitate Sally.

Finally, Lindsey used tweezers to meticulously collect fibrous debris from around Sally's bruised neck. She placed the delicate samples into plastic cassettes to be examined under a microscope.

"Any particulates on her skin or clothes from the assault location could be invaluable evidence," Lindsey said. She worked with clinical precision, preserving every minuscule shred that could illuminate Sally's tragic end.

George observed the exhaustive evidence collection, understanding how critical these specimens could prove. Lindsey's skills were giving them the best chance to unravel what happened once the samples reached the capable hands of their forensic scientists. Step by step, they would expose the truth—no matter how difficult it was to face.

"Thank you for this, Dr Yardley," Luke said as he nodded, his jaw clenched. "We'll chase this down hard. Good catch."

Lindsey gave a thin smile at the acknowledgement. "Wish I could offer more. I know you're all eager for progress on this."

Beaumont's stony expression mirrored the cold fury Mason felt smouldering inside. When he spoke, his voice resonated with banked anger. "No doubt she suffered terribly. We'll see the animal pays for it."

Lindsey continued methodically highlighting contusions and lacerations scattering Sally's slender limbs. Bruises also marred her hips and lower back, suggesting the killer had pinned her down cruelly. George's stony expression grew thunderous.

Luke clenched his jaw so hard it ached. His gut churned with impotent rage, the primal need to make someone hurt as she had suffered.

Abruptly turning away, the DI tugged off his gloves and gown with sharp, jerking motions. He raked both hands roughly through his greying hair, exhaling harshly. Get hold of yourself, Luke, he admonished silently. This reaction won't help find the culprit. Justice first. Vengeance later.

Across the table, George seemed to wage his own inner battle. The muscles in his bearded jaw bunched as he ground his teeth. But he kept his burning gaze rooted on Sally's battered form. Bearing witness for her when she could not.

George watched as she and Luke discussed the logistics of transferring Sally's body to the funeral home. He only half listened, preoccupied contemplating Lindsey's findings. The level of violence directed solely at Sally pointed to an intensely personal motivation. And the deliberate gag indicated the assault had been cruelly drawn out, intended to torment and silence her. Chilling implications swirled in George's mind.

George peeled off his gown and gloves with slow, deliberate motions and bundled them into the hazardous waste bin, turning from the body. His rugged features were carved from stone, but Mason glimpsed the anguish lurking in his piercing green eyes.

After Lindsey departed, George turned to Luke, green eyes burning with conviction. "This was personal, whatever the motive. Our killer wanted to inflict maximum suffering on Sally specifically before killing her."

Luke nodded, scrubbing a hand over his salt-and-pepper

hair. "Aye. He damn near pulverised her, the vicious fucker." George could hear the disgust thickening Luke's Lancastrian accent.

"If it's who I think…" Luke bit out harshly before catching himself. He shook his head.

"Let's not jump to conclusions yet. I just hope forensics can give us something actionable to nail down the bastard."

George understood Luke's visceral reaction but knew they needed level heads to solve this rationally. "Agreed. We follow where the evidence leads, not assumptions."

Yet privately, a name lurked in George's mind that he could not ignore. Ethan Holloway. The sadistic killer who slipped through their grasp over a decade ago, leaving a trail of violated, lifeless women behind. George shuddered at the thought of Holloway's savagery turned loose again after so long.

No, he told himself firmly. Supposition helped no one now. Only steadfast professionalism would bring them closer to the truth of what happened to Sally in her final hours. George closed his eyes briefly, centring himself for the relentless slog ahead.

When he opened them, he saw Luke watching him intently. George recognised the tension etching Luke's worn face. This case already dug into old wounds that never fully healed for either of them.

George steeled himself. Their failure then didn't have to doom them now. Sally deserved justice. And together, he and Luke would find it for her.

George extended his hand, gratified by Luke's firm grip as they shook. No words were needed. The solidarity bolstered them both, fuelling their determination as they parted ways

CHAPTER EIGHTEEN

to pursue the subsequent avenues of investigation.

Chapter Nineteen

The late afternoon sun streamed through the car windows as Luke navigated the busy streets back towards the station. In the passenger seat, George stared contemplatively out at the bustling city, Sally's case file open across his lap. The image of her battered body seemed seared into his mind after today's examination—so much cruelty inflicted for reasons still unknown.

The shrill ring of George's mobile pierced the pensive silence. Checking the screen, he saw it was Detective Superintendent Jim Smith calling for an update. George answered briskly.

"DCI Beaumont here, sir. Just wrapping up at the morgue with Dr Yardley." He exhaled heavily.

"OK, George," Smith replied sombrely over the speakerphone. "We owe it to Sally to find some answers about why this happened."

George's jaw tightened. "Yes, sir. Yardley took extensive samples and will expedite the forensic results. And we're pursuing every lead on Holloway's whereabouts and known associates."

"Good, stay on top of it," Smith said. He paused before asking the question lurking ominously between them. "Do we think this is the same killer as before? Back to his old ways after so long unseen?"

George considered the question, Atkinson's gaunt face flashing in his mind. "A revenge killing is possible. But the MO feels... different. More brutal, more personal. I'm starting to wonder if we're looking at a copycat." He paused. "That or the killer has changed their MO so we think it's a different person." He hesitated before adding, "Using the same rituals but amping up the violence even further. Like he's trying to surpass whoever was the killer twelve years ago and outdo their savagery."

Across the line, he heard Smith humming thoughtfully. "A copycat... I hope you're wrong, son, but it's looking that way to me. We need to catch this bastard before he can strike again."

George thought of Lindsey's disturbing postmortem discoveries. Whoever did this did so intending to inflict maximum suffering. His hands curled into fists.

"It wasn't Holloway or a copycat. It was Atkinson," George said bluntly, unable to contain himself any longer. "We both know that's where the evidence will lead if we follow it honestly."

An uneasy pause followed. George could sense Smith's consternation through the phone.

"Now's not the time for unfounded speculation, George," Smith said carefully. "I know you have... a history with Atkinson. But the priority is finding Sally's killer through proper investigative work, not assumptions."

George's jaw tightened, hearing the evasion in Smith's response. "With respect, sir, we can't ignore a potential suspect with intimate knowledge of the original murders. If Atkinson is back—"

"You found the girl's body today, son," Smith interjected, an edge entering his voice. "Stay focused on Holloway for now. I am watching Atkinson personally, so he's irrelevant to you at this stage."

The rebuke stung, but George bit back a sharp retort. Pushing would get him nowhere. He scrubbed a hand down his face, exhaling frustration.

"Understood. We'll continue pursuing Holloway's trail for now," he acknowledged tightly. "I'll keep you apprised of any developments."

Smith seemed to sense he had gotten his point across. "Good man. And George... we'll get to the bottom of this. The truth always comes out eventually. Just be patient."

The call ended with a resolute click. George sat in brooding silence as Luke navigated towards the station through late afternoon traffic. Outwardly, he presented a façade of professional focus, but inwardly, doubt festered.

If Atkinson really was involved in this murder, then the clock was ticking before he struck again. George swallowed back a surge of anger at the injustice.

For now, he could only follow orders and stay vigilant for the first cracks in the façade. When they came, George would be ready to bring his full force down and expose the rot within West Yorkshire Police once and for all.

He owed that much to Sally Jenkins. And her death would not be in vain if it finally brought down those who hid behind tarnished badges while enabling the wicked. George silently renewed that unrelenting vow yet again. However long it took, justice would be done.

* * *

CHAPTER NINETEEN

George's team gathered around the scuffed table, case files and notepads at the ready. He studied their faces—Candy biting her lip, Jay jiggling his leg nervously, Tashan stone-faced as ever—and felt the weight of responsibility on his shoulders. They were all looking to him for direction and answers he did not have.

At the head of the table, George cleared his throat. "Right, let's get started. As you all know, Dr Yardley completed the postmortem on Sally earlier today." He paused, remembering her battered body with a tightness in his chest.

"The exact cause of death was manual strangulation. But no signs she had been tied up or restrained for any extended period." George chose his following words carefully.

"Yardley's analysis suggests Sally likely knew her attacker and may have gone willingly with him at some point preceding the assault."

A charged silence followed as the implications sank in. Alexis and Luke exchanged a subtle, knowing look. Yolanda shook her head in confusion. "But why go willingly if he intended to kill her?"

"That's the question we need to answer," George said grimly. He held back his suspicions about Atkinson, lacking solid proof. But the senior detective's intimate knowledge of the rituals used pointed to his involvement in George's mind.

Hoping to refocus their momentum, George prompted, "Right, DS Williams, let's start with you. What have you learned digging into Holloway's history?"

Yolanda straightened, glancing down at her notebook. "He was released from Ranby, a men's prison in Retford, Nottinghamshire, in 2010 after serving eight years for aggravated assault."

"I already know that much, Yolanda," said George. "I want to know what he's been doing the last twelve years!"

She looked back up at George. "He disappeared, sir. No tax records, license renewals, or medical visits. It's like Holloway ceased to exist after 2012."

George's jaw tightened. "He's out there somewhere, living off the grid. We just have to find what rock he's hiding under."

He turned his attention to his youngest detective. "DC Scott, what are you learning from Council Tax and business registers? Any properties listed under Holloway's known aliases?"

Jay sat up straight, eagerness shining through his unease. "Still waiting on the council records, boss. Local Government moves as slowly as treacle. But I've got tech sweeping for utility bills tied to his aliases and cold calling agents about commercial spaces rented under those names over the years." Jay's brow furrowed. "One promising lead is a mechanics garage leased under his cousin's name since 2012. I've got a plain clothes team staking it out for any activity."

George nodded, clamping his shoulder briefly. "Good initiative. Let me know if you find anything actionable on that garage or other locations. He had to be holed up somewhere all this time."

Sergeant Greenwood spoke up next. "My uniformed teams have canvassed the neighbourhoods around Holloway's last known addresses but turned up nothing useful yet. Neighbours can't recall seeing him for at least the last decade. But we'll keep up the search."

"Appreciate that, Sergeant," George acknowledged. He surveyed the room, seeing the faith and determination pushing back against their doubts. This was his team, united by a shared purpose. Together, they would find the truth.

"Right, you all have your assignments regarding Holloway," George said crisply, rising from his chair. "Keep digging and leave no stone unturned. He's out there, and we're going to find the bastard."

As the briefing concluded, George added, "And remember, our priority is locating Holloway and connecting him to Sally's murder. All energy needs to remain focused there for now."

He held Alexis and Luke's gazes meaningfully—a silent reminder to set aside assumptions and personal grudges for the sake of the investigation. With a curt nod of dismissal, George sent the team back into the fray. Step by step, they would unravel the tangled threads until justice for Sally emerged. Of that much, he was certain.

* * *

George and Tashan were greeted by the faint antiseptic tang of sterility and rows of gleaming equipment lined up with meticulous precision as they entered the lab.

At the back of the spacious room, forensic scientist Maya Chen looked up from a monitor displaying chromatic graphs. She set down a stylus and clipboard, striding over to meet them. Her sleek black hair swung neatly just above her shoulders, and her dark brown eyes glinted with sharp intellect.

"Detective Chief Inspector, Detective Constable," she addressed them briskly. Though the two tall men dwarfed Maya's slight frame, she exuded no-nonsense competence. "I have the results of my analysis on the evidence from the photographs and envelopes."

George inclined his head. "Let's have it then."

Maya launched right in, her naturally succinct manner well-suited for delivering findings.

"Starting with fingerprints found on the first two photos, you already know they belong to Arthur Grimes. I've found nothing on the third photograph."

George nodded and Maya referred to her notes. "Moving on to DNA analysis. I swabbed the envelope seals in case saliva remained from licking them shut. Again, the profile matched that of Arthur Grimes for the first two photos, but there's nothing from the third. One because there was no envelope, and two, whoever printed it was extremely careful."

George nodded slowly, arms folded across his broad chest. It suggested the third photo was sent by the killer, which they'd already theorised.

"The trace evidence proved more fruitful," Maya continued briskly. "I discovered minute fibres embedded in the seal of the outer envelope of the newer third photograph, DCI Beaumont."

She tapped her clipboard. "They appear to be polyester with a distinctive red and black chequered pattern. I've sent a sample to our textile experts for identification. If we can pinpoint the exact material, it may indicate where the envelope was stored prior to delivery."

"Good work, Maya," George said approvingly. It wasn't much, but even slender threads like this could eventually weave into breakthroughs.

Tashan's dark eyes narrowed with interest as he jotted a note. George knew he was already contemplating how such fibres might trace back to their suspect. No detail escaped Tashan's methodical mental filing system when piecing together puzzles.

Maya concluded her report with the chemical analysis findings. "The printer ink and paper stock for the third photo are relatively common, I'm afraid." She shut the folder with an air of finality. "I'll keep you updated if our experts can ID the fabric or source. Please let me know if any other evidence arises for analysis."

George nodded decisively. "Appreciate your thorough work as always, Maya. We'll be in touch."

As they exited the lab, Tashan murmured, "Back to square one, it seems."

George clapped a hand on his shoulder. "Every case has its share of dead ends. But remember, it appears Grimes is trying to help us. We just need to find him."

* * *

Later that night, Alexis Mercer quietly latched her daughter's bedroom door and paused in the hallway, heart heavy. Georgia had finally drifted off to sleep after a day of escalating meltdowns. The 11-year-old had refused to get dressed or eat breakfast that morning, overwhelmed by some unseen force. Alexis' usual bag of sensory tricks and comforting routines failed to soothe her daughter's frayed nerves. Hence the frantic morning that made Alexis late for work yet again.

Leaning against the wall, Alexis took a few deep breaths to steady herself. The phone call from Georgia's school advisor replayed in her mind. Georgia's outbursts and shutdowns had increased in frequency, disrupting her classes. They wanted Alexis to consider adjusting her ECHP or even switch to a specialist school.

Alexis scrubbed a hand over her face. Georgia made it

abundantly clear this morning she had no intention of going to school. Alexis couldn't bear to force her traumatised daughter anywhere she felt unsafe. But homeschooling would require Alexis to take indefinite leave from her job. Even with reduced hours, balancing her demanding detective role with caring for Georgia was barely feasible as it was.

The thought of sacrificing her career tore at Alexis' soul. She had worked relentlessly to earn the respect of her mostly male colleagues and rise to the rank of detective constable. Her pragmatic competence was a point of hard-won pride, proving she could handle high-pressure cases with equal skill despite being a single mother. Letting all that slip away felt unthinkable.

Yet when Alexis pictured Georgia's tear-streaked, fearful face from that morning, she would move heaven and earth to soothe her daughter's hurts. Nothing mattered more than Georgia's happiness and security. If becoming a full-time carer was the only way to provide that, so be it.

Alexis worried her lower lip pensively. Perhaps she was getting ahead of herself. They could try different accommodations and therapies before drastically changing Georgia's school environment. Her psychologist had mentioned a promising new technique to help ease Georgia's sensory overload. Alexis would do anything within her power to avoid disrupting the comforting routine her daughter depended on.

While it pained Alexis to even entertain stepping back from police work, being there for Georgia came first. She could only pray that an alternative presented itself, a way forward allowing her to maintain both halves of her identity—the devoted detective and loving mother.

Alexis started down the hall towards the living room, movements heavy with the weight of responsibility. She sank onto the sofa and closed her eyes, but the noises started up again, blaring from the baby monitor on the coffee table.

Half an hour later, now 3 am and her daughter sleeping peacefully, Alexis powered up her laptop to research local autism therapy programs.

The website's cheerful stock photos of children playing felt jarringly disconnected from the reality she and Georgia endured each challenging day. Georgia rarely interacted with other kids at school, preferring to stay within the safe and familiar confines of her mind.

Alexis' heart constricted, wishing for the hundredth time she could simply fix whatever wiring had gone awry in her daughter's brilliant but tormented mind. But real life was far more complicated.

However long the journey took, Alexis silently renewed her vow to walk every step of it by Georgia's side, navigating her daughter's unique challenges with unconditional love and patience. Her little girl was perfect exactly as she was, and Alexis would ensure Georgia knew that truth every single day.

Come what may, they would tackle this latest hurdle together, Alexis resolved as she typed notes on therapy options. Her pragmatic nature refused to dwell on unanswerable what-ifs. The future was unclear, but today she could listen to, comfort, and support her daughter. And sometimes, that was enough.

Chapter Twenty

Early morning sunlight filtered into George's office as he and Luke Mason sat across from each other, nursing steaming mugs of coffee. Luke could see the weary tension etched in his friend's rugged features after another long night pursuing leads.

"I'm telling you, Luke, Atkinson is wrapped up in this somehow," George said, an edge creeping into his gravelly voice. "The violence, the intimate knowledge of the original murders' rituals—it points to an inside man."

Luke tilted his head. "But some key elements were absent this time. The lack of runic symbols at the scene doesn't fit the original killer's MO."

George raked a hand through his hair in frustration. "Because he's changed the methods now! Amped up the savagery to throw us off." He leaned forward intently. "It has to be Atkinson. After Sally told us she overheard him admitting to the cover-up of the Gildersome case and then turning up dead? That's no coincidence."

Luke pondered this as he sipped his bitter coffee. George did seem convinced of Alistair's guilt. And Luke knew all too well how corruption festered within their ranks. He'd witnessed the wreckage bad apples left behind, the lives ruined.

CHAPTER TWENTY

"You really believe Atkinson would take such a risk now if he got away with it in the past?" Luke asked carefully, playing devil's advocate.

"I know how it sounds," George admitted wearily. "But you haven't dealt with him like I have. Atkinson feels untouchable because he's been protected for so long. And these ritualised murders are compulsive for him—he can't stop even after all this time."

Luke saw the certainty etched on George's face. There would be no changing his mind. And perhaps he was right to follow his instincts. Luke knew from experience that evil rarely stayed hidden forever.

"What about Detective Superintendent Smith? Does he share your assessment of Atkinson's involvement?"

George's face darkened. "He refuses to even consider it. Ordered me outright not to pursue that angle." He shook his head bitterly. "I used to trust Smith to have my back. But it's clear he's more concerned with PR than truth. If Atkinson takes us all down in the process, they'll find a way to cover that up, too."

Luke frowned, troubled by the implications of high-level stonewalling. It did not bode well for true justice being served.

"So where does that leave us?" Luke asked quietly. "I assume you don't intend to let this go?"

"Not a chance in hell," George said vehemently. "The second I find concrete proof tying Atkinson to Sally's murder, I'm taking it public. Smith and the rest of the brass can't bury this if it's exposed."

Luke held his friend's burning gaze, seeing the unwavering conviction there. He knew George would stop at nothing to bring down corruption and avenge Sally's death. Luke just hoped it didn't come at too great a personal cost this time. George had more than his career to consider now, with a young family waiting at home.

"Just watch your back, son," Luke cautioned gravely. "You're playing a dangerous game if you keep pursuing this against orders."

George's expression softened slightly. "I know, and I appreciate your concern. But I don't have a choice, Luke. I swore an oath to protect the innocent. If I have to cut out rot to fulfil that oath, so be it."

He clasped George's shoulder. "Whatever comes, you can count on my support, son. That's a promise."

"I know," George said, covering Luke's hand with his own. "That means everything. Thank you."

Luke leaned back in his chair, steepling his fingers contemplatively. "Playing devil's advocate here, but could Atkinson possibly be getting framed?"

George raised a sceptical brow. "Framed? That seems a stretch. The intel implicated him directly."

"True," Luke conceded. "But we know Atkinson is a right bastard. Could someone have a grudge and be setting him up to take the fall?"

George frowned, turning the idea over in his mind. He remained convinced of Atkinson's guilt, but Luke had a point—they had to consider other angles. Rushing to judgment could derail the investigation if they pursued the wrong man.

"I suppose it's possible," George said slowly. "But who would have that big a vendetta against him while also having intricate knowledge of the Gildersome case?"

Luke shrugged. "Old enemies from past collars gone wrong? Victims of his abuse looking for payback?"

CHAPTER TWENTY

He arched a brow meaningfully. "Colleagues who got wind of his corruption?"

George tensed, thoughts jumping to Alexis Mercer's unrelenting contempt for Atkinson. She had both knowledge and motive if she caught wind of his misdeeds. But surely framing a senior officer would be beyond even Alexis' drive for justice.

"It would take someone equally as ruthless as Atkinson to orchestrate such an intricate setup," George said carefully. "Not sure I see that level of cold calculation in his known detractors."

"Fair enough," Luke conceded. He studied George shrewdly. "But promise me you'll keep an open mind to other possibilities. I know you and Atkinson have history making it personal."

George held Luke's piercing gaze unflinchingly. "I promise to follow the evidence objectively wherever it leads."

Inwardly, though, George harboured no doubts about where it led—straight to Atkinson's door. The sadistic violence in Sally's murder fit him like a glove. Smith's orders be damned, George knew with bone-deep certainty that Atkinson was their man.

Which left George with a moral quandary. He couldn't officially investigate Atkinson without raising red flags. But letting him walk free to kill again was unthinkable.

Perhaps it was time to discreetly recruit help under the radar, George mused—someone tenacious who shared his drive for justice over politics. Tashan was too by-the-book. But Alexis...

"Just tread carefully, George," Luke said solemnly, as though reading his thoughts. "I know that look. Don't go kicking hornets' nests without backup."

George met his friend's concerned gaze unflinchingly. "I'll be careful; you have my word. But I swore an oath to protect the public, no matter the cost. If hunting monsters in our own ranks is the price, so be it."

Luke blew out a heavy breath, brow furrowing. But he gave a grudging nod of understanding. They both knew this wasn't the first snake pit George had stared down within the police force's walls. "Keep me in the loop, son," Luke cautioned as they shook hands. "And know I'll stand with you whatever comes."

George's stern expression softened fractionally. "I know, Luke. Your support means everything with the storm on the horizon." Then something occurred to him. "You still thinking about retiring?" George ventured carefully. "Have you and Elaine discussed it further?"

Luke exhaled heavily, looking down as he spun his mug between weathered hands. "Aye, it's all we discuss lately. Her dementia is progressing faster than expected. The specialist says she needs round-the-clock care soon." He shook his head, grief etched in every crease of his worn face. "I can't do that for her with the long hours here. And I'll not have her shut away in some facility. She deserves better than that."

George's heart ached for his friend. Luke had been devoted to Elaine for over thirty years. Facing this cruel illness eroding her vital mind was devastating.

"I'm so sorry, Luke," George said. "You definitely should do what's right for your family. No one would fault you for retiring now."

Luke gave a sad half-smile. "Oh, some of the old guard will call me weak. But sod 'em all. My Elaine is all that matters now." He looked directly at George then. "Will you be alright with one less old warhorse around? I worry I'm leaving you short-handed on top of the instability lately."

George waved a hand dismissively despite the kernel of truth in Luke's words. "Don't go fretting about that. Your priority is caring for Elaine. We'll manage things on the job end."

Privately, though, George lamented the void Luke's absence would leave, both professionally and personally. They had been a formidable team for so long. Life at the station would feel off-kilter without his friend down the hall to confer with as he'd grown accustomed.

But George would never begrudge Luke for choosing his wife's welfare first. The job made profound sacrifices of officers and their loved ones. It was past time for Luke to focus on his family now.

"Just promise you won't become a stranger," George added gruffly. "Come round for dinner as soon as you're settled. Olivia would love to see her Uncle Luke and Auntie Elaine again. She enjoyed your company on Christmas Day."

Luke smiled warmly. "Wild horses couldn't keep me away. I expect regular updates on my little lass."

He studied George pensively. "And how is Isabella doing? Will she return to duty once you find a replacement for me?"

George exhaled slowly, weighing his words. "She seems ready for it mentally. Throwing herself into reviewing case files and news. I know I shouldn't share information with her, but she misses the job." He shook his head ruefully. "But she also feels torn about leaving Olivia." George hesitated. "Last night, Livvy stayed with my mum, and I saw the guilt in Izzy's eyes when Livvy clung and cried at drop-off." He rubbed his tired eyes. "And that's when she stays over at Nanna's. Can you imagine if we need to find a childminder?"

George met Luke's knowing gaze. "So I haven't pressed the issue yet. I don't want Isabella rushing back before she's ready. Family comes first, as you well know."

Luke nodded sagely. "You're a good man, George. And a good father, never doubt that." He tilted his head, assessing. "But have you truly considered what Isabella's return might mean for your dynamic here? Things can get... complicated."

George raked a hand through his hair with a pensive frown. Luke had a point. Isabella's confident manner had already raised some jealous hackles. The wedding was this year, and George could already foresee tensions within the upper echelons.

"We'll maintain professionalism, of course," George said. "But you're right, there could be challenges. I'll need to tread carefully to avoid any hint of impropriety or undue influence."

"You will, as always," Luke said with an affirming clap on his shoulder. "Just watch each other's backs. Not everyone wishes you well."

George nodded gravely. Between Isabella's return and Luke's retirement, the winds of change were stirring with unpredictable consequences. He would need to redouble efforts to stabilize the team amidst the coming transition.

But gazing into Luke's steady eyes, George felt reassured. They would navigate the path ahead as they had every past challenge, with courage, integrity and mutual support. All would be well so long as those unshakable bonds remained.

Chapter Twenty-one

The brisk autumn air nipped at Candy's cheeks as she hurried down the pavement of Town Street, weaving between other pedestrians. She was on a mission to pick up sandwiches for the team from a nearby deli before they reconvened to discuss new leads in the case.

Town Street in Beeston was a bustling hub of activity this Saturday afternoon. People streamed in and out of shops, their laughter and chatter mingling with the distant rush of traffic. Candy brushed past a woman pushing a pram, offering a quick "Excuse me" as she checked her watch. She was cutting it close if she wanted to get back to the station with the food before the briefing.

The smell of fresh bread and roasting meat drew Candy toward the door of The Bread Basket Case sandwich shop, which was no doubt named after a song by Candy's favourite band. Or so she'd hoped; she'd never actually asked anybody at the sandwich shop the origin of their name. The team was no doubt already gathered and waiting impatiently.

Weaving her way up to the counter, Candy placed an order for an assortment of sandwiches. As the teenage boy behind the counter assembled the sandwiches, Candy's gaze drifted to the display case of plump cookies and fresh creams. Maybe she'd pick up something sweet as a treat for the team's hard work, too. They'd earned it.

Ten minutes later, arms laden with two bulging paper bags, Candy pushed out the door with her shoulder, the merry tinkle of the shop's bell signalling her exit. She blinked against the sudden sunlight, pausing to get her bearings.

Candy had only gone about twenty paces down the pavement towards her car when she sensed movement behind her a split second before a heavy blow slammed into her back. Candy staggered, bags flying from her arms as she threw them out to break her fall. She collapsed to her knees on the hard concrete with a cry.

"Hey!" Candy yelped, twisting around. Pain radiated from between her shoulder blades where she'd been struck. She glimpsed a figure in dark clothing, and a hood yank back the way they'd come, quickly vanishing into the lunchtime crowds.

Candy grimaced, gingerly touching her back. Her fingers came away wet with blood. The bastard must have clubbed her or maybe used a blunt knife. Shock quickly gave way to anger. She struggled to stand, intent on giving chase, but a wave of dizziness sent her crashing back to the pavement.

By the time Candy's vision cleared, her assailant had disappeared from view down a side street. Cursing under her breath, she fumbled for her mobile to call for backup and medical assistance. Her head was still spinning, and she could feel blood soaking into her blouse beneath her jacket.

Before Candy could hit dial, a small crowd had gathered around her, faces peering down in concern. "Are you alright, dear?" an elderly lady asked.

Candy blinked hard, trying to focus through the encroaching

CHAPTER TWENTY-ONE

grey fuzziness at the edges of her vision. "I'm a police detective," she managed to grit out. "I need backup and an ambulance to Beeston Town Street, near The Bread Basket Case sandwich shop."

Even as Candy answered the concerned questions being fired at her, she mentally catalogued details of the assault that might identify her attacker. She'd sensed only one assailant, average height and build from what she glimpsed—no distinguishable accent. But what was most telling was the vicious efficiency of the ambush.

This had been no random act of violence; Candy felt certain. Which meant she—or someone on the team—had been targeted deliberately. The implications sent a chill through Candy that had nothing to do with her growing lightheadedness.

By the time the wail of sirens split the air, Candy's vision was spotty with dark splotches. The jostling crowd's voices sounded strangely muffled, their faces blurring together. As strong hands carefully eased her onto her back, Candy managed to rasp out one last instruction before the world faded away.

"Call my boss, DCI Beaumont... tell him..."

But the blackness rushed up to swallow her words, leaving that ominous warning unfinished.

* * *

The Incident Room at Elland Road police station buzzed with restless energy as DCI George Beaumont, DI Luke Mason, and DC Tashan Blackburn gathered around the central table. Stacks of files and curling pages of notes littered every surface, evidence of the long hours poured into both the Jenkins and Gildersome investigations. The sharp scent of stale coffee permeated the stale air.

George raked a hand through his hair, exhaling frustration. "How much longer for those damn lab results on the medals found at the Gildersome scenes?"

Luke shuffled through a disorganised pile of paperwork. "They said possibly today or tomorrow at the latest when I checked in this morning."

"It's already mid-afternoon," George grumbled, crossing his muscular arms. "We're losing momentum on the Gildersome killer while we chase the Jenkins murder."

"I know it's frustrating, but there's only so much they can rush," Luke placated. Though tension pinched the corners of his eyes. Luke checked his watch for what felt like the hundredth time, his wiry frame radiating restless energy. "That lass should have been back by now. Those sandwiches can't take this long."

Jay Scott didn't glance up from his rapid typing. "You know how chatty Candy is. Probably got caught up talking the server's ear off." But faint creases of concern marked his brow.

Tashan straightened where he sat, scanning digitised files. "We shouldn't downplay the importance of those medals, sirs. The symbolism indicates a ritualistic motivation, and identifying their origins could be key to the culprit's psychological profile."

George exhaled through his nose, jaw tight. He respected Tashan's analytic eye, but time was slipping away. "You're right, of course. But we've been waiting too long."

Luke blew out a slow breath. "Forensics has been over-

CHAPTER TWENTY-ONE

whelmed processing evidence from the Jenkins scene. It's been all hands on deck."

The three men sat in tense silence for a moment, the weight of their dual investigations bearing down. Lives hung in the balance with a ruthless killer still at large. Yet the very evidence needed to catch him eluded their grasp.

Pacing to the evidence board, George studied the photos of the small, worn medals discovered buried at the Gildersome sites. Their uniform size and mysterious engraved symbol nagged at him.

"Tashan's behavioural analysis suggests these medals hold special meaning for the culprit," George mused. "His taunting escalation makes cracking this symbolism crucial."

Tashan said, "Which also makes it all the more interesting why one wasn't found at the Jenkins crime scene."

"Excellent point, Tashan." George turned back to the others. "Have we gotten anywhere tracing the insignia design or metal composition? Anything to hint at their origins?"

Luke shook his head regretfully. "Hit dead ends so far. No matches in any heraldry or military registries. Though alloy analysis did confirm a high silver content."

George's jaw tightened. "There must be some significance to these objects beyond mere souvenirs of the killer's work."

He thought of the victims' anguished families seeking answers that maddeningly eluded him. George felt the weight of wasted years, of justice denied. Never again, he vowed.

Tashan straightened, a thought apparently occurring. "What if it's the number that matters? Three interlinked medals left deliberately, one at each decades-old crime scene." He raised his dark gaze. "A ritual leaving his macabre signature, perhaps?"

George froze, pinned by the implication. "The third medal at the third site...bloody hell. You could be onto something." The medals as a numerical calling card at each murder location fit the obsessive nature of their suspect's escalation. But how did the three medals relate to Detective Foster's medal left at the Bramley Woods murder scene?

George asked his team that exact question, but was met with blank faces.

Except for DI Mason.

Frustration simmered beneath Luke's composed expression. "If we're right about the significance, it makes identifying them immediately critical. We must anticipate where he'll strike next as the sequence continues."

Just then, George's mobile vibrated with an incoming call. Checking the screen, his pulse quickened—it was Maya Chen. He answered briskly. "Please tell me you have news, Maya."

The forensic scientist's voice was apologetic but urgent. "Sorry for the delay, but I've uncovered something. I need you and your team down here now."

George signalled sharply to Luke and Tashan. "We're on our way."

Suddenly, the Incident Room door banged open. A uniformed sergeant rushed in, face grim. "Sorry to interrupt, sir, but we just got a call. DC Nichols was assaulted on Town Street in Beeston twenty minutes ago."

George froze, breath catching in his throat as the words sunk in. Candy attacked? His gut twisted with dismay and anger.

Luke straightened abruptly from where he leaned against the table.

Jay's head jerked up, fingers stilling over his keyboard.

CHAPTER TWENTY-ONE

"What?" Jay blurted, paling beneath his haphazard dark hair. "Is Candy OK? What happened?"

The sergeant shook his head. "Injured badly enough that witnesses called for an ambulance. She's being transported to the hospital now."

"Give us details, Sergeant!" George demanded; his gravelly voice was sharp with tightly leashed concern.

The officer relayed the few known details—head trauma from a blow to the back, no ID yet on the assailant who fled. George's jaw tightened, fury simmering beneath his calm facade.

"This is ridiculous," Jay bit out, beginning to pace. "Who would want to hurt Candy? She's never got mixed up in anything dodgy."

"My thoughts exactly," George said. He scrubbed a hand down his bearded jaw, anger simmering just below the surface. "The timing feels... significant, given our current caseload. But speculating is useless until Candy can provide details."

Jay nodded, though his hands still flexed and curled at his sides, as though longing to strike out at whoever had harmed his colleague—the love of his life.

"Any description of the suspect?" Tashan asked sharply, already rising from his seat. His sudden stillness reminded George of a predator scenting prey.

"Just someone dressed all in dark clothing with a hood up. Fled the scene quickly after striking her from behind." The sergeant hesitated. "But witnesses say DC Nichols indicated it was likely a targeted attack before she lost consciousness."

A chill swept through the room at those ominous words. George's hands curled into fists where they rested atop the table. His jaw tightened, green eyes blazing.

"Right, get all available units locking down that scene immediately," George instructed tersely. "I want witnesses interviewed and any shred of evidence collected. And keep me updated on Candy's condition."

George studied the young detective constable. Beneath Jay's casual, lively exterior beat a fiercely loyal heart. "Go to the hospital," George said decisively. "Offer any support you can until we get more information. And call in with any updates on her condition."

Relief flashed across Jay's face. "Of course, I'll head there straight away." He turned towards the door but then hesitated, glancing back. "We'll find who did this, right, boss? Make them pay?"

The fervent concern in Jay's voice resonated within George's own simmering anger.

"Absolutely," he said resolutely, holding Jay's gaze. "I protect my own. Rest assured, whoever is responsible will regret ever laying a hand on Candy." George's voice was stone, every word a solemn vow.

Jay gave a sharp nod, jaw clenching, before striding out with renewed purpose. Alone again, George forced himself to sit, inhaling slowly. But his hands still tightened into fists against the tabletop.

Candy was more than just a colleague—she was family. And George would move heaven and earth to keep his family safe. For now, he could only wait helplessly for updates, the damned case files forgotten.

Chapter Twenty-two

Detective Chief Inspector George Beaumont stared down at the defaced photograph clutched in his gloved hands, a mix of emotions roiling within him—shock, anger, and concern for his colleague Alexis Mercer. The image, a Christmas card of Alexis and her young daughter with their faces violently scratched out, conveyed a disturbing threat.

Alexis, having not long arrived from her lunch break, stood frozen beside George, hands covering her mouth, eyes wide with horror.

Alexis Mercer felt the room tilt around her as she read the chilling words scrawled inside the defaced Christmas card. A poem alluding to danger coming for her and her daughter Georgia by name. She gripped the edge of the table to steady herself, chest tight with fear.

Georgia. Her innocent eleven-year-old child pulled violently into the darkness surrounding this case. Alexis felt gutted by the implication. She fumbled for her mobile with trembling hands, desperate to hear her daughter's voice and confirm she was safe.

George gently grasped Alexis' wrist before she could dial, the touch startling her. His green eyes were steady but filled with compassion.

"Alexis, wait," he urged quietly. "Take a breath. I know you're terrified for Georgia right now. But we need to be smart."

Alexis searched his face frantically. "I have to call her school, get her somewhere safe. She's not picking up her mobile, what if—"

"Shh, listen to me," George soothed. "Georgia is fine. No one can get to her at school."

Alexis hesitated, wavering on the edge of panic; the visceral fear of any threat to her only child was overwhelming.

George's steady voice cut through the haze of dread. "Hey, look at me. I swear to you we will keep Georgia and you safe, no matter what it takes. But right now, I need you to hold it together so we can make a plan. Can you do that for me?"

Alexis sucked in a ragged breath, then another, until the initial paralysing shock began to subside. She managed a jerky nod. Having George's calm strength to anchor herself against was the only thing keeping her afloat.

"Good, you're doing brilliantly," George encouraged. He gave her wrist a gentle squeeze. "Now, the first priority is getting Georgia someplace secure without raising suspicion."

Alexis exhaled shakily. Removing Georgia from danger was all that mattered. "Yes, please. I don't want her scared, though. I want to be there with her." She paused. "And it'll have to be home because she doesn't do well in unknown places."

"Home." George nodded. "Of course. And you'll be protected round-the-clock as well until we end this threat," he promised. "I swear to you, we will find who is responsible and make them pay." His eyes smouldered with banked fury.

Alexis managed a tremulous nod of gratitude. But inside,

CHAPTER TWENTY-TWO

she was at war with herself. Could she continue aiding this investigation when it had turned savagely personal? The thought of leaving George short-handed at this critical juncture tore at her.

Yet, was it fair to Georgia to stay involved and potentially draw more danger towards them? Alexis didn't know how to reconcile her duelling professional duty and maternal instinct.

As if reading her turmoil, George drew up a chair beside her. His voice was gentler than Alexis had ever heard it.

"Whatever you need to do to feel your daughter is safe, we'll support you one hundred per cent. Don't worry about the investigation. Focus on your family first."

Alexis' eyes welled up, the compassion in his words cracking her fragile composure. She nodded jerkily.

"I just...I don't know if I can stay on the case," she whispered brokenly. "Not with Georgia at risk. I'm so sorry..."

"You have absolutely nothing to apologise for," George emphasised, clasping her shoulder. "I can't imagine the fear you're feeling as a mother. Despite only working together for a few days, you're one of the finest detectives I've worked with, Alexis. But if you need to step back now, I understand completely."

Alexis swiped at her eyes, simultaneously relieved and ashamed. "I want to see this through. I do. But Georgia has to come first." Her voice was scarcely audible.

"Of course she does," George said firmly. "Your daughter needs you. Take all the time you need away. Your position will be waiting whenever you're ready to return."

Alexis managed a wavering smile, the reassurance easing her anguish somewhat. She knew George meant every word. They would weather this storm, and she would emerge stronger—as a mother and a detective.

"One battle at a time," George said steadily. "Today, you focus on Georgia's safety. We'll fight the rest of this war. You have my word."

George, stepping to the door, called, "Tashan!" sharply. "Get in here immediately, and bring an evidence collection kit."

Moments later, Tashan Blackburn hurried in, his imposing figure radiating alertness. His dark gaze immediately fixed on the defaced photograph on George's desk. Tashan's expression hardened as he took in the violent mutilation of Alexis and her daughter's faces.

Pulling out his phone, he quickly took a picture of the photograph and then turned to Tashan. "Secure this as evidence and get it to forensics straight away for analysis," George instructed. His gravelly voice was tight with restrained emotion. "And speak of this to no one else yet."

Tashan nodded, his focus absolute as he carefully bagged the photograph. "Consider it done, sir." His usually stoic demeanour could not mask the concern in his eyes as he regarded Alexis.

As Tashan swiftly departed with the evidence, George turned his full attention back to Alexis. She seemed diminished somehow, arms wrapped around herself, the vibrant confidence drained away.

A chill crept down George's spine as the implications sank in. This was no random act of cruelty—it was a calculated threat aimed directly at his colleague, Alexis.

George gently guided Alexis to a chair. "I cannot imagine how violating this must feel," he said gravely, keeping his voice low and steady. "But we are going to uncover who is

CHAPTER TWENTY-TWO

behind this, I swear to you."

Alexis' voice was nearly a whisper. "It's Georgia, my daughter. She's only eleven, George. If someone wanted to hurt me, they've destroyed the one thing I can't..." Her words dissolved into quiet tears.

George crouched before Alexis, waiting until she met his gaze. "Listen to me. No one is going to harm Georgia or you. I promise." His green eyes blazed with conviction.

Alexis searched his face and seemed to find resolve reflected back at her. She wiped her eyes and gave a tremulous nod.

"We will post an officer outside your home immediately for extra security," George continued gently. "And I want you off active field duty for now, just as a precaution."

Alexis drew a shaky breath but didn't argue. She knew George was right; she was in no state to be of use until this threat was neutralised.

The room around George faded into the background as his mind raced, piecing together connections. A sudden realization hit him like a thunderclap. This photograph, placed deliberately in Candy's bag, had to be linked to her assault. It was too much of a coincidence otherwise.

Alexis glanced up at George from where she sat hunched in the chair, arms wrapped around herself protectively. Her face was still etched with shock, but she searched his expression. "You've realised something," she said hoarsely. "This is connected to Candy, isn't it?"

George nodded, his jaw tight. He crouched before Alexis again, holding her distressed gaze. "I believe whoever attacked Candy left this photograph intentionally. It suggests the cases are linked."

Alexis paled further. "Why? Why target Candy to threaten

me?" Her voice broke.

George squeezed her shoulder. "I don't know yet. But we will find out, I swear to you." His green eyes blazed with conviction. Inwardly, his mind spun with unanswered questions. What twisted agenda was at play here?

Yolanda frowned. "Left deliberately to threaten Alexis? Why?"

"That's what we need to determine," George said grimly.

A brisk knock preceded Luke Mason sticking his head in the door. His weathered face creased into a concerned frown as he took in Alexis' traumatised expression.

"What's happened?" Luke asked tersely. "I just heard Tashan rushed off with an evidence bag."

George pressed his lips into a thin line, anger simmering beneath the surface. He passed Luke his phone, who inspected the image on it closely. His eyes widened, then narrowed, mouth thinning into an enraged line.

"Bloody hell," Luke bit out, his expression thunderous. "This was no random street crime, son. Someone wanted us rattled." He turned to George and said, "What are you thinking?" before crouching next to Alexis.

George folded his arms. "I think the photograph confirms the attack on Candy was meant to deliver a message. But the motivation and desired outcome remain unclear."

"We'll find who did this, lass," said Luke. "No one hurts our people and gets away with it." The fierceness of his tone seemed to steady Alexis slightly. She managed a slight nod of acknowledgement.

Alexis spoke up, voice tight but steady. "It seems I'm being targeted, but through Candy instead. Why not come directly for me?"

CHAPTER TWENTY-TWO

Yolanda suggested, "Maybe sending a warning first? Implying they can get to all of us?"

George nodded slowly. "Perhaps. They're playing psychological games instead of a straight-up assault." His jaw tightened. "But we cannot let fear force us off this case. That's what they want."

Around the table, resolute expressions answered him. Luke said gruffly, "Too damn right. We don't scare easy."

George felt a swell of pride for his team. Even rattled, they remained committed to pursuing justice and protecting their own. It was that unbreakable loyalty and courage that would see them through this darkness.

George squared his shoulders, green eyes gleaming with determination. "We won't rest until we expose whoever is behind these vicious attacks. And when we do, they will regret ever threatening us. That's a promise."

His gravelly words resonated with solemn promise. For George, this had turned deeply personal. And he would go to any lengths to shield his people from harm. Failure was not an option.

"Let's get you home to Georgia, alright?" George suggested.

Alexis nodded.

As Luke helped Alexis up and escorted her from the office, George sank heavily into his desk chair. He braced his elbows on the wood surface, scrubbing both hands down his bearded face. This case had taken a dark, personal turn.

In his mind, George re-examined each detail of the photograph and Candy's assault, searching for connections. Why leave such a disturbing image specifically for Alexis to find? The chilling warning implied she might be the next target. But the fact Candy was attacked first didn't fit. It was like a puzzle missing key pieces.

* * *

The late afternoon sun bathed the exterior of Adwalton Primary School in a warm glow as Detective Inspector Luke Mason, and Detective Constables Tashan Blackburn, and Alexis Mercer arrived. But none felt any warmth as they entered the building on their solemn mission to retrieve Alexis' daughter, Georgia.

Walking briskly down the empty hall, their footsteps echoed off the walls decorated with children's art. Alexis fought to keep her composure, fearful of alarming her sensitive daughter.

Luke placed a steadying hand on Alexis' shoulder. "We'll keep Georgia safe; I promise you that," he avowed gravely. Alexis managed a tight nod of gratitude.

Eventually, they were allowed through reception and to a room deep within the school, where they were told to wait by the Head Teacher, Amanda Collins, a woman in her early 50s with a graceful, willowy figure.

Her face was all gentle curves—high cheekbones, a button nose, and a mouth often quirked into a sympathetic smile. Yet her hazel eyes could flash sharp behind wire-rimmed glasses when doling out reprimands.

Ten minutes later, Georgia's teacher, an older woman with a salt-and-pepper tidy bob grazing her shoulders, greeted them with a concerned frown. The teacher wore simple pearl earrings and a matching necklace. Her attire was understated but smart—tailored trousers with a pressed, white blouse and low-heeled pumps. A colourful silk scarf added a splash of

CHAPTER TWENTY-TWO

vibrancy. "Miss Mercer, is everything alright?"

"There's been a threat at work, Mrs Bruff, so I'm taking Georgia home early as a precaution," Alexis explained tightly. "Thank you for allowing us to do this."

The teacher's eyes widened, but she nodded in understanding. "Of course, her well-being is paramount. She's in the sensory room when you're ready. I'll gather her things."

As the teacher disappeared, Alexis took a deep breath, mentally preparing herself. A gentle hand gripping her arm made her turn. Tashan offered an encouraging smile. "You've got this, Alexis. We're right here with you." His steadfast support eased her nerves slightly.

When they entered the room, Georgia sat rocking slightly in a beanbag chair, fingers over her ears, her teeth nibbling the end of a red and black striped tie. At the sight of her mother, she leapt up and rushed into Alexis' waiting arms.

"Mummy, who are these people?" Georgia whimpered, her tiny body tense. "What's going on?"

Alexis crouched down, brushing a blonde curl from her daughter's face. "I know this is frightening, sweetheart. But some bad people are threatening Mummy at work. These officers are very good friends of mine." She paused. "We need to take you home and keep you safe until the scary people go away."

Georgia's blue eyes, so like Alexis' own, welled up. "I'm scared, Mummy," she whispered shakily.

Alexis had to choke back tears of her own. "You don't need to be, baby girl. We're going to be safe, I promise."

Georgia searched her mother's face, lower lip quivering. Finally, she gave a slight, jerky nod. Alexis exhaled in relief, hugging her daughter fiercely. Luke and Tashan watched the poignant scene, hearts aching.

After gently explaining the arrangements, Alexis took Georgia's hand and led her outside to the discreet police vehicle. Georgia tensed up when Luke reached to buckle her in, withdrawing from his touch.

Alexis shot him an apologetic look. "Here, let me get her settled." With soothing words and caresses, she eased Georgia into her seat and secured the belt. Luke and Tashan climbed into the front seats, leaving Alexis in the back with her daughter.

Alexis kissed her forehead, swallowing the lump in her throat. "I love you so much, Georgia. Never forget that."

"Love you too, Mummy," Georgia whispered back.

"Everything is going to be OK, I promise you."

Chapter Twenty-three

The Incident Room hummed with tense energy. Detective Chief Inspector George Beaumont stood at the head of the room, jaw tight with fury.

"The attack on Candy and the threat on Alexis and Georgia confirm this perpetrator is targeting our team strategically," he announced, green eyes steely. "They know our strengths and are trying to fragment us by striking at our most vulnerable points."

Murmurs rippled around the room. Detective Constable Tashan Blackburn suggested hesitantly, "It's got to be somebody within the West Yorkshire Police, right, sir? With that level of intimate knowledge?"

Luke and Tashan exchanged a subtle glance. George's throat tightened with anger, but he kept his tone even. "We have to consider every possibility. But for now, stay focused on leads related to known suspects." His look forestalled further discussion of certain senior officers.

After dismissing the team to pursue their assignments, George retreated to his office. Isabella and Olivia were still heavy on his mind. After the disturbing photograph and attack on his team, concern for his own family's safety gnawed at him. He couldn't bear the thought of anything happening to them because of this case.

George paced back and forth in his office, phone in hand. His forehead was creased with worry lines, and his jaw was tense. He pulled up Isabella's number and hit dial, raking a hand through his blond hair as it rang.

"Hi gorgeous," Isabella's warm voice greeted after a few rings. "Was just giving Livvy her bath. Everything OK?"

George smiled despite the circumstances, picturing his fiancée and baby girl. "Yeah, all fine here, my love," he said, aiming for a casual tone. "Just wanted to check in since I'm missing you."

He hesitated, unsure how much to reveal of the escalating threats. Isabella could read him like a book.

Sure enough, her tone shifted, soft but probing. "George, what's wrong? And don't say nothing—I can hear that worry creeping in."

George sighed, sinking into his desk chair. He should have known better than to attempt to evade her. "It's this damn case, Izzy. Things have gotten... personal lately. Threats made against the team." He scrubbed a hand down his bearded jaw. "I just need to know that you and Olivia are safe."

Isabella inhaled sharply. "Threats? Of what sort?" He could hear her maternal concern surging to the forefront.

"Photos and notes alluding to danger to our families. And Candy was assaulted today." George's voice tightened at the memory. "It was meant to intimidate us off the case. But I'll be damned if I let that happen."

"Oh, George," Isabella murmured, and he could envision her brows drawing together in that way that made his chest ache. "That's terrifying. Are you all taking precautions?"

"Round-the-clock security at their homes," George assured her. "But right now, I need to know you and Olivia are safe where you are. Is your grandad's house still a fortress?" he asked tongue in cheek.

Isabella exhaled slowly. "Yes, you know how he is. Cameras everywhere, doors like vaults. I've never felt unsafe here." In the background, George could hear Olivia's delighted squeals as Isabella talked. The sound eased his spiking pulse.

"Well, he does live in Miggy, so that's the standard to keep safe," George said with a chuckle. "I'm just glad you're both OK," he said, rubbing the back of his neck. "Any chance you could stay there a while longer until this madness ends? I know the wedding's soon, but..."

"Of course, anything to keep Olivia safe," Isabella said without hesitation. "My grandparents understand; this crazy job of yours has to come first right now." Her tone softened. "Just promise you'll be careful, love. We need you in one piece."

Emotion clogged George's throat. "I promise, sweet. And I swear I'll get this bastard and make him pay for threatening us."

Isabella made a slight sound of acknowledgement. "I know you will, George. No one is more relentless about protecting others than you." Her faith, despite the circumstances, heartened him.

In the background, Olivia babbled happily, and George's heart ached to hold her. "Give Livvy a big kiss for me, will you? And take care of each other."

"Always do," Isabella promised warmly. "And you look after yourself as well, gorgeous. Come round when you can for a much-needed cuddle with your girls."

George smiled, some of the weight on his shoulders easing.

"Nothing could keep me away. I love you both to the moon and back."

"We love you too. Forever and ever. Now go catch some bad guys." Isabella's tone turned playful, but he could hear the thread of concern beneath it. They exchanged a few more tender parting words before reluctantly ringing off.

George sat for a moment, scrolling through photos of Olivia on his mobile. Her bright eyes and delighted giggles melted away some of his encroaching darkness. He was reminded of what truly mattered—protecting the innocent lives that gave his own meaning.

Whatever it took, he would shield his girls from the evil threatening those he loved. When it came to his family, George's relentlessness knew no bounds. And heaven help anyone who dared try to harm them. He would rain down hellfire on anyone who threatened his loved ones.

* * *

The shadowy figure sat alone in the dark, rage simmering beneath the surface. Successfully eliminating one target was gratifying, but the real victory lay in seeing the fear take hold in the eyes of Detective Chief Inspector Beaumont and his team. Their false confidence was already beginning to crack, exposing the weaknesses underneath.

A cruel smile twisted their lips as they replayed each strategic move in their mind—the mutilated photograph, the savage assault on the young redhead. Such exquisite suffering they had orchestrated, and still only the opening acts. Soon, the real spectacle would begin, each scene choreographed for maximum devastation.

CHAPTER TWENTY-THREE

George Beaumont would learn the meaning of torment before the final curtain fell. The arrogance in those piercing green eyes stirred a visceral fury within them. Beaumont embodied everything corrupt and hypocritical about the force. He paraded as a hero while hiding sins as black as any criminal. The seething anger and thirst for vengeance had driven their meticulous scheming these many months, awaiting the perfect moment to set chaos in motion.

And now, the pieces were clicking flawlessly into place. The anticipation was electric, each small victory stoking the sadistic excitement for what lay ahead. There was a perverse artistry to orchestrating such exquisite suffering. Soon enough, Beaumont's smug confidence would morph into anguished helplessness.

The thought sent a pleasurable thrill down their spine. Imagining the anguish on proud Isabella's face when her beloved George was ripped away also stirred twisted ecstasy. They had devoted endless hours to learning every intimate detail of Beaumont's world, probing for the most vulnerable points to strike when the time was right. The game was exhilarating, requiring infinite patience and cunning. But the rewards would prove exquisite.

A pleasant ache had settled in their muscles after the savouring of these dark thoughts. A run along the rural Country Way would provide a euphoric release for the simmering energy. The night called, its cloak of shadows a comfort and ally on the hunt.

Pulling on dark athletic gear and trainers perfect for silent movement, they slipped outside unseen. A faint mist clung to the isolated pavement, muffling any distant sounds of the sleeping city. Each breath emerged in soft white puffs as muscles warmed and loosened. Then the steady rhythm found its cadence, feet pounding out a driving beat accompanied only by the rush of blood in the ears.

The run transported them into an almost meditative state like a predator effortlessly coursing through its territory. Their focus turned inward as the plan took shape in their mind. The next strike must land soon to keep the fear from abating.

As the paved road gradually gave way to gravel, they felt an impulsive desire for connection. For an audience to share in the intoxicating thrill of the game. The need for recognition, to be known, flickered briefly beneath the surface before being ruthlessly suppressed. Such weakness could prove fatal to the grand design.

Still, the yearning remained. Perhaps a tiny taste of complicity without risk of exposure. They pulled out a burner mobile, satisfaction curling their mouth into a smirk.

The danger and domination were exquisite. And the game was only just heating up in earnest. Dark currents of excitement swept them onwards down the silent road, muscles burning pleasantly from the sustained exertion. Anticipation for the next brutal master-stroke unfurled within like an exquisite flower.

* * *

A soft rap at the door heralded Jay Scott peeking in, hollow-eyed and tense. "Hey, boss. I just got back from the hospital. Candy's stable but pretty banged up." His voice was subdued, lacking its usual exuberance.

George studied the shaken young officer sympathetically. "How are you holding up, Jay?"

CHAPTER TWENTY-THREE

Jay just shook his head jerkily. "I just don't understand who would target Candy, you know? She doesn't have an enemy in the world."

George's jaw tightened. "I know. But we're going to find out who did this. Did the hospital say when she might be able to talk to us about the assault?"

"Few days at least," Jay answered dully. "She took a pretty bad blow to the head. But she's doing pretty good." He paused, and George sensed the hesitation.

"What's wrong? Other than the obvious."

"I was wondering whether I could have some time off tonight to spend with my mother, sir," he said. "I know we're swamped, but I—"

"Oh, it's sir now, is it, DC Scott?" George interrupted.

"I'm sorry, boss, I just—"

"Get out. Leave. Go see your mum." George grinned. "That's an order."

"Thanks, boss. I mean it."

"Go on. Get out!" George winked. "Before I change my mind."

* * *

Tashan Blackburn reclined on his sofa, laptop balanced on his knees as his girlfriend Amara's face filled the screen. Her umber skin glowed in the flattering light of her bedroom, and Tashan drank in the beauty of her features—wide-set eyes, high cheekbones, full lips curved into a smile.

"I miss you," Amara sighed, a faint pout turning down her mouth. "Feels like it's been ages since we spent real time together."

Tashan nodded, wishing he could reach through the screen and caress her cheek. "I know, sweetheart. The cases have been all-consuming lately." His eyes traced over her pixelated image, trying to commit every detail to memory. "Just have to get through this rough patch at work, and then I'm all yours again."

Amara's dark eyes softened. "I'm proud of you, Tash. I know how hard you're working to get justice for that poor woman." She worried her bottom lip. "But don't run yourself into the ground, OK? I need my man at full strength."

Tashan chuckled, warmth blooming in his chest. Amara always knew just what to say to lift his spirits. "I'll be sure to save some energy for you, don't worry." He arched a teasing brow.

Amara's answering laugh was musical. "See that you do!" She paused, tender sincerity replacing the mischief in her eyes. "In all seriousness, be safe out there. I worry about you."

Tashan's expression turned solemn. "I know. And I promise I'll come home to you, no matter what this psycho throws at us. Nothing could keep me from my best girl."

Amara lifted her hand to the webcam, and Tashan matched the gesture, wishing he could twine their fingers together. For now, the separation was finite; he would hold her in his arms again soon. Their bond could weather any storm.

* * *

Jay Scott hovered in the doorway of his mother's hospital room, observing her fragile form dwarfed by tubes and machines. Guilt gnawed at him that work kept him away so much as her health failed. He should be here more. Should make time, no matter how consuming the caseload got.

Approaching the bed quietly, Jay eased into the chair beside her, gently gripping one thin hand in his own. Her skin felt like crinkled tissue paper, so delicate. Jay swallowed hard.

"Hi, Mum," he murmured, even though she slept on. "Brought you some biscuits from that bakery you like. Chocolate chip, your favourite."

Jay wished she would open her eyes, would squeeze his hand back. But the rhythmic beep of the monitors reassured him she was stable, holding her own a bit longer. He studied her paper-fine eyelids, remembering her eyes so vividly—pale grey ringed with blue, full of lively mischief once upon a time. Before the cancer drained that vibrant spirit away, reducing her to this fragile shell.

"I miss talking to you, Mum," Jay confessed softly. "You always knew how to make me laugh, no matter what." He exhaled a shaky breath, gripping her limp hand tighter. "I'm trying to stay positive, but it feels like I'm losing you a bit more each day."

Jay leaned in, lowering his voice as if sharing a secret. "We've got a real monster to catch right now. Attacked one of our own. Candy. The one I told you about. The one I love. I won't rest until we have the bastard locked up." Jay felt that familiar thirst for justice stirring, parching his throat. "Wish you were still here to tell me your crazy stories, keep me smiling. I could use that about now."

Jay lapsed into silence then, listening to the oxygen pump's rhythmic hiss and the beep-beep-beep of the heart monitor. Those sounds were a metronome counting down the precious time left with his mum. He clung to her hand like an anchor against grief's rising tide.

"I love you, Mum," Jay whispered finally, throat tight. "I'll be back soon, I promise. And I'll find a way to smile more, like you always told me to."

He stood reluctantly, brushing a soft kiss over her cool forehead. Then Jay slipped away as quietly as he'd come, carrying the echo of the monitors' refrain with him.

Chapter Twenty-four

Detective Constable Connie Turner perched on the edge of her desk, absently twirling a lock of auburn hair around her finger as she stared at the message on her phone. The glowing screen was a beacon in the otherwise empty office, most other detectives having already left for the day. But Connie had lingered, finishing up paperwork on a recent case.

Now, the mundane details of her report were forgotten, curiosity swimming in her mossy green eyes. The message was from a detective she used to partner with at community outreach events. But seeing their name pop up so late, suggesting meeting for drinks in Gildersome of all places, was decidedly odd.

Connie bit her lip, contemplating the invitation. She hadn't socialised much with colleagues since returning to her hometown a few months back. The move was meant to be a fresh start after... well, after everything in the city fell apart. But old ghosts followed, shadows clinging to her even here. Like the faint distrust she still glimpsed in familiar faces around town.

With a sigh, Connie pushed off from the desk, the movement sending her long auburn braid swishing behind her back. She slid on her navy pea coat, fingers working the mismatched buttons into place. The coat was vintage, picked up at a local shop when she first returned to Gildersome. Connie preferred pre-loved items, each scuff or stain hinting at unknown stories.

* * *

Isabella Wood reclined against the pillows in her childhood bedroom, phone propped on her knees as Olivia babbled happily on the mattress beside her. On the screen, George's rugged features softened into an adoring smile at the sight of his girls.

"There you are, my two favourite ladies in the whole world," he rumbled, the affection and warmth evident in his tone even through the tinny speaker. Olivia gurgled gleefully at the sound of her father's voice, reaching a chubby hand toward the screen.

Isabella's heart clenched. "She misses her daddy," she said wistfully. "We both do. When can you visit next?"

George's expression turned regretful, the case lines etched around his eyes seeming to deepen. "Tomorrow night, hopefully." His gaze was tender but also worried, the threats against his family still looming. "I'll come and spoil you both rotten."

Sensing his unease, Isabella forced a playful tone. "Just don't spoil Livvy too much! She's already got you wrapped around her little finger." Isabella tilted the camera to catch Olivia crawling determinedly toward the screen, seeking her father's face.

George chuckled, the sound filled with warmth and love. "Too right. That one. She's as clever as her mum." He touched

CHAPTER TWENTY-FOUR

his fingertips to the screen. "Be good for your mummy, little one. I'll see you both very soon."

Isabella's throat tightened with emotion. Even with chaos and danger all around, this connection kept their family intact. "Stay safe, gorgeous," she implored softly. "Come back to us in one piece."

George held her gaze, verdant eyes intense even through the small screen. "Always."

* * *

The cosy interior of The Tipsy Hog enveloped Connie Turner in warmth as she stepped inside, the door thudding closed behind her. The pub's dark wood-panelled walls and low lighting created an intimate atmosphere, while the babble of patrons' cheerful chatter lent the space a pleasant feel. Connie paused just inside the entrance, hands tucked into the pockets of her fitted navy pea coat as her mossy green eyes roved over the lively scene.

The Tipsy Hog had been one of her regular haunts as a teenager, a place to nestle into the corner booths with schoolbooks spread out, soaking up the lively energy around her. Now, twelve years later, Connie found comfort in the familiarity of the surroundings. The well-worn umber leather booths lining the walls, the gleaming oak of the bar stretching along the back, the faded murals depicting countryside scenes—it was like stepping back in time.

Weaving her way through the cluster of patrons gathered near the entrance, Connie claimed an empty booth tucked in the far corner beneath a painting of grazing sheep. She slid onto the bench seat facing the door, allowing her an unobstructed view of the pub. Connie knew her colleague would be arriving shortly, though the reason for their impromptu invitation remained unclear. She sensed an air of secrecy surrounding the meeting that set her instincts humming.

While waiting, Connie unbuttoned her coat but left it on, comforted by the protective layer it provided.

Connie watched the pub's entrance discreetly as she waited, curious who might wander through on this week-night. The Tipsy Hog attracted a diverse mix of locals and regulars from surrounding villages. She recognised a few faces—Billy, the postman regaling the bartender, Nathan, with some tale, bespectacled Joyce from the library giggling with a friend in the opposite corner. Comfortingly familiar, yet distanced by the passage of years.

The pub door swung open again right on cue. Connie spotted her colleague instantly, their enthusiastic wave and crooked grin stirring conflicting emotions. She offered a slight smile in return, tamping down her misgivings. Their insistence on meeting here this late to 'talk' smacked of an agenda, one Connie wasn't sure she wished to entertain. But curiosity won out as her colleague slid into the booth opposite her.

"Thanks for coming, Connie," they enthused, scrubbing a hand through tousled hair. "Wasn't sure you'd show up on such short notice. Especially as I invited you through text."

"Of course," Connie replied lightly. "What's a quick pint between colleagues on a week-night?"

But her attempted humour felt hollow, a flimsy facade over churning unease. Connie studied her companion surreptitiously across the nicked tabletop, searching for clues to explain their furtive urgency around this meetup.

They made idle small talk as two IPAs were delivered,

condensation beading the glasses. Connie nursed hers slowly, ever observant as the conversation meandered. But the longer they danced around the subject of this impromptu gathering, the more Connie's instincts screamed something wasn't right.

Finally, her colleague leaned conspiratorially across the table, dropping their voice. "Honestly, Connie? I wanted to pick your brain about the Gildersome case."

Connie went utterly still, her IPA frozen halfway to her mouth. She lowered the glass slowly, throat constricting. "What?"

"All this renewed interest since the medals were found," her colleague continued, oblivious to Connie's reaction. "And that fourth recent crime scene matching details from the original murders..." They shook their head, eyes round with lurid fascination.

Connie's stomach soured, insides clenching at the unwelcome trip down memory lane. Even after twelve years away, Gildersome's shadows continued haunting her.

"With your history, I figured you might have insights to help my own amateur investigation," they were saying enthusiastically.

Connie stiffened, hands curling into fists in her lap beneath the table. "My history was being wrongly implicated due to coincidences," she ground out, struggling to keep her voice even. "I was cleared of all suspicion related to those cases." She paused. "You know that more than anybody."

"So why were the medals found?"

"All I have to do is scream really loud and my friends here will all come over and see what's wrong," said Connie.

Their face fell slightly. "Right, 'course, sorry. Didn't mean to dredge up bad memories." They chewed their lip. "It's just so fascinating, this killer who evaded justice and now seems to be escalating again. You heard about Sally Jenkins. Right?"

They leaned in, dropping their voice lower, excitement sparking in their eyes once more.

"Some even say the Gildersome killer never left town. That the murders twelve years back were only the beginning of something bigger. So I'd be careful if I were you."

A chill crept down Connie's spine, raw pain constricting her chest. The terror that gripped Gildersome during that string of horrific killings had nearly devoured her whole, the accusations shattering Connie's world. She still awoke some nights drenched in sweat, screams echoing in her ears.

Gently but firmly, Connie redirected the conversation to mundane topics, deflecting each attempt to probe the Gildersome case. Her colleague looked disappointed but surrendered, apparently sensing Connie had reached her limit.

They parted ways outside the cosy pub sometime later, her colleague waving enthusiastically before sauntering off into the night. Connie watched them pensively, fresh doubts swirling. What had motivated the probing into past traumas? Had this simply been an academic curiosity for them or something more?

The night air held a sobering chill, so Connie tugged her coat tighter against the creeping cold, her mind still spinning from her colleague's ominous words about the Gildersome killer.

After two IPAs on an empty stomach, tipsiness fuzzed the edges of her senses. Connie fumbled for her mobile, recognising it would be wise to call a taxi for the short ride home rather than walk in this state.

As she attempted to focus her vision on the screen to dial

CHAPTER TWENTY-FOUR

the number, the pavement seemed to tilt and sway beneath her feet. Connie staggered, bracing one hand against the brick exterior of the pub until the spell passed.

Finally, she managed to tap the taxi company's icon and bring the phone to her ear sluggishly. But just as the call connected and Connie opened her mouth to provide the address, a figure emerged from the darkness of a nearby alley.

Before she could react, the assailant was upon her, one arm hooking brutally around her throat while the other shoved a cloth over her nose and mouth.

Connie struggled desperately, terror and confusion crashing through her muddled thoughts. But the cloying chemical scent overwhelmed her senses. Against her will, an insidious greyness seeped into the edges of her vision, her limbs growing numb and uncoordinated.

As Connie slipped into unconsciousness, her mind latched onto one final, futile thought—I never should have come here alone...

Chapter Twenty-five

The faint chirp of birds stirring at sunrise gradually pulled George Beaumont from sleep. He lay still for a moment, staring up at the ceiling of his bedroom. The empty space beside him in the bed felt cavernous, the sheets cold without Isabella's comforting warmth.

With a sigh, George sat up, scrubbing a hand over his face. He already missed falling asleep and waking up entwined with his fiancée. And their baby daughter Olivia's delighted giggles were a daily dose of joy he craved. But he understood Isabella's decision to stay with her grandparents in Middleton until the danger from this case passed. Keeping his girls safe had to be the priority.

Glancing at the clock, George hauled himself out of bed. His morning workout regimen beckoned. Throwing on shorts and a vest, he made his way to the small home gym setup to start his routine.

The clank of weights and rhythmic pounding of feet on the treadmill helped clear the lingering unease from another restless night. George embraced the burn in his muscles, channelling his emotions into productive energy.

By the time an hour had passed, a sheen of sweat coated his skin but his mind felt sharper. After towelling off, George opted for a brisk shower, the hot spray easing any lingering tension.

Cleaned and refreshed, George selected one of his usual work ensembles—crisp white collared shirt paired with a smart navy suit, blond hair neatly combed. He brewed coffee but opted for a protein shake instead, gulping it down as he gathered his keys and coat.

Settling into the driver's seat of his Mercedes, George pulled out his mobile and hit Isabella's number. Her warm voice greeted him after a few rings.

"Hi gorgeous, how are you holding up?" she asked gently.

George smiled. "Morning, sweet. Doing alright. The house just feels too empty without my beautiful girls here."

Isabella made a sympathetic noise. "I know. It's so quiet here without my handsome detective to chase after Livvy while I make breakfast."

They chatted idly until George broached the subject on his mind. "So I've been thinking more about us finding a new place. Maybe a fresh start, away from the past." He hesitated. "I know the timing isn't ideal, but that house in Middleton you mentioned could be perfect."

Isabella hummed thoughtfully. "It would be nice to find our forever home. Although..." She hesitated delicately.

George's shoulders tensed. He knew she was considering the complication posed by his ex Mia still living in his East Ardsley property. Isabella said gently, "We don't have to decide now. Just promise me you'll consider what's best long-term for our family."

"Of course, sweet. You're absolutely right." George raked a hand through his hair. The last thing he wanted was to cause further hurt over his past failings as a partner and father.

Perhaps it was time to make a clean break, he mused. But doubt still gnawed at him. Jack needed stability and familiarity right now as much as possible. Tearing away the only home he'd known felt unwise, no matter how tangled George's history was with Mia. He sighed, the winding road towards resolution unclear.

"I know it's complicated, love," Isabella said gently, intuiting his turmoil. "We'll work through it together. There's no rush."

George's heart swelled with gratitude at her patience and understanding. "Have I told you lately that you're a saint for putting up with me?" he asked wryly.

Isabella's answering laugh lightened the mood. "Only about a hundred times. But feel free to remind me again." Her voice softened. "We're in this together, George. Always."

The certainty in her words anchored him. With Isabella by his side, they could weather any storm. "Together," George echoed, a vow and a promise.

After a few more tender words, they reluctantly ended the call as George pulled into the station's car park. He sat for a moment steeling himself for the challenges that awaited inside.

Stepping through the familiar doors, George felt the weight of leadership and responsibility settle fully upon his shoulders once more. Lives hung jeopardy, and his team was relying on him to guide them through the darkness. He could not afford to waver.

Striding into the Incident Room, George was greeted by his detectives' determined faces. There was fear and fatigue shadowing their eyes, but resolve still burned bright.

CHAPTER TWENTY-FIVE

* * *

Luke Mason rolled over with a muffled groan, squinting against the sunlight filtering through the curtains. Beside him, Elaine remained curled on her side; wispy grey hair fanned over the pillow. Luke stroked a hand down her arm, exhaling heavily.

"Morning, love," he rumbled, voice still gravelly with sleep.

Elaine stirred, blinking up at him in momentary confusion until recognition cleared the fog in her pale eyes. She managed a faint smile. "Luke... you stayed."

His chest constricted at the surprise in her voice. This illness made her lose track of so much lately. Made her forget he never left her side now except when duty called.

"Of course I stayed, Laney," Luke soothed, thumb grazing her cheek. Elaine just gazed up at him for a long moment before her eyes began to drift closed again. Luke's heart fractured a bit more.

He slipped quietly from the bed, pulling on a t-shirt and padding to the kitchen. The specialist's words echoing in his mind were an unrelenting refrain—the dementia was advancing rapidly now. Elaine's moments of lucidity were fleeting, her frail body failing.

Luke braced his hands on the counter, head bowed under the weight pressing down. Each day brought Elaine's decline, their dwindling time ticking away. He was losing her by increments to this cruel thief stealing her memories, her essence.

And yet Luke still clung to hope of halting fate's steady march. Just a little longer, please, he begged the universe. Grant them a few more days before the light in Elaine's eyes dimmed forever. He would pay any price for a reprieve from this excruciating helplessness.

Straightening, Luke inhaled a steeling breath. He forced his despair down deep and compartmentalised, walling it off. Today, Elaine was still here; he would cherish each fractured moment. The rest they would face when it came.

Squaring his shoulders, Luke prepared Elaine's tea just how she preferred and brought it to her along with toast and jam. Her responding smile upon seeing the tray ignited a brief flare of warmth in Luke's aching chest.

"My beautiful Laney," he murmured, carding a hand through her wispy hair. Luke kept his tone light, reminiscing on cheerier days as they shared a simple breakfast. All else could wait—the doom creeping closer, his own conflicted heart. For now, Elaine was still here. And Luke would soak up every second fate allowed them.

* * *

Alexis Mercer awoke to something tickling her face. She blinked groggily in the pale morning light, vision focusing on her daughter Georgia's hand resting inches from her nose. The 11-year-old must have crept under the covers in the night again, as was her habit when unsettled.

Propping herself up on one elbow, Alexis gazed down at her daughter's angelic face, all her fierce maternal love welling up. Georgia looked so peaceful in sleep; the usual tension smoothed away. Awake, her beautiful mind never stopped churning, struggling to process the stimuli bombarding her. But like this, she seemed free for a moment.

Alexis gently smoothed back Georgia's mussed blonde curls,

CHAPTER TWENTY-FIVE

heart aching. Her brave, brilliant little girl wrestled daily with challenges most couldn't fathom. Yet she persevered, finding wonder in small joys—the texture of a fuzzy blanket, the colours in a kaleidoscope, the rhythm of raindrops on the window. Georgia was Alexis' inspiration to appreciate the snippets of beauty around them, no matter how dark things seemed.

Leaning down, Alexis placed a feather-light kiss on her daughter's forehead. "I love you to the moon and back, baby girl," she whispered. Georgia's only response was a soft sigh, features perfectly relaxed. Alexis treasured these glimpses of her little one at peace.

As carefully as possible, Alexis slid from the bed to avoid waking Georgia. She lingered a moment more, imprinting this image of tranquillity in her mind. Then Alexis slipped from the room to prepare Georgia's favourite hot chocolate and breakfast.

* * *

The persistent hum of ringing phones and rapid clicking of keyboards permeated the Incident Room as the investigation team gathered around the central table. The space felt charged with restless energy, the detectives eager to make headway on leads even as fatigue shadowed their tense features.

At the head of the table, Detective Chief Inspector George Beaumont straightened the already orderly stacks of notes before him. But his jaw remained tight with tension as his thoughts strayed constantly back to Isabella and Olivia. Were they truly safe staying with Isabella's grandparents? He gnawed his lip, second-guessing the protection protocols in place.

George forced himself to tune back into the conversation as Detective Constable Alexis Mercer presented the latest findings on their prime suspect, Ethan Holloway. He noticed the strain around her eyes as she detailed the exhaustive search efforts coming up empty. No trace of Holloway in any government or medical system for over a decade now. He might as well have vanished into thin air after his prison release.

"It's like chasing a ghost," Alexis concluded with a frustrated huff, raking a hand through her golden hair. "I can't find anything at all!"

Around the table, the mood grew even more sombre at this update. They had hoped the renewed focus on Holloway would finally yield his location after so many fruitless years.

Detective Inspector Luke Mason scrubbed at the fresh stubble lining his jaw. "Bastard must've reinvented himself under the radar. New name, new documents and all." He shook his head bitterly. "Needle in a bloody haystack trying to sniff him out now."

Alexis turned her piercing blue eyes on George. "We've exhausted all conventional search methods, sir. Where do we go from here?" The others regarded him expectantly as well.

George blinked, realising he'd missed Alexis' question, thoughts consumed once more with concern for Isabella and Olivia's well-being. He hesitated, grasping for an appropriate response.

Alexis' head tilted, reading his distraction instantly. She spoke gently, "Is everything alright, sir? We're happy to pick this up another time if you need a break."

The others glanced between them, noting the exchange.

George cursed internally, hating that he was letting personal anxiety disrupt the briefing. He forced what he hoped was a reassuring expression. "I'm fine, just worn down like the rest of you. Let's keep the momentum going."

Alexis looked unconvinced but simply nodded. "It's your family, isn't it?" she asked.

George nodded.

"You're worried about them," she said softly. "Understandably so, given the threats. But we'll find who's responsible, sir. Try not to let it consume you."

George scrubbed a hand down his bearded jaw. "I could say the same to you, Alexis," he said. "Why are you here? Why are you not with Georgia?"

"She's safe at school," Alexis said with a shrug. "It's the safest place for her to be fair. And DSU Smith has amended my hours so I can leave to pick her up."

Alexis' directness took him aback. But he appreciated her empathy and discretion. The compassion in her azure eyes reminded him of Isabella.

"Makes sense," George acknowledged. "And being here will take your mind off her. Right?" He offered Alexis a grateful glance before briskly redirecting the conversation.

"Right."

"OK, where were we? Detective Constable Scott, any insights from informants on Holloway's potential aliases or recent activities?"

The team followed George's lead in resuming the briefing, but he sensed their lingering concern. He was grateful no one openly objected to his obvious distraction. Though he knew he needed to compartmentalize better with so much at stake.

As the meeting progressed, George's thoughts continued

drifting to Isabella and Olivia. Was Smith providing secret surveillance of them, as he had for Alexis? The lack of transparency gnawed at George, but he recognised the logic in discretion. Still, the urge to personally ensure his girls' safety itched relentlessly beneath the surface.

When they finally adjourned, George pulled Alexis aside discreetly. His voice was low and tense. "Thank you for understanding earlier. My mind hasn't been fully here..." He trailed off, jaw tightening.

Alexis touched his arm lightly. "No need to explain, sir. Your family's safety is priority one." She held his gaze unflinchingly and then smiled softly. "Believe me, I know all about that."

Chapter Twenty-six

Detective Superintendent Jim Smith's secretary waved George straight through with an understanding smile. He wondered fleetingly how many other spouses and partners had sat in her chair anxiously awaiting updates over the years.

Smith stood from behind his wide oak desk to greet George, his salt and pepper hair neatly combed as always. But his eyes were shadowed with fatigue, telling of the toll this case took on them all.

"George, come in. What's the latest from your team downstairs?" Smith asked without preamble.

George sank into the chair across from him with a frustrated sigh. "No progress on Holloway's current identity or location yet. He's a ghost for all intents and purposes." George scrubbed a hand through his hair. "My team is hitting dead end after dead end trying to trace him over the past decade."

Smith hummed pensively, leaning back in his chair. "So he reinvented himself completely after your suspicions before. Not surprising for someone that twisted." His grey eyes sharpened on George. "But we knew this bastard would be tough to sniff out when we reopened the case. Keep at it."

George nodded tightly. "I know, sir. But with two lives hanging in the balance now, I'm feeling the urgency personally." He met Smith's knowing gaze. "Are my family under discreet surveillance? After the home invasion—"

Smith held up a placating hand. "Don't worry yourself over that right now. Just stay focused on the investigation." He offered a thin smile that didn't reach his eyes. "We're handling security protocols."

George bit back a flare of annoyance. He needed certainty Isabella and Olivia were truly protected, not more evasions. But challenging Smith's authority was unwise, so he simply nodded curtly. They would revisit this issue soon, whether the Superintendent wished to or not.

Smith briskly changed topics. "We need fresh angles on Holloway if digital records are turning up nothing. You've got skilled investigators downstairs. Have them start re-interviewing known associates from his past crimes."

George leaned forward. "Actually, Alexis Mercer mentioned she has imaging software that can digitally age photographs to show how Holloway may appear today. It could really help with canvassing potential sightings."

"Excellent initiative," Smith said approvingly. "Put Mercer on the photograph straight away. This is our best bet for a break right now."

As George stood to leave, reluctant to let his earlier concerns about Alistair Atkinson go unvoiced, Smith pinned him with a sharp look. "Remember, Holloway stays the priority. No veering off on personal vendettas, George. The evidence will lead us to the truth."

What evidence? George thought as he bristled internally at the warning. He kept his tone neutral when he said, "Of course, sir. My team understands that Holloway is our prime suspect."

CHAPTER TWENTY-SIX

Inwardly, though, George still harboured suspicions about Atkinson's potential involvement. But challenging Smith's directives now seemed unwise, even if it was confusing George. He could only quietly work other angles in hopes of uncovering corroborating evidence against Atkinson and his connections.

Descending the stairs, George girded himself mentally to lead the briefing. Focusing his team's energy productively was crucial despite his own lingering distractions. He refused to fail Candy and Alexis like he had past victims.

As George outlined the plan to have Alexis age Holloway's image to aid the search, his detectives absorbed the instructions with a sombre focus. Around the room, fatigued faces lifted with fragile hope at this new strategy. George let that shared sense of purpose centre him. By coming together, they would navigate this darkness.

Alexis readily agreed to take point generating the aged likenesses. Luke and Tashan began compiling comprehensive lists of Holloway's known associates to re-question, hoping time had loosened lips. The palpable gloom of recent days cautiously gave way to renewed momentum.

After George dismissed the team to pursue their assignments, Alexis lingered, straightening the piles of reports spread before her. When the others had departed, she met George's eyes directly.

"We're going to find him, sir," she said simply. Her unwavering faith heartened George like sunlight piercing storm clouds. "However long it takes, Holloway will make a mistake. And we'll be ready."

George nodded, throat tightening unexpectedly.

***

George stood at the head of the Incident Room, broad shoulders squared, prepared to provide direction to his team. But before he could speak, the door swung open abruptly.

Detective Sergeant Yolanda Williams strode in, face flushed from rushing up from the digital forensics lab. "Sorry to interrupt, sir, but I have something critical," she announced without preamble.

George nodded for her to proceed, interest sharpening his rugged features. The others turned in their seats to give Yolanda their full attention.

"Security footage retrieved from a betting shop neighbouring the sandwich shop where DC Nichols was assaulted," Yolanda explained rapidly. "Their camera captured the attack from across the street."

She quickly queued up the video on the monitor along the back wall. The team crowded around, a palpable tension gripping them as the footage began rolling.

The busy pedestrian street scene looked innocuous at first. Then, a figure in dark clothing with a hood up could be seen striding purposefully through the midday crowds. They trailed closely behind a woman the team instantly recognised, despite her back being to the camera, as Candy from her distinctive mane of red curls.

When Candy stopped to check her watch, the ominous figure seized the opportunity and closed the gap swiftly. Before anyone could react, a vicious blow landed squarely between Candy's shoulders. Cries erupted from surrounding pedestrians as she collapsed to her hands and knees. But her attacker had already yanked their hood up and melted back

CHAPTER TWENTY-SIX

into the throngs of people.

"Can we get a clear shot of the bastard's face?" Luke Mason demanded gruffly.

Yolanda shook her head, frustration etching her features. "No. The hood and angle obscure it completely."

The team absorbed this disappointing update, watching grimly as good Samaritans on the video footage helped Candy to her feet before the ambulance arrived. It was difficult witnessing the violence inflicted so ruthlessly on their colleague and friend. It also made him doubt the culprit was Atkinson. They were too small.

"Right then," George said decisively, snapping them out of their dark reflections. "We need uniforms re-canvassing that entire street straight away, focusing on businesses with exterior cameras. Somebody else must have caught a better angle on our attacker."

Yolanda stepped forward eagerly. "Let DC Scott and I coordinate the canvas, sir. We'll go door-to-door along the full block if that's what it takes."

Her assertiveness surprised George, accustomed to Yolanda's reserved demeanour. But he sensed her determination to take more initiative on the case, perhaps feeling eclipsed by Alexis' rapid rise. George knew such professional jealousies were common; he would need to foster cooperation between the two driven women.

"Excellent initiative, DS Williams," George affirmed. "You and Scott work closely with Sergeant Greenwood's team to widen the CCTV search. Leave no stone unturned."

Jay Scott perked up at the prospect of pairing with Yolanda, his innate friendliness balancing her cool professionalism. "You got it, boss. We won't come back until we ID the scumbag who hurt Candy."

Yolanda shot him a quelling look, but George understood the young man's thirst for justice. It echoed the fierce protectiveness boiling in his own chest.

"Just remember, safety first out there," George cautioned. "We don't need anyone else getting ambushed because we let emotions override caution. Approach each person professionally but gently. And go out in pairs!"

Yolanda nodded curtly while Jay bobbed his affable head in acknowledgement. But George glimpsed the determined set of their jaws beneath the deferential demeanours. They would probe relentlessly until Candy's assailant was brought to light.

As the pair departed to assemble the canvassing teams, George surveyed the remaining detectives. "Right. In their absence, we proceed digging into Holloway's history. There must be clues about his present-day identity we've overlooked."

Around the table, fatigued bodies straightened with renewed purpose. The video footage was sickening, but it had injected fresh urgency into the stagnated case. George clutched that fragile momentum like a lifeline. Each minute that passed could bring them closer to exposing whoever was behind the vicious assault on Candy—and, by extension, the threats against all of them.

United by the shared mission, the team dispersed to their individual assignments. Step by step, they would tighten the net around the shadowy culprit. And their unwavering dedication gave George faith that, together, they would drag the perpetrator into the light and see justice done. The risks they faced daily only strengthened their camaraderie and

CHAPTER TWENTY-SIX

courage when challenged. And they would need every ounce of both to defeat the gathering darkness.

* * *

The faint hum of the radiator was the only sound piercing the silence of George Beaumont's office. He sat hunched at his desk, poring over the sparse notes and forensic reports related to the perplexing medals discovered at the crime scenes. Fatigue blurred the words on the pages as evening shadows stretched across his office. But George stubbornly resisted the urge to rub his gritty eyes, fearful of losing his tenuous grasp on the elusive clues.

The shrill ring of his mobile phone nearly made him jump. Snatching it up eagerly, George saw the call was from the forensics lab. "Maya, tell me you've got something," he greeted without preamble, pulse already quickening. Even a fragment of new evidence could re-energize the stagnated case.

Forensic scientist Maya Chen's voice was apologetic but tinged with excitement. "Sorry for the delay analysing those medallions, DCI Beaumont. The intricate designs and unique metal composition required expert consultation." She paused, and George could practically hear her weighing how to frame a significant discovery.

"But using scanning electron microscopy and comparative analyses, we established a definitive link between all four medallions." Maya's words came faster, unable to contain the revelation any longer. "The expert we consulted identified them as badges worn exclusively by members of an obscure fraternal organization called the White Rose League. They were active here in Leeds in the late 1980s and 90s."

George straightened abruptly, sending his chair wheeling back from the sudden movement. This was the first promising break in days. "The White Rose League, you said? What more do we know about them?" He began hastily scribbling notes, thoughts already churning through implications—was the League connected to the White Roses, a group Grimes investigated back in his early days on the force?

"Very little, unfortunately," Maya admitted regretfully. "They seemed to operate in secrecy, leaving minimal records behind. But our analyst indicated exclusive membership was limited solely to detectives within the police force at that time."

George's pen stilled as he absorbed this. The police. Detectives. Secrecy. He thought of Sally Jenkins, her recording, and Alistair Atkinson. His gut urged caution at the alarming possibilities.

"We're digging through archives and historical department records for more details on the League," Maya was saying. "And discreetly reaching out to retired personnel who may recall something about their activities back then."

George leaned back in his chair, scrubbing a hand over his bearded jaw. "Right. Well, excellent work, Maya. This connection, however tenuous now, could prove pivotal if we can illuminate it further."

After expressing his profound thanks for her diligence, George ended the call, weariness momentarily forgotten. His gaze fell to the four photographs of worn medallions pinned to the case board. What sinister secrets might you reveal if given voice? he mused grimly.

Mind racing, George began jotting down conduits for imme-

CHAPTER TWENTY-SIX

diate exploration. He would instruct Tashan to comb methodically through archived department records for any glimpses of this White Rose League. Yolanda and Jay could subtly probe retirees from that era, seeking whispered knowledge of the group's existence and activities without causing alarm just yet.

And—George tapped his pen decisively—they needed an urgent team briefing to assimilate this new intelligence. Fresh eyes examining the implications could spark investigative angles not apparent to him in isolation.

Pushing up from his desk, George rolled his shoulders to alleviate the strain of hunching over files for endless hours. He needed to shake off the creeping defeatism and refocus his energies on the hunt. Maya's breakthrough was the jolt they needed to re-engage a case that had grown stagnant and convoluted, so he headed to their Incident Room.

"I know the last few days have been frustrating, filled with dead ends that sap our energy," George began sombrely. "But staying focused on the truth is imperative, even when the path there is obscured."

He held each of their gazes in turn, radiating quiet empathy. "Perseverance gets results."

Around the table, heads lifted marginally at his words. The gloom did not lift entirely, but George glimpsed a fragile spark of renewed purpose kindling in their eyes. It was something to nurture going forward.

Turning first to Tashan Blackburn, George invited updates, keeping his tone light but firm. "Let's recap recent developments, see if we can spot any openings we've overlooked. Tashan, your team revisited Grimes' place in Gildersome yesterday?"

Tashan exhaled heavily, an acknowledgement of disappointment even before he voiced it. "Yes, but it was a dead end. The house was abandoned weeks ago. Neighbours had nothing useful to add." He spread his hands. "Apologies, but it seems a wasted effort."

George nodded solemnly. "You did well to follow through. Now we can decisively refocus our resources elsewhere." He offered an encouraging glance, hoping to temper Tashan's discouragement. Morale was fragile enough without dwelling on lost time chasing empty leads.

As the briefing continued, each update highlighted how entrenched their frustrations had become. Records on Leonard Beedham proved opaque, merely placing him briefly with Arthur Grimes but providing no substantive leads. Likewise, extensive background checks on Beedham and his known associates kept turning up nothing suspicious or illuminating.

When Luke Mason and Yolanda Williams described exhausting all avenues with Ethan Holloway's inner circle to no avail, George felt the creeping weight of futility threatening to smother the room's atmosphere entirely. He understood now the hushed voices and defeated shoulders that had greeted him earlier.

"This damned phantom Corsa that's taunting us but leaving no solid trace," Jay Scott was saying when George tuned back in, having drifted into pensive thought. "The enhanced photo didn't give us any definite location to scrutinise. I'm running out of ideas, boss." He brushed back an errant strand of brown hair; frustration etched in his boyish features.

George absorbed this final dead end with a slow exhale, leaning back in his seat. The hollow silences awaiting his response echoed loudly in the confined space. He saw the

CHAPTER TWENTY-SIX

flagging hope in his team's faces, their relentless efforts rewarded only with frustration. Boosting their battered morale would take finesse, care, and honesty.

Rising from his seat, George moved to stand before the evidence board, the team swivelling to follow him. "I understand why the constant setbacks feel dispiriting," he began, letting his gaze trace over the photos of victims and suspects pinned there.

"But we cannot measure our success only in breakthroughs. Progress lives also in the thoroughness, the determination we bring to each lead, no matter how tenuous." He turned back to face them directly. "What matters most now is retaining belief in the purpose guiding our steps. OK?"

Around the room, spines straightened almost imperceptibly as his words resonated. George pressed onward, bolstered by the responsiveness.

When George finally resumed his seat, the atmosphere had lightened, if only marginally. His words seemed to have rekindled the gutted candle flames of determination in his team. There was a shared purpose, realigning their fatigued bodies toward hope again.

"The second reason I wanted you here was to share that we've had a major forensic development," George announced without preamble. His commanding voice carried a current of urgency that compelled attention. Detectives halted conversations, heads swivelling towards their superior.

George surveyed the room, ensuring he had their complete focus. "The medals we recovered have been conclusively linked to a secretive fraternal organization called the White Rose League." He paused, letting the significance permeate the heavy silence.

"They were active here in Leeds during the eighties and nineties until apparently disbanding, leaving minimal information behind," George elaborated. Around the room, his team absorbed this bombshell revelation with startled looks.

Detective Constable Tashan Blackburn broke the uneasy silence. "Do we know who the members were or what activities this League engaged in, sir?" His rich baritone rang with analytical curiosity. Trust Tashan to spear straight to pragmatic questions.

George's mouth flattened into a sombre line. "Very little so far. But clarifying those points is now priority one." He surveyed the room, shoulders squared with conviction.

His words resonated through the cramped space. George glimpsed his own steely determination mirrored back in the eyes of his team. Good—they understood the gravity of pursuing justice, even within their own ranks.

Turning to Tashan, George began issuing directives. "Tashan, I need you mining department archives for any references to the White Rose League. Comb personnel registers, case logs, anything that could indicate who was involved."

Tashan dipped his head. "Consider it done. I'll cross-reference names, dates, and locations, following any threads connecting to this group." George knew Tashan's methodical nature made him perfect for unravelling obscure historical details.

Next, George addressed the cocksure Jay Scott and level-headed Yolanda Williams. "You two will discreetly reach out to retired personnel from the eighties and nineties. See what whispers you can gather about this secret brotherhood."

Jay grinned, rubbing his hands together in anticipation,

CHAPTER TWENTY-SIX

while Yolanda offered a curt nod. "We'll keep things subtle, boss," Jay affirmed, to which Yolanda added pointedly, "No need to stir up trouble before we know more."

George acknowledged her prudence with an approving glance. He would need Yolanda's composure to balance Jay's over-eager tendencies during sensitive inquiries.

"This requires utmost discretion," George stressed, holding them both in his piercing green gaze. "We don't want our questions getting back to the wrong ears prematurely." The warning resonated through the room, the team nodding solemnly. Probing the dark recesses of their own force's history would require delicate steps.

Resuming his pacing, George surveyed the tense faces around him. "Time is critical. This White Rose League likely holds the key to definitively connecting our cold cases to present-day events. Find me something actionable fast."

The briefing concluded with a flurry of movement as his detectives sprang into action. George tracked Tashan gathering notebooks and historical case logs with focused intensity. Yolanda and Jay huddled, heads bent in intense discussion, no doubt strategising their approach to interviewing cagey retired personnel.

Chapter Twenty-seven

Detective Inspector Luke Mason called out as George passed. "Those background checks on Sally's boyfriend came up empty. Nothing out of the ordinary there that could explain her disappearance."

George nodded curtly in acknowledgement without slowing his stride. Liam Rhodes had seemed genuinely troubled by Sally's disappearance when Alexis interviewed him. Still, they needed to investigate every possibility in her inner circle, no matter how unlikely.

The familiar chaos of the shared office greeted George as he strode briskly through the door. His sharp gaze swept over the crowded space, the ringing phones and clicking keyboards fading to background noise. It had been a long day of chasing the sparse few leads in the Sally Jenkins case without results. George craved the quiet of his personal office for some uninterrupted thinking before another gruelling team briefing.

Finally reaching his office door, George slipped inside and eased it shut, muffling the persistent ringing and low voices. Sinking into his worn leather chair, he allowed his eyes to drift closed for a moment. But his mind continued churning relentlessly, gnawing at the confounding lack of leads or

CHAPTER TWENTY-SEVEN

forensic evidence.

With a sigh, George straightened and woke his computer. Might as well catch up on emails while he had a free moment, he thought. Perhaps one would yield a surprise breakthrough.

He clicked through the usual mundane department announcements and meeting invites. One subject line caught his eye—'Postmortem Findings: Sally Jenkins' from Lindsey Yardley. His pulse quickened.

The pathologist's overview was concise but thorough in documenting her examination and evidence collection. George carefully scanned the details, picturing each step in his mind. There wasn't much different to what they already knew.

The email concluded with mention of coarse fibres discovered in Sally's mouth, indicating a crude attempt to gag her. Lindsey noted the samples had been rushed to the lab for expedited analysis.

An attached message from Maya Chen detailed the results— the fibres were identified as originating from a silk tie. The lack of manufacturer tags or unique stitching meant the exact scarf could not be traced. But its improvised usage as a gag stood out given the precise and methodical nature of the strangulation.

George leaned back in his chair, contemplating the implications. A makeshift tie gag suggested opportunism by Sally's attacker, possibly contradicting the controlled and meticulous way she was strangled. This apparent inconsistency intrigued George and was a detail worth probing further.

The strangulation indicated preparation, while the spur-of-the-moment gag implied hastily silencing an unexpected outcry from Sally. George's sharp investigative instincts told him that dichotomy could prove pivotal in reconstructing the chain of events preceding her death. The truth often lay in subtle contradictions.

Scrolling down, George spied another new message from Maya Chen that explained the lab had rushed analysis on the distinctive red and black polyester fibres discovered. Experts identified the material as a polyester blend commonly used for school uniforms.

Maya noted regretfully that the generic fibre composition matched uniforms from over twenty different schools in Leeds alone and countless more nationwide. Without unique dyes, weave patterns, or manufacturer tags, tracing the fibres to a specific location or uniform would be impossible.

George's initial surge of anticipation evaporated as he absorbed this latest dead end. Twenty schools, most likely a mix of primary and secondary, were far too many people to interview and look into. The tantalising clue of fibres now appeared merely another fruitless thread. He leaned back with a frustrated sigh, scrubbing a hand down his bearded jaw.

The ubiquity of the school uniform fibres meant they likely originated anywhere in the country. No definitive location could be traced—just another vague, impossible-to-decipher taunt from their sadistic tormentor.

The more George turned the scant evidence over in his mind, the more convinced he became this clue had been left deliberately. The killer knew the indistinct fibres would send them chasing futile leads and breed doubt. Psychological manipulation seemed fundamental to his vicious sport.

Jaw set, George resolutely tamped down the insidious frustration. This only strengthened his resolve to keep digging. However cunning their opponent, a persistent bloodhound would eventually sniff out the truth. And George could be relentlessly patient when justice was at stake.

After jotting down detailed notes, George typed quick replies to both Maya and Lindsey. He expressed profound gratitude for their exhaustive efforts while requesting notification immediately if further insights arose.

George understood that answers rarely emerged from nothing. They were gradually woven together through each investigator's unique skills and determination. Pathologists, forensic scientists, detectives—each played an integral role in constructing the elusive narrative. By weaving together multiple threads, the truth slowly emerged.

Leaning back in his chair, coffee forgotten and long-cold, George contemplated his next steps. He decided the team would need to be briefed on these updates immediately. Perhaps the fresh perspectives of his diverse detectives could glean angles or possibilities he failed to identify. There was always value in collective wisdom when grappling with complex puzzles.

The phantom image of Sally Jenkins seemed to hover at the edge of George's awareness, a reminder of the flesh-and-blood woman reduced to a case number and grim crime scene. He had not known Sally well, yet felt the profound duty to illuminate the tragic circumstances surrounding her death. She deserved justice, and George would walk through fire if that's what it took to unravel the sinister truth.

Rolling his shoulders to ease the building tension, George gathered up his notebook and stale coffee. The answers were waiting somewhere in the sparse evidence recovered so far. Each cryptic detail was a clue whispering the solution if they listened closely enough. And George knew his team would probe tirelessly beside him until the whispers swelled to a deafening chorus of truth that could no longer be ignored.

Justice required great patience and resilience. But when paired with unwavering dedication, the light of truth would emerge, no matter how long and serpentine the path leading to it. Head high, George pushed open his office door to brief the waiting team. There was much yet to unravel, but they would untangle it together, one fragile thread at a time. He was certain of that much.

Chapter Twenty-eight

The persistent hum of the heating unit was the only sound piercing the silence of George Beaumont's office. Evening shadows stretched across his desk as he sat hunched over personnel files and forensic reports. But despite the lateness of the hour, sleep remained out of reach while concern for his injured team member lingered.

Scrubbing a weary hand down his bearded face, George reached for his mobile. He pulled up Jay Scott's contact and hit dial, knowing the affable young detective was staying by Candy's side.

Jay answered briskly after two rings, his naturally buoyant voice subdued but still underlaid with its characteristic warmth. "Boss! Everything alright?"

"Just calling for an update on Candy," George replied, tension creeping into his gravelly baritone. "Wanted to check in given the severity of her injuries. How is she doing?"

Jay's response carried a trace of relief, hinting at the depth of his own unease. "She's pretty banged up and exhausted, but you know our Candy—tough as old boots. Doctors have given the OK for her to go home as long as she's got someone to help out."

George leaned back in his chair, scrubbing a hand down

his bearded jaw. "That's reassuring to hear. Glad she's been discharged home if she's stable enough." He knew Candy's independent spirit would baulk at extended hospital confinement.

"Yeah, I'll be staying over at hers for a few days to keep an eye on things," Jay affirmed. George heard the devotion beneath the casual words and felt a pang of empathy.

"I appreciate you looking after her, Jay," George said sincerely. "Please pass along my warm regards to Candy. And let her know her teammates are all wishing her a swift recovery."

"Will do, boss!" Jay promised. "I know it'll lift her spirits to hear you checked in personally."

After exchanging a few more words, George ended the call, comforted by the positive update. Knowing Candy was safely recovering and surrounded by support eased some of the helplessness still churning inside him. But an undercurrent of fury lingered beneath his calm facade. Whoever dared harm his officer so sadistically would not evade justice for long, George silently vowed.

Leaning back in his desk chair in the muted solitude of his office, the day's stresses weighed heavily on George's shoulders. He pressed the heels of his hands against tired eyes, mind drifting. So much uncertainty still swirled around Candy's vicious assault and the threats that continued plaguing his team. He despised feeling constantly two steps behind an invisible enemy.

Yet in times like these, their solidarity and loyalty to one another shone brightest, George mused. No matter how dark the forces allying against them, the bonds between his team would prevail. Their commitment to protecting each other

CHAPTER TWENTY-EIGHT

and serving justice did not falter, even amidst profound fear and doubt. It was that unrelenting spirit that would guide them through the darkness.

And so George clung to cautious optimism rather than dread in this quiet moment. Each small comfort and show of encouragement were beacons lighting the way forward through the surrounding gloom. Step by step, they would find their way through together. George just prayed the road ahead would lead not to further pain but to long-awaited justice and closure.

After ending the call with Jay, George Beaumont lingered at his desk, gazing pensively into the empty shadows of his office. The relief upon learning of Candy's recovery only partially eased the tumultuous emotions swirling within him— lingering helplessness, smouldering rage at her unknown attacker, gnawing worry for his team's safety.

Scrubbing a hand down his bearded jaw, George considered his options for the evening. Part of him craved the mindless escape of going straight home to collapse into oblivious sleep. But the thought of the empty house only amplified his isolation and stress.

Making a decisive choice, George powered down his computer and gathered his coat and keys. He would make a quick stop for some hot takeaway and then head to the comforting sanctuary of family. Even a short visit could recharge his flagging spirit.

The aromatic scent of hot fish and chips filled the car on the brief drive to Isabella's grandparents' house. George felt his tense shoulders already loosening in anticipation of seeing his girls. He hadn't realised how much he needed this until now.

Pulling up outside the modest brick home, George smiled seeing Isabella's grandmother Anne peeking through the lace curtains. After Anne's friendly greetings and enthusiastic hug, George followed her down the cosy hallway lined with family photos.

"Eric's just nodding off in the living room," Anne said over her shoulder. "But Izzy and the little one are so excited you're here! It's a lovely surprise."

Before George could reply, hurried footsteps preceded Isabella appearing cradling a delighted Olivia. George's heart swelled at the sight.

"Look Livvy, Daddy's here!" Isabella cooed. Olivia babbled gleefully, pudgy hands grabbing for the grease-stained bag of takeaway.

Chuckling, George relieved Isabella of Olivia's wriggling weight and kissed his daughter's round cheek. "Keen nose on this one. Definitely takes after her mum." He shot Isabella a playful wink.

Isabella just rolled her eyes, smile radiant. "It's so good to see you, gorgeous." She wrapped her arms around George and Olivia in a fierce embrace.

The stresses of the day melted away at that moment. Tension seeped from George's body as he held his girls close, breathing in the comforting scents of lavender shampoo and baby powder. This was what truly mattered, he was reminded – life and light.

Over steaming fish and chips at the kitchen table with Isabella and Anne, George almost felt transported back to simpler times before darkness invaded their haven. Laughter flowed easily again in the welcoming warmth of family.

And when Olivia curled against his chest, George cradled

her close, savouring this stolen moment of peace. He pressed a soft kiss to her downy hair as she dozed. Here, with his most cherished loved ones, he remembered who he was fighting for and why he could never give up hope.

The visit was a balm to George's battered spirit, replenishing reserves of resilience to face the challenges ahead. Too soon, he was reluctantly bundling a sleepy Olivia into her cot.

Isabella's playful voice at the doorway drew George's gaze up as he finished tucking a sleeping Olivia into her cot. "Leaving me so soon, Detective Inspector Beaumont?"

Despite the strains of the day, George felt the corners of his mouth curve into an answering smile. "Wouldn't dream of it, future Beaumont," he replied warmly, matching her light-hearted tone. After one last gentle caress of his daughter's downy hair, George padded into the hall, pulling the door partially closed behind him.

Isabella was waiting, hands tucked into the back pockets of her fitted jeans, eyes dancing with mischief and affection. Just being near her had tension already seeping from George's shoulders.

Taking his hand, Isabella led him along the short hallway and down the stairs to the cosy living room. The golden glow of the table lamp cast a welcoming ambience over the well-worn furniture and family photos lining the walls.

As George settled onto the sofa, Isabella curled into his side, tucking her legs beneath her. The comforting familiarity of her body tucked against his kindled a profound sense of peace and homecoming.

They sat in easy silence for a few moments, George idly twirling a lock of Isabella's dark hair between his fingers, but the tension in George's shoulders lingered. Then Isabella tipped her head back to study his pensive expression. "That case still weighing on your mind, gorgeous?" she asked knowingly.

George nodded, exhaling heavily. Isabella had always been able to read him so effortlessly. "Just feeling frustrated by all the dead ends lately. We finally got a solid forensic lead today, but it opened up more questions than answers."

"Tell me all about it," she said gently, wrapping George in a fierce hug. He sighed, leaning into her embrace, the day's stresses seeping away in her arms.

"We're just continually hitting dead ends," he admitted when they parted. "I know we're missing a vital piece that connects everything. But damned if I can figure out what it is."

George began recounting the convoluted details that plagued him. The missing retired DI Arthur Grimes and his hidden office... The mysterious Vauxhall Corsa tied to retired Inspector Langton... Sally Jenkins' explosive claims against Atkinson, and George's own fears about his colleague... The cryptic insinuations from the retired judge. With each twist revealed, he saw Isabella listening more intently, eyes sharp.

"Izzy, what is it?" George asked when he finally paused for breath. "You look like... you look guilty of something."

"I've been working on something, something behind your back," Isabella said, holding up the palm of her hand to stop George from interrupting her. "But let me explain, OK?"

George simply nodded.

"Thank you." She paused. "Where to begin?" She rolled her tongue across her lips as she began, "I've been thinking about how I could help you solve the case, and I figured the best way to do that was to figure out whether the cold cases you were looking into and the recent death were committed by the same killer."

"We had the same thoughts back at the station," admitted George.

"And what did you come up with?" asked Izzy.

"Not much other than the lack of medals at the recent crime scene and the apparent disregard of said medals at the three crime scenes from twelve years ago," George explained.

"By forensics, you mean?" asked Isabella, and George nodded. "I have a theory about that."

"Go on."

"I think whoever handled the search team twelve years ago disregarded the medals on purpose," Isabella explained.

"That makes sense as Detective Foster found one at the Bramley Woods murder scene in the nineties that also didn't get logged as evidence," George said.

"Which suggests the same murderer and similar murders being covered up, right?" asked Izzy.

"I guess," said George. He explained about the White Rose League and Operation Redwood.

"I know about them both already," she said. "So I've been looking into Laura Hughes, Sarah Jennings, Emily Thompson, and Sally Jenkins, to see what the common denominator is."

"How?"

"I've been trading favours with old friends in Wakefield," she explained.

"What the hell, Izzy?"

"Don't get mad, just listen."

"How can I not get mad?" He paused. "Did you leave the house?"

She nodded.

"You're supposed to be at Anne and Eric's looking after Olivia. You're supposed to be here, safe. You know my team has been personally attacked. What the hell!"

"Please, George," she requested, scrunching her nose.

George said, "I'm not promising anything. Just tell me."

"Alistair Atkinson is one dodgy bastard," was all she said.

George frowned. "Tell me something I don't already know."

"He's involved in this. I'm sure." She paused. "Even if he's not the killer, he knows more about the case than what he's letting on."

"Go on," he prompted, a note of wry curiosity in his tone.

Isabella hesitated. "I've been discreetly looking into the four victims' backgrounds, including digging through old personnel records and case files." She took a breath before continuing. "Turns out, Laura, Sarah, Emily, and Sally all lodged formal complaints early in their careers against the same senior officer—Alistair Atkinson."

George stiffened, eyes narrowed. "What sort of complaints?"

"Claims of sexual harassment, intimidation, coercion," Isabella revealed quietly. "But according to the files, each complaint was dismissed rapidly without investigation. Swept under the rug by Atkinson's superiors." She met George's gaze. "The pattern suggests an organised cover-up spanning years. Protecting Atkinson even back then."

George absorbed this bombshell, scrubbing a hand over his bearded jaw. "Jesus. That bastard was terrorising women even early in his career, and ranking officers just turned a blind eye."

His green eyes blazed with fury. "It aligns far too neatly to be coincidence. This has Atkinson's fingerprints all over it."

CHAPTER TWENTY-EIGHT

Pride swelled in George's chest as Isabella laid out the intricate threads she had woven together behind the scenes. Once again, her keen insights and unrelenting dedication had illuminated the path forward when the way seemed hopelessly lost.

Over tea and biscuits, they delved deeper into past events and motivations. Isabella possessed a natural knack for spotting subtle connections that George had missed when too close to the details. He valued her fresh perspective, free of preconceptions.

"Have I told you lately that you're brilliant?" George said, only half-teasing. "We'd be stumbling around blindly if not for you, sweet."

Isabella waved away his praise even as she smiled. "I just wanted to help move things along. Though I shouldn't have gone behind your back..."

"True, but you've helped massively." Pulling back, George grasped Isabella's hands, expression turning solemn. "But this needs to stay between us for now. Atkinson clearly has connections running deep, as does whoever is puppeteering him which puts you at risk, Isabella. These are dangerous people we're provoking."

Isabella's eyes glinted fiercely. "I knew the risks going in. And I believe in this investigation. In you." She squeezed his hand. "Whatever comes next, we'll face it together."

Her courage and conviction never failed to inspire George. With Isabella by his side, he felt encouraged to press onward; however dark the road ahead appeared. Her love anchored him through the storm. He considered himself profoundly blessed to have such a partner—loving and passionate, yet sharper than any detective he'd worked with. However their personal and professional paths wound together going forward, George knew he could weather any storm with Isabella.

As the conversation meandered, George found himself sharing his anxieties about change on the horizon—Luke's retirement, Isabella's return to work, and the upheaval this case promised. And eventually, the threat of Mia taking Jack away from him.

"There's something else worrying me, Izzy. It's about Jack."

Isabella turned to face George, concern creasing her brows. "What is it?"

George scrubbed a hand over his face. "Mia called yesterday, angry I haven't been around for Jack with the demands of this case. She threatened to file for sole custody."

Isabella inhaled sharply. "Oh, George, I'm so sorry. That must have been awful to hear." She grasped his hand. "What can I do?"

"I don't know," George admitted heavily. "Part of me knows she's justified in being upset. I should make more time for my son." He looked at Isabella helplessly. "But I can't just abandon this investigation either."

Isabella squeezed his hand. "Of course not. But maybe you can compromise? Schedule one evening a week for you and Jack, no matter what. He needs that consistency."

George nodded slowly. "Having a standard night might work, but what if something comes up? Something important?"

"But that's why you're a Detective Chief Inspector now. You can delegate tasks to your team. You trust them, right?"

George nodded. "More than anything."

"Well, there you go."

CHAPTER TWENTY-EIGHT

"OK, I'll talk to Mia; make sure she knows I'm trying despite the chaos of this case." He managed a faint, grateful smile for Isabella. "Thank you for the advice, sweet. I don't know what I'd do without you."

Isabella wrapped her arms around George, holding him close. "You'll work this out; I know you will. And I'm always here if you need to talk or vent. We'll get through this together."

George pressed a fervent kiss to her hair, emotions swelling.

Eventually, talk turned to happier topics, like their hopes for the house in Middleton. Isabella had managed to arrange a viewing for tomorrow. Isabella's hazel eyes shone as she described ideas for decorating the nursery and spacious garden.

"A place that's truly ours, for our family," Isabella said softly, lacing her fingers through George's. "A fresh start."

George traced his thumb across her knuckles, surprising himself with a rush of emotion. After years in his East Ardsley house shadowed by memories of his broken relationship with Mia, the promise of a new sanctum with Isabella felt miraculous.

As they speculated about furniture arrangements and dreamed up schemes for the cottage's cosy nooks, George basked in the novel sensation of optimism. For once, thoughts of their upcoming wedding, of beaches, of suits and white dresses and declarations of love, didn't feel marred by lingering darkness. He and Isabella deserved this bright future together.

Isabella must have glimpsed the sheen of tears George hastily blinked back. She touched his cheek tenderly. "Hey, you alright?"

George turned his face into her palm, pressing a fervent kiss there. "Just feeling so damn grateful for you, sweet," he rasped. "For being my rock, my light through all the madness."

Isabella's eyes softened with emotion. "Right back at you, gorgeous," she whispered. "I can't wait to stand up in front of everyone and pledge myself to you for life." A playful smile lifted her lips. "Reckon you can put up with me that long?"

Chuckling, George drew her into his lap. "Forever wouldn't be long enough," he murmured before capturing her lips in a slow, tender kiss.

As the old clock on the mantle chimed half-eleven, they reluctantly parted. George knew morning's demands awaited, the real world beckoning him back. But tonight had replenished his reserves of strength and hope. With Isabella lighting his path, he could weather any darkness ahead.

At the front door, Isabella wrapped her arms around George's shoulders, gazing up at him sombrely. "You'll figure this out, love. But just remember to take care of yourself along the way. You don't have to carry every burden alone."

George enfolded her in his embrace, breathing in the scent of her hair. "I know," he whispered. "You and Livvy give me something to fight for and come home to. That's what keeps me going through everything."

They shared one last lingering kiss before parting, fingers entwined until distance forced them to let go. As George navigated the sleeping streets toward home, the memory of Isabella's tender faith remained wrapped around him like armour, shielding him from doubt and fear. He would find a way through for those he cherished—for his team, his family, for himself. Step by step, the light would come. He just had to

CHAPTER TWENTY-EIGHT

keep believing it existed.

Chapter Twenty-nine

Early morning sunlight filtered softly through the half-drawn blinds of the hospital room. The rhythmic beep of monitors and hiss of oxygen punctuated the silence as Jay Scott tiptoed over to the bed holding his slumbering mother. Her frail form looked dwarfed amidst the stark white linens and maze of tubes and wires. Jay's heart constricted at the sight.

Moving carefully to avoid disturbing her rest, Jay eased into the visitor's chair beside the bed. He studied his mother's pallid features, so delicate now like tissue paper stretched over her bones. The aggressive chemotherapy had sapped away any plumpness from her, leaving behind this diminished shell. Jay swallowed hard at the painful transformation cancer had wrought on the once lively, smiling mother he cherished.

Gently, Jay took her thin hand in both of his, cradling it as though it were glass. Her fingers were limp, skin cool and paper dry. Jay remembered when these hands had been strong and nimble—kneading bread dough, flying across piano keys, or tousling his hair playfully. Now, they seemed as fragile as a baby bird's.

"Hi, Mum," Jay whispered, knowing she likely couldn't hear him but taking comfort in the one-sided conversation. "I brought you some biscuits again, your favourite."

CHAPTER TWENTY-NINE

He watched her face for any reaction but saw only the fluttering of veined eyelids as she continued dozing. Not wanting to disturb her rest, Jay lapsed into silence, gently rubbing his thumb over the prominent ridges of her knuckles. He wished desperately his mum would open her eyes, would squeeze his hand back even fleetingly. But the steady beep of the monitors reassured him she was hanging on, still fighting.

Jay wasn't sure how long he sat keeping vigil when a knock at the door made him turn. A willowy nurse he recognised from past visits stood there holding a small glass vase of colourful gerbera daisies.

"These just got dropped off for your mum downstairs," the nurse said kindly as she stepped inside. Her name badge read 'Claire.' "Aren't they lovely? We wanted to bring them straight up to brighten her spirits."

Jay blinked in surprise but gave Claire a grateful nod. "That's so thoughtful. Thank you for bringing them up." He accepted the vibrant bouquet when she handed it over. "Any idea who they're from?"

Claire shook her head apologetically. "Sorry, no name or card attached. But it's always nice to see patients receiving some cheer, especially those undergoing intensive treatments." She gestured to an empty spot on the bedside table. "I can grab a vase and some water for those."

While the nurse slipped out, Jay inspected the bouquet, searching for any hidden note but finding nothing. The unexpected gift was perplexing yet oddly touching.

Jay continued chatting to fill the silence, describing inconsequential details about work and mutual friends' lives, avoiding mention of her illness. He wanted these moments to feel as normal as possible, untainted by grim reality.

Nearly two hours passed enjoyably this way until his mother grew noticeably fatigued, her brief periods of lucidity fading. Jay stayed a while longer, holding her hand as she dozed, appreciating every second they still had together. But eventually, he knew visiting hours would be ending soon.

Rising reluctantly from the chair, Jay leaned down to brush a feather-light kiss over his mother's cool forehead. "I'll be back to see you very soon, Mum," he whispered. "I love you so much." Jay lingered a moment more, fingers interlaced with hers, before forcing himself to pull away.

Pausing in the doorway, Jay gave the nurse Claire a grateful smile and wave as she passed in the hall. But as he turned back, his pulse stuttered at the sight of two items left atop his vacated chair. Sitting conspicuously on the faded vinyl was a photograph depicting a smiling young policewoman Jay didn't recognise and a VHS marked simply 'Watch Me.'

Jay froze, thoughts racing. None of the nurses had entered recently, and his mother had been sleeping. That could only mean someone had slipped inside unnoticed and deposited the tape. But who? And why?

Pulse hammering, Jay, following in the footsteps of his boss, pulled a disposable glove from out of his pocket and picked up the VHS gingerly, half expecting it to burst into flames or spew acid. But the small black rectangle remained stubbornly inert. Turning it over, Jay saw no other exterior markings, just those two disturbingly ambiguous words scrawled in black marker.

Mind reeling through possibilities, Jay knew he couldn't ignore such a strange event, especially amidst the threats surrounding their current case. This felt too deliberate, too unsettling to be random. Jay's instincts screamed it was

CHAPTER TWENTY-NINE

connected somehow.

Glancing back at his slumbering mother, unease trickled down Jay's spine like icy water. If someone had breached hospital security and made it unnoticed into her room, how vulnerable was she really? Sudden fear for his defenceless mum gripped Jay's chest. He needed to get this tape analysed immediately in case it posed any danger to her.

Hastily gathering his things and the mysterious VHS, Jay scribbled a quick note for his mother, explaining he got called away for work unexpectedly. He hated leaving her unguarded but had no choice until he could get a protection detail assigned here.

Striding rapidly from the room, mind racing, Jay moved swiftly toward the nurse's station, pulse thrumming. The middle-aged nurse looked up from her computer, eyes widening at the urgency radiating off Jay as he approached.

"Excuse me, when was the last time someone came into my mother's room?" Jay asked without preamble, pointing towards his mother's room.

The nurse blinked, taken aback. "Oh, um, just us nurses during regular rounds, dear. Every few hours to check vitals and such. Why?"

Jay exhaled harshly, raking a hand through his messy hair. "Are you sure? No other staff or visitors stopped by in the last two hours or so?"

At the nurse's confused head shake, Jay leaned closer, keeping his voice low and steady with effort. "Listen, I just found something very alarming planted in my mum's room that could impact her safety. We need to limit access immediately until it's secured."

The nurse sat up straighter, distress creasing her plump

features. "Oh goodness! Should I call security?"

Jay hesitated, weighing options rapidly. His gut screamed this incident was connected to their spate of unsettling threats at work. He needed to inform DCI Beaumont immediately and get the tape to forensics for analysis.

"Not just yet, but please don't allow any non-staff into the room for now until my colleagues arrive," Jay instructed firmly but politely. "And thank you for your help."

Jay pulled out his mobile, found George's number and hit ring. He tried to keep the burgeoning panic from his voice when his boss answered briskly.

"Boss, it's Jay. Listen, something strange just happened at the hospital with my mum," he said in a rush. "Someone left a VHS tape marked 'Watch Me' and a picture of a policewoman I don't recognise in her room while I was visiting."

He quickly explained the other odd deliveries and the tape's ambiguous message. "I've got a really bad feeling about this, boss," Jay finished anxiously. "It seems too sinister to be random, especially with everything happening lately."

On the other end of the line, George inhaled sharply. "I agree; this feels significant, given everything, so take a picture of the photo and email it over ASAP," he said grimly. "Also bring the tape straight here, but don't watch it yet until we can analyse it safely. I don't want you exposed to anything traumatic alone."

Jay nodded even though George couldn't see him. "I'm on my way now. And, boss, I'm worried whoever left this might try getting to my mum again. She's so frail. Could we get police protection assigned to her hospital room straight away?"

"Absolutely, consider it done," George affirmed decisively.

CHAPTER TWENTY-NINE

"I'll call dispatch now and have uniforms dispatched immediately. We'll keep your mother safe, Jay, I promise you."

Profound relief washed over Jay, easing some of the icy tension gripping his chest. "Thank you, boss," he rasped. "I'll be there within half an hour."

Ending the call, Jay said, "My DCI is sending officers here straight away to get this sorted."

The nurse nodded anxiously as Jay turned and strode rapidly toward the lifts.

Jay was eager to have the unsettling VHS out of his possession. But dread still roiled in his gut. What sinister purpose was behind taping a disturbing video in his vulnerable mother's hospital room? What darker message was this unknown messenger trying to send by invading Jay's family tragedy?

Jay didn't know yet, but he intended to find out. And heaven help whoever had threatened his mum because they had no idea the fire they'd ignited within usually easy-going Jay. When it came to protecting his loved ones, Jay's devotion knew no bounds.

Reassured his mother would be secured, Jay headed for the lift. But his thoughts churned as he descended to the entrance hall. Who had managed to infiltrate the hospital unseen? And what sinister purpose lay behind filming and delivering a tape specifically for him to find?

Mounting anxiety gnawed at Jay's gut as he took a step forward, not leaving the lift. What if that person was still upstairs? What if they had a knife? What if...

Jay turned on his heel and pressed the button, the door closing swiftly, the lift dragging him up. "Please don't be too late."

* * *

Detective Chief Inspector George Beaumont stood at the head of the Incident Room, his expression grave. Part of his team was gathered before him—Detective Sergeant Yolanda Williams, Detective Inspector Luke Mason, and Detective Constable Tashan Blackburn. A tense silence filled the cramped space.

"I have some disturbing news," George began grimly. "There has been an incident involving Detective Constable Scott's mother at the hospital."

He proceeded to explain the troubling discovery of the VHS tape left anonymously in Jay's mother's room. "Clearly, this implies a potential threat and intrusion of privacy. As such, I have arranged for police protection of Mrs Scott effective immediately."

The team exchanged startled and worried glances. An invasion into one of their personal lives felt ominous given recent events.

George saw their obvious unease. "Rest assured, we are taking precautions," he said solemnly. "The priority now is determining the purpose of that tape and securing Mrs Scott from harm."

"Absolutely, sir," Yolanda agreed, her youthful face creasing with concern. "Please tell Jay we stand ready to assist however we can, both professionally and personally."

The others murmured their heartfelt agreement. As a tight-knit team, they felt Jay's crisis deeply.

George acknowledged their support with an approving dip of his head. "I know we all share concern for Jay and his mother." His piercing green eyes hardened. "But the mission holds—we stay laser-focused on tracking down Holloway."

He pressed a button and grainy CCTV footage appeared on the monitor behind him. It showed a nondescript figure in a cap and hooded sweatshirt. "This was recorded near that Leeds mechanic shop Jay flagged. The gait and profile match our suspect." George pointed with the remote in emphasis. "He was seen casing the garage, possibly indicating a drop point or safe house location."

"Clever timing on his part, too," Tashan observed. "Came on a rainy night when foot traffic was minimal. Knew how to avoid drawing attention."

Luke gave a grudging nod. "Bastard was always a slippery one. But we'll tighten the net with this new intel."

"Too right," George said. "I want tech running facial recognition through our criminal database along with age progression software to confirm it's Holloway. And get CCTVs scanned along that entire block for any other glimpse we can analyse."

He turned to address Yolanda directly. "Where do we stand on the list of known associates, DS Williams?"

Yolanda straightened. "I have interviews scheduled with several starting this afternoon. We know they protected Holloway in the past; I intend to apply pressure until someone cracks." Her eyes sparked with conviction despite her usual reserved manner.

"Excellent. Remind them obstructing this investigation carries stiff penalties." George's expression brooked no argument. He moved to stand before the team; arms crossed firmly over his chest.

"Holloway has evaded justice for years using intimidation and exploiting weaknesses. But his past crimes breed mistrust, and time erodes loyalty." George's jaw tightened, a determined light entering his eyes. "If we shake the right trees, compliant informants will scurry out."

Around him, the detectives nodded with fired-up focus. George was pleased to see them rallying despite the external chaos.

"It's a chess match now," he concluded. "Let Holloway make his next move; then we counter decisively." George held each of their gazes, radiating steadfast purpose. "Stay vigilant, and we'll catch him off-guard soon enough."

* * *

The door clicked shut behind DI Luke Mason as he entered DCI George Beaumont's office, immediately noting the strained tension evident in his boss' taut posture. George gestured brusquely for Luke to take a seat across the cluttered desk strewn haphazardly with case files and notes.

"Thank you for coming quickly, Luke. I have a sensitive task requiring discretion." George leaned forward intently, voice low despite the enclosed privacy.

Luke nodded. "Of course, son. How can I help?"

George exhaled slowly. "I need someone to quietly investigate any potential connections between Alistair and the Gildersome victims."

The DCI hesitated momentarily, not wanting to get Isabella into the shit, but deciding he trusted Luke like no other. He proceeded to briefly explain Isabella's insights tying the original Gildersome murder victims to Alistair Atkinson.

Luke's brow creased thoughtfully as he listened. When George finished, Luke replied without hesitation, "I'll get started immediately, son and leave no stone unturned in uncovering any possible connections."

"Thanks, Luke," George acknowledged, leaning back. "I appreciate it. And your discretion."

"Understood." Luke stood swiftly, determined purpose etched across his lined features. "I'll begin digging through old personnel files and case databases, cross-referencing known associates. And I'll discreetly reach out to some retired CID members who might have insight on Atkinson and the victims from their heyday."

George inclined his head approvingly. "Cheers, Luke, and keep me informed, yeah?"

"Yeah."

Luke departed with a crisp nod, mind already spinning ahead to the complex task at hand.

Chapter Thirty

The sterilised coolness of the hospital security office enveloped Jay Scott as he stepped inside. Rows of monitors covered the far wall, displays glowing faintly in the dimmed lighting. A paunchy guard glanced up from his newspaper, brow furrowing.

"Can I help you?" he asked Jay gruffly.

Jay straightened his lanky frame, adopting a professional demeanour. "Detective Constable Scott, West Yorkshire Police," he introduced, briefly flashing his warrant card. "I need to review your CCTV footage immediately."

The guard's eyes widened slightly as he sat up straighter. "This about that odd delivery left in a patient's room?" At Jay's sharp look, he elaborated, "Your DCI rang and filled me in. Got the tape cued up for you."

Jay moved closer as the guard wheeled his chair over to the controls. "Much appreciated. We're eager to identify who made the unauthorised drop-off."

The guard's face creased apologetically as he tapped a few commands. "Cameras sweep that hall every thirty seconds. Doubt we caught much."

Jay contained his spike of impatience. "Let's have a look then."

CHAPTER THIRTY

With a nod, the guard started the footage from that morning, time stamp 07:14 blinking in the corner. Jay watched the deserted hallway intently as the camera panned left to right every half minute. He willed some identifying detail to appear on-screen.

During the first several cycles, only staff moved briskly along the corridor. Then, during panning at 07:26, a figure emerged from Jay's mum's room, closing the door swiftly behind them. Jay tensed, leaning closer.

The hooded figure kept their back angled away from the camera's view as they hurried off down the hall out of frame. Jay cursed under his breath. "Back it up and play again slowly."

The guard obliged, both men scrutinising each pixel as the brief scene replayed. But no identifying characteristics were visible beneath the hooded jacket and baseball cap obscuring their form.

"Best shot would be the entrance cameras picking him up on exit," the guard suggested. Jay nodded tightly, mind churning. The sparse footage stirred more questions than answers, but perhaps they'd get a decent facial shot downstairs.

"I'll need that footage burned to a disc," Jay decided. "Along with all feeds from the hallway for time stamp 07:10 to 08:00. Our technical team may be able to enhance it."

The guard readily complied, clearly eager to assist the police investigation. As the disc burned, he glanced at Jay curiously. "This delivery, was it dangerous material left unsecured?"

Jay debated how much to divulge. "No clue yet, but whatever it was, it was meant to intimidate us, it seems."

The guard shook his head, features clouding. "Can't believe someone would invade a vulnerable patient's room for something so malicious. Your mum's lucky to have you looking out for her."

Jay managed a thin but grateful smile at the sentiment. He knew the warm support of his police family surrounded him even in the darkest moments. Whatever sinister forces conspired against them, Jay and his team would expose the truth together, encouraged by their unbreakable bonds.

With the disc finally in hand, Jay bid the guard a brisk thanks before heading for his hatchback. Sliding behind the wheel, he allowed himself a moment to process, tipping his head back against the seat. Lingering nausea churned his gut from witnessing the sadistic hospital tape. Its invasive violation left Jay rattled, but also hardened his resolve. This shadowy enemy clearly underestimated his devotion to protecting loved ones and upholding justice. Jay refused to let fear force him or the team off course.

With a weary sigh, Jay started the engine, thoughts turning to his ailing mum. At least forensics and round-the-clock police protection now secured her room, easing Jay's immediate concerns for her safety. She likely remained blissfully oblivious, lost in morphine dreams that dulled her pain. Jay envied that peaceful escape from grim reality, if only temporarily.

* * *

The dull rays of the winter sun cast an ominous ruddy glow across George Beaumont's office as he sat hunched over personnel reports and crime scene analysis documents. Fatigue blurred the lines of text, but a nagging sense of unease kept sleep at bay. He was worried for Jay and his mother, for Alexis

CHAPTER THIRTY

and her daughter, for his fiancée and his daughter. And for his relationship with his son. Those, and that the investigation felt mired, progress elusive, despite endless hours poured into each slender lead.

When his mobile suddenly shattered the silence, George snatched it up swiftly, tension coiling tighter at the sight of Maya Chen's name. "Please tell me you've got something," he greeted without preamble, gravelly voice taut.

The forensic scientist's usual crisp authority sounded muted over the line. "Apologies in advance, DCI Beaumont. But I've thoroughly analysed the image you provided, and..." Maya hesitated delicately before continuing. "Unfortunately, I could find no usable fingerprints or DNA traces. Whoever handled the photograph knew how to eliminate evidence."

George exhaled harshly, scrubbing a hand down his bearded jaw. He felt violated enough without confirmation an intruder had penetrated his privacy and erased their tracks with meticulous expertise.

Maya was still speaking, her regret clear despite the professional neutrality. "I utilised every viable enhancement technique on the image itself, searching for distinctive markings, reflections, anything that seemed anomalous..." She huffed softly. "But it remains simply an unremarkable photograph on standard print paper stock."

In the taut silence, George could sense her tacit frustration at the investigation hitting yet another wall. He managed a terse but sincere, "I understand, Maya. And I appreciate you deploying every asset available. We'll find another thread to pull."

After extending further gratitude and disconnecting— more to escape the pained sympathy in Maya's tone than brusqueness—George found himself gripping his mobile fiercely enough to whiten his knuckles. This dead end wasn't merely about delayed justice or a stalled case. It intimated a stranger worming intimate access to his private world without impediment. And that raised implications far more ominous.

George wrestled against an unfamiliar undercurrent of vulnerability. Police work meant accepting the lack of control and embracing the variable chaos of each day. But this felt personal in a way that pierced his usual poise. Someone had rifled through his life unseen, their motives cloaked in sinister shadows. It shook George more profoundly than expected to confront how fragile even his own bastion of security proved against a cunning enough adversary.

* * *

Hours later, bleary-eyed and shoulders knotted with frustration; Luke could only scowl at the results of his exhaustive search. No official records existed of any complaints lodged at Atkinson by Laura Hughes, Sarah Jennings, Emily Thompson, or Sally Jenkins. He hadn't expected them to be there, of course. But it sickened him that the only conclusion he could come to was that the upper echelons had covered all the complaints up.

Luke leaned back, pinching the bridge of his nose against an incipient headache. He had combed every database and archive possible, even calling in favours with retired CID colleagues to pick their memories. But not a shred of evidence linked Atkinson with the four women in any tangible way. Their paths appeared never to have legitimately crossed.

CHAPTER THIRTY

Yet Luke's instincts screamed that some connection lurked below the surface. He just had to dig deeper, find the hidden threads so they could speak with Atkinson officially. Luke refused to accept he had hit a dead end. The truth was out there somewhere. He only had to look hard enough.

Straightening with renewed determination, Luke turned his focus to less traditional channels—yellowed newspapers, microfiche reports, personal journals donated by retired coppers. If Atkinson had covered official tracks expertly, perhaps traces lingered elsewhere. Luke became a man possessed, chasing the faintest wisps of memory and speculation that might illuminate the sinister man's hidden past.

* * *

The persistent hum of ringing phones and rapid clicking of keyboards filled the air as Jay Scott wound his way briskly through the crowded shared office. After the dead end at the hospital CCTV office, he was eager to deliver the footage disc to Detective Constable Alexis Mercer for enhancement. Tension coiled in his gut, hoping desperately they could eke some identifying detail about his mother's sinister visitor from the grainy images.

Jay spotted Alexis seated at a workstation, staring intently at her monitor. Pausing, Jay stepped closer and saw she was scrutinising the photograph left at his mum's bedside, the one depicting a smiling young policewoman Jay didn't recognise.

"Any hits on facial recognition?" Jay asked without preamble.

Alexis started slightly, drawn from her intense focus. She swivelled to face Jay, azure eyes clouded with frustration.

"You got the original for me?"

Jay nodded and handed over a plastic bag. "Thanks."

"So, any hints?" asked Jay impatiently.

"None yet," she huffed, blowing a wisp of golden hair off her forehead. "I'm trying every parameter combination, but she must not be in our databases." Alexis crossed her arms. "This will help," she explained, nodding at the original photo. "How did the CCTV analysis go?"

Jay grimaced, holding up the disc in his grip. "Sparse footage, and too obscured to ID the suspect. Hoping your imaging software can enhance it."

Alexis gave a thoughtful hum. "I can start on that next; provide a fresh perspective in case Yolanda missed any angles." Her determined expression lifted Jay's spirits slightly. He was continually impressed by Alexis' tireless dedication.

"Appreciate you looking into this footage too," Jay said earnestly, sensing her unspoken support. "We'll catch a break soon if we keep digging."

Alexis offered a brisk nod, and Jay continued on his way, grateful for his teammates' unwavering commitment to finding the truth. Their resilience never faltered, no matter the darkness challenging them.

Inside the Incident Room, Jay quickly summarised the hospital CCTV situation for Detective Sergeant Yolanda Williams. She readily agreed to prioritize scrutinising the sparse footage, determination glinting in her dark eyes.

Stepping out of the Incident Room to find the boss, he wove briskly past clusters of focused detectives until a familiar gravelly voice called his name.

"DC Scott! How is your mum faring?"

Jay turned to see Detective Inspector Luke Mason regarding

him solemnly from a corner desk—his craggy features creased with concern beneath his close-cropped grey hair.

Crossing over, Jay offered a weak smile. "She seems alright, luckily oblivious to everything happening around her." He scrubbed a hand through his rumpled hair. "I hate feeling so powerless to protect her while she's confined there vulnerable."

Luke gripped Jay's shoulder bracingly. "You're doing everything you can, lad. And George has officers on her room day and night now." His mouth flattened into a grim line. "We'll find the sick bastard, lad. I promise."

Jay managed a jerky nod, gratitude swelling in his chest. Luke's uncompromising dedication to justice was precisely why Jay admired him so much as a mentor.

"How're you holding up otherwise?" Luke asked, sharp eyes searching Jay's face. "That was a heavy burden dumped on you earlier."

Jay exhaled slowly, the images from the unsettling tape still seared into his mind. "Honestly? Feeling rattled," he admitted. "But also more determined than ever to protect Mum and take these bastards down."

Luke gave an approving grunt, clapping Jay's shoulder firmly before releasing it. "Too right. We won't be intimidated or deterred." He held Jay's gaze unwaveringly. "Whatever comes, know you have the full support of your team and me. Understand?"

Emotion clogged Jay's throat at the steadfast reassurance. He managed a jerky nod, which Luke correctly interpreted. The DI gave Jay's shoulder a final bracing squeeze. "Chin up now, lad. We've got work to do."

Galvanised by Luke's stalwart presence, Jay continued on to

the Incident Room, where the rest of the team were gathered around a projection screen. He slipped inside quietly, not wanting to interrupt.

On-screen, silent security camera footage showed a figure emerging from a hospital room, face obscured. Jay realised with a start it was the CCTV clip of his mother's violation. The team must be reviewing it for any telling details.

As the figure hurried away down the hall, Jay scanned the room. Faces reflected degrees of shock and unease as they studied the unsettling scene. Jay cleared his throat awkwardly, drawing startled looks.

"Oh Jay, I'm so sorry you endured that," Alexis blurted, her pretty features creased with dismay. Murmurs of sympathy rippled around the room.

Jay held up a hand self-consciously. "It's fine, I'm managing." He reached back to rub his neck. "Just hope the footage yields something useful."

"We'll keep viewing it from every angle, see what turns up," George affirmed from his position beside the projection screen, expression sober. "And the disc is now with our technical team for enhancement."

Jay dipped his head in acknowledgement, moved by their collective determination to support him. "I appreciate everyone working so diligently on this. Really means a lot."

"Of course, lad," Luke grunted. "You're family. We protect our own." Heartened murmurs greeted his steadfast proclamation.

George cleared his throat, redirecting the briefing to case details. But Jay only half-listened, inner reserves bolstered simply by standing shoulder-to-shoulder with his team. Their bonds of loyalty and trust could withstand any darkness.

CHAPTER THIRTY

Together, they would drag the villains threatening their own into the light to face justice.

After the briefing, Jay pulled George aside discreetly in the hall. "How's the analysis going on that depraved tape left in my mum's room?" he asked tightly, stomach-churning just at the memory.

George's jaw feathered, eyes glinting with banked fury. "The technical team is still enhancing and scrutinising, but we're keeping the contents tightly restricted for now." George assessed him a moment before conceding. "You've handled this admirably, DC Scott. But the offer stands if you need to talk. No judgments, only support."

Unexpected emotion clogged Jay's throat. "Thank you, truly," he managed hoarsely. "Just knowing I have people to lean on makes all the difference."

George clasped his shoulder firmly. "Always, Jay." He gave Jay's shoulder a final affirming squeeze before heading off.

Jay watched him go, heart full of fierce affection for his colleagues who felt more like family. With their unconditional support lifting him up during even the darkest hours, Jay knew he could endure anything.

Chapter Thirty-one

The persistent ringing of phones and rapid clicking of keyboards filled the air as the investigation team worked diligently at their desks in the Incident Room. An undercurrent of urgency charged the space; there was a sense of momentum regained after the unsettling deliveries at the hospital.

Leaning against the doorframe of his office, Detective Chief Inspector George Beaumont surveyed the focused activity with a glimmer of pride. This was his team—resilient and relentless even in the face of ominous threats. Seeing their determination reawakened George's own energy and conviction. Together, they would prevail through tenacity and trust.

Spotting Detective Inspector Luke Mason conferring with Sergeant Tashan Blackburn, George crossed over. "Any progress enhancing that CCTV footage from the hospital?" he inquired without preamble.

Luke shook his head regretfully. "Our lab's technician worked every imaging trick possible, but the original feed was just too low quality." His mouth flattened into a grim line. "Bastard knew where to stand to avoid the cameras."

George nodded, jaw tightening. "He's cautious, but we only need one mistake. Stay on it." As Luke dipped his head in acknowledgement, George added, "And check in with Jay soon.

CHAPTER THIRTY-ONE

He's shouldering a heavy burden."

"Of course," Luke agreed gruffly. "I'll ring him later; make sure he's holding up alright." George knew Luke's directness and empathy could bolster morale in the lowest moments.

Leaving Luke to manage Jay's emotional needs, George headed toward Alexis Mercer's desk where she sat frowning at her monitor. But before he reached her, Alexis suddenly stood, clutching a sheet of paper in her hand.

"Sir, I think there's a situation," she said urgently as she met him halfway across the room. Alexis' face reflected deep unease as she quickly summarised.

Placing a hand on the DC's shoulder, George asked, "Are you sure you should be here, Alexis?"

"Yes, sir, Georgia is safe at school and I'm safe here with you."

George nodded. "What situation?"

"I just received notification that Detective Constable Connie Turner didn't report for duty this morning. She left work yesterday evening but never made it home." Alexis chewed her lip. "Given everything happening lately, this feels significant."

Alarm sparked through George as the implications sank in. Turner's disappearance coinciding with their threats couldn't be random. His gut screamed the events were connected.

Around the room, heads had swivelled towards Alexis at her rushed announcement, and an unsettled ripple spread through the team. George noted their expressions reflected heightened concern now that one of their own was unaccounted for.

"When was Turner last seen?" George demanded tersely.

Alexis checked her notes. "Not last evening but the evening before around half eight, leaving Elland Road police station.

Her house is empty, the car is still parked out front. No communication since she went off-shift." Alexis paused. "She was on annual leave yesterday which is why we haven't been informed."

"Right, we need all hands searching straight away," George decided grimly. "Get Sergeant Greenwood coordinating search teams to canvas the town and surrounding countryside."

As Alexis hurried off to muster resources, adrenaline flooded George's veins. They desperately needed to locate Turner before trails grew cold. He prayed they weren't already too late.

Turning on his heel, George strode back to where Luke and Tashan remained gathered. "You two, take the lead pursuing any leads on Turner's case history, known whereabouts, potential suspects," he directed decisively.

"If she ties back to the Gildersome cases or Sally Jenkins' murder somehow, I need to know immediately. Don't leave any stones unturned."

Luke and Tashan exchanged a loaded glance but simply nodded and moved briskly into action at George's uncompromising tone. They knew better than to question him when lives hung precariously in the balance, and the clock was already ticking.

As the two detectives got to work, Alexis reappeared at George's shoulder. "Search teams are assembling now under Greenwood's oversight," she reported briskly. "And I'm coordinating efforts here to follow any digital leads."

George gave a curt nod of approval. "Excellent. Let me know the instant anything substantive comes up." As Alexis returned swiftly to her workstation, George added, "And good job for informing me straight away about Turner's disappearance. Time is critical now."

Alexis flashed him a small but gratified smile at the acknowledgement of her quick thinking before focusing back on her urgent search. George knew Alexis never sought acclaim, only justice, and those pure motives earned his profound respect.

Mind racing, George retreated to his office to compile detailed background information on Connie Turner and formulate a strategy. If her disappearance did tie back to Sally Jenkins' murder, his priority was recovering Turner safely and swiftly. He refused to lose another colleague to this sadistic killer.

Not thirty minutes later, a brisk rap at his door heralded Alexis stepping into his office clutching a file folder. "I've got Turner's personnel record and an old academy portrait, sir, in case you want the photos to compare against each other," she explained without preamble.

George waved her over impatiently, shuffling the stacks of papers atop his desk to make space. His pulse quickened. If his theory proved correct, this could be the break in the case they so desperately needed.

Alexis placed a personnel photo of Detective Constable Turner beside the unsettling landscape scene depicting the young officer left at the hospital. George grabbed them both; green eyes narrowed intently.

His gaze tracked back and forth repeatedly between the images, analysing every minute detail. The bright smile and youthful features in the informal countryside photo starkly contrasted with the staid portrait in Turner's file. But the auburn hair, slender build, and distinctive mossy green eyes were unmistakably identical.

"It's her," George declared grimly after a taut moment. He slapped the photos down decisively. "This proves Turner is linked somehow to the bloody hospital threats."

Alexis' eyes widened fractionally at the startling conclusion, but she gave a jerky nod of agreement. "It certainly suggests she's entangled in this web, whether willingly or not."

George's fingers curled into fists, fury bubbling up inside him. "Which means she's now in the gravest danger if our culprit believes we're onto something." He shot to his feet, nerves thrumming with adrenaline. "We have to find Turner before it's too late. She clearly knows something pivotal."

Storming to his office door, George bellowed for Luke and Tashan. Across the room, heads jerked up at his urgent tone. The two detectives in question hurried over, tension radiating off them.

"You're both now solely dedicated to finding Turner," George declared without preamble. "Whatever resources you need, you'll have. But I want actionable leads in front of me within the hour." His tone brooked no argument.

Luke and Tashan chorused understanding before rushing off, weariness shaken by the fresh urgency in their boss' voice. George watched them coordinate briefly with Alexis at her desk before scattering to pursue different angles. Around the office, the energy had shifted into high gear at the day's alarming developments. Exactly as it should be, George thought fiercely. He wouldn't settle for complacency while a colleague's life hung precariously in the balance.

Turning on his heel, George retreated to his office before he could snap at the lack of progress or answers. There was nowhere productive for the restless energy boiling inside him right now. Pausing inside the doorway, he forced himself

CHAPTER THIRTY-ONE

through a series of slow, deep breaths as Isabella had coached him to do during moments of peak stress.

When his immediate agitation finally ebbed slightly, George moved to his desk and sat. He steepled his fingers together tightly and focused on constructive actions. First, he needed to personally visit the floor where Turner worked, her last known location, for insights. He couldn't simply pace his office, waiting for updates.

Snatching up his notebook, George quickly scribbled down all the pertinent details on Turner's background and disappearance. Questions without answers still outnumbered facts, but he methodically outlined the slim leads they had thus far. The very act of committing the convoluted case to paper helped impose order on the chaos in his mind.

Finishing his notes, George leaned back in his chair and shut his burning eyes for a brief moment. Turner was one of their own, and he felt her disappearance like a physical blow. Worse still was imagining what she might be enduring now if their perpetrator believed she had betrayed his twisted cause.

Jaw set, George banished the darkest speculations from his mind. Turner needed them sharp and hopeful, not blinded by dread. Each minute that passed could bring her closer to salvation if they refused to squander it. That persistent faith had to fuel them forward.

Pushing determinedly to his feet, George grabbed his coat and keys. He would start by examining Turner's last known location himself. Some vital clue could be waiting there to seize the precious momentum they needed. One way or another, George was going to drag the guilty party out of hiding soon. Justice would be swift and certain—he was resolved on that point.

George stepped out of his office with crisp purpose etched into every fibre of his military-straight posture. Around the room, his team observed DCI Beaumont radiating that formidable presence which both steadied and inspired them. Spines straightened instinctively at the sight.

Before leaving, George paused by Alexis' desk, where she was coordinating digital searches. "Keep me informed, Alexis," he said solemnly, holding her gaze.

Alexis' chin lifted, pride flashing briefly at his confidence in her skills but quickly replaced by stoic focus. "I'll keep digging until we find that clue to bring Turner home safe, sir. You have my word." Her vow resonated with fierce determination.

George gave a terse nod and left her immersed in databases and records, trusting Alexis' unwavering dedication to be their lifeline. No matter how deeply buried, she would unearth the truth. Blazing with restless energy, George exited the station into the bracing cold. He finally had a purpose for the raging helplessness—finding justice for Connie Turner, no matter the cost.

Later, the persistent clicking of keyboards and low hum of conversation filled the Incident Room. But an undercurrent of tension charged the space as DCI George Beaumont's team worked urgently to unravel the disturbing web surrounding Detective Constable Connie Turner's disappearance.

At her workstation near the back, Detective Constable Alexis Mercer sat scrutinising grainy CCTV images on her monitor. She zoomed in and out minutely, adjusting filters in attempts to sharpen the footage showing the hooded figure who had invaded the hospital room of Detective Constable Jay Scott's ailing mother.

Though the video lacked definitive identifying details,

CHAPTER THIRTY-ONE

Alexis knew their sophisticated imaging software might detect subtle characteristics she could cross-reference against suspects. She just needed one telling marker to emerge that could ID the ominous figure and hopefully explain the threats against their team.

After spending nearly two hours applying various enhancements without success, Alexis finally sat back, stifling a sigh of frustration. Rubbing the strain from her eyes, she contemplated her next approach.

Perhaps she should run comparisons between the footage and suspects' known images, seeing if any points overlapped. The idea sparked renewed hope. Quickly bringing up the case files of Ethan Holloway and Alistair Atkinson, Alexis queued their mugshots to analyse against the grainy hospital assailant.

Starting with Holloway, she began painstakingly matching measurements and features, searching for similarities. But after exhaustive scrutiny, Alexis leaned away from the monitor, disappointment sitting heavily on her shoulders.

None of Holloway's structural characteristics sufficiently aligned with their target image. Alexis realised with a pang that she'd have to relay the unsatisfying results to DCI Beaumont soon. He was counting on her skills to move this investigation forward.

Closing Holloway's file, Alexis pulled up Alistair Atkinson next. As the image of her former mentor filled the screen, she froze, old wounds tightening her chest. Atkinson had taken a promising young Alexis under his experienced wing, mentoring her path in policing. His later betrayal still cut deeply, leaving her guarded and suspicious.

Quickly cross-referencing Atkinson's photo against the

grainy hospital assailant didn't yield definitive common markers either. She sat back heavily—another dead end when Beaumont was depending on her skills.

Shutting down the files on her monitor, Alexis gathered her notes to deliver the disappointing update. Dread festered in her gut, worried she was letting the formidable DCI down on a critical lead. His steely green eyes seemed to stare from her memory, demanding results she couldn't deliver yet.

Exiting the labyrinth of workstations, Alexis wound through the open office toward their Incident Room. Through the ceiling-to-floor glass pane, she glimpsed him standing at a desk, muscular arms crossed as he studied the Big Boards intently. His focus was palpable even at a distance. Alexis hesitated, hating to disrupt him without substantive progress to report. But delaying would only deepen his dissatisfaction later.

Squaring her shoulders, Alexis stepped forward and entered, clutching her file to her chest like a shield. His piercing green eyes immediately turned her way, brow furrowed.

"Sir, I've completed suspect comparisons on the hospital footage against Holloway," Alexis began without preamble, pulse thrumming with anxiety. "Unfortunately, his facial structure and measurements simply don't align conclusively."

Beaumont stared at her, stone-faced, as she summarised her unsatisfying efforts. When Alexis finished, silence hung heavily for a taut moment before he responded. "Your diligence is appreciated as always, Alexis," Beaumont said finally, though his gravelly voice held no warmth. His expression remained impossible to read. "Exhausting those possibilities was necessary, of course. We'll just have to keep digging."

CHAPTER THIRTY-ONE

Alexis released a quiet breath, shoulders loosening slightly. She'd expected more overt disappointment at the lack of progress. But Beaumont merely turned back to studying the case boards, tacitly dismissing her.

"Of course, sir," Alexis acknowledged. "Did you find anything on the floor below relating to Connie?"

Beaumont didn't look back at her. "No. Nothing." His curt tone brooked no argument.

Alexis slipped silently from his office, chastened. She'd let Beaumont down by failing to identify their suspect. But even lower hung the shameful relief she felt at not having told George about her comparisons against Atkinson. Alexis still recalled his coldly calculating eyes all too vividly. Her objectivity fractured around the man who'd once been her most trusted mentor.

Back at her desk, Alexis slowly opened the personnel file she'd started on Alistair weeks before when initial suspicions arose. She traced a finger over the image of Atkinson shaking her hand the day she graduated from the academy, so proud to be selected as his junior partner. Was that manipulative monster already lurking inside him then?

* * *

"Unfortunately, it's a dead end, son," Luke concluded reluctantly some hours later across from George's desk. "No documented connection between Atkinson and the Gildersome victims exists that I could find."

George's brows lowered pensively. "Nothing at all? That seems... unlikely."

"I thought the same, which is why I kept digging beyond

the usual channels," Luke agreed. "But it's like they occupied different worlds entirely. Atkinson never worked a case involving the four victims, nor did they even have any shared friends." He hesitated briefly. "Either there truly is no link, or someone erased all traces expertly." Luke paused. "Are you sure that Atkinson isn't being set up? Are you sure you and Isabella are not being used?"

Rubbing his bearded chin, George considered Luke's words in silence. The possibility of a cover-up Luke couldn't penetrate was deeply troubling, implying high-level corruption. And the theory that he and Isabella were being used was indeed alarming. He exhaled slowly. "Right then. Keep monitoring less official sources, Luke. This bears deeper scrutiny."

"Absolutely, son," Luke affirmed immediately. "I have some retired CID friends who are gossip goldmines. And I'll recheck jacket files and reports for any threads we may have overlooked."

George clasped Luke's shoulder warmly. "Good work despite obstacles. Thank you, Luke. I mean it."

Luke offered a small smile. "No bother, son. I appreciate the trust."

Alone again, George brooded over this latest setback, eyes shadowed. The lack of evidence somehow felt almost more unsettling than discovering a legitimately documented connection. It hinted at corruption running deeper than he imagined, choking off avenues of truth.

Chapter Thirty-two

Needing a break from the stuffiness, George opened the door to the stairwell.

As he started to walk down the steps, the stairwell echoed with the sounds of voices. A male voice and a female voice. Voices he was sure he recognised. Though the echo didn't help.

"Is everything OK?" the man asked.

"No. You're not being careful," the female voice said.

"Of course I am. It just appears somebody is trying to out me," the man said, a nervousness in his voice.

The female voice took on a tone, one of authority, one that showed she was angry. "Who? Whoever it is, you need to get rid of them ASAP."

"I've no idea who it is yet," the nervous man replied.

"Which is why I'm telling you you're not being careful!"

"I've emptied both desks of anything incriminating," the male explained. "There wasn't much, anyway."

"So, who's sending the photos? Other than Grimes?"

Grimes? thought George. Were they discussing the Gildersome case? As silently as he could, the DCI headed down the stairs.

"Like I said, I've no idea yet." The male paused. "Have you

found Grimes yet?"

"No, but I'm working on it. There's heat on me too, you know."

A long, suffocating pause drew out for what was probably ten or twenty seconds but felt like hours before the nervous man spoke once more. "Heat? Nah. Not as much as me. I know from those higher up I'm suspected, yet your name hasn't come up once." He paused. "Perhaps it should come up—"

"Are you threatening me?"

"No, I'm just saying you need to find somebody else to blame rather than letting people look at just me."

"They're not just looking at you."

"No, they're looking at Holloway. That man's like a ghost!"

"Wait, what?" the woman asked, a nervous tone edging her question. "You said... I thought you said you'd silenced him—"

"Well I lied, OK. I've no idea where the hell he is," the man said, clearly now in control.

"No wonder Beaumont can't find him."

At the mention of his name, George decided to risk another level and silently headed down. The voices were getting louder, but he still couldn't quite figure out who they belonged to as it wasn't as if they were Geordie or Lancastrian. The accents were just Yorkshire accents, accents he heard daily.

A hollow laugh came from the male, and George was sure the tables had turned. The man was now the one commanding the conversation rather than the woman. "I need George's team to focus on someone else. To forget about Holloway. To—"

"To stop focussing on Alistair Atkinson?" the woman asked.

CHAPTER THIRTY-TWO

"Exactly." The man paused. "I need Beaumont to focus on someone tangible. Someone easy. Perhaps Foster."

"Foster's as guilty as anyone," the woman said.

"Exactly."

"And they know Langston's dead."

There was another suffocating silence. "Yep."

"Have you decided on your third?" the woman asked.

There was a laugh, a laugh that got louder the longer it went on. "I have, and it's brilliant," the man uttered, the sound of his voice low and mournful.

"Who?"

George didn't know quite what to do, but the mention of a third victim boiled his blood. He sprinted down the stairs, his heavy steps carrying up and down the stairwell, and when he got to the bottom, there was nobody there.

He pulled out his mobile and called Detective Superintendent Smith, asking for two uniformed officers to be stationed outside Isabella's grandparents' house. Just in case.

* * *

Alexis Mercer sat hunched before her monitor, eyes burning from endless hours of scrutiny. The Incident Room's frenetic activity had gradually quieted as evening shadows stretched across desks. But Alexis refused to halt her tireless analysis of the CCTV footage from the hospital room invasion. Somewhere in the grainy pixels lurked the clue that would expose their sadistic adversary's face. She just had to keep digging.

Rubbing gritty eyes, Alexis magnified the footage once more, determined to analyse it millimetre by painstaking millimetre. The key details were waiting to be unearthed if she could just maintain relentless patience.

She was so engrossed in her focused scrutiny that the sound of someone softly clearing their throat at her shoulder nearly made Alexis jump from her chair. Glancing up sharply, she found Detective Constable Tashan Blackburn regarding her from over the cubicle wall, his dark eyes gently amused.

"Got a minute for an update, Alexis?" he asked. His baritone was low and measured compared to the edgy energy charging the rest of the team lately. Alexis nodded for him to continue.

Tashan's expression grew serious, voice still pitched discreetly as he summarised new developments. "That lead on the location of Connie Turner's mobile phone paid off. I've tracked down an address where we believe she's being held captive based on the ping data."

Alexis straightened in her chair, pulse kicking as the significance registered. This could be the breakthrough to rescue their endangered colleague.

"Luke is assembling an armed response unit as we speak," Tashan continued solemnly. "We move out within the hour to secure and search the location. I wanted you to be informed, but please keep details strictly confidential for now."

Alexis nodded rapidly. "Of course, operational security is critical. Thank you for the update, Tashan." She offered a faint, hopeful smile. "Sounds like we may have our first solid break thanks to your methodical tracking skills."

Tashan dipped his head modestly at the praise before his expression shifted and grew more serious. He held Alexis' gaze. "Whatever we uncover tonight will likely be difficult," he said gravely. "I want you to prepare yourself mentally for that."

Alexis tensed. In her excitement, she hadn't considered the

potential horrific outcomes if they were too late. But Tashan's quiet compassion reminded her this operation carried grave risks that could haunt them all.

"I understand," she acknowledged solemnly. "My thoughts will remain with all of you out there until your safe return. And I deeply hope Connie will be coming back unharmed along with you all."

Tashan studied her a moment as though confirming her steadiness in handling the unknowns ahead. Apparently satisfied, he simply offered a small smile and nod before moving off to finish preparations.

Alexis watched him confer briefly with DCI Beaumont across the room, their voices low and urgent. Beaumont's piercing green eyes were ablaze with banked intensity, his muscular frame nearly vibrating from tightly leashed adrenaline. When Tashan finished briefing him, the DCI shook his hand briefly but firmly in gratitude. Even from a distance, Alexis could sense Beaumont's fierce determination radiating powerfully. There would be justice tonight, one way or another. Failure was not an option.

As the two men parted ways, Beaumont crossed to confer last-minute details with Luke at his desk. Alexis felt unexpectedly overwhelmed by emotion. They were so close to answers now, but at what cost still remained uncertain. The risks weighed heavily on her as she observed the team prepare to depart into the dangerous unknown.

Turning back to her frozen monitor, Alexis stared sightlessly at the grainy figure who had sparked this turmoil what felt like lifetimes ago. She willed the pixels to rearrange into telling details that could spare her friends walking needlessly into peril. But the sadistic orchestrator of their pain remained obscured, taunting her.

As the men disappeared around the corner, the hair on Alexis' neck prickled with dread. She said a silent prayer for the team's safe return with Connie. But premonition whispered this night still held dark and tragic revelations yet to be unveiled.

* * *

An hour later, George Beaumont strode briskly into the Incident Room, cradling Connie Turner's smartphone in an evidence bag. The grim resignation on his rugged face told the story before he even spoke—the search of Leeds Country Way had only turned up more hollow misdirection.

As his team gathered round, George held up the bagged mobile. "This was left conspicuously near a footpath, wiped clean so no prints..." he ground out. "The phone's locked for now, too, until digital forensics get a look at it. So we're back to square one on Connie's location."

His piercing green eyes smouldered with banked fury over yet another taunt by their sadistic adversary. Around George, his detectives mirrored his frustration, weary shoulders sagging under the news.

Alexis Mercer stepped forward tentatively; folder clutched to her chest. Her azure eyes lacked their usual vibrancy. "Actually, we may have a solid lead on Connie's whereabouts now," she ventured carefully.

At George's startled look, she explained, "After exhaustive digital searching, we finally traced the footage on the VHS to an abandoned farmhouse east of Gildersome that looks highly suspicious on satellite." Alexis opened the folder to reveal

CHAPTER THIRTY-TWO

grainy aerial shots circled in red marker.

George's sharp gaze honed in on the images even as annoyance flared briefly. "And why wasn't I told of this sooner?" The harsh words escaped before he could soften them.

But Alexis displayed no defensiveness, merely contrition. "Apologies, sir, our technical team only pieced it together in the last hour," she clarified gently. "I didn't want to distract the search party without hard confirmation first."

Chagrin swept George, and his flash of annoyance evaporated. Alexis deserved commendation for her initiative, not irritation at the timing. This was how breakthroughs emerged—fragmentary clues coalescing into revelations when properly nurtured.

George softened his brusque tone markedly. "No, I'm really sorry. Your work here is exemplary, as always, Alexis. This insight on the farmhouse could be the lifeline we desperately needed."

Her faint answering smile conveyed a wordless understanding of the stressful uncertainty spurring his impatience. By unspoken consensus, the momentary tension dissolved into a united purpose.

George immediately began issuing rapid instructions for reconvening their response and gearing up to hit this new location swiftly and decisively. He refused to waste another instant now that a solid lead pointed to Connie's whereabouts. And Alexis had earned her place spearheading the tactical planning based on that critical intel.

As his detectives erupted into action gathering equipment and the coordinates for the abandoned farmstead, George crossed to Alexis amidst the chaos. Clasping her shoulder in emphasis, he met her gaze directly.

"Your relentless analysis gave us back lost hope today," George said gravely. "We move on that farmhouse within the hour thanks to you. Whatever happens next..." He inhaled slowly. "I won't forget what it took for us to reach this point."

Alexis read the deeper sentiment and managed a tremulous half-smile even as her eyes glistened suspiciously. But her voice rang steady enough replying simply, "Let's bring our girl home safe, sir."

George could only nod gruffly, throat unexpectedly tight. But his swirling thoughts steadied into crystalline conviction. However tortuous the road that delivered them here, by damned he would see their loyal devotion pay off. They would have resolution tonight, somehow. Even if his own soul shattered irrevocably in the seeking.

* * *

The late afternoon sun cast an ominous burnt umber glow across the weed-choked fields surrounding the derelict farmhouse. DCI George Beaumont stood motionless beside the sagging split-rail fence, sharp gaze assessing the structure's eerie stillness through narrowed eyes. All seemed abandoned. Yet instinct screamed something far more sinister festered inside the crumbling walls.

Beaumont turned to Alexis Mercer beside him, her youthful features carved with stoic intensity. "Stay sharp," he cautioned under his breath.

Alexis flashed a curt nod, hand hovering near the retractable baton on her belt.

Moving toward the sagging porch with swift precision, Beaumont gestured for Alexis and two uniformed officers to cover alternate entry points as he swiftly broke the stubborn front door. The resounding crack pierced the heavy silence enveloping the farmstead like a gunshot, signalling the start of a race.

That race's outcome would reveal itself soon enough. But foreboding weighted the stale air in George's lungs as he slipped inside, torch beam slicing the gloom. The front rooms proved empty aside from the detritus of squatters and vermin. Yet dread intensified with each cautious step deeper into the derelict structure. Where was their colleague if not here? Had the exhaustive search led merely to another dead end? George refused to accept that, striding forward relentlessly.

Until Alexis' choked cry froze him mid-step. Swirling, he spotted her slight form silhouetted in a doorway, torch dangling limply from her hand. Two long strides carried George to her side, sharp gaze following the beam of light to illuminate the nightmarish tableau rooted there.

George's breath arrested in his chest, the air sucked violently from the room. There, suspended grotesquely five feet off the grimy floorboards on a makeshift wooden cross, hung the savaged body of Connie Turner. Her mouth gaped in a gruesome silent scream; limbs splayed at awkward angles by the cruel iron spikes pinning her naked flesh. Dark, coagulated blood caked the wooden beams and floor below her dangling feet.

It took long seconds for the dreadful scene to pierce the protective numbness allowing George to function. When it did, the pain was as savage as a physical blow. Little remained of the bright spirit, and sly humour that had defined Connie Turner beyond the anguished rictus of her ruined face. George's gut lurched as much at the callous desecration of her humanity as the gruesome manner of displaying her stolen life. This was beyond murder—it was annihilation.

At George's side, Alexis made a raw, wounded noise low in her throat. Before he could react, she stumbled forward, hands outstretched toward Connie. "Oh God...Connie..." she choked, tears spilling down her cheeks. She looked poised to embrace Connie's lifeless body suspended there.

The contact would destroy precious trace evidence. George reacted on instinct, catching Alexis' slender wrist before her fingertips could graze Connie's bruised flesh. "Don't touch her!" George commanded sharply. Then he registered Alexis' devastated expression. His tone softened by degrees. "You mustn't contaminate the scene, Alexis."

She peered up at him with devastated azure eyes, the professional facade shattered. George glimpsed the anguished woman behind the stalwart investigator for the first time then. Overwhelmed himself, he drew Alexis gently back from Connie's body and enfolded her in his arms. He felt her tears soak through his shirt as she clung to him.

"I knew her, sir. Connie. We worked together for... for..."

"I'm so sorry, Alexis," George rasped thickly. "So damned sorry..." He couldn't tear his gaze from Connie's broken figure, emotion stoppered behind his sternum threatening to rupture his ribs. Alexis only shook silently against him for endless moments.

Finally, her low words filtered up, muffled in his shirtfront. "How could anyone do such a thing?" The question was rhetorical and naive in equal parts. They both knew too intimately what depths human cruelty could plumb. Yet somehow, this violation cut deeper still. They had failed to reach Connie in time.

CHAPTER THIRTY-TWO

The distant wail of sirens split the evening air, heralding grim professional duties that could no longer wait. George loosened his embrace and held Alexis by both shoulders, ducking his head to catch her downcast eyes.

"We will get justice for her," George vowed raggedly. "For what happened here today." His burning gaze bored into Alexis beseechingly until she gave one short, jerky nod and swiped at her cheeks. The steel core of her spirit glinted beneath the sheen of tears.

They parted then wordlessly as Stuart Kent and his forensics team arrived, their usual levity grave and pained. Grim purpose descended as they documented and collected samples from Connie's desecrated shell. More would come to bear witness. But none would view the horror through the same intimate lens of failure as George and Alexis in this moment. Theirs was a private anguish never to be fully excised.

As George slipped outside and saw the encroaching crime scene investigators, the slanting sunlight proved a mockery of nature's indifference. He gazed sightlessly across the rustling fields, the grass a gold ocean around him. But all he envisioned was Connie Turner's vibrant, laughing eyes. Now extinguished forever, their last flickering over his face in a silent, tragic accusation.

Chapter Thirty-three

An oppressive pall clouded the atmosphere within George Beaumont's car, the silence absolute save for the hypnotic thrum of tyres on the tarmac. In the passenger seat, Alexis Mercer stared dry-eyed out the window, azure orbs hollowed of their usual vibrant intelligence. The horrific scene at the farmhouse had drained all softness from her youthful features, leaving behind only bleak devastation.

George kept his own gaze fixed grimly ahead, jaw clenched tight enough that a headache pulsed at his temples. But physical discomfort barely registered through the raw anguish searing his psyche. Connie Turner's mutilated corpse seemed seared onto his retinas; her ruined face an eternal indictment.

By unspoken consensus, George and Alexis closeted their roiling emotions during the grim ride back to the city, the space between them weighted by unvoiced recriminations.

Alexis stared numbly out the passenger window, barely seeing the grey city streets flowing past. Her anguished eyes seemed fixed on some distant nightmare.

The walls of the Mercedes felt suddenly claustrophobic, mirroring the shrinking options available once corruption poisoned the ranks. George could scarcely draw breath for the rage and futility filling his lungs.

CHAPTER THIRTY-THREE

But George finally broke the heavy silence as they stopped at a traffic light. "Why didn't you tell me you knew Connie personally, Alexis?" His voice was raw yet gentle. "I could have shielded you from the worst of that back there if I'd known."

Alexis' shoulders hunched defensively as she turned her hollow gaze toward him. "I didn't expect to react that way; so unprofessional", she whispered. "I thought I could handle it, that my skills would make the difference..." Her voice broke.

George's expression softened. "You're far from the first to misjudge how trauma impacts us." His eyes grew distant, full of ghosts. "I made that mistake once or twice myself over the years."

The light changed but George didn't accelerate yet. He gripped Alexis' rigid shoulder. "If experience has taught me anything, it's that we're all only human beneath the job's harsh demands," he told her solemnly. "Don't punish yourself for that humanity, Alexis. And let your team help shoulder unbearable burdens—that's why we endure together."

Alexis' eyes shone wetly. She nodded without speaking, a wealth of emotion passing silently between them. George finally nudged the car forward again through the deepening night. They travelled onward together with a shared purpose now instead of isolation. And perhaps that made all the difference.

Back at the station, he gathered the shell-shocked remainder of his team with brusque efficiency that brooked no argument. When all had assembled, George scanned their pale faces, seeing his own anguished desolation reflected back at him from each tightened jaw and wounded gaze. This tragedy had tapped the very heart of their family.

"By now you've all been informed of Connie's... discovery," George began heavily, the mere utterance like jagged gravel on his tongue. He gave a brief factual overview of her condition, more for the official record than for their benefit. Every acid detail was already seared into his brain, never to be forgotten however fervently he might wish it.

When Alexis flinched almost imperceptibly at the clinically graphic description, George gentled his tone by increments. "I know the shock is profound for us all. But we must stay laser-focused despite emotions running high if there's to be any justice for Connie." Around the room, devastated eyes lifted with fragile hope towards promised redemption. George clung to that fervent faith like a drowning man to flotsam. It was all that kept the darkness at bay.

He doled out investigative assignments, trying to match skills with fit. Luke Mason's bulldog tenacity would aid in knocking on Connie's neighbourhood doors, however fruitless. Tashan Blackburn's methodical nature was well-suited to assisting Luke. Young Jay Scott's creative thinking might spot fresh connections in her background.

"I won't insult anyone by demanding calm," George concluded solemnly. "Rage, guilt, fear—I share it all. But we must channel those emotions constructively into the tenacious pursuit of truth, however elusive. We owe Connie that much." He skewered each detective with his piercing green eyes until receiving affirming nods one by one around the room. They would stay the course, somehow.

As his team reluctantly dispersed, the Incident Room felt suddenly cavernous. George's roiling thoughts kept savage time to the clock's relentless ticks echoing off the barren walls. Despite resolute words bolstering his fractured people,

CHAPTER THIRTY-THREE

hollowness gaped within George's chest.

* * *

Gold and crimson hues from the setting sun filtered through the slatted blinds of the Incident Room, casting bars of light across the tense faces gathered around George Beaumont. He studied his team in the melancholy glow—the fatigue etched around Jay Scott's eyes, the tight set of Alexis Mercer's delicate jaw, the furrow between Yolanda Williams' brows—seeing his own bone-deep weariness reflected back.

George turned to Jay Scott, noticing new hollows beneath the lad's eyes from hours hunched over files. "What have you learned about Connie's connections?"

Jay straightened, amber eyes brightening. "Connie worked closely with Sally Jenkins a few years back, and much longer alongside Detective Chief Inspector Alistair Atkinson and other senior brass."

He rifled through messy notes. "Some retired now or passed away. But she had deep roots in the department."

"What else do we know of Connie's relationships?" George pressed Jay. "Past collars with grudges, jealous ex-partners, shady connections?"

"Still piecing together her history, boss." Jay raked restless fingers through his dishevelled hair and scrubbed gritty eyes with the heel of his hand.

George absorbed this, thoughts churning. Connie's ties to pivotal figures like Jenkins and Atkinson felt too significant to dismiss as coincidences. Especially Atkinson. He was involved in this somehow; George knew it, and a shadowy part of George whispered that rotten trees still bore poisonous fruit.

But open speculation poisoned cases as surely as corruption soured justice.

He clapped Jay's shoulder. "Good work. Keep digging into Connie's history here and reach out discreetly to former colleagues. We need the full picture."

Jay dipped his head, stifling a yawn as he moved to gather his things.

Just then, the Incident Room door banged open, admitting a blast of cold air and Luke Mason's imposing frame. Tashan Blackburn loomed behind him, their matching grave expressions electrifying the room's energy.

Luke squared his shoulders. "We've got a development on Connie's last night. Owner of The Tipsy Hog in Gildersome confirmed she was at his pub and met a mysterious fella no one knew." He quickly elaborated on eyewitness reports of Connie drinking and conversing intently with an unidentified man.

George leaned forward intently. "Was he someone known to her?"

Tashan shook his head, frustration creasing his youthful brow. "Unknown, sir. Average build, dark clothing. They seemed friendly at first, but then it got a bit awkward apparently before parting ways, according to other patrons."

"Any usable footage for identification?" Alexis asked urgently. The first spark of real interest had entered her drained eyes.

"Already being analysed," Tashan rumbled. "Pub owner's emailing security tapes. If our bastard's face wasn't obscured, he's done because we struck gold—multiple camera angles showing this stranger cosying up to Connie, apparently." His deep voice resonated with gathering momentum. "With some image enhancement, we'll have our bastard dead to rights if he's got a record."

Anticipation prickled the stale air as the team absorbed these slim developments. The investigation's lumbering momentum felt poised to avalanche forward suddenly just as their stamina reached its frayed end. George knew well the pendular nature of enduring cases—interminable inertia of chasing wisps abruptly swinging to frenetic action when threads crossed at last. This revelation, coming so late in their grim day, felt weighted by omen.

"Expedite that enhancement work and Facial Rec sweeps," George ordered decisively. "I want eyes on this pub meeting ASAP."

Around him, grim nods answered George's steely tone. After endless missteps, the investigation teetered fatefully on the edge at last. Now to guide its final path towards justice or ruin. Spines straightened almost imperceptibly as the profundity of imminent revelation took hold. For better or worse, the search would soon end one way or another.

* * *

Pale moonlight filtered through lace curtains in the cosy sitting room as George Beaumont settled back against the worn sofa beside Isabella Wood. A heaviness still clung to his shoulders despite the warm, welcoming comfort surrounding them at her grandparents' home. The bittersweet case weighed relentlessly on his mind even here.

Isabella nestled into George's side with a contented sigh, one slender hand wrapped loosely around her rose-patterned teacup. The aroma of tea and symphony of muted night sounds couldn't entirely drown the echoes of horror witnessed today. The ghosts followed.

"Olivia go down alright?" George murmured absently, rolling tense shoulders. The investigation's darkness constantly intruded somehow, tainting even these stolen moments of peace.

Isabella watched him knowingly. She stroked his forearm. "I've already told you she did, George." She paused. "I know it's easier said than done, but enough thinking about work for tonight, love. You're carrying the world again."

George forced a half-smile. She knew him far too well. "It's Alexis," he admitted tiredly.

"You're thinking about your new blonde, gorgeous detective constable whilst in the presence of your fiancée, Beaumont?" Isabella asked over the dainty rim of her cup with narrowed eyes. "I always knew you preferred blondes to brunettes."

George nearly choked on his tea. "You what?" he sputtered, eyes wide.

Isabella bit her lip, suppressing a grin at his flabbergasted reaction. "Just having you on," she said, hazel eyes dancing playfully. "You should see your face right now!"

"You little shit," George huffed, but his mouth twitched despite himself. He gently poked Isabella in the ribcage, eliciting a squeak. "Is that any way to address your future husband? Challenging my honour so scandalously..."

Isabella pretended to look contrite, poorly disguising her smile behind her teacup. "Terribly sorry, husband-to-be. I suppose I deserved that poke for my cheekiness."

Her eyes softened then, resting a hand on George's arm.

"You deserve a lot more than just a poke with my finger,

CHAPTER THIRTY-THREE

future Beaumont," he said, "but I'm not sure your grandparents would appreciate us taking this upstairs." George paused. "I can't wait for you to come home."

"Then solve this bloody case," she said with a grin.

"I'm trying."

Isabella nodded. "I can see the toll this case is taking on you, and with that I can see it must be affecting the whole team."

George covered her hand, expression sobering slightly. "You know me so well," he admitted ruefully.

"I might be able to help you reduce the stress," Isabella said.

"I'm not sure your grandparents would appreciate—"

"Stop being a perv and listen," Isabella interrupted, a grin flashing across her face. "When you told me about Connie, I decided to look into her as well," Isabella explained.

"The team can't find anything. I put Alexis on it, but she came back with nothing."

"Well, I got in touch with my contacts in Wakefield again." She paused, considering. "And they got me in touch with a lower-ranking officer, troubled by Atkinson's cover-ups."

"Go on."

"The lower-ranking officer is going to act as a whistleblower if we decide to take this further, George," Izzy explained.

"How?"

"They've found emails and files hidden away by retired detectives. It appears that despite Atkinson having cultivated relationships with influential figures within the West Yorkshire Police, some don't trust him."

"Maybe Atkinson has something on them?"

"Like blackmail?" Isabella asked.

"Exactly!"

"It makes sense," Isabella said. "Anyway, Connie also put in a complaint, which I believe reveals a pattern of misconduct by Alistair. It also reveals the systematic way the higher-ups suppressed them."

She paused.

"What are you not telling me?"

"I have people willing to put official statements forward tomorrow, George," Isabella explained. "Colleagues of Alistair who are willing to provide their accounts." She smiled. "I'll have two of my detective friends with me, so I'll be safe. And Olivia will be here with my grandma and grandad, OK?"

"That's... That's incredible," George said appreciatively. The swell of tenderness nearly overrode frustration at this revelation. "So why didn't Alexis discover that already? She's worked for the West Yorkshire Police for years. As long as you have. Surely if you did it from home, she could do this from the office?"

Isabella shook her head. "As the one who saw the aftermath of Connie's murder first-hand, she's probably shattered. Still wearing her professional mask when with you all. But haunted."

George recalled Alexis' ashen face and clouded blue eyes. "You may be right. But that was crucial. I can't afford missed steps now." He sighed. "I'll need to address it straight away."

Isabella touched his cheek gently. "Go carefully, though, gorgeous. She likely feels inadequate already. Overcompensating through relentless work." She swirled dregs of tea, gazing through the scattered leaves speculatively. "Best not to pressure her unless absolutely necessary."

George lifted their joined hands to his mouth, brushing his

lips across Isabella's knuckles. She knew exactly how to shift his mood. "It's fine; I'm not going have a go at her. I'll just ask her to look deeper, see if she can find anything to corroborate what you eventually find." He paused and then explained what he'd overheard between Alexis and a colleague a couple of days ago.

"Did I say how thankful I am, Izzy?"

"No," Isabella smiled tenderly, "but what are partners for?" Her hazel eyes held understanding and acceptance that never failed to pierce George's very soul. "I'm always in your corner, George."

George grabbed her hand and pressed a reverent kiss to her palm. Then he hugged her close, cheek resting against curly hair, finding sanctuary, however briefly. "Don't know what I ever did to deserve you, you know?" he admitted hoarsely. "But I'll spend every day proving worthy if I can."

Isabella nuzzled against George's shoulder. "Oh hush, you silly sausage, you already do. Every day."

George allowed his eyes to drift shut, soaking up her soothing presence. Anne and Eric wouldn't mind if he stayed over. In fact, last night, they'd asked him why he was staying in Morley when Isabella's bed was king-sized, anyway.

"I think I might stay tonight, actually, Izzy," George said before his phone began ringing. "It's Yolanda. She's working late. I'd better get this."

* * *

While George was discussing the case with Isabella, the Incident Room's persistent background hum faded to muted periphery as Detective Sergeant Yolanda Williams scrutinised the CCTV footage from Connie Turner's fateful last night. With utmost care, she advanced the grainy recording moment by painstaking moment, sharp eyes cataloguing each nuanced gesture and expression for subtle tells.

The grainy video showed Connie entering The Tipsy Hog pub, pausing momentarily with hands tucked into the pockets of her fitted navy pea coat, before moving to sit in a corner booth, weaving her way through the cluster of patrons gathered.

While waiting, Yolanda saw Connie unbutton her coat but left it on, intrigued. Did she leave it on in case she needed to escape? Or was there another reason?

It was then that her pulse raced nearly loud enough to drown the trilling phones and clicking keyboards as a familiar imposing figure entered the frame beside Connie —Detective Chief Inspector Alistair Atkinson.

Yolanda studied Atkinson's swaggering posture as he leaned toward Connie to speak; her body language grew markedly closed off—shoulders hunching, head angling away from him. Yolanda's eyes narrowed. Connie didn't seem to welcome Atkinson's overtures, judging by her pronounced discomfort.

The recording lacked audio, forcing Yolanda to parse meaning from their stilted interaction alone. Atkinson gestured forcefully several times while speaking to Connie, whose reactions shifted from defensive to conciliatory in gradual measures. Yolanda wished fervently she could hear the nature of Atkinson's intense address that had Connie alternately clenching her fists beneath the table or nodding placatingly.

Connie then set the glass down with exaggerated care, throat visibly constricting. Her hands curled into fists beneath the table.

CHAPTER THIRTY-THREE

Atkinson continued his intense address, punctuated by forceful gestures. Connie reacted alternately with tension or placating nods, appearing increasingly discomfited. Finally, she shook her head sharply and stood, clearly denying some demand from Atkinson.

Checking the timestamp, Yolanda noted it was nearly 10 pm. She loaded additional footage from outside cameras, picking up Connie exiting the pub on unsteady feet. Atkinson followed shortly after, waving enthusiastically before departing opposite.

Yolanda tracked Connie tugging her coat against the night chill, fumbling for her mobile, likely to call a cab rather than walk in her impaired state. Yolanda tensed as Connie neared the alley. Then suddenly, a figure lunged out, brutally grabbing Connie from behind, likely forcing a chemical-soaked rag over her face as she struggled violently.

Swallowing bile, Yolanda froze that final devastating frame. Then she snatched up her desk phone with trembling fingers while Connie's muted, desperate struggle replayed mercilessly behind her eyelids. The vivid imagery confirmed Yolanda's worst fears.

DCI Beaumont answered on the second ring. "What is it, DS Williams?" His gravelly voice already carried exhaustion and grief's eroded edges. Yolanda winced internally at the news she was duty-bound to deliver that would carve away more of his spirit. But justice allowed no compromise.

"You need to review this footage, sir," Yolanda said urgently. "Atkinson was with Connie directly before her attack."

A bleak affirmative was George's only reply before disconnecting. But Yolanda sensed the gravity of her call's implications crashing down on his burdened psyche. Their reckoning was at hand.

Chapter Thirty-four

Pale dawn light filtered through ivory linen curtains as George Beaumont gradually awoke, momentarily disoriented by the unfamiliar warmth nestled against his side. As drowsy synapses sparked connections, a wry smile lifted his bearded face. Isabella. The comforts of home felt impossibly far removed from the grim revelations that awaited him back at the station. For a blissful interlude, waking with his beloved soothed the relentless churning in George's mind.

But the outside world inevitably clawed back his consciousness, spectres of tragedy pursuing him even here. George sighed, easing from beneath Isabella's slender arm draped across his chest. She made a tiny sound of protest but quickly lapsed back into peaceful dreaming. George paused, drinking in her delicate features smoothed of any cares. Selfishly, he wished they could hide from harsh reality a while longer.

But duty called. With utmost care not to rouse Isabella further, George slipped from beneath the duvet and reached for yesterday's rumpled clothing with no time to stop home for fresh clothes or even shower at the station. Yesterday's earth-shaking revelations awaited his singular focus.

Settling gingerly on the edge of the mattress to lace his shoes, George's thoughts raced ahead to the station and

Detective Superintendent Jim Smith's ominous SMS received at 3 am: the recording of Alistair Atkinson's interview now awaited George's intense scrutiny on the secure server. His pulse quickened just anticipating the coming hours.

Pausing at the bedroom door, George allowed himself one last hungry look at Isabella's sleeping form burrowed into his vacant pillow. Her sweetness never failed to pierce his battered spirit. He committed this nurturing image to memory like a talisman against gathering darkness before forcing himself to exit silently.

The roads remained nearly empty as George navigated the familiar route on autopilot, thoughts consumed by spiralling questions.

Arriving at Elland Road station's car park, George took a fortifying gulp of the to-go coffee picked-up route. Caffeine hummed through his system, honing focus for the onslaught ahead. Striding briskly inside, George pulled up short scanning morning briefing notices, but there was still no word from Sergeant Greenwood on Adwalton CCTV around the traced mobile number's last location. George scrubbed the scruff lining his jaw harshly. One bloody crisis at a time. He continued onward with an intensifying purpose.

The familiar chaos of the main office area remained muted this early, particularly with most resources diverted to Connie's case or protecting would-be targets like Jay's mother in the hospital. George preferred the solitude for absorbing crude truths off the record. His office called urgently.

Booting up his PC, George logged directly into the secure case file server and cued the recent addition: 'Atkinson, Interview 1.' Settling back as the recording flickered to life on-screen, George watched the Wakefield detective superintendent read monotonously through the standard spiel. Opposite him, Alistair sat with the negligent patience of a man untroubled by the outcome.

* * *

Detective Superintendent Ian Dalrymple studied the seated Detective Chief Inspector Alistair Atkinson across the sparsely furnished interview room table. Atkinson appeared relaxed despite the stark fluorescent lighting, smiling easily back at Dalrymple. If he felt any trace of nerves at the unexpected summons here from neighbouring Leeds, Atkinson concealed it flawlessly.

Clearing his throat, Dalrymple began. "Thank you for coming in voluntarily, DCI Atkinson. As you know, your colleagues are investigating DC Connie Turner's disappearance and subsequent murder. Your interactions at The Tipsy Hog pub directly preceded concerning events, so we have some questions."

Atkinson spread his hands innocently. "Of course, happy to assist however I'm able. Poor Connie—such a senseless tragedy happening to one of our own." His slack posture and easy smile conveyed utmost unconcern at being called in. If he felt any nerves over the unexpected summons regarding Connie Turner, Atkinson concealed them flawlessly.

Clearing his throat, Dalrymple launched straight into questioning. "Let's start with your account of the night in question. Connie Turner disappeared shortly after you were observed interacting with her at a pub."

Atkinson inclined his head cooperatively. "Of course. On the evening in question, as you know from looking through my phone, I invited Detective Constable Turner to The Tipsy Hog pub because I wanted to pick Connie's brain." He paused as if thinking, then added, "We ordered an IPA each and made idle small talk until they arrived."

"And once they arrived?"

"Like I said, I wanted to pick her brain about the Gildersome case."

"Forgive me, but I didn't realise the Gildersome case was something you were working on," the DSU said.

"You realise right," said Atkinson. "Neither of us were working on it, in fact, which is why I thought it OK to bring up out-of-work hours."

"What else did you discuss?"

"Not that much," said Atkinson. "You know from watching the CCTV that we managed two drinks each, and to be honest, we downed the first ones at such a rate we barely had time to chat."

"Why drink them so fast?"

Atkinson grinned. "I was thirsty. I cannot comment for Connie." He turned to Detective Superintendent Smith, who was sitting next to him. "Sir, do I really need to answer such ludicrous questions."

"You're here voluntarily, Alistair. Answer what you see fit, but it's getting late."

"What is the nature of your relationship with Connie Turner?" asked Ian.

"I used to be her mentor twelve years ago when I was a DI."

"How would you describe your interactions with her prior to her disappearance?"

"Isn't that the same question as before, but reworded?"

"Just answer the damn question, Alistair, so that we can

leave," said Smith.

"Sorry, sir," Atkinson said with a grin. "I asked her again about the Gildersome murders, specifically what she knew about Sally Jenkins."

"Why the interest in Sally Jenkins?" asked Dalrymple.

"I'm a murder detective, sir," Atkinson stated. "I just wanted to make sure Beaumont was giving the case the recognition it deserved."

"Speaking of DCI Beaumont," Dalrymple said, "there's clear discomfort on CCTV. Why would Connie be uncomfortable in your presence if you were her mentor?" He paused. "I've seen the way Connie stiffened, her hands curling into fists in her lap beneath the table.

Atkinson insisted he meant no harm with his solicitations. "I can be a bit brash; she was probably startled. But nothing inappropriate occurred between colleagues, I assure you," he added sincerely.

"So what occurred that wasn't inappropriate?" asked Dalrymple.

"I brought up Connie's history, of course," Atkinson explained.

"You're referring to when she was implicated in the Gildersome murders twelve years ago?"

"Correct."

"But she was cleared of all suspicion related to those cases. Because of you."

"You're correct that I provided her an alibi, but I assumed she must have had some intel I didn't." Alistair shrugged. "Clearly I was wrong." Atkinson pointed to the CCTV stills Dalrymple had printed out. "I remember being apologetic about that. Check the CCTV. You'll see. I just simply find it so fascinating that the killer who evaded justice seems to be escalating again."

Regarding his swift departure afterwards, Atkinson clarified he was expected at his girlfriend Eleanor's home that night. "I even invited Connie along to talk more, as Eleanor lives in Gildersome, but she declined. My whereabouts can be fully accounted for once I leave the pub if you require confirmation. Her mobile number's in my phone if necessary."

Dalrymple nodded. "We've already spoken with Eleanor Smith, and she has confirmed your alibi."

Dalrymple pressed play, and the TV in the corner showed Atkinson proceeding directly to Eleanor's flat a short ways off, remaining there through the morning.

"So, if you have an alibi for me, why am I here?"

"You're here voluntarily, DCI Atkinson," said Dalrymple. "And I still hold a higher rank than you, so some respect is expected."

"I apologise, sir."

"Were you aware of Connie Turner's plans after leaving the pub? Did she mention where she was going or who she was meeting?"

"No, sir."

"How did Connie seem to you that night? Did she appear distressed, anxious, or afraid?"

"Connie's state of mind had seemed troubled but not paranoid, sir. And I didn't observe anything peculiar about her demeanour."

"OK, fair enough," said Dalrymple. "Were there any physical interactions between you and Connie Turner that night that might explain any forensic evidence we might find?"

The question caught Atkinson off guard despite it being

routine. "Every interaction leaves a trace. I leaned in close so strands of my hair may be on her. I handled her IPA pint glasses, so again, traces may have... how do I word it... may have contaminated her."

Dalrymple frowned. "Contaminate?"

"I mean that you won't find any link between myself and harm coming to the poor girl," he stated flatly. "I pray you uncover who committed this horrific crime and find justice for Connie."

DSU Dalrymple made a note and then asked, "Were there other individuals present during your interaction with Connie Turner who can corroborate your account?"

"No, sir. Not unless you count the witnesses in the pub. Connie may have known the people there, but I did not."

"Has there been any previous instance where your professional conduct towards Connie or others has been called into question?"

Atkinson hesitated again. "Yes."

"Yes?"

"Yes, sir."

Dalrymple scowled. "Elaborate, Atkinson."

"She accused me of being..." He looked at DSU Smith.

Jim said, "Unprofessional, I believe the word was Alistair."

"Yes, unprofessional. I was trying hard to help Connie become a police detective as she was getting tired of being a scene of crime officer, and it appeared, in her opinion, I overstepped." Atkinson held up his hands. "However, I must say everything was investigated, and I was exonerated."

"Twice."

"Yes, sir. Twice."

"With another young female detective who is currently

investigating the Gildersome case."

"Correct, sir. But as you say, I was acquitted."

"Have you been involved in any activities or associations recently that might be relevant to this investigation?"

"No, sir."

"Yet I have here your recent run-ins with DCI Beaumont and PC Jenkins."

"I assure you this cover-up nonsense is just that, nonsense." Atkinson turned to Smith. "There's no proof the tape existed. Am I right, sir?"

"You are correct, Alistair." Smith looked at Dalrymple. "Can we finish this soon, Ian?"

"Of course, Jim. Just a few more questions."

"I have here an official complaint lodged recently by a detective working at Elland Road station."

"That's who you were referring to earlier, sir," said Atkinson. "Alexis Mercer. An absolute nightmare. She was obsessed with me. In fact, she becomes obsessed with anybody who gives her a slight bit of attention. You can ask Beaumont all about that."

Smith turned sharply to Atkinson. "What's Beaumont got to do with this?"

"Ask Beaumont about 12 years ago and the party we attended together. He'll tell you exactly what Mercer's all about, though she was named Alexandra Bickerdike back then." Atkinson turned to Smith. "I'm amazed Beaumont is happy working with her to tell you the truth."

"OK, that's all. Thank you for coming." DSU Dalrymple stood and offered his hand to both Smith and Atkinson, both shaking rigorously.

Exiting afterwards, Atkinson offered Dalrymple a placid

smile that didn't reach his hooded eyes. Dalrymple watched him depart pensively, unable to shake nagging doubts about his flawless answers. But without evidence, and his tight alibi, only suspicions remained, and those never stood up in court.

* * *

A maelstrom of emotion roiled within George Beaumont as the interview recording ended abruptly. He stared sightlessly at the darkened monitor, thoughts ricocheting wildly. The smug nonchalance Alistair Atkinson exhibited while an esteemed colleague lay mutilated felt like shards of glass under George's skin.

Yet even more unsettling were Atkinson's parting remarks casually impugning Alexis Mercer's credibility over some party apparently attended together 12 years prior. George wracked his memory but could dredge no recollection of Alexis from that era, certainly nothing to validate Atkinson's sly character assassination, but he did know the name Alexandra Bickerdike. He just couldn't think from where.

George surged from his desk chair, raking both hands roughly through his hair. He began pacing the confines of his office, the walls suddenly feeling constraining. Blind rage warred with gnawing disbelief and disgust in his gut. How could corruption's insidious tentacles have penetrated so deeply into an institution sworn to integrity?

Pausing at the window overlooking the ice rink, George grimly acknowledged his naive faith in the system had allowed complacency regarding rot festering for ages untold. Willowy Alexis Mercer was merely Atkinson's latest intended victim, her earnest face swimming in George's mind beside dozens of others sacrificed by ruthless evil. Never again, George silently vowed.

He swallowed down the sear of fury, fighting for clarity of thought and strategic calm. Proof remained intangible as smoke, but George's gut screamed Atkinson was intricately tied to Connie Turner's sadistic murder somehow. Eleanor Smith's convenient alibi felt manufactured, even viewing their mundane CCTV footage. But conjuring motive from thin air proved impossible.

Unless... George froze, synapses firing rapidly. What if Atkinson wasn't the sole orchestrator but merely an instrument wielded by someone wishing to punish past sins? George began piecing connections—the medallion symbolism indicating ritualism, Connie's inside knowledge from the Gildersome inquiry, and her agitation when meeting Atkinson. Too many subtleties aligned to dismiss.

George scrubbed both hands hard down his bearded face, exhaling slowly. If a copycat were mimicking crimes tied to the White Rose League, intimate familiarity suggested an original member sending some twisted message. And who better to employ as a ruthless proxy than Atkinson? Outmanoeuvring adversaries who anticipated all countermoves demanded cunning and a moral flexibility George lacked.

For now, though, progress fluttered tentatively within reach at last. George clung fiercely to that fragile hope. If Alexis Mercer truly were this 'Alexandra Bickerdike' from their past, perhaps looking into their shared past would help them solve the current case they were struggling with.

Yet George dreaded what other bleak revelations might lurk down that rabbit hole. Because piercing veils of conspiracy never ended cleanly. And those revelations always came at a

CHAPTER THIRTY-FOUR

price...

Chapter Thirty-five

George Beaumont strode purposefully towards the Incident Room. Despite the early hour, the team was already gathered and waiting expectantly. All except one. George noted Alexis Mercer's absence with a pang of unease, but he refrained from commenting as he took his place before the room.

"Thank you for assembling promptly this morning," George began, meeting each team member's gaze in turn. "I know these rapid developments have been taxing, so I appreciate your professionalism and dedication."

He paused, pursing his lips. "Let's address the elephant first. DCI Atkinson was interviewed last night regarding his interactions with Connie prior to her disappearance. His alibi checked out." George held up a hand to forestall reactions. "I know how that sits with many of us, myself included. But we must respect where the evidence leads, not emotions or hunches. I trust Atkinson's activities will remain under scrutiny, but for now, we must widen our focus beyond one individual."

Murmurs rippled around the room, but no one challenged George openly. DI Luke Mason and DS Yolanda Williams exchanged loaded glances. DC Jay Scott's jaw clenched while DC Tashan Blackburn merely listened impassively, arms

CHAPTER THIRTY-FIVE

folded across his chest.

"Here is where we stand," George continued briskly. "We have a sadistic killer still at large. Our duty remains bringing justice and closure for Connie Turner and her loved ones. That requires examining this case through fresh eyes."

He began handing out assignments. "DI Mason and DS Williams, re-examine events leading up to Connie's disappearance. Was anything or anyone overlooked? Triple-check timelines and verify alibis."

Both nodded, scribbling notes. George went on. "DC Scott, dig deeper into other connections in Connie's life—friends, family, anyone she might have confided in regarding the investigation or her own actions that night."

"You got it, boss," Jay acknowledged, though his eyes remained troubled.

George turned to Tashan. "DC Blackburn, meticulously re-review forensic evidence collected so far. Look for any fibres, prints, or DNA that may provide new leads."

Tashan inclined his head. "I'll go over it with a fine-toothed comb, sir."

George surveyed the room. "I know recent revelations have bred doubts and speculation. But we must remain focused on facts, not hearsay. Justice for our fallen comrade depends on it."

He deliberately avoided any mention of Atkinson's allegations against Alexis Mercer—or rather Alexandra Bickerdike—not wanting to fan speculative flames. George still struggled internally to square the earnest detective he knew with this name dredged from a fragmented past. Some quiet investigation was required before voicing vague accusations, no matter their source.

"Remember, eyes open, minds open," George emphasised. "And to quote my favourite American cop, 'Details matter!' We may have become fixated on certain avenues and lost objectivity. Take a step back and re-question all assumptions through an impartial lens." He paused, holding each gaze solemnly. "Dismissed."

As the team dispersed, low conversations resumed, an undercurrent of tension palpable in Mercer's unexplained absence and the unaddressed rumours swirling around her alleged past identity. But they departed with renewed vigour to their assigned tasks.

Alone again, George sank into his desk chair, scrubbing a hand over his bearded jaw. This complex web of deception kept ensnaring more innocents while the spider lurked elusively out of sight. George feared speculating over Mercer could irreparably damage the team's cohesion, especially in the absence of concrete facts.

He decided some discreet digging into Mercer's background was required first. George reluctantly acknowledged that ignoring Atkinson's cruel remarks completely could allow doubts to fester. But a measured, evidence-based unveiling would cause less turmoil than reacting rashly now.

* * *

Yolanda Williams strode briskly beside Luke Mason towards the car park; brows furrowed in thought. "That was interesting," she remarked neutrally as they exited the building into the pale morning sunlight. "Quite the pivot."

Luke grunted non-committally, fishing for his keys.

Yolanda eyed him sideways. "Odd Mercer not being there,

though, you must admit. No explanation or anything." Luke just offered a distracted shrug.

Sliding into the passenger seat, Yolanda pressed on. "Did you catch how quickly the boss shut down discussing her? It was like there's something he didn't want to talk about in front of everyone."

"Come on, Yolanda, you know George's a straight shooter," Luke chided as the engine rumbled to life. "He wouldn't hide anything important from us."

Yolanda arched one brow sceptically. "If you say so." She saw the muscle in Luke's jaw tick but didn't push it. Changing tack, she scanned her notebook, pen poised. "Let's start with re-interviewing that barman, Nathan. See if his story lines up or if he remembers anything useful."

Luke nodded, some of the tension easing from his posture as he guided the car towards Gildersome. "Good idea."

Yolanda uttered a non-committal sound, gaze drifting unseeing out the window. Something in their boss' demeanour back there niggled her instincts in a way she couldn't quite define.

* * *

Jay Scott gulped tepid coffee in the break room, steeling himself before approaching the victim liaison team's office area. Re-interviewing Connie's loved ones so soon after her horrific murder felt like picking at wounds that needed time to even begin scabbing over. But if they held any previously overlooked clues that could break this case open, Jay would endure the discomfort gladly.

Striding down the hall, Jay rapped twice on the half-open

door before poking his head inside. The petite brunette PC assigned as Connie's family liaison glanced up from her paperwork-strewn desk, surprise flickering across her plain features at Jay's unexpected presence.

"DC Scott, what can I do for you?" she greeted politely, though caution lurked in her brown eyes. FLOs took their protective duties seriously.

Jay adopted his most non-threatening posture. "Morning, PC Marsh. I know they've barely had time to grieve, but we urgently need to re-establish contact with Connie's inner circle—friends, relatives, anyone she might have confided in leading up to that night."

Marsh nodded slowly, gauging him. "That's a bit soon for intruding again, but I understand the urgency here." She scribbled something on a notepad and passed it over. "Here are the names and numbers for Connie's parents, brother, closest friend, and ex-boyfriend. Tread lightly, but hopefully one of them knows something helpful."

Jay accepted the list gratefully. "Thanks, I appreciate it. And the cooperation despite the imposition." He offered what he hoped was a reassuring smile. "We just want to ensure no stone goes unturned finding who did this."

Marsh eyed him levelly. "I know. Just remember there are real people on the other end of those calls, detective. Folks who had their world shattered overnight."

Jay nodded solemnly. "You have my word. I'll handle this with the utmost sensitivity and respect."

He departed swiftly, steeling himself before dialling the first devastating number. As the line connected, Jay exhaled slowly. However unbearable this proved for Connie's loved ones, it was nothing compared to what she had endured at the hands of a monster. That truth fortified Jay's resolve to keep digging, no matter how painful.

* * *

The relentless trill of Alexis Mercer's mobile continuously ringing rather than being answered filled the tense silence of George Beaumont's office, underscoring her unexplained absence. Brow furrowed, George ended the call after the eighth unanswered ring, the device clicking loudly in the ensuing stillness.

Something about this situation sat ill with his investigator's instincts. After contacting Adwalton Primary looking for reassurance of Mercer's daughter Georgia's safety, the school receptionist's startling revelation was the last straw. Basically, there was no student named Georgia Mercer, and the receptionist wouldn't answer any other questions without a warrant due to data protection and safeguarding concerns.

George exhaled harshly, raking a hand through his hair. Getting stonewalled citing data protection protocols only heightened his disquiet. He needed answers, and quickly.

Striding to his office door, George spotted DC Jay Scott passing by. "Jay, got a minute?" George called, beckoning him inside.

Settling in the spare chair, Jay regarded him attentively. "What's going on, boss?"

George hesitated, debating how much to reveal. Atkinson's sly impugning of Mercer's credibility during his interview still grated, yet protocol demanded discretion regarding ongoing inquiries. Still, something about Mercer's sudden absence felt ominous. George chose to confide in the dependable Jay.

"This is in absolute confidence," George emphasised gravely. Jay nodded without hesitation. George inhaled slowly. "It's about DC Mercer. She's been mysteriously absent, and I'm... concerned."

He quickly summarised the worrisome phone call to her daughter's school. "The receptionist claims no student named Georgia Mercer even exists there. When I asked for clarification on Alexis' daughter's name, I was stonewalled." George scrubbed a hand over his bearded jaw, exhaling harshly. "Something's clearly amiss."

Jay's eyebrows shot up, but he simply nodded attentively. "That's definitely alarming, sir. How can I help get to the bottom of this?"

George considered him carefully. "During DCI Atkinson's interview, he made vague allegations about... Alexandra Bickerdike." Jay's eyes widened fractionally in recognition. "You know that name, I see," George noted.

"Only whispers over the years, sir," Jay replied neutrally. "Rumours without substance, as far as I ever knew."

George nodded slowly. "Just so. However, Atkinson implied that Bickerdike and Mercer are one and the same." He held up a hand, forestalling Jay's shock. "I have no actual evidence, only suspicions fuelled by Mercer's sudden disappearance and that bizarre school call."

Jay digested this silently.

"You understand the sensitivity here," George continued gravely. "I need someone discreet yet dogged uncovering Mercer's full background, quietly. Every detail—schooling, previous employment, family." He held Jay's gaze intently. "Most importantly, find out the truth about this 'Bickerdike' and her daughter. But utter secrecy is paramount."

CHAPTER THIRTY-FIVE

Jay met his stare levelly. "You can count on my absolute discretion. I'll report only to you until we understand exactly what we're dealing with." He stood swiftly. "I'll get started straight away."

"Tread carefully," George warned as Jay reached the door. "And keep me informed of each discovery, no matter how small. If I'm wrong, the fewer people know, the better."

Jay nodded. "Mum's the word, boss." The door click echoed with strange finality as he departed.

Alone again, George released a harsh breath. Familiar self-doubt crept in regarding his handling of this investigation's endless pitfalls and convoluted knots. His duty to protect the victims wrestled ceaselessly with his simultaneous role as his team's caretaker, their leader. George despised this constant tension.

* * *

Jay Scott slid silently into the records room, swiftly locating the cabinet containing archived personnel files. He scanned the tags rapidly until he finally spotted one reading 'Mercer, Alexis.' Jay slid the slim folder carefully from inside.

He flipped it open, hungry eyes devouring the paltry contents. Just a sparse service record, commendations for sharp detective work closing complex cases, and psychiatric evaluations consistently deeming her fit to serve despite some obsessive tendencies and difficulty with interpersonal boundaries—nothing to validate Atkinson's innuendo so far.

Jay turned next to the computer, initiating a meticulous records search on variations of Alexis Mercer's name and birthdate. He first attempted cross-referencing 'Alexandra

Bickerdike,' but no officer by that name emerged. Next, he searched historical databases of police trainees and cadets, hoping to dredge up any previous identities.

"Come on, where are you hiding..." Jay muttered, fingers flying across the keys. After over an hour of relentless digging, finally, a single hit populated: Alexandra Bickerdike was listed among recruits joining the West Yorkshire Police from the Leeds Police College in 2007. The academy photo showed a fresh-faced young brunette who, despite the different hair colour, was undeniably a much younger Alexis.

"Bingo," Jay breathed. He quickly searched for any documentation explaining the name change but came up empty. Scrubbing a hand down his face, Jay considered his next avenue of investigation. School records could be enlightening if accessible.

Pulling up the Ministry of Education's portal, Jay first located Alexis' schooling history in Leeds, then attempted tracing the enrolment of any daughter named Georgia Mercer in Leeds. Once again, the system yielded zero results for both females. Frustration mounting, Jay logged out and swiftly departed before his illicit searching drew attention, more puzzled than ever by the elusive detective's obscured past.

* * *

Upon returning to the bustling HMET floor upstairs, Jay was intercepted by a stern-looking DS Williams. "Where have you been all morning?" she demanded without preamble. "You were meant to be re-interviewing Connie's inner circle."

Jay affected an abashed look. "Apologies, Sarge, got waylaid chasing down a sensitive lead for the boss." He leaned in

CHAPTER THIRTY-FIVE

conspiratorially. "You know how he is once he gets focused on an angle. I'll get straight back to those interviews now."

Yolanda eyed him shrewdly but merely jerked her head towards his desk phone blinking with unheard voice messages. "See that you do, then. And don't forget to log your tasks promptly, including this mysterious assignment." With that parting warning, she strode off.

Jay hid a sigh of relief as he sank into his desk chair and woke his computer. Glancing secretively around to ensure isolation, he opened a new message to George and typed rapidly:

'Boss, initial searches yield confirmation on an Alexandra Bickerdike in 2007 upon joining the West Yorkshire Police. No daughter enrolled here under Georgia Mercer. Currently working on tracing schools both attended next. Will proceed with utmost care. Could Alexis have gotten married, boss? Hence the surname change? Let me know if you want me to look. Please advise. -JS'

He clicked send and promptly shut down the email program, not wanting to risk any glimpse of their clandestine correspondence. Returning Yolanda's pointed look, Jay picked up his desk phone and began dialling, steeling himself to resume intruding on those poor, grieving loved ones left shattered in this investigation's wake. The sooner they uncovered the truth, the sooner healing could begin for so many wounded souls.

* * *

Hours later, as the old floorboards creaked underfoot, George studied the sparse personnel file contents Jay had discreetly left on his office chair. He took small comfort noting the psychiatric evaluations consistently deemed Alexis fit to serve despite some obsessive tendencies. Perhaps those very traits lent themselves to her dogged dedication solving difficult cases.

A brief knock interrupted George's musings. He hastily closed the file as Jay slipped inside. "Boss, apologies for the interruption, but I wanted to update you straight away." At George's nod, Jay continued. "I've confirmed Alexis Mercer was originally Alexandra Bickerdike when she joined West Yorkshire Police in 2007. No documentation on why the name change. The Royal Courts of Justice are taking the piss in providing details."

He hesitated briefly. "Also no indication of any daughter named Georgia Mercer attending school here in Leeds. I'm still attempting to trace where each of them was educated, but access to records is understandably restricted."

"What names have you tried?"

"Georgia Mercer and Georgia Bickerdike," Jay explained. "I tried Georgina Mercer, and Georgina Bickerdike. I even tried Gee, George, and Georgie with both surnames, but I'm completely flummoxed."

George digested this silently, gaze distant. "Good work, Jay," he finally acknowledged. "Keep following this thread discretely. There's something significant here; I feel it." He refocused fully on Jay. "But utter secrecy remains essential. The team is already on edge with these constant new shocks. Morale is fragile."

Jay nodded. "You have my word, boss." He turned to leave but paused, hand on the doorknob. "For what it's worth, I don't sense malicious intent from Alexis. Just someone trying to outrun the past." Jay met George's gaze. "We all have chapters we'd rather forget."

George inclined his head gratefully. "Too right, unfortunately. We can only move forward as best we're able, making amends where possible." He managed a wan smile.

"Too true, boss." Jay departed quietly.

Chapter Thirty-six

The trill of a third straight call to Alexis Mercer's phone going unanswered did little to ease the pit of unease in George Beaumont's gut. Scrubbing a hand down his face, he exhaled harshly and reached instead for the handset on his desk.

"Smith," came the terse reply.

"Sir, it's George. Just checking in on the status of that warrant request for Mercer's records."

DSU Smith grunted. "You know the wheels of bureaucracy, George. Could be days before it worms through the proper channels."

George's jaw clenched. "This can't wait, sir. We have a brutal killer roaming free and an officer's reputation at stake."

"I'm well aware of the stakes," Smith replied coolly. "But some stones won't be hurried in turning. Keep your shirt on, and we'll be in touch." The line went dead.

George slowly replaced the receiver, a mix of frustration and unease churning in his gut. Needing answers was one thing; manoeuvring the convoluted system was another matter entirely. He exhaled harshly, raking both hands through his hair.

A brisk rap at the door interrupted his brooding. DS Yolanda Williams entered, DI Luke Mason close behind.

CHAPTER THIRTY-SIX

"Afternoon, sir," Yolanda greeted crisply, though she eyed him with a touch of wariness. "Got a development to share after speaking with the pub staff and patrons from the night Connie disappeared."

George straightened, motioning them to the chairs across from his desk. "Go on then."

Yolanda flipped open her notebook. "The barman, Nathan, didn't have much to add about Connie and Atkinson's interaction. But he did reveal she was considered an outcast by most regulars due to her past involvement in the original Gildersome murder investigation twelve years back."

George maintained a neutral expression despite his instinctive dismay. "Is that so?"

"We did some more digging into Connie's background," Luke added. "Speaking with older community members, it turns out she was deceased Inspector Alfred Langton's granddaughter."

George struggled not to react to that chilling detail, keeping his voice level. "I see. Very interesting." His thoughts raced. Langton died not long after retiring. Was he assassinated? Or was George becoming paranoid?

"We thought so too, sir," Yolanda agreed, oblivious to George's internal turmoil. "But we're not sure of the implications here or if it provides any solid leads."

George considered for a long moment, debating how much to reveal. At last, he said, "Look into Inspector Langton more deeply then. Focus on any connections to the other Gildersome victims." Yolanda and Luke exchanged a surprised glance at the abrupt shift, with Luke noticing the slight nod from Beaumont.

"Will do, son," Luke affirmed after a moment. "We'll shake

the trees and see what falls out." He and Yolanda moved briskly to depart, questions lingering in their expressions.

Alone again, George dropped his head into his hands, exhaling harshly. This tangled web grew dense with every passing day. And then there was the fact that Alexis Mercer, or whatever she was called, was AWOL.

* * *

Yolanda slid silently into the records room, nostrils flaring in the musty air as she located the file she was looking for.

"Let's see what skeletons you've got hidden, Inspector Langton," Yolanda muttered, lifting carefully bound ledgers and personnel files marked simply with dates. She spread her haul across the dust-shrouded table. Sinking into the rickety chair, Yolanda donned gloves and a mask to begin delicately turning crackling pages, scanning for any mention of Sally Jenkins.

But finally, buried amongst cryptic case notes, one brief reference surfaced. The delicate cursive described Langton questioning a schoolgirl named Sally back in 1997 regarding claims of harassment by an unknown man. A postscript indicated no further action was taken. Yolanda quickly jotted down notes before returning the materials to their untouched hiding place.

Blinking against the harsh sun outside, Yolanda hurried back to her desk and typed a quick email update to George, who was nowhere to be seen:

'Sir, I found a cryptic case note from Langton in '97 mentioning speaking with Sally Jenkins about unknown man harassment claims. First connection found between them. Continuing to dig. Let me know how you'd like me to proceed—YW'

She tapped send just as Luke approached her desk, shaking his head. "Another dead end on my end so far, Yolanda. Langton's files are almost non-existent."

"Keep at it, sir," she encouraged. "I just found one thin thread to Sally Jenkins, at least. We'll unravel this knot sooner or later."

Luke's eyes sparked with renewed vigour. "That's promising, then. We just have to keep picking at loose ends until the whole tapestry comes undone." He strode off with fresh purpose.

Yolanda allowed herself a small smile before waking her computer again. Their boss clearly suspected more than he was letting on about Langton, Atkinson, and whatever connected past to present here. But old cops' secrets never stayed buried forever.

* * *

George paced, lost in thought. A brief knock interrupted his brooding. George glanced up as Luke slipped discreetly inside. "Sorry to bother you, son, but we've hit a bit of a dead end trying to connect Langton to the victims. Records must have been scrubbed intentionally." His frustration was evident. "What's our next step?"

George considered for a long moment. "Keep pressing friendlier sources for anything not documented officially," he finally instructed. "Surviving relatives, unlisted mobile numbers, safe deposit rentals—even the smallest lead often unravels the larger tapestry."

"Good thought, son," Luke agreed, a touch of renewed hope in his eyes. "I'll scour diaries, photo albums, even greeting cards for mentions. And have another chat with those CID retiree gossips over pints."

He made to leave but turned back with a moment's hesitation. "Are we any closer on the Mercer situation, son? The team's growing concerned."

George's jaw tightened briefly before he replied. "I'm doing everything possible on that front, believe me. But secrets don't unravel overnight, as this case keeps reminding us." He held Luke's gaze. "For now, we stay patient and trust the truth finds a way eventually. That's all we can do."

Luke searched his face briefly, then nodded. "Of course, son. We'll keep the faith." The floorboards creaked faintly under his retreat.

* * *

After another spate of calls that yet again went unanswered, George Beaumont exhaled harshly and reached for the handset on his desk instead.

"Smith," came the terse reply.

"Sir, it's George again. Just checking in on the protective detail you have on Alexis Mercer's home."

DSU Smith grunted. "Round-the-clock watch as requested—Constable Jayden Porter has the day shift, PC Samira Patel covers nights."

George jotted the names quickly. "And have either reported anything concerning so far?"

"All's been quiet last I heard," Smith replied. "But you know I'll have their heads if they've been lax."

CHAPTER THIRTY-SIX

"Too right," George muttered. "I appreciate you arranging security on short notice. Hopefully just a precaution, but with her situation so uncertain..." He paused. "Can I have Porter's and Patel's mobile numbers?"

After providing them, Smith made an ambivalent noise. "Trust me, those constables understand the precarious stakes here. Any developments arise, you'll be my first call."

"Thank you, sir. I'll be in touch." George rang off, exhaling slowly. His gut nagged that relying on second-hand reports wouldn't suffice. He needed to see Alexis' situation for himself.

Picking up the desk phone again, George dialled PC Jayden Porter's mobile number. It rang five times before clicking over to voicemail. George hung up heavily, equal parts frustration and deepening concern churning in his chest. He was stressing, and probably for no reason. He dialled Jayden again, but once more, it was five times before clicking over to voicemail.

What was it that Einstein said? The definition of insanity is doing the same thing over and over and expecting different results.

George decided he needed to do things differently, so he strode urgently from his office in search of DC Scott. Spotting Jay exiting the break room, coffee in hand, George beckoned him over.

"Jay, I need you to accompany me to Alexis Mercer's home straight away," George said in an undertone, glancing around. "Her protective detail isn't responding, so we're doing a welfare check ourselves."

Jay's eyes widened slightly, but he nodded. "Of course, boss. Give me two minutes to grab my things."

"Meet me at the car. And not a word to anyone else," George added pointedly. Jay inclined his head and moved swiftly towards his desk.

En route to the car park, George attempted Jayden's mobile again with the same lack of response, his mounting unease manifesting in a throbbing vein at his temple. He had to see Alexis' situation for himself.

Jay arrived minutes later, sliding silently into the passenger seat of George's Merc, his brow furrowed. George quickly relayed the sparse details as he pulled out of the station car park. "Her home security isn't answering. Something feels off."

Jay nodded grimly. "Let's assess her place then. Could just be a false alarm…" But his tone lacked conviction, anxiety creeping in around the edges.

They drove on in tense silence, the clicking of the indicator unnaturally loud in the stillness when George turned down Alexis' street. His pulse spiked, noting the empty marked car outside her property. This felt all wrong.

Pulling the Merc by the curb, George and Jay approached the front door warily. George rang the bell twice, but no response came. At his terse nod, Jay rapped sharply on the door. "Police! Open up!" Only ominous silence answered.

George tried the handle to no avail, then crouched to peer through the letter box. Nothing stirred within the dim interior. He straightened slowly, dread pooling in his gut. Wherever Alexis was, it wasn't here.

He turned to Jay. "We need to get inside." He pointed towards the marked car. "I believe there's a risk to two police officers and possibly a minor."

"I agree, boss."

CHAPTER THIRTY-SIX

"Do the honours, DC Scott."

"Wait a sec, boss," Jay said, pulling his backpack from his shoulder. "I think we should do this cautiously rather than going in all guns blazing if you know what I mean."

"What did you have in mind?"

Jay knelt and made quick work of the simple lock with his pocket kit. He pushed the door cautiously open.

"Well, colour me impressed; I had no idea you had such a skill set, DC Scott."

Jay grinned. "There's a lot you don't know about me, boss."

They cleared each empty room with mounting unease. Her toothbrush still lay beside the sink, and her important prescription medicine was on the side. Their wardrobes were undisturbed. And no sign of Alexis or Georgia themselves or indications they had left.

Returning to the kitchen, George stared grimly out of the back window overlooking a small, barren garden, weeds poking persistently through the cracked patio. His mind spun furiously with the implications of Alexis' inexplicable, outright disappearance despite protection. How had every precaution failed so entirely?

A floorboard creaked behind George. He turned to see Jay regarding him sombrely. "No signs of struggle or forced entry that I could see, boss," Jay reported. "It's like she just vanished."

George's jaw tightened. "Or was taken. Right from under our noses, despite the safeguards." His hands curled into helpless fists at his sides. "How could I have missed this? I should have protected her..."

Jay stepped closer, meeting his self-recriminating gaze. "This isn't on you, sir. We all missed indications that Alexis was at risk." His amber eyes reflected George's own haunted guilt and fury. "But we will find her."

George scrubbed a hand over his face, regaining composure. "You're right. Speculating solves nothing." He checked his watch. "We need to widen the search, starting with CCTV on her street. Discreetly."

Jay nodded. "I'm on it. We'll retrace her movements leading up to this." His expression turned steely. "The truth is out there somewhere. However well hidden."

George clasped Jay's shoulder briefly in wordless gratitude. However bleak the situation, his team remained united.

Or it did until a bloodied Police Constable Jayden Porter stumbled through the back door, with a knife sticking out of his back.

Chapter Thirty-seven

George and Jay rushed to Porter's aid as he collapsed onto the kitchen floor. Blood spread across his uniform from the knife lodged between his shoulder blades.

"Jayden! What happened?" George demanded, quickly assessing the wound.

Porter gasped for breath, face contorted in pain. "Ambush... a masked man took Georgia..." His words came out choked.

Jay applied pressure to stem the bleeding.

"I'm calling this in officially," George said tersely, already dialling 999 on his mobile. When the desk sergeant answered, he wasted no time. "This is DCI Beaumont. I need all available units dispatched to DC Alexis Mercer's address immediately. Officer abducted, possibility of a minor in danger." He paused. "PC Jayden Porter is critical!"

The dispatcher gasped audibly. "Ambulance is on it's way, sir!" He paused. "Sergeant Greenwood can have a team there in ten minutes."

George rang off and looked at Jayden. "Just hang on; help is coming. Do you know who attacked you?"

Porter shook his head weakly. "Came out of nowhere and got a hold of the girl... too fast... Alexis went willingly because of daughter..." His eyes fluttered closed.

Sirens wailed faintly, approaching fast as George kept the pressure on the wound. Alexis was abducted, and an officer grievously wounded right under their noses. How had things gone so horribly wrong?

The paramedics rushed in, immediately taking over Porter's care as police secured the scene. George stepped back, scrubbing a shaky hand over his face.

"This wasn't just a random home invasion," Jay said grimly beside him. "Alexis was targeted. We need to identify who would want to take her and why."

George's jaw tightened, fury simmering beneath his shock. "You're right. And we start with tracking down DSU Smith. He has some explaining to do about this compromised protective detail."

Jay nodded, eyes glinting. "We'll get answers, one way or another. And find Alexis, no matter what it takes."

The two detectives shared a look of steely determination. This assault on their own wouldn't stand. And neither would whoever took Alexis Mercer. Justice would be swift and uncompromising.

* * *

Detective Chief Inspector George Beaumont kept his jaw set in a hard line as he surveyed Alexis Mercer's empty house. He and DC Jay Scott had found no signs of the missing detective constable or her daughter, only an ominous absence. The implications sat like rocks in George's gut.

As George continued watching the paramedics work on Jayden, Jay wandered through the silent rooms like a ghost. His amber eyes were haunted. In the living room, Georgia's

CHAPTER THIRTY-SEVEN

stuffed animals lay scattered across the sofa, abandoned mid-playtime. The sight pierced Jay's heart. They had to find Alexis and her little girl before it was too late.

Tyres crunching on gravel signalled the forensics team arriving promptly. George waved them inside as their supervisor, Stuart Kent, approached, metal cases in hand.

"Walk us through what you've observed so far," Stuart requested, snapping on gloves.

George quickly summarised the ominous lack of signs of struggle contrasted with Alexis and Georgia's unexplained disappearance. "Just do a thorough sweep for any indication where they might have gone or been taken," he concluded grimly. "We're working blind until something substantive turns up."

Stuart nodded. "We'll go over every inch. If there's anything here to find, we will."

As the forensics team dispersed through the house, George returned Sergeant Greenwood's call, having gotten voicemail earlier.

"Greenwood here, sir."

"Status of the canvassing team?" George demanded without preamble.

"En route to you now, sir. I've got uniforms Markham and Lewis taking your street and Reynolds and Banerjee covering adjacent blocks."

"Good. Have them show Alexis and Georgia's photos to all the neighbours. Someone must have seen something useful."

After confirming the door-to-door team's imminent arrival, George rang off and quickly dialled DSU Smith next, knowing he would need to update the superintendent ASAP.

Smith answered tersely. "What is it, Beaumont?"

"It's Alexis Mercer, sir. She and her young daughter appear to have been abducted from their home." George quickly outlined the ominous lack of evidence within the house.

Smith cursed vehemently. "How the hell did this happen on our watch?"

"I don't know, sir," George ground out. "But now we need all hands searching."

"Consider it done," Smith affirmed decisively. "I'll get additional uniforms and reach out to neighbouring forces for urgent assistance." His tone hardened. "We'll turn over every bloody rock in Yorkshire if that's what it takes to bring them home safely."

George acknowledged Smith's assurances grimly before ending the call, which made him less suspicious of the DSU. But dread still pooled in his gut like icy water. Whoever orchestrated this had managed to outmanoeuvre their every safeguard with terrifying ease. And with each minute that passed, the odds of recovering Alexis and Georgia unharmed worsened.

Striding back inside, George spotted DC Scott in the kitchen, staring sightlessly out the window above the sink. His lean shoulders were slumped in defeat.

George gripped his shoulder bracingly. "We'll find them, Jay," he rasped, willing his own fragile faith to take root in the shaken young detective. "Whoever's behind this has no idea who they're messing with."

Jay managed a jerky nod, jaw clenching with renewed conviction. "Too right, boss."

Just then, George glimpsed Sergeant Greenwood's marked car pulling up outside. The reinforcements he desperately needed had arrived. It was time to mobilise every resource at

CHAPTER THIRTY-SEVEN

his disposal before the trail went cold.

"Let's get these officers briefed up and canvassing immediately," George said briskly. "We're losing daylight."

He quickly outlined Alexis and Georgia's descriptions to Greenwood's team, stressing the critical window to gather eyewitness accounts before memories faded. The four uniformed officers nodded gravely, clutching printed photos of Alexis and Georgia before dispersing up and down the suburban street.

With the urgent door-to-door search underway, George pulled out his mobile again, dialling Detective Sergeant Josh Fry's direct line at the station. When Fry answered, George dispensed with pleasantries.

"Josh, I need you to get into Alexis Mercer's work computer straight away. Go through her files, emails, everything."

"Sir? DC Mercer's system?" Fry asked, confusion lacing his voice. "What exactly am I looking for?"

"Anything pertaining to where she might have gone or who might have taken her," George clarified tersely. "Leave no digital stone unturned. Any clue could be vital."

"Understood, sir," Fry acknowledged, steel entering his tone. "I'll start digging through Mercer's data immediately. And let you know the second I find anything significant."

George scrubbed a hand down his bearded jaw after ringing off; tension coiled tightly beneath the surface. With Fry scouring Alexis' digital history and uniforms canvassing the area, they were finally mobilising every asset available. Yet nagging helplessness still plagued George. Alexis had been right under his nose—he should have protected her.

When his mobile rang an hour later, George snatched it up swiftly. "Talk to me, Greenwood. Any leads out there?"

The uniform sergeant's response was apologetic but urgent. "No eyewitness accounts yet of anything concrete, sir. But one neighbour's security camera shows a dark blue Transit van driving by multiple times yesterday. I'm sending the footage through now."

George's pulse kicked as he opened the video clip, depicting a nondescript van cruising past at slow speed as if casing the street. He quickly ran the number plate through the database.

"That plate trace came back as stolen," George muttered bleakly to Jay.

"Another dead end, then, boss," Jay sighed, dragging both hands through his already dishevelled hair.

"Not necessarily," George said. "Get on the phone to Tashan and ask him to run it through ANPR. It might just lead us to where Alexis and Georgia are."

He gazed out at the suburb street bustling with purposeful uniforms as tensions mounted. We're coming, Alexis, Georgia, he silently vowed. Just hold on a little longer.

* * *

"This is my fault."

Jay glanced over from the passenger seat to where DCI Beaumont was gazing out of the Merc's windscreen, manoeuvring the car at great speed.

"It isn't, boss."

"It is," George insisted, not turning. I should have seen it sooner. I should have known about it sooner." George's hands tightened on the wheel. "I kept calling and calling her. I should have just gone to her house sooner."

"You weren't to know, boss. We weren't sure she was a

target at that point."

"Bollocks, Jay," George said, not turning to look at the DC. "As soon as another policewoman became unreachable, I should have done something."

A long, suffocating pause drew out for what was ten or twenty seconds before George spoke once more. "We're going to make it right, Jay," George told him. "We're going to find Alexis and Georgia."

"How? Where? We don't have any idea where he took her!" Jay snapped. "Not a fucking clue."

"Then we figure it out," George barked back.

* * *

George paced the confines of the Incident Room like a caged tiger, tension radiating from his broad shoulders. With each pass, his piercing green eyes flicked to the clock, watching precious minutes tick away.

It had been over two hours since Alexis Mercer and her young daughter Georgia had seemingly vanished. Two hours of George mobilising every asset in a desperate search for clues, all amounting to frustrating dead ends so far.

He paused by the Big Board, staring sightlessly at the images pinned there. Somewhere out in the sprawling city, two lives hung precariously in the balance. And George could do nothing but wait helplessly for forensics or CCTV footage to produce a lead.

The inaction clawed at him. He should be out there knocking on doors, turning over every stone. Instead, protocol dictated he remained cooped up here coordinating remotely. It was maddening.

George's mobile rang abruptly, an unknown number flashing on the screen. He snatched it up quickly. "DCI Beaumont."

"DCI Beaumont, it's Hughes from the forensic team at Mercer's house." The woman's voice was crisp and professional. "We've conducted a thorough sweep and collected all viable evidence. I just wanted to update you personally that we're still awaiting results from the lab."

George closed his eyes briefly, fresh frustration swirling. "Thank you for the update, Hughes," he managed evenly. "Please expedite those findings by any means possible. We're racing the clock here."

After exchanging a few more terse words, George hung up heavily—bloody forensics. Even the most experienced team needed days, if not weeks, to analyse samples thoroughly. Time he feared Alexis and Georgia did not have.

The Incident Room door swung open, and DS Yolanda Williams hurried in, clutching a notepad. George turned to her expectantly.

"Council CCTV didn't reveal much, unfortunately," she reported briskly. "Traffic was light around Mercer's home for the time frame in question. Just one dark sedan noted circling the area off and on."

George's jaw clenched. "Any clear shots of the plates or occupants?"

Yolanda shook her head in frustration. "Camera angles were poor. But I've got the footage queued up if you want a look."

Scrubbing a hand over his bearded jaw, George waved off her offer. More blurred images lacking concrete details would only compound his helplessness. He needed progress, not dead ends.

"Keep monitoring for any glimpse of transit from her house

to elsewhere," he decided tersely. "And pull satellite imagery as well in case we spot something useful overhead."

Yolanda dipped her head and departed swiftly, tension evident in her hurried stride. Alone again, George resumed pacing, gaze returning compulsively to the ticking clock. The enforced inaction was pissing him off. He needed to act.

Grabbing his overcoat off the back of a chair, George made for the door. Returning to Alexis' house himself could stir some new angle not apparent from stale CCTV footage. It beat this useless pacing, waiting on others.

His desk phone suddenly shrilled, a jarring sound in the tense room. George hurried over, pulse kicking. "DCI Beaumont," he answered curtly.

"Sir, it's DS Fry." The man sounded slightly breathless with suppressed excitement. "I've accessed Mercer's work computer and found something critical pertaining to her disappearance."

George straightened abruptly, senses hyper-focusing on Fry's words. "What is it, Josh?" he demanded urgently. "What did you find?"

"Her iCloud account was still open, including the 'Find My' app," Fry explained rapidly. "Someone deleted the location history yesterday, so today's data is there for all to see."

George's grip tightened on the phone as Fry continued. "That incomplete record showed two active AirTags, likely Mercer's phone and her daughter's, moving from their house to a remote area out past Gildersome. Sending the coordinates now, but I think we can track them."

For an instant, the revelation froze George's racing thoughts. Then hope ignited fiercely within his chest, a bright flare dispelling the gloom.

"Brilliant work, Fry," George rasped. "Get all available units en route to those coordinates now. Priority rescue op. I'll meet them there."

Fry confirmed the mobilisation of backup before George slammed down the phone. In mere seconds, his despair had transformed into razor-sharp focus and momentum.

No time could be wasted. Georgia and Alexis were out there, and he would move heaven and earth to reach them in time. Nothing mattered except getting to that location.

George flew down the staircase two steps at a time, coat flapping behind him. Hitting the car park at a dead sprint, he flung himself into the driver's seat. The engine roared to life as George punched the location Fry had sent into his GPS. Wheels screamed on the tarmac as he blazed out of the car park.

Chapter Thirty-eight

Pain exploded through Alexis Mercer's skull, jolting her awake with disorienting intensity. She gasped, vision swimming. Her head felt consumed by fiery agony, a crushing pressure radiating from the back of her skull. Gritting her teeth against the searing pain, Alexis forced her eyelids open.

The room was dim, lit only by the faint orange glow of a nightlight near the door. As her bleary eyes adjusted, she realised she was inside what looked to be an abandoned farmhouse. The scuffed wooden floorboards beneath her bare feet were gritty with years of accumulated filth. Alexis grimaced, the potent musty odour of mould and rot thick in her nose. She lifted her head slightly to take in more of her unfamiliar surroundings. Shafts of golden light speared through gaps in the weathered planks covering the windows, faintly illuminating the peeling floral wallpaper of the dingy room. A moth-eaten sofa sagged against one wall, coils of stuffing erupting from gashes in the faded fabric. The place looked utterly derelict, decay eating away at the corners and crevices.

Clenching her jaw against the percussive throbbing in her skull, Alexis shifted carefully. She was bound to some sort of wooden cross, ankles also immobilised. Alexis twisted her wrists experimentally, but coarse rope grazed her skin.

Fresh panic constricted her chest. How had she ended up restrained in this unfamiliar place?

Fighting past the jackhammer pulse of pain in her skull, Alexis strained to recall her last moments of freedom. She had been at home, preparing hot chocolate. There was a knock at the door... Georgia! Where was her daughter? Terror surged anew for her child's safety.

Alexis jerked against the restraints in desperation. She had to get free, get to Georgia! But the ropes only cut deeper, slickened by her blood. Chest heaving, Alexis forced herself to be still. Blind panic would only tighten her bonds. She needed to keep calm and get her bearings.

Soft footsteps in the hallway sent Alexis' pulse rocketing. She froze, breaths rasping loudly in the silence. The intruder paused just outside the cracked door, a menacing silhouette limned by the dim glow behind him. Alexis' heart hammered against her ribs. Somehow, her tormentor had discovered her covert investigation and switched targets. This was where it ended.

The door creaked open slowly. Alexis' muscles coiled, straining uselessly against her restraints. She thought wildly of Georgia, George, and the team—would she ever see them again? A face appeared, black pits for eyes. He took a deliberate step into the room.

It was him.

He'd figured out what she'd done, and he'd switched his final target. What else could it be? Why else would she be here?

This would be the end of her.

He stepped closer, each step slow and agonising, until she

CHAPTER THIRTY-EIGHT

saw his gloved hands.

He stretched out his fingers. He'd strangle me too, she thought, just like the others.

"You should never have betrayed me, Alexandra."

"It's good you're awake," he murmured, creeping closer. "I prefer them awake."

Revulsion curdled Alexis' gut. She had to keep him talking, distract him. She had plenty left to lose—everything, in fact—and screaming was only going to panic him or make him angry. She didn't want him panicked, and she definitely didn't want him angry.

She could get through this. Somehow, she could get through this. She just had to stay calm. "Why me?" she asked hoarsely. "I thought Isabella Wood was your final target." Alexis raised her head, pulling her neck in close. Making it a smaller target.

The killer grinned, the expression made monstrous by his bloodshot eyes. "She was. But then I learned about your betrayal." He ran a gloved hand down Alexis' cheek in a perverse caress, his fingers thick and strong as they rubbed away a stray tear. She cringed away, tasting bile.

He grinned again. "Does this tear mean you're scared?"

There was no point trying to pretend otherwise. "Yes," Alexis told him.

The vicious fingers of his left hand clamped her hair. "You were a fool to cross me!" he bellowed. Alexis' scalp ignited in agony. She bit back a wail. "I thought we were a team, but you wanted me to take the blame!"

Blame? Comprehension sparked through Alexis' pain-fogged thoughts. "Where is my daughter?" she gasped out.

The killer cocked his head, hand loosening slightly. "Our daughter, you mean?" he taunted.

When she didn't reply, he yanked harder on her hair, forcing her eyes to meet his.

Rage temporarily overrode Alexis' fear. "Don't you dare threaten Georgia!" she spat. "Leave her out of your twisted games."

The killer leaned closer, acrid breath hot on her cheek. "But you involved her by betraying me, darling."

Revulsion churned Alexis' gut.

His right hand abruptly closed around her throat, sadistic excitement burning in his eyes. "I'll show liars like you what happens," he hissed, squeezing brutally.

"P-please," Alexis sobbed, the pain burning through her scalp and lighting up her brain. "Leave Georgia out of this."

She could smell his breath even more now. It smelled strongly of alcohol. Combined with the sour stench of his body odour, it made her want to gag.

"Georgia is currently half mine, but when George and the team find you, Alexis, she'll be all mine!"

"But they already know it's you!"

"Bullshit!" He held his breath and cocked an ear. "Hear that?"

"No."

"EXACTLY!" he roared, his other hand clamping onto her throat. "That's a lie. You're a fucking liar, just like the rest of them!"

He pushed his weight on her, pushing his open palm onto her throat. Alexis' eyes bulged as she coughed and spluttered, her body instinctively fighting for air. Her head tingled. Darkness crept in, shadows closing at the edges of her vision.

Just when she thought she was about to pass out, he eased off enough for her to gulp down a breath. She wheezed in and out, eyes streaming, chest heaving, breath coming in frantic, uneven rasps.

"I'm going to show you what happens to fucking liars like you."

* * *

Streetlights streaked by in phosphorescent smudges as George wove expertly through sparse traffic. He flashed his lights, warning cars to clear the way. The speedometer crept higher as the open road unfurled before him.

George's hands were steady on the wheel despite emotions threatening to choke him. Lives were on the line, and every second brought possible salvation closer or stole it irrevocably away. Outwardly, he appeared a model of icy control. But inwardly, frantic prayers looped endlessly.

Please hold on, Alexis. Georgia. I'm coming. Please just hold on a little longer.

The desolate stretch of road eventually gave way to rolling rural landscape on the outskirts of Gildersome. George eased off the gas pedal slightly, not wanting to miss the unmarked side road that would lead to them.

There, the innocuous gravel turn-off nearly escaped his notice in the waning light. Making the sharp turn threw up a plume of dust in his wake as he careened down the lonely road, tyres bouncing harshly on the uneven track. Lush greenery closed around the car, hemming them into nature's indifference.

George's pulse roared in his ears, nearly drowning the ping of his GPS indicating arrival. Slowing the car to a crawl, his sharp gaze scoured the thickly wooded area for any signs of life. Less than a kilometre, Fry said. They had to be close.

There, a faint animal trail wending off among shadowy pines. It could be the path to salvation or damnation, but George knew he had no choice but to follow wherever it led.

Parking hastily outside the decaying farmhouse he knew from twelve years ago, George grabbed a torch and exited the Merc.

* * *

The rusted knife clanged dully as the killer placed it atop the bedside cabinet. He positioned it deliberately, angling the pitted blade so it remained in Alexis' eyeline. She watched warily as he laid out his sinister tools with disturbing precision—a larger serrated knife, a pair of bloody pliers, and a roll of masking tape.

Alexis' pulse thundered, breaths rasping loud. She was bound helplessly at the mercy of a depraved monster who clearly savoured ritualised torture.

He'd set the tape down with a clunk, then thought better of it and pulled off a strip that he'd then placed over Alexis' mouth and slapped firmly to make sure it stayed stuck. "What?" he'd asked. "I don't have a spare tie, sadly," he remarked with chilling nonchalance. He tried to caress her cheek again, but she jerked away from his touch, skin crawling.

The final muted rays of sunset trickled through the grimy window. The killer glanced up as though evaluating the lighting conditions with an artistic eye. "You'll look spectacular covered in shadows and moonlight," he murmured. "I'll take photographs to commemorate our intimate time together." He hesitated. "It hurts that no one's going to know it was me, but that's how it goes."

Revulsion churned Alexis' stomach. She craned her neck, instinctively testing her bindings, but the ropes only scratched her wrists. Pain blazed through her shoulder as she strained against the restraints.

The killer cocked his head, tone turning conversational. "Your team thinks quite highly of you, Alexandra. Especially young Jay. Does he have an infatuation, do you think?" He clucked his tongue. "Tsk. Well, I suppose battering poor Candy would dash any romantic notions."

Alexis froze.

"No comment?"

Alexis couldn't have replied, even if she'd wanted to. She found her gaze returning to the serrated knife, then creeping sideways to the pliers.

He ripped away the tape, and Alexis spat at him. He used his sleeve to wipe the phlegm away, grinning. "I'd better get rid of that in case forensics come running, eh?" He cocked his ear and smiled. "Then again, nobody knows where you are."

When she remained defiantly silent, the killer reached for the rusted knife and then paused. "Actually, I think I'll use my bare hands instead. Much more... intimate." His leer raised bile in Alexis' throat.

"Ah, shit. The camera," he admonished himself. "It's downstairs," he whispered, caressing her bruised face. Alexis recoiled violently, eliciting a chilling smile.

He placed his hand on her face again, ran it down over the purple bruising on her neck, and then brushed it lightly against one of her breasts. "I miss your body, you know? I wondered whether you'd let me play with you one last time."

"Over my dead body!" she screamed.

The man grinned. "Have it your way!"

"You wait right there, darling," he told her, smiling at the way she flinched at his touch. "I'll be right back."

The instant his footsteps descended the creaking stairs, Alexis began frantically working her right wrist, twisting and tugging against the fibres. Agony blazed through her chafed skin, but she bit back whimpers, breath coming in panicked grunts. Please, God, just a little more...

Heavy footfalls sounded on the stairs again. With a final wrenching effort fuelled by desperation, Alexis felt the rope slacken around her bloody wrist. Seconds later, her tormentor loomed into view, clutching a ball pein hammer in his right hand and a Phillips-head screwdriver in his left, grinning as he closed the distance.

"My father was obsessed with these tools. I've no idea why, but he was obsessed with Sutcliffe. Even more so than Finch." He paused. "You know, my father would have been proud of Finch, and that got me thinking. My father never once told me he was proud of me, Alexandra. Not once. Do you have any idea how that feels?"

But Alexis couldn't speak. She didn't want to draw attention to herself and the fact she'd managed to loosen her bonds whilst the man still chatted amiably about his father's demented obsessions.

Instead, Alexis tuned out the madness, feigning continued submission while covertly straining her freed hand against the remaining bonds.

As the killer leaned in, vile excitement contorting his features, starbursts exploded in Alexis' vision as she choked for air. A smile split the killer's face. But just before darkness claimed her, a faint sound pierced the ringing in Alexis' ears—

CHAPTER THIRTY-EIGHT

the creak of a floorboard.

The killer's head jerked up, his choke hold loosening.

Alexis made her move as the bedroom door exploded inward off its hinges to reveal a powerfully built silhouette.

With a primal scream, she whipped her loose arm up and raked her nails violently across his face. The killer howled, staggering back and clutching his savaged cheek. Alexis twisted like a wild animal, grappling for the rusted knife on the cabinet.

Her attacker recovered quickly, lunging to grab her wrist. But Alexis was faster—she grasped the handle and slashed blindly. A spray of hot liquid hit her face as the serrated blade found its mark. The killer's agonised wail was cut short as he fell back.

Alexis sagged, drawing ragged breaths. She blinked, vision clearing enough to recognise the man's blond hair and determined set of his broad shoulders as he grappled furiously with the man, pushing him to the ground.

Gasping raggedly, Alexis sawed at the remaining bonds until she finally tore free. Swaying unsteadily, she limped towards George, the floor slippery with blood. "George!" Alexis rasped out in dizzying relief. The Detective Chief Inspector didn't spare a glance up, absorbed in his ruthless struggle. With an enraged roar, George landed a crushing right elbow to the killer's throat.

And then, in a flash, George had the man pinned down.

"It's over, Atkinson," George snarled; the moonlight streaming in through the wooden beams revealed Alistair Atkinson's face. He had a scratched face, a split lip, and a slash to his eye that was oozing blood. Revulsion and shock warred within Alexis.

Breathing hard, George turned to Alexis, his gaze gentle. "Let's get you home safe and reunited with Georgia," he said softly.

Alexis nodded, overwhelmed with gratitude. She wanted to embrace George in relief but knew their ordeal wasn't over yet. Not until Atkinson was secured in cuffs and behind bars.

She turned away from George to smile; she'd won, but a sudden blur of movement in her peripheral vision made Alexis whirl in alarm. Atkinson, his face contorted in animalistic rage, baring his teeth, managed to push George off him and get up.

He lunged towards her.

Acting on pure instinct, Alexis snatched up the serrated knife from the floor. She squeezed her eyes shut and mindlessly thrust the blade forward with all her might. A sickening, wet impact vibrated up her arm.

Alexis' eyes flew open to see Atkinson staggering back, the knife protruding from his stomach. Shock registered on his face for a fleeting second before his legs buckled. He collapsed like a puppet with cut strings.

Alexis stood frozen in horror, the bloodied knife dropping from her nerveless fingers. A strong hand grasped her shoulder, steadying her.

"It's alright, Alexis. You're safe now. He can't hurt you any more," George soothed, though his piercing green eyes remained fixed warily on Atkinson's motionless form. After a tense moment, he stepped forward and knelt to check Atkinson's still wrist for a pulse. Looking up at Alexis, he gave a slight nod of his head. Atkinson was still alive, though barely.

Alexis released a shuddering breath, the adrenaline draining

CHAPTER THIRTY-EIGHT

from her body and leaving her limbs leaden. She couldn't tear her eyes from the growing crimson stain surrounding the body of the man who had tormented her. But strangely, she felt no regret, only bone-deep exhaustion.

Sensing her inner turmoil, George gently guided Alexis from the room. "Let's get you out of this place," he murmured. Downstairs, the relieved voices of the rest of the team reached them as backup finally arrived. Alexis felt a profound sense of peace and safety envelop her despite her battered body and shattered nerves.

Leaning heavily on George's solid strength, Alexis limped from the house where she had narrowly escaped death. She was battered but alive, thanks to George's tireless pursuit of the truth. And Alistair Atkinson would finally face justice for his heinous acts. Alexis squeezed George's hand, pulse settling for the first time in days. The long nightmare was over for many, but for her, it had only just begun.

Chapter Thirty-nine

The shadows deepened in Detective Chief Inspector George Beaumont's office as dusk settled over the city, the space still holding the lingering tension of the day's traumatic events. Two lives had hung precariously in the balance only hours ago. And though Alexis Mercer and her daughter were safely recovering now thanks to his team's efforts, the larger sinister puzzle still plagued George's weary mind.

Leaning back in his desk chair, spine knotted with fatigue, George scrubbed both hands down his bearded face. So much remained unresolved despite the danger passing. Whilst the orchestrator of the vicious threats and abduction was now caught, Alexis' full motives and connections to the twisted scheme continued mystifying George.

A sharp rap at the door jarred him from his brooding. "Come in," George called brusquely, straightening in his chair.

The door swung open, and Detective Inspector Luke Mason stepped inside, his salt and pepper hair impeccably combed as always despite the late hour. But tension lined the Lancastrian's unsmiling face. Wordlessly, he crossed the office and placed a folder on George's desk.

George raised one blond brow but accepted the folder. "The background records for Alexis Mercer, I presume?" About

CHAPTER THIRTY-NINE

bloody time, he thought tightly, noting the Royal Courts of Justice seal stamped prominently on the cover.

Mason simply inclined his head in affirmation. "This just arrived priority post. I'll leave you to review the contents privately, son." He exited as briskly as he had entered.

Alone again, George's pulse quickened as he considered the folder's contents. What long-buried secrets might finally come to light about Alexis Mercer's obscured past? The answers were literally at his fingertips, but trepidation stayed his hand a moment longer. Once this door opened, there was no closing it again. Was he prepared for where the revelations might lead?

Steeling himself, George flipped open the file, senses hyper-alert. His sharp gaze immediately homed in on a single detail, and his breath arrested in his chest. There, on the scanned birth certificate, the name listed for Alexis' daughter was Georgia Atkinson. George stared, momentarily unable to process the implication of Detective Chief Inspector Alistair Atkinson being named the child's father.

Alistair Atkinson. Georgia's father. Alexis had never mentioned it on either her personal or professional record. The surreal shock momentarily fractured George's usual poise. What the hell? His thoughts spun wildly, struggling to assimilate this staggering development.

Georgia was Alistair's daughter. The same Alistair who had been under intense suspicion just yesterday regarding the sadistic threats against their team and the person they had just arrested. George's gut churned as scattered fragments realigned into a disturbing new pattern, one hinting at betrayals far more intimate and destructive than he had imagined.

The sharp crack of his office door bursting open snapped

George from his stunned reflections. Detective Constable Jay Scott hurried in, eyes wide and movements jittery. "Boss, we just got word—" Jay pulled up short, reading the evident distress on George's face. "What happened?" he asked worriedly.

George sat motionless, the birth certificate gripped tightly in one hand. "Close the door," he rasped hoarsely. Jay complied swiftly before crossing to perch on the chair across from the imposing desk. His youthful features were creased with concern, but he waited in patient silence for George to gather himself enough to explain.

Finally, George met the detective constable's gaze directly, seeing his own hollow shock reflected back at him. "I just received Alexis Mercer's background records," he ground out, voice rough. "And there's something you need to see."

Jay straightened, senses alert as George slid the birth certificate across the desk towards him. He scanned it quickly, confusion crinkling his brow. Then his eyes widened in stunned disbelief reading the father's name.

"Bloody hell..." Jay breathed, shooting an incredulous look at George. "Atkinson? Her daughter is his?" Jay dragged a hand roughly through his perpetually messy hair, blowing out a long breath as the revelation sank in.

"This changes... well, everything, doesn't it?" he eventually managed, amber eyes burning with questions.

George nodded grimly, the room's atmosphere seeming to press down with suffocating weight. "Aye, lad. The layers here just got exponentially more complex." He shook his head, anger and dismay churning beneath the surface. "Alexis Mercer hid her connection to Atkinson. Which implies intimate knowledge of his activities." George met Jay's troubled gaze. "She betrayed our trust. Same as he did."

Jay blew out another harsh breath, shoulders slumping. "Never saw that coming, boss. She always seemed so dedicated to the job, to getting justice..." Jay chewed his lower lip pensively before his expression hardened. "But you're right. She lied to our faces. Used our resources under false pretences." His voice turned flinty. "Alexis owes us some answers."

"Too right," George affirmed vehemently. His piercing green eyes blazed with banked fury. "I mean to get them straight from the source." His hands curled into fists atop his desk. "No more evasions. Time to stop hiding behind half-truths and expose what she knows about Atkinson's involvement."

Jay gave a wordless nod of agreement, jaw set. They had been patient, even protective, of Alexis throughout the investigation. But that trust had been irrevocably shattered if she knowingly concealed intimate ties to the culprit. The Alexis they thought they knew no longer existed. Probably never did.

George glanced at the clock, noting the late hour. Visiting hours at the hospital were long over, but he would pull whatever strings necessary to get access tonight. The need for answers brooked no delay.

Striding around the large desk with sharp, decisive movements, George shrugged on his overcoat. His piercing green eyes reflected icy determination beneath furrowed brows. "Stay by the phone, Jay," he instructed tersely. "I'll ring as soon as I have a full statement from Mercer."

Jay straightened in his chair, sensing the gravity of this confrontation. "Do you want me there as an impartial witness?"

he offered.

But George shook his head, equal parts fury and sorrow etching the lines of his rugged face. "Best I do this alone, lad. Get the full truth without her lawyering up right away." His gravelly voice turned bleak. "Never imagined it coming to this. But too much is at stake now."

Jay nodded solemnly. This reckoning had been building for a long while, seeded in secrecy and nurtured by betrayal. He only prayed that shattering facades now could lead to eventual healing, both for Alexis and George. The wounds ran deep.

Pausing with his hand on the doorknob, George glanced back at Jay. The young detective constable read the silent message in his superior's eyes—this was the point of no return. Once George stepped through that threshold, lives would be irrevocably changed, for better or worse. But truth offered the only path forward from ruin. However painful the process, redemption waited on the other side.

Jay met George's gaze steadily, letting his absolute faith shine through. "You've got this, boss," he affirmed simply. "Do what needs to be done."

* * *

The chill unique to hospitals at night seeped under George Beaumont's skin as he marched down the bustling hallway, jaw set like granite. The gruelling events of the last 24 hours weighed upon him with each crisp step, amplified by grief and betrayal churning ceaselessly in his gut. But George relied on sheer, stubborn will to propel him forward when his spirit felt flayed to aching rawness. The truth lay ahead now. He would claw his way to it or die trying.

CHAPTER THIRTY-NINE

Nodding briskly to the officer stationed outside Alexis Mercer's room, George slipped inside quietly. The steady beep of monitors and hiss of oxygen filled the dim, depressing space. And there, tucked in the stark bed, looking impossibly fragile, lay Alexis. Her usually bright azure eyes were closed in fitful slumber, bruises still livid across one side of her wan face—the violent imprint of recent trauma.

George experienced an instinctive pang seeing her so diminished after coming so terrifyingly close to death. But bitterness quickly flooded back in, and the image of her daughter's birth certificate burned into his psyche. She had betrayed them all with her deception, and the time for mercy had expired.

Closing the door firmly, George crossed the small space to stand at Alexis' bedside. Up close, her visible injuries appeared even more graphic against the pallid backdrop of sheets. George steeled himself against sympathy, focusing on the interrogation ahead.

"Alexis," he called sharply, needing answers more than her rest. When she didn't stir, he gripped her shoulder through the thin hospital gown, giving it a small shake. "Alexis, wake up."

She dragged her eyes open sluggishly, glassy gaze struggling to focus. "George..." Alexis rasped, tongue darting out to try and moisten cracked lips. "What are you doin' here?" Her words slurred from lingering anaesthesia and pain medication.

George pulled over a chair but remained standing, using the height advantage to loom intimidatingly over her. He kept his piercing green eyes fixed unwaveringly on her face.

"I'm here for the truth, Alexis," he informed her bluntly.

When she simply blinked up at him in groggy confusion, George pressed on ruthlessly. "The whole truth this time. No more evasions or half lies."

Alexis struggled to prop herself up on one elbow, wincing as the movement tugged at tender incisions and bruises. She shook her head a bit, still fighting to clear away the clinging fog. "What... what are you talking about?"

George's gravelly voice turned deadly quiet. "Your daughter's surname. Atkinson." He spat the name like venom. "You've been concealing your connection to Alistair this entire time."

The colour abruptly drained from Alexis' face, leaving her ghostly pale against the sheets. Her eyes darted sideways, throat convulsing.

"So you don't deny it," George surmised grimly. "He's her father." His piercing eyes bore into her. "Did you know about Alistair's involvement in all this from the start? Or were you just protecting him once you found out?"

Alexis turned her face away, body language screaming shame. Her silence told George everything he needed to know. Jaw clenching, he slammed a fist down on the bed railing, the sharp crack splitting the air. Alexis flinched.

"Dammit, Alexis, he nearly killed you!" George roared. "You and an innocent child! How can you still be protecting that monster?"

Her voice, when it finally emerged, was nearly inaudible. "You don't understand..."

"Then explain it to me!" George demanded harshly. "Make me understand!" His fury simmered just below the surface. He wanted—no, needed—to understand her motivation.

Alexis shut her eyes briefly. When she opened them again,

CHAPTER THIRTY-NINE

azure orbs glistened with unshed tears.

"I was ashamed, alright?" she admitted tremulously. "Ashamed of the mistakes I made then. Of the hold Alistair still had over me." She dashed the traitorous tears away angrily. "I thought I could make things right quietly. Protect Georgia from her father's sins."

George searched her face, seeing the anguish etched there beneath the truth. But doubt still lingered. "That maybe explains concealing his paternity," he allowed grudgingly. He leaned down, voice dropping. "Did you help plan this, Alexis? Try to frame Atkinson for your own sick purpose?"

She reared back as though he had struck her, eyes huge. "No! I swear, George, I had no idea what Alistair was orchestrating." Alexis sat forward urgently. "I made mistakes, but I've only ever acted to get justice like you."

Her raw pleading eroded George's anger slightly. But he still needed concrete facts, not emotions.

"Then tell me everything from the beginning," he demanded implacably. "No more omissions or selective sharing. If you want even a chance at forgiveness, lay it all bare now."

Alexis gazed up at him for a long, taut moment. Then her slender shoulders slumped in defeat. Haltingly, voice rasping with pain and shame, she began recounting it all—the wide-eyed recruit lured in by Alistair's flattery, the charismatic superior she fell for despite every warning sign, the birth of their child Georgia, and Alistair's explosive reaction driving Alexis to change her name and sever all contact.

"I thought I'd escaped his influence," Alexis explained wretchedly. "That my Georgia could have a fresh start and a life free from his toxicity." She drew her knees up tightly to her chest. "I had no clue he was involved in any of this." Tears leaked silently down her cheeks. "Then all the old panic came flooding back. I knew I had to get away to protect Georgia from him. But it was already too late."

She dissolved into quiet sobs, the toll of reliving past trauma taking its full devastating toll. George remained frozen in the bedside chair, thoughts and emotions at war within him. The bitterness bred from her deception still festered. But witnessing Alexis' naked anguish made his black-and-white judgements muddle into shades of grey. She had tried desperately to rewrite the story of her own life, only to become trapped in the original tragedy repeating. Was driving her further into ruin truly justice? Or was it just avoidance of the scars each of them carried?

George held her watery gaze, voice low but steady. "The way forward won't be easy for either of us after this. But the fact you're still here, surviving everything he did, proves your strength, Alexis."

He offered a faint smile before straightening slowly, joints cracking. Glancing at his watch, he hesitated reluctantly. "I should let you rest. It's late."

Alexis bit her lip. "Wait... will you stay? Just a bit longer?" She flushed, sounding suddenly much younger and more vulnerable. "Hospitals unsettle me at night. The shadows..." she trailed off self-consciously.

George felt his chest constrict, imagining how the pitch darkness and isolation must magnify grim memories. Perching on the edge of the bed, he gave Alexis a gentle shake of his head. "There are officers outside, so try to sleep if you're able, and I'll see you tomorrow."

"Bye, George."

The midnight silence in Alexis' hospital room was abruptly

shattered by the jarring ring of George's mobile. He fumbled the device from his coat pocket, pulse kicking as he noted Jim Smith's name flashing urgently on the screen. Apprehension gripped his gut in an iron vice. Nothing good ever came from middle-of-the-night calls.

Stepping hastily into the hallway, George answered with blood roaring in his ears. "Sir? Everything alright?" He dispensed with polite preamble, Smith's tone already conveying something had gone terribly wrong.

But the detective superintendent's solemn words still somehow blindsided George completely. "There's been an incident, George. The surgeons tried their best, but Atkinson was just pronounced dead."

George sagged back against the cold hallway tiles, shock momentarily arresting his ability to comprehend language. "Dead?" Atkinson was gone just like that, without ever confessing? The reality fractured George's already crumbling foundations. It left nothing but questions swirling in the wreckage.

He gradually became aware of Smith repeating his name sharply in concern. George blinked slowly, the present re-emerging from numb fog. "What happened, sir?" he managed hoarsely. "His injuries weren't that severe..."

Smith sighed heavily over the line. "Looks like a pulmonary embolism brought on by the trauma. The blood clot must have ruptured suddenly." He paused. "I know this robs us of the closure we needed, George. But sometimes justice finds another way in the end."

George scrubbed a shaky hand down his bearded jaw, emotions at war within him. He should feel vindicated that Atkinson could never hurt anyone again. But denial of the truth he'd sought left only a hollow void where answers should have been.

"I suppose some might call it karma," George eventually replied bleakly. "Though it doesn't feel much like justice to me right now." He hesitated. "What's the situation there? Do we need to manage public response?"

"The scene is contained," Smith assured briskly. "And we can restrict the narrative for now until you're ready. Take tonight to process this, and we'll craft our statement in the morning."

George rasped an affirmative, the simple conversation taxing his depleted reserves. After Smith promised to keep him updated on any developments, George ended the call and slumped against the wall, despair crashing through the bulwarks of composure.

Atkinson was gone. Just like that. Without ever giving George the confession or clarity he so desperately craved. Intellectually, he knew death sometimes circumvented human justice. But emotionally, it felt like the final, taunting victory of a man who had slipped his grasp for decades. George pressed the heels of his palms against burning eyes, sucking in an unsteady breath. The universe felt off-kilter, cast adrift. He needed an anchor before the darkness swallowed him whole.

Forcing iron rigidity into his spine through monumental effort, George moved to grasp Alexis' door handle. She deserved to know her tormentor's fate as soon as possible. Though it offered cold comfort now, at least Atkinson could never hurt Georgia again. They would find a way to move forward from this hollow ending.

CHAPTER THIRTY-NINE

* * *

From inside the hospital room, Alexis carefully strained her ears. She heard the words: 'Dead', 'What happened', and 'His injuries weren't that severe'.

That was great news.

She grinned.

And at the movement of the door handle, she closed her eyes and pretended to be asleep.

* * *

Stepping wearily back inside the dim hospital room, George gently shook Alexis' shoulder. There would be little sleep for what remained of this bleak night. But they would endure it as they always did, as old ghosts were put to rest at last. The lingering shadows eventually had to cede to dawning light. But George couldn't help but hear echoes in the silence.

About the Author

From Middleton in Leeds, Lee is an author who now lives in Rothwell, West Yorkshire, England with his wife and three children. He spends most of his days writing about the places he loves, watching sports, or reading. He has a soft spot for Pokemon Trading Cards, Japanese manga and anime, comic books, and video games. He's also rather partial to a cup of strong tea.

You can connect with me on:
- https://www.leebrookauthor.com
- https://www.facebook.com/LBrookAuthor

Subscribe to my newsletter:
- https://leebrookauthor.aweb.page/p/cfff8220-7312-4e37-b61a-b1c6c2d15fc2

Also by Lee Brook

The Detective George Beaumont West Yorkshire Crime Thriller series in order:

The Miss Murderer

The Bone Saw Ripper

The Blonde Delilah

The Cross Flatts Snatcher

The Middleton Woods Stalker

The Naughty List

The Footballer and the Wife

The New Forest Village Book Club

Missing: Michelle Cromack novella

The Killer in the Family

The Stourton Stone Circle

A Halloween to Remember: The Leeds Vampire novella

Shadows of the Ripper: The Long Shadow novella

The West Yorkshire Ripper

The Shadows of Yuletide

The Shadows of the Past

The Echoes of Silence

More titles coming soon.